I0718965

Survival *From The* Start

The Misadventures of Mekkâr

SAAVO

Contents

Forward

Names of people, teams, and places have been changed to protect the innocent [Dragnet TV show 1951-1970]. I want to avoid any legal hassles in the litigious society that is all around us and appears to be getting worse each day.

These stories are based on a real person and different experiences of the main character. The fortunate thing is the author is one of the few people who can converse with the person behind the premier character and in his native language. There is not any interest on his part to put his experiences in print, but he is fine with me doing so. There is still his strong belief in old fashioned traditions of passing down stories by oral means alone. Neither one has the desire to present any of his heroes in a negative or embarrassing light while still getting the story across. Meanings and interpretations can be made any way the reader would like, that is up to you.

The original premise of this collection of stories was to be a partial semi-autobiography of the main character. However, while writing it the intent changed to a theme of hope of possibility, adventure, & opportunity. The idea was aimed at anyone, especially young people, who could dream of participating in various and exciting life events. It could be applied to people anywhere whether one is from the Andes, Northwest Territories in Canada, Siberia, the Himalayas, and even to the remotest regions of the earth. Individuals do not have to just accept a routine and ordinary life nor be stuck in a rut no matter where they are located.

Many thanks to Thesaurus.com, OnlineConversion.com, online spell correction, and a few others. This is always a tolerance of a lot of distractions during this whole process. A process that included turning incoherent concepts, scribblings, and notes converted into written form to become accessible to read. Written English is contrary to many other languages in that it is very different from the spoken words used in interpersonal interaction. Also, writing a novel or creative non-fiction is a far cry from composing and constructing a college paper on any subject, which to me is

95% B.S. and 5% filler. Hope you like it because there is more to come as I have many more stories to complete.

Any input and writing helps, suggestions is appreciated, but please be merciful as I am attempting to improve my writing skills in a language that is not native to me. I know that I am not a great writer, but just a beginner. Specifics and examples are most beneficial for me. One that has a hard time grasping the practical aspect of the concept of how to write to show, not just tell a story. It is much easier said than done.

I am in a fight against increasing age, concussion related brain injury, and forgetfulness of some stories that might be lost if no action is taken now. There are even many more past events that have been lost to the sands of time that I will probably never remember again. I have no control of the writing "flow" as I call it, along with what presents itself in my conscious mind to be written down. It can arrive at any time and disappear just as suddenly as it showed up.

I have also had a very difficult time finding a quality, reliable co-author, editor, etc. over a period of years.

Thanks for reading,
Saavo

Main Character Descriptions

The main characters in his life:

Sirga – Mekkar's mama. A beautiful six-foot two-inch dark haired woman with a slightly darker Arctic native complexion. She was a part time professional model, ran the family businesses, worked at the main government building, and also for an airline. She was a fiercely independent woman who spoke twenty four languages and forty eight dialects. A very take charge person and definitely not a procrastinator. Sirga was a workaholic, highly educated with an advanced degree in business. She had a feisty disposition; was very outspoken, and extremely blunt. She was not afraid to say anything to anyone. Sirga acquired these traits from her mother's side of the family. Also, she could curse worse than a sailor and had a few close friends that were pretty much like her.

Henrik – Mekkar's papa. A handsome six-foot seven-inch two hundred and fifty pound muscular outdoor type. He was a former athlete and a logger. At first glance he looked intimidating, but he had a mellow disposition. Henrik was a workaholic and had an advanced degree in business. Later on he became an international marketing and sales executive with a multinational conglomerate company.

Alf – Mekkar's brother, but not the youngest sibling. He grew up to be a six-foot seven-inch lanky very light blond haired athlete. He was big into the martial arts, ninja, and samurai disciplines. Alf was like his papa with an easy going disposition, but he was quieter. He was quite different at his work where he started as a teenager and now gets to travel around the globe. He is fluent in at least seventeen languages and a workaholic also.

Lasse – Mekkar's best friend. They grew up together except that Lasse is about a year older than Mekkar. He stands six-foot four-inches tall and averages about two hundred forty pounds of solid muscle with blond hair and blue eyes. Lasse is an athlete with a nasty disposition toward strangers. If he doesn't know you, he doesn't like you. He has a photographic memory and later became an accountant. He is well educated and smart as a tack. He has a penchant for making trouble when he gets together with Mekkar and later on Alf. Lasse's mother is good friends with Sirga.

Mekkar – The oldest sibling of the three boys in his immediate family. He is about three and a half years older than Alf and approximately seven years older than the youngest Niillas. Since he was born a little more than three months early, he is unlike the other members of his family in size. Mekkar is five-foot seven-inches in height with brown colored hair and blue-gray eyes. He also inherited the feisty disposition from his mama. Initially raised as a reindeer herder, he became educated and has two Bachelor of Arts degrees. He is tough as nails, athletic, and gives the impression of a real fierce individual. He is a person who doesn't take any mistreatment from anyone and will fight to the death if he has to.

Birth of Mekkar

According to the native practice of relating stories through oral tradition, his grandmamma told the boy, along with some his friends, the story of his entrance into the world. She believed in the honored tradition of passing on these sagas in this manner. Plus, Mekkar's grandmama loved the attention of anyone who would listen to her speak. Having an audience made her feel respected or at least she believed that it did. That is how her grandson perceived it.

Mekkar leaned over to his best friend sitting there and whispered, "If any baby pictures of me are displayed to my friends, then I am out of here as soon as possible. I do not need to see my bare bottom, neither do my friends."

The birth of Mekkar: Now the story begins...

There was darkness along the horizon, except for the thick blanket of snow that provided the only light. The quietness was ever present throughout the area. All one could hear were the sounds of hooves and boots penetrating the white powder. Fortunately, for the first time in days no blizzard had come to pass to affect the journey. It was decided that this was a good time to set up camp.

Camp set-up began amongst the clicking sounds of boots and hooves in frenzied activity. Adults, as well as children maneuvered materials, food, and animals into position. Tepee poles were raised, first the curved ones for the inner base. Next, the straight ones were placed to rise above the base. After that specifically cut layers of reindeer skins were wrapped around the tepee frame.

In its finished form an opening was formed at the top of the tepee. This was to provide an outlet for the smoke created from the fire inside. A tepee was set up for each family. Some could "house" up to 10 people. A heavier structure ordinarily made of small logs or large formed wood pieces, along with other materials, would be used for the sauna tent. Camp was usually set up in an area where there had been one before, similar to times long past. A previously constructed, permanent structure built into the side of a hill might also be nearby. Many times those shelters could be quickly modified and used for the relaxing hot room instead.

The camp itself was normally arranged in a type of semicircle with a centralized common area, but the layout could be altered according to the surroundings. Normally, there are only a couple of options for establishing a camp site, either a circular placement or a relatively straight line. The settlement formation was chosen after thoughtful analysis by the tribe's leaders and based on historical tradition. Final selection is determined by various features of the surrounding landscape.

Some of these chosen locations and places include access to readily available water and food sources, ground levelness, and mobility ease for continued transport. Basically, how easy is it to get to and later on back out on the trek? It was a very efficient process that took place and the whole camp setup was usually completed in only a couple of hours. This stop was just a short rest for the trekkers to replenish themselves as they were behind schedule. The trek leaders felt it was a good way to get back on the path as soon as possible to catch up according to their original plan. When mid-evening appeared the group gathered everything, packed it all up quickly and began to set off again through the darkness of night.

Early the next morning the group was still on the move. The movement of gear and animals, as well as, muted voices of a few individuals were the only sounds in the darkness. Soon, it was overcome by the now labored breathing and noise stemming from one source, one young woman. That woman was Sirga, six months pregnant with child. Unexpectedly, it was evident that she was about to deliver her child right there. It wasn't going to wait for the full span of time as planned. Plus, there were still many miles to reach the nearest modern hospital facility. There was the realization that this risky premature birth would take place in an unscheduled manner and according to the old way.

Forward movement of all in the group, as well as the animals stopped and was now in hesitation mode with the tents still packed up. It seemed that the whole tribe was going to take a brief rest after all whether they liked it or not. Most other activity for the most part ceased altogether. Specifically, the children were not as loud and animated within their game movement as normal. Many adults, especially the older ones, were standing or sitting around discussing the current state of affairs over cups of fresh hot coffee or other drinks. There was anticipation in the air. At the same time, some commotion was stirring, as a few individuals hastily scrambled to gather some needed items for the event to commence!

After a small mound of snow was gathered and evened out, it was covered with some of the finest tanned reindeer skins that were usually made for trade or for sale. The smoothed-out area was quickly constructed and setup. The young Sirga was placed by a couple of the attendants on the makeshift snow bed, since none of the tents had been set up yet. She was told to lie down and encouraged to relax, as much as possible. While others in the tribe attempted to make her as comfortable as they could.

Even though the birthing was very premature and the child quite small, there was still suffering experienced by Sirga. This was noticed by some of the other women who had previously given birth themselves. They could relate to the situation by listening and understood the difficulties of a woman going through her first such milestone.

The event had taken longer than expected. Finally, the newborn child had arrived and took his first breath, while the sun was still approaching along the horizon. The background consisted of a light snow fall, surrounded by a couple of reindeer, and a few important members of the tribe. Those individuals that were present for the event included the shaman, the chief's wife, the husband, and some additional midwives.

Sirga was now considered a real woman since she had now ascended into motherhood. She was very exhausted, proud, and even seemed to radiate. Henrik, the father of the child, suggested that Sirga looked even younger at that particular moment than her age would indicate. However, even before this event many people incorrectly guessed Sirga's age because she had always looked much younger than she really was.

Many in the tribe described Sirga as a beautiful young woman. She possessed a medium round face with high cheekbones, deep set light bluish-gray eyes, dark brown hair, and a warm smile that transported others in her presence. In addition, she exhibited smooth, flush skin with not a wrinkle in sight. On top of that, Sirga possessed a tall, medium to slender figure. However, it was not considered to be one fashioned for motherhood or so it was thought. Those features, mainly owing to family genetics dictated why the young woman appeared much more youthful than her true age. This would always be the case throughout her whole life.

The new parents then and there conferred upon the little one the name of Mekkar that was alluded to the previous October. A cultural custom was every day of the year has a few specific common names assigned to that particular day. In this instance the name was chosen on that specific day before the birth took place. Some parents also choose one of those names for their newborn that are listed among the choices on the specific day of the calendar the child is actually born. The practice is a borrowed one from the dominant culture that enveloped the whole area.

But, the name Mekkar was only a small part of the boy's full name. His name encompassed many names handed down through the family lineage. One part of the little child's namesake was taken after the person who helped in the delivery; that occurred on the tundra in the Arctic mist. It was the tribe's medicine man, spiritual leader and shaman all rolled into one person, Aslak Mekkar. Thereafter, the child would always just be referred to as Mekkar from then on to make it easier for everyone to identify him.

In typical native fashion, only a few hours after the birthing process, Sirga gathered herself, as well as, her personal items. She and Mekkar continued on the trek with the rest of the tribe, animals, and belongings.

A few days later, the story of this event was retold during the sauna tent storytelling session. It was ironic that no one could pinpoint the exact spot where the birthing event took place, just the general area. Now, this might have been solved if the whole tribe backtracked along the same route just taken. That is, by following the footprints and other indicators they left behind. Yet, this action was not going to happen due to lack of extra time and other physical constraints. Nevertheless, it was predetermined that there was a schedule to keep and the trek to their destination couldn't be interrupted. The tribe didn't want to overburden the resources provided by the land in that specific location. So, sustained movement at this time was necessary for the continued existence of this Arctic tribe on the journey.

Anyhow, the skins that were laid out for the birthing episode were left behind in that spot. Either the hides were forgotten in the rush of activity or left behind because of the blood and placenta matter remaining on them. The usual practice was to bury the furs in the snow or store them in a hard to access place, but there was little time for that. By the time dusk arrived scavenger wolves had approached the now deserted location. As the animals noticed the birth contents on the skins they began to feast on the blood matter. After the lead male wolf had devoured some of the left behind remnants, he started to have convulsions and howled uncontrollably.

The wolf pack shouts emanating from the spot could be heard from a great distance throughout the valley.

By the time the journey had reached a sizeable city that had modern practitioners of medicine, the newborn child Mekkar had lapsed into a coma. It was learned that Mekkar was much too small, due to being so premature. The doctors wondered how the young one could endure a continued non traditional existence. His mama brushed aside these cautions and boldly replied that Mekkar would be a fighter and a survivor. She flatly stated that Mekkar would not lose this battle for his life. Not now, not here.

Mekkar had to be taken further away where increased medical attention could be given to him. Arrangements for transport to a city in this region were made. However, it was not a large metropolis but a town with a few thousand inhabitants. For this territory in the middle of the Arctic that is considered a big town. Trouble was, the city put his group on a modified route that ventured the tribe far off the regular path. So Mekkar's mama and papa had to stay with the little one as the tribe went on without them.

Well, Mekkar did awake from his stillness and the future showed that Sirga was right after all. She couldn't have been more accurate in proving the doctors predictions wrong. It was determined that the baby would be separated out at this point. That is, until his growth could be accelerated enough for him to catch up with other babies in the normal stages of infant development.

He surprisingly surpassed other children throughout his early years and eventually grew in stature. This occurred despite many who continued to predict that Mekkar wouldn't survive very long in the harsh Arctic environment. A few of these forecasters had the nerve to persist in speaking this way to Sirga too, but she would hear none of it.

Addition to the Family

Then, one day, Bam! Out of nowhere and unexpectedly, Mekkar overhears a young lady tell another that they hear that Mekkar's mama is pregnant and about to have another child. This was a dramatic turn of events "floored" little Mekkar, who was young himself. He was surprised and bothered about this news and its possible affect on him. He thought, "How could this happen to him!" and was disappointed that nobody warned him ahead of time.

He was confused about how he should react to the news of this event, as well as, how he would have to help care for the young sibling. Also, he felt that he wasn't old enough to do this and be a "big brother". He was furthermore upset that no one would pay as much attention to him anymore, since he currently was "the cat's meow". It seemed to Mekkar that his upcoming brother would become the "new special one" and that Mekkar would be the forgotten one.

Later on, when the little brother had arrived, Mekkar was still jealous and even a little bit resentful of Alf. This is where the competition begins between the brothers. Mekkar attempted to take care of his little brother from time-to-time, but didn't always know how to make this small creature understand and relate to him. Mekkar was thought to be mature for his age, but his "real immaturity" was revealed in these situations because Mekkar would get easily frustrated with Alf.

No matter what Mekkar believed, he couldn't comprehend that infants were not able to communicate in a similar manner as fully developed individuals. Added to the fact, that even though Mekkar was learning many languages at this time - he still was not even close to being "fully evolved" yet. However, eventually in time, Mekkar would come to appreciate his sibling and Alf's affect on him!

Beginnings

As Mekkar grew and became further advanced for his age, both in body and mind, he was required to experience integral certain cultural rituals. One was such that occurred when Mekkar reached the age of 4. Mekkar felt he was ready for the induction ceremony, as he had seen a previous similar one beforehand. This ceremony existed for a few reasons that he couldn't figure out. Mekkar would fully understand later on in adulthood, that this ceremony began an experience and process for cultural and "self-life preservation". While at the same time, come out of a need for practical reasons.

The feeling was that in a nomadic culture, if one, no matter how small, young, or insignificant they thought a person seemed - that individual had to contribute to the tribe, in a physical manner, as part of a whole. The thinking was that if each part "pulled their weight" the whole would go with increasing smoothness. Otherwise, non-contributors would become a burden to entire group and negatively affect the collective.

Thus, the reasons behind why those who are so physically or mentally challenged, the infirm, and those too old to contribute are left behind. Usually, left to freeze to their last breath in the winter or sent to any relatives outside the region that can accommodate them. This selective Darwinism is according to the nomadic cultural thinking necessary for survival of the whole tribe. Otherwise, like a domino effect, those who cannot pull their own weight can put the whole group in grave danger and cause unnecessary suffering.

Although this application of selective Darwinism is considered cruel by modern society, the opposite affect could be total annihilation for the whole group. The reasoning behind this was that the surrounding Arctic environment is so fragile. It is quick to reattribute against such problems such as over-population through lack of food supply. Mekkar listened to, but did not comprehend, these words during the nightly sauna discussions by the leaders of the tribe.

Many methods of action, carried out by a collection of a certain society's members, are attributed through their cultural beliefs and environment.

Another basic belief by the tribe was that you only take what is needed at the current time. So, that the environment could resupply the tribal members the next time they journeyed through a specific area. This is due to the slow recovery, and possible irreparable damage that could be done if over-used.

Added to the belief was the agreement that no modern technology could change this state of affairs. Possibly, because of the massive expense and potential of little profitable gain to justify the investment. Also, there is the notion that the more advanced the technology used - the more havoc would be created. This presumption is based on a degree of further distancing itself from the original provision of nature. An example referred to is the 20th century situation in Antarctica.

These were biases that would influence and shape Mekkâr's thought processes for the rest of his life. He would understand, at a later time, the purpose for this ceremony. Additionally, match it with the conversation pieces he had heard during the past few days leading up to the event.

It was seven days prior to Mekkâr's birthday. The place was in a valley near a semi-iced over river. The river, was more a large stream, was beginning to flow a bit, next to the bank. The top layer of ice, in the center, continued to thin out. This region was "caught" between the big hills and small mountains, to the north and south. No one had a map of the area, as the tribal leaders had been through this place many times, and so knew their way.

All the members of Mekkâr's family were present - his mama Sirga, father Henrik, and little brother Alf. Others on this trek were Sirga's parents, the village chief Raauno, the shaman Aslak Mekkar, and of course, other members of the group.

For this important event, Mekkar appeared in a brand new winter costume. The tunic was in a deep blue and had brightly colored stripes on the shoulders. The pants were made with still tough reindeer skin and needed to be stretched or broken in a bit. The shoes were warm, dry and full of fresh, matted straw-grass in them. They were water-proof and made with an upward curve on the toe to slip-on cross-country skis, if desired. The hat straight, and standing tall - even slightly dwarfing the inductee's head. These special clothes, as well as, all of Mekkar's clothes were made by his mama or grandmama.

A few ditties were sung by the surrounding group, at the same time one preformed by Mekkar himself. After that, the shaman proceeded over the event and carried out specific duties that were required. Rituals, such as the sprinkling of the reindeer blood on and around the altar. Another instance was the recipient wearing the "helm of horns" as he approached the altar to the rythmatic beat of the shaman's drum. The altar itself was made of stone and was a permanent structure. Various tribal symbols surrounded the outdoor shrine. In a short period of time the ceremony was completed. Mekkar now was treated differently as a result of graduating to this stage. Then, his working career had begun.

Speaking for Papa

Mekkar's papa had to conduct a business trip to the United States. The father directed his oldest son to ready himself for the journey ahead. Yet, Henrik didn't reveal any other details about the journey to come. Mekkar was even unaware of the destination or the nature of the trip at all. He thought this was odd, since usually his papa normally prepared him just in case Mekkar's help was needed in any way.

They drove from the village on a bright sunny day to the closest airport, which was a little over one hundred miles (160.93 Kilometers) away. This trip by vehicle normally takes a couple of hours, in good weather. Right away, Mekkar began the journey speaking with his papa regarding a variety of subjects. Mekkar felt the give and take of conversation would make the drive pass more quickly. However, the reality set in, about fifteen to twenty minutes later Mekkar's eyelids got heavier and he began to nod off. Soon the youngster, in the front passenger seat, fell asleep to the hum of the car's motor.

Henrik continued to navigate the vehicle in a non-vocal manner. Mekkar slept all the way to their destination and awoke when they reached the long term auto parking area at the airport. Now, he needed to be alert to avoid mistakes and be at the right gate to board the correct flight. The boy thought it was good that his papa was a detailed individual who handled those minute details for him.

After waiting in the lounge for about thirty minutes to hear a voice over the speaker, it was time to get on the plane. Mekkar joined his papa, Henrik, in their first class seats. His papa never flew economy class. For a few main reasons: Flying coach would create an image that would negatively affect the company Henrik worked for. Secondly, the trips were usually long ones and there is more to be done. Not to forget Henrik, at six foot seven inches (2.0066 meters) tall, had a build that was larger than most people. Personal comfort was always a consideration. Henrik said that, for him, being at ease improved his business interaction and success rates. On forays with his papa, Mekkar was a beneficiary of this projection of appearances due to his papa's beliefs. The boy was not going to complain in the least. It was also the same when arriving at different places with his mama, Sirga, too. Both of Mekkar' parents permanently spoiled him in this regard. Mekkar preferred travelling in style and had gotten a small taste of the good life. No return would ever be acceptable. Mekkar would only now fly economy on an air carrier that has no availability of better accommodations.

The first leg of the voyage was about a three and half hour flight to a much larger city to change planes. It is part of the airline's hub and spoke timed interchange flight connection system. The larger metropolises are the hub where all flights meet and funnel out of spoke out to smaller destinations. Airlines claim it saves money and provides more service. Not surprisingly, many flyers are skeptical about those assertions.

This was not the first time Mekkar had been on this particular route. He had done this previously with Sirga. There was only a short wait until the next departure and that would be of a much longer duration. The pilots would direct them, high in the sky, over the polar route to Los Angeles. Mekkar watched a couple of movies, grubbed away, and napped some more. Fighting boredom was a difficult task. The youngster was aware of the fact there are a limited number of activities available inside a tube hurdling through the sky. Plus, due to their elevation he couldn't see much out the windows of the jumbo jet either. At least, it was more comfortable in the non-coach area of the aircraft.

It was nighttime when they at last arrived in Los Angeles. Still, the city illuminated the evening horizon. Henrik and Mekkar's body clocks needed to adjust to the local area. Both the boy and his papa were tired of travelling all day. Henrik figured they had logged a minimum of ten thousand global air miles in the past twenty four hours. Henrik told Mekkar that sightseeing of the famous movie industry and other locations would only occur after the main tasks were completed.

Accommodations had already been made to stay at one of the nicer local hotels. Mekkar knew that his papa would avoid a reservation too close to a busy airport like LAX. Thus, to be further away from the constant aviation landing, takeoff, traffic, and crowd noise. Avoidance of shaking and rumbling windows, as well as, the scream of powerful engines soaring into the night can affect a person's sleep habits. The next morning, a limousine, it was more like a shuttle van, came to pickup Henrik and Mekkar outside the hotel main entrance to take them southward toward San Diego.

In the van Mekkar's papa only revealed their destination but little else. Henrik told him in a language that no one else there could understand them about this the situation. He said that this was a secret meeting involving a military nature. Henrik also mentioned from this point on, Mekkar could not speak of anything related to this matter for many years to come. The boy misinterpreted his papa's warning, assuming that he must keep silent about the tasks ahead, forever. Mekkar was fine with that particular stand. Yet, he was still a curious boy. The shuttle dropped off a couple of people and picked up only one other person, a uniformed military man. Henrik figured that this individual must be going to the same place down south as they were. For the rest of the drive there were no more stopovers.

Mekkar had some scant knowledge of his papa's flight skills and military training. Most of what he did know about his papa in those areas was from listening to stories told between the other adults in the sauna. Henrik would, once in awhile, contribute to the historical discussions and tell his own adventures that he participating in. Much of the conversation went back to World War II because their village was directly affected by it. However, Henrik was much too young to be of any effective armed resistance during that great-war period.

The oldest son, Mekkar, was proud of the fact his papa was the only accomplished jet pilot in the village. Airborne crop sprayers and small plane recreational flying was dismissed by Mekkar, in his mind. Only top-notch commercial jumbo and air force supersonic jets would suffice in the boy's equations. After hearing these stories about his papa, Mekkar began to elevate his papa on a pedestal. Equaling him at the same level as other great historical flying aces and famous battle tested pilots of earlier times. Mekkar thought his papa was so cool and put him in his own category, a master of the air. Similar to the Red Baron, the boy read about in books.

However, the adolescent declined each time Henrik offered him a plane ride with him in the speedy aircraft he was required to test out. Mekkar was not excited by the possibility of losing his last meal, be rendered unconscious by the g-forces involved, or being inside a plane that was not fully tested. The boy didn't want to suffer embarrassment, due to a failure to hack it. Also, Mekkar had a feeling if that were the case, the word would get back home and the teasing wouldn't end for a long time. Thus, Mekkar never took advantage of any requests to go up into the sky. Still, Henrik continued to ask every so often if his son wanted to fly with him. Yet, he was always rebuffed by Mekkar. Henrik's attitude was ok but you are missing out on a unique experience. Mekkar interpreted it as a probable plane crash would be a rare event also.

Henrik was required during these assessment flights to conduct maneuvers to demonstrate the flying machine's full capacities. His job included an evaluation process to be done in these prototype jets. Questions must be answered whether the planes functioned as they were originally intended and which improvements were required before full production. Henrik would test the limits of these original aircraft far before they reached full capacity status. After a number of flights or more Mekkar's papa would land the plane, then get out, and pointed out flaws to improve the flying mechanism's capabilities. He would also suggest needed upgrades and other aspects based on his electronics and avionics expertise. If other pilots were involved, the cockpit might be reset back to normal. As they were modified to accommodate the large physical specimen that Henrik was. Mekkar's papa, as a full grown adult, was considered too large to be a pilot according the size and space restrictions of the time. Despite his body structure Henrik was adaptable and could take the controls of just about any aircraft in the skies. Even if the instrumental panel labeling was in an unfamiliar language, he had the knack to figure it out anyway.

On the other hand, Sirga was always worried that she would be the recipient of bad news. She expected that one day she would see an unwelcomed government official or military officer. Sirga continually worried about an approach to the front door of the family home with news that her husband's test plane had crashed. She was afraid of that dreaded announcement regarding his death as a result of an accident. The good thing is that it never happened. Mekkar and his mama mainly thought that Henrik was fortunate or just lucky perhaps. From time to time, Henrik would fill in and join the crews of the national airline. Henrik flew their commercial jets on various travel routes just because he loved to fly and he was great at it. The company smartly took advantage of his services due to a seeming shortage of good pilots. Once in awhile, Mekkar went along on a few of those flights to destinations all over the globe.

Even though he can't recall who first mentioned it, Mekkar had previously been told by someone about his papa's exploits as a fighter pilot. Part of the epic included Henrik as a young air enemy hunter in the Korean conflict on the side of the United States and United Nations led Allied forces. Henrik's true age was fibbed so he could appear older to manage the jets of the time. Otherwise, technically he would have been considered too young to participate in dogfights. Mekkar had heard about his papa's past air war activities from others. The son was also aware of Henrik's extensive study, knowledge, and insight about Soviet made aeroplanes, especially the MiG. Over the years Henrik defeated a good number of those enemy planes in various aerial encounters.

What was remarkable was a promising and daring young Henrik had a more experienced co-pilot right behind him in the cockpit. The other aviator with Mekkar's papa had the ability to converse in the same communication language of the Allied operations. Many difficulties were avoided because Henrik did not speak the main language of the commanders at all. It was a smart move to put a compatriot with Henrik that comprehended and spoke English. While at the same time, the co-pilot translated commands and instructions for Henrik. Some things never change and exposed the reason a young Mekkar was on this itinerary with his papa. He needed a translator for him to relay valuable information to his audience. In this area, Henrik displayed a portion of his stubbornness. He never felt the need to learn English because he frequently used other tongues instead while conducting business affairs. Yet, this was a special undertaking and Mekkar would be part of it. Sirga's plan for Mekkar to learn English for the tourist business back home paid off in other ways also.

When the transport limousine reached a security gate at the military base, Henrik roused Mekkar from his nap. They passed through the first layer of security and encountered more soldiers at the next checkpoint. One of the guards had a clipboard in his hands with a list of names on it. He had anticipated the passenger van after seeing it arrive at the front entrance. The young boy spoke up to the security person and told him he was there to translate because he papa did not speak English. The soldier responded back to Mekkar, "My list has your father's name which matches his identification plus his son. Okay, you may proceed." There weren't many strange glances at them, thought Mekkar. He figured it was like military bases at home when the troops would bring their families with them. The youngster concluded that, here like back home, the sight wasn't uncommon either.

After reaching the main building, papa and son ventured down a fairly long hallway. To the left, Henrik opened a door to what appeared to be a classroom. Mekkar recognized one, even though he had not been present in a formal classroom setting. Various uniformed personnel began to file in. The adolescent boy tried to recall if he could identify their ranks, etc., but he failed to do so. After about ten minutes or so, Henrik was all setup and primed to give his presentation with students who were ready to receive it.

Henrik spoke first and Mekkar followed by telling the group who they were in English. Mekkar explained that since there was nobody else available to perform his role, it was up to him. He asked the audience to bear with him. Mekkar pointed out the fact that despite having only a few years in their language, he would do his best to translate properly. Mekkar continued on and said, "My papa has instructed me to convert exactly what he says to the best of my ability. He says there will be items, aspects, & concepts of a nature that you will understand. However, I am not familiar with most of these things. Also, my papa has pictures and will draw pictures to illustrate some of his points. This session should take about an hour or so."

The presenter, Henrik, started in and shortly drew a diagram with a black marker on a large white sheet of paper. Mekkar thought to himself, wow! My papa can draw really well and detailed too. On the stand there were many large white sheets that could be flipped over the top and continue on to the next one. The stand dwarfed Mekkar due to its largeness, yet Henrik towered over the helpful tool.

The developing boy had no inkling of what message his papa's sketches were conveying to the group, by looking at them. Mekkar only comprehended a little more when it was his turn to deliver the words to the audience. It dawned on him right about then, that this could be what his mama was trying to inform him, the day before. Sirga was right again, when she said to him yet again, "If you had a brain you would be dangerous." Mekkar realized, by helping his papa get some of this information across to a number of the best U.S. military jet pilots, he fulfilled that remark made by his mama. In this particular case, Mekkar was dangerous, especially if an enemy were operating Soviet-made aircraft.

Due to Mekkar's capability and value in helping his papa on this mission, the boy later received the added benefit of further trips with his papa. Henrik would later on have his oldest son accompany him on three separate trips to the Hawaiian Islands and other places to conduct sessions of a similar vein. For Mekkar, the best part of being involved with those assignments was the time spent with his papa afterward. The two would have fun with sightseeing, theme park rides, and more after the job was completed. The bonding between papa and oldest son increased as a result.

Henrik has a specific business philosophy of extensive early preparation, follow the plan set out, get the work done, then play time begins. On these trips, Mekkar gained an understanding of why his papa was very successful and enjoyed his job so much. Another bonus was the perks of frequent worldwide travel to fulfill Henrik's widespread duties. Mekkar enjoyed the travel part most of all.

Further North

Mekkar had a relative from his mama's side of the family who lived even further north than he did above the Arctic Circle. When Mekkar was young, he and his younger brother Alf would travel with Sirga to visit her relatives in that area. Most of the time his papa wouldn't accompany them on their infrequent journey near the top of the continent. In those days there wasn't even a paved road between the closest small town and the small inlet village on the other side of the island where Gretta lived. This was especially hazardous during the latter part of the calendar year when the road was basically plowed snow pack. Very much like a dirt road to make it accessible to vehicle traffic at all. Frequently, it was easier to get there by boat.

The inlet was a small fishing village of people who gather their livelihood from the nearby Arctic Ocean. That is, when the waterway approaches were not frozen over. The area hasn't changed much since then, except for local animal observation tours that cater to travelers. Many tourists hope to see rare wildlife that inhabit a cluster of islands nearby.

The boy played in deep snow in the open area next to Gretta's house. It wasn't really a flat field in the usual sense, but a series of small hillsides to climb on. Most of the houses and the small number of businesses were mainly located on one strip of land. Otherwise, the surrounding landscape was fairly barren with just brush plants. Trees are unable to gain roots and grow on the rocky hills that are mostly confined by water. At least, that would be the average visitor's perspective. Those same rocky plains would be blanketed in snow during wintertime. At times, the powder could be up to little Mekkar's waist. For him that was one way to interact with a few of the local kids in outdoor activities. The choices were extremely limited as there wasn't many people living in this area to start with.

Every so often, polar bears would arrive on the shoreline from one ice flow or another. Their goal was to scour around on land looking for any scraps of food they could find to fill their aching bellies. One time, Mekkar saw a rare event that was not only remarkable, but showed him the power possessed by these animals. A regular bear had arrived this far north on the tundra, which was out of the ordinary. Mekkar wondered why that bear was there when there almost no trees of any significance to forage on. Usually, many land animals don't travel this far north of the forest areas due to the lack of available game. Mekkar thought that this fairly large brown bear must have gotten lost somehow and was way out of his element. It might possibly be delirious from hunger. When Mekkar eventually spotted this scene, he tapped some of the other kids on their shoulder. He wanted the whole group's attention and warned them to be aware. The kids began to send signals between them and whispered to each other to be quiet. The hope was that the wandering unexpected visitor wouldn't notice their presence very easily.

Of course, neither Mekkar nor any of the other children on that snowy hillside were stupid enough to yell at the lost animal. They definitely didn't want to attract its attention. It was a good thing that bear was way over on the other side of the inlet and far enough away from them for any real danger to occur. The youngsters continued to keep their wits about them. Still, none of the now huddled children saw the large polar bear arrive into their view until it was nearby the lost brown bear. The other bear must have come upon the floating ice from another direction, thought Mekkar. Everyone assumed both were both males in gender because no cubs were there. However, when both animals were almost face-to- face one could see the arctic beast was much larger in size and towered over his counterpart. Someone pointed out that a territorial confrontation was about to occur. The polar bear then suddenly moved forward while still standing straight up on his hind legs. What an imposing figure he was. The two of them wrestled for a bit. Next, the arctic animal raised its hand and gave a back-handed swat to the lost brown bear's head. A separation and decapitation occurred. The now deceased beast's head went flying away from the torso for a few feet. After that, the smaller bear's whole body fell to the ground with a resounding thud that sent tiny shockwaves.

Wow! The kids thought with the mouths aghast. They only whispered their surprise under their breaths in the cold air. This reaction was not only due to their frightened state, but because they were hoping to avoid the attention of the victorious animal. Too late! The lighter colored bear had used its keen sense of smell and could easily smell the little ones from a distance. It was decided among them, the kids should now respond with action and Mekkar led the group of kids back to the houses in the village.

They figured the adults would know what to do to scare off any aggressive animals. They immediately began functioning on pure adrenaline. Full awareness with regard to exercising the fight or flight response and other undeveloped human mechanisms within their little beings. Soon, they all reached their destination back to the village structures. By the time they all reached their destination, each of them was completely out of breath. Yet, they didn't seem to notice. Mekkar felt that the group did not care at this point. The desire was for the curious children to be in a secure place and out of harms way.

Ceremony & Trek Survival

After awhile of Mekkar's growth development from birth we have the ceremony. This is where one goes to work. The thing with this is you start early as compared to the modern work world. You have a ceremony at this stage because it is an honor. It shows that you have grown up enough to do work that is valued.

It is odd from the modern sense because if you look at other modern nations like the United States, kids are not expected to work until they get older in life. This was due to the abuse and exploitation by companies prior to the 1920's.

But here in the native Arctic environment if you don't pull your own weight you are considered a drag on the society. The native thinking and practice is you do not want to become a burden that negatively affects the whole. The whole is the most important thing because the whole group, the whole tribe, whatever terminology one wants to use - fits into the environment as part of the whole realm. Most native cultures adapt to their environments and circumstances while modern cultures seek to dominate theirs which natives see as to their detriment.

If something deviates from that perception, from the norm, there is the harsh reality of the environment to catch your attention. What is affected is not just that one deviation but the whole is also affected, everyone feels it in some way.

It is very intertwined there and it has to be, so that is why certain practices are frowned upon and other are followed. Such as when one is on a reindeer trek you always have to keep moving. The thinking is that you don't want to eat up all the food and animal food supply that the earth provides in one place.

Otherwise the food won't grow back quick enough to sustain the herd and you the next time the group is in a specific area. Which is important for the next season when you need it for feeding? If you don't consider this factor, the next time you are in that area you will starve due to lack of foresight.

You let the earth go through its cyclical natural order, in other words — the whole. That's the whole idea and viewpoint if you and your people want to survive there. The tribe or group is part of a whole big puzzle, a greater life cycle and that is why these things must be always considered.

Anyway, at the ceremony. The shaman is into his routine, beating his drum with his related items and used in situations like this. There is an alter made of stone and earth in which you have reindeer antlers adorning it and on the top of a hat. Mekkar will have to wear this headpiece as the ceremonee or the person as the focus of this particular ceremonial ritual on this day. The blood is sprinkled on the alter, along a few other items there that symbolize this realm and the blood of life.

The blood of life, there was a realization there on Mekkar's part that without any blood there is no life. Since the basis of blood is water and without water, which the body is at least seventy percent of, there is once again no life. Any ritual is an interesting thing in that a person learns from their environment and how to deal with it through rituals. One learns how to adapt and their own limitations. This applies to all societies and all cultures. Neglect of this understanding results in destruction.

You think it is part of a cycle as life and rituals is also of a cyclical nature that reminds us that being part of the whole is the key. The whole has to fit within the environment whether it is the whole tribe or group. It must fit together in a unified way to be successful for all of those involved.

For instance, an example from the environment which is so harsh there during the winter is that if you are on the trek and you let the animals eat all of the food in one place. As well as you don't move on, the food has little chance of growing back in time or takes much longer than expected. Then, the when you need it next time there might be nothing for you and you are up a shit creek without a paddle. If you have to go there in the future you will go hungry and starve to death. Not just you but the animals you are counting on also.

The group comes back to that location later on expecting any food supply in that area but it might not be there. The fault was yours due to earlier short-term greedy thinking regarding what Mekkar likes to call resource management. Similar to the impatience of stock markets around the world today. The tribe over used the land and resources available to them and didn't think ahead for the long term future.

Everything and everyone is part of a great big puzzle. You have to fit in and consider the whole environment. When Mekkar speaks of the whole he is thinking of the whole group of people. People are just one smart piece of this huge realm, just like all the seas of the planet are a tiny portion of this dimension.

A star in the sky seems small to us, but we seem small to the star in the heavens. The sun that gives the earth warmth and light is considered by many scientists to be a fairly small star. It seems large to earthlings due its position which is very close to the earth. The thing with that is that is the whole point! People place more importance on themselves and think that they are greater than they really are.

Mekkar felt privileged at this point in the ceremonial event because he was the center of attention. He liked being the center of attention once again. He felt that he regained this status being here in the ceremony.

After his little brother was born only a few months earlier before this ritual, Mekkar exclusively enjoyed being the focus of many people and he thought everything in his own little world revolved around him. He was probably developing a sense of arrogance there.

Now with a sibling Mekkar wasn't the number one anymore. He was now not it and was frustrated by this!

His little brother Alf was now the cats meow. So in that way Mekkar resented him a bit or at least for awhile. Plus, Mekkar had his own dog as a pet. Mekkar eventually saw in another respect that hey here is someone I can help shape and mold his character any way that I want through his influence upon him. Mekkar felt whatever I want as a companion or lifelong friend as well as a relative for life.

Mekkar, even though he was young, was brilliant and highly intelligent. He had questions in his mind during the ceremony. However, wisely he kept his mouth shut for most of it. Yes, I am blessed but there is so much of the world I don't know Mekkar thought to himself. Thus, Mekkar's mind was continually flooded with more questions than answers. The more you find out, the more you know you don't know (a modified quote of Socrates). For a small child that's a brilliant deduction, but then Mekkar wasn't like anybody else and rapidly absorbed many things shown him by his elders.

The thing with that is there is a reason why the ceremony, which usually happens on your fourth birthday, was happening for Mekkar even a week earlier. It was because his papa had to go on a business trip and papa is required to be there if he is alive. How little did Mekkar know that his papa was also working on his behalf right as the ceremony was going on.

Some of the individuals there observing the ceremony were friends of his papa. He was the person who took care of him and arranged for Mekkar's first employment experience. Mekkar knew what was ahead because he was warned that there were many burdens to come and much responsibility. But, he didn't know exactly how it happen. Maybe that was a good thing because he might not have wanted to forge ahead on this course. Especially if he knew the future difficulties and struggles laid out for him or would befall upon him.

This is what bothers Mekkar even as an adult to this day. Okay, well his papa worked it out and about a month later Mekkar was on his way to the sea off of the coast quite some distance to the west. The sea there has very cold water and is very unforgiving along with being an inducer of hypothermia.

Well, Mekkar was about to work on a boat of a crew of about twenty five people. He had the lowliest job but he was the littlest and thus was at the bottom of scale in regards to wage also. Some of the fishermen had been doing this job for more than twenty years and some much longer. Plus, because of their experience they also knew this area where they were fishing very well. Also, the boat was not the most modern one on the high seas nor was it a modern operation because the owners didn't put much money back into the operation. It was a lack of funding for maintenance and operations which sounds like many companies today.

The good thing was that more of the profits were funneled back to the actual workers on the boat instead which is rare. There was a lot of cash to be made for hard work and a successful catch. Henrik felt this was a good experience for Mekkar but it would place many undue burdens upon the young boy.

Mekkar's job was to swab (mop and clean) the decks and other cleanup duties. There were some long days, it seemed to Mekkar to be at least a few twenty hour shifts. That is a long time for a small boy but his papa thought it would help to toughen him up a bit. Mekkar was deluded. Even he at times thought that he was a man. Then, reality struck him hard that he was not. It was hard for him to keep up with some of these people and crew members who had been doing this type of work for a long time.

Originally there was not even a crank for pulling back in the fish nets. You had to position the boat so it would make it easier for the crew. Some of which would become divers into the cold water (brrr!) to help hook the net to another boat on a similar path and be able to pull the net in, full of fish. This is very difficult and dangerous work. There were other options such as to use another item to help the crew pull it in or you eventually have to align the positioning against the rocks while approaching back to shore. The result was you would always lose some of your fish catch. It was easier just to use another boat alongside at a specific distance.

This seemed to Mekkar to happen for months on end. Fill up the nets, come ashore, sell the fish, load the nets back onto the boat, and get paid. Not stay on shore too long and go back out to sea. The more trips out to sea usually meant more paydays for all. At first, Mekkar felt sick and he was very uncomfortable. There was no stillness even when he slept due to the constant rocking of the water.

It was a nuthouse during the day and Mekkar had to get used to the continual rocking of the boat at nighttime to finally get some shuteye. Early mornings, as Mekkar would later find out, were hard for him since Mekkar was not a morning person. He is more of a night owl and usually more productive at night also.

Late evenings while always trying to keep up with the others on the crew was hard for Mekkar. The physical labor was intense, especially for the little boy, the feeling was that maybe he would in time get used to it. The near freezing cold ocean was very dangerous, but he made good money.

Once on land, Mekkar would send most of the cash to his parents so they would put it into a bank account back home or at least save it somewhere for him. Later, he could get the stuff he wanted when he got back. In addition, Mekkar felt that he owed his parents something for taking care of him and even spoiling him a bit. He had this sense even though they both had good employment and each had their own money at their disposal.

That was just the inducement of the rituals included in their culture. The thinking was you have to pull your own weight otherwise you are a burden and you are unproductive. This way of thinking was the reason, as like in other places at the turn of the twentieth century, for the institution of child labor laws and protections to prevent abuse. This was not an issue in Mekkar's culture.

You were still part of the whole, not just an individual, and you have to produce and contribute in some way if you could. Otherwise the whole group could be affected in a negative manner. Thus, that is the way the thinking is. It sounds cruel, but certain people who do not pull their own weight are sent away. It does not matter whether the issue is a genetic reason, a physical handicap, or any similar type of thing. Sometimes older people, and if you are familiar with native people and tribes in general, many times those individuals go out themselves during wintertime to freeze to death. Many of those who go out to die already have an indicator that their time is up in this life or that it is almost over. Some see a vision, hear a voice, or have a dream, a premonition, or some similar experience.

It sounds very harsh according to viewpoint of the modern world. This is a society that relies on a majority of pure people and animal power to keep them alive, along with the whole tribe, in the harshest of environments. It was even more true in a time and area where not a lot of machines are used.

It was a necessary thing. They natives there must have been doing something right as they have been living in the same manner for thousands of years and still survive. No matter who has tried to wipe out the people and their culture many times in the past. Even though Mekkar didn't understand these things at that time he later would and ponder about them in a deeper way. There were many things racing through his mind.

When his time was finished working on the boat, the operation had been slightly modernized. All of the boats received motorized cranks to pull in the nets from the water. Mekkar also had made a fair amount of cash and there weren't a great number of choices or opportunities to blow his money. Of course he didn't understand and consider yet what he would spend it on or even what to do it. He left it for his parents to help him decide on that later.

Mekkar was not grown up enough at this point to fully understand the worth and value of money, but he soon would! His parents were pretty smart, so he turned to them for their advice. They both had college degrees and were wise in the ways of the world.

Mekkar's parents were not in the business of reindeer herding for the money because they both didn't think it was sustainable as a full time occupation for the family in this time and age. The herding was done more as a hobby and to keep the option of reindeer herding in the eyes of the national government, where they resided. The natives who herd these animals and their direct family members would forever lose their reindeer herding rights if they stop and fail to have their offspring continue the occupation.

The boy heard from adults that laws like these are just other ways to curb, and in the future, eliminate the native customs and culture that have been there for thousands of years. This is done through what some have called strict legal maneuvers, in other words trickery by using law statutes.

Regrettably, tactics such as these have been used against native living and cultures since the beginning of time.

His papa once again started working his own two jobs while Mekkar was still young. His mama was also working; it seemed to Mekkar, all of the time. They both were workaholics and enjoyed that euphoria rush that came with the constant activity around them. Mekkar would also help out at the small family restaurant and he felt that he should to do his part to contribute some of his efforts toward the family, tribe, and village. It is still part of the mental makeup of his native culture instilled into him.

Mekkar eventually would be weaned off of just participating in tasks restricted to the village and would move on to greater horizons. When he was done with this period of experience in his young life, Mekkar parents felt that he was grown up enough to expose him to other things and gather other work experience.

Sometimes his mama would take him along with her to one of her jobs. When she did a little modeling and similar tasks once in awhile others would give him goodies and pat him on the head. Mekkar did not care too much of the head patting because he felt that is what you do to a dog. Others would tell him what a wonderful little boy he was.

He did his best to behave but it was a hard thing to always be on his very best behavior. However, what probably kept him in line was the fact that he did like being spoiled and once again being the center of attention. This is another aspect of Mekkar's character whether he wanted to admit it or not. Mekkar didn't always want to accompany his mama on some of the trips because he thought he might get bored. Sirga had other plans however. On a few of the journeys she would take him to her work with her and he would be assigned responsibilities also.

They would get up early on these occasions to travel and get on an airplane. The destination flight, to Mekkar, would seem to take forever sometimes. On the other hand, Mekkar like these new experiences and it made him feel free in a different way from being on a nomadic trail or reindeer trek. But still when they finally got to where they were going cold hard reality stuck him.

Mekkar encountered lots of different people and foreign tongues speaking in phrases that he didn't understand. This is probably, in his mind, the maximum languages in existence at that time and place. There were quite a few people there that were very different from him. While he was helping his mama, a couple of rude individuals would yell at him. He would think to himself, why? I didn't do anything bad to you; I am trying to help you and my mama. Do you understand what I am saying?

Mekkar, while working at the airport with his mama, would have contests and races between them. She would try to make it interesting but the boy always lost and had to pay up, treat his mama special in some manner, or meet one of her requests. Sirga was always working hard and thus expected Mekkar to do so also. She had a no loafing policy around her and did not tolerate it from anybody.

He felt that this is time he was able to spend with his mama, rare that it was, even if he had to go to do work alongside her. Mekkar would also go to work with his papa too. Mekkar now understood because they work so much this might be the only quality interaction he could have with each of his parents.

In an odd way they all needed to enjoy each other in their family and if this was the only way to do it so be it. This was however, not a normal thing in the native cultural environment Mekkar grew up in. Plus, Henrik was not a native, he just married into it.

Mekkar, of all people would always accept her challenges and he would race against his mama. He thought it was great. He would see if he could tag his bags, actually they were passenger check in luggage he was working with that came onto the conveyer belt, quicker than his mama could check the airline passengers in at the ticket counter.

Sirga could type extremely fast and a bad day for her was typing at a rapid pace. At least one hundred eighty five words per minute. This was one of those bad days. Well the thing with Mekkar is that he always tried to do the best he could, no matter what he did. He had this standard of himself. Mekkar's own work ethic was instilled into him through the observation of his workaholic parents and family as a whole.

In that vein, Mekkar started to think more highly of himself. His mind was telling him that I'm special and that I better do things in the special way. That is better than the norm. It was an internal conflict trend that began to grow right there. The attitude of standing out due to his own pride and hyper individualism perspective that was in contrast to his native belief system and upbringing and even the national country culture at large.

The modern society had taken root in Mekkar even though he did not see it as a shaping source upon his personality. He was starting to analyze more and more like this. This trend would in time become the force to question everything you had previously learned before. He had heard of the saying that ninety five percent of a person's personality is created by the time they are five years old. Now, that belief was being formed in him.

Mekkar was not far from that. Still some aspects of his personality and why he thought the way that he did, react the way he did was beyond his understanding. He would not be able to grasp it for awhile. On top of that, there are certain aspects he still has not figured out to this day. Mekkar referred to it as unknown mysteries of our inner being.

Mekkar knew he was special, in which way he still had no idea, but he figured there had to be a reason why he had survived so far up to this point. With this belief, he always tried to perform everything he did in a special way, a thorough way that would fit a special person. Maybe that was the stimulus for the many things he been exposed to and had learned in his young life.

He felt like I am doing stuff that nobody else, especially at his age, does. In his still developing mind he also thought that none of my friends do these kinds of things and have these adventures. I am getting to see things that they only dream about. Of course, he would tell his brother and friends the stories when he would go back. He tried to hold back and didn't want to brag, but he had the great urge to share the details with them. So, they could have a little taste of what he had seen and heard.

When Mekkar came back home he would hang out a lot with his best friend Lasse. Lasse was also in the same culture as Mekkar. However, Mekkar considered his best friend was not as much of a native as himself because Lasse's family raised him in a more non-native manner unlike Mekkar despite the physical location. Lasse never went on a reindeer trek along with his best friend. Mekkar's opinion was that Lasse's parents might have already decided he would eventually move away from the area on a permanent basis, but how did they know the future?

Lasse's papa was not native as Mekkar's was not either. But, both of their mama's were fully native and their papa's joined their families up here in the far north through marriage. Lasse spoke the language of the indigenous people just as good as Mekkar, yet it was not his primary one in his own house. Make no mistake, Lasse was still very familiar and exposed to the fundamental ways through contacts like Mekkar.

Lasse was no dummy and could be a great teacher Mekkar thought. After all, even though he is a one and a half years older, he still teaches Mekkar some things once in awhile. Lasse is a little obnoxious sometimes and rowdy at others. Mekkar thought he was a little crazy, but so was

Mekkar. Adults would comment that Lasse was still a good boy and not as blunt as Mekkar. They both still grew up in the same environment with different viewpoints, perspectives, and a few varied influences.

Lasse would share aspects and features from the non-local dominant culture with their group that some individuals might not have exposed to. Lasse liked to tell stories just like his buddy. This is how they shared their special bond as they grew up together. Parents are familiar with how little boys are in their mischievous moods. At other times, the boys would go play army or games like that, at least it is good training for when they get older and have to do it for real.

The boys would participate in many things together with their friends in the village. This would include jokes, tricks, and pranks too. There were not many people in general populating this area, so it was a good idea to get along due to a lack of choices. The amount of people would increase greatly, even sometimes doubling the local population when tourist season hit. This was also true when reindeer trekking was in full swing and on their migrations to whatever destination. On occasion they would stop for supplies and rest.

Mekkar and Lasse would take on everyone else even during activities on the ice. It was at times like them against the world. This is how Mekkar thought of the relationship with his best friend and was of the opinion that they were a like minded pair. Even if that was far from reality.

There are two facets of living in a small town or village. Everyone pretty much knows everyone else, even if no one is all up in your business in a nosy sense. The second is a kid, especially during childhood, makes a few very close friends that you do almost everything with. The reason is because the selection is limited and in fact is that it is a numbers game, otherwise the alternative is a very lonely existence.

People in Mekkar's area have a different philosophy, attitude, and outlook on true friendship. It is harder to pierce the steadfast guardedness, but once past that you have a friend for life. You don't lose your friendship as easily as in other places just because the two of you have a disagreement or piss one another off. It is much deeper than that. Even the language has a better description of the level of interaction between people who know one another better.

At times, Lasse would just be overwhelmed by the stories that Mekkar told. Sometimes he believed him, sometimes he didn't or until he could confirm their validity with one of Mekkar's family members. He thought that Mekkar exaggerated a bit regarding some of the tales told by his best friend. But, isn't that commonly used for effect when boys are that age? Lasse would even approach Sirga and ask her about the truth in Mekkar's stories.

After awhile he gave up because he found it to be the case that Mekkar was telling the truth and not totally full of falsehood. Mekkar would just spit it out and try to be fascinating at the same time. Mekkar liked to tell various tales of what happened during the most recent trip. Sometimes he would go into too much detail or get sidetracked easily. But, you know it is just exploration of your surroundings and how one describes them. Everyone has their own biases. Of course, he would mention the bad stuff that went on too! So, there was kind of a sense of balance there.

That it, life and living, is not all easy and rosy, not all fun and games. There are negative aspects also. But, Mekkar didn't think of those categories when reciting the accounts of his adventures, he would just let it all fly. Well, everything that he could recall like a boy his age could. Lasse eventually grew up to be a big physical specimen, much larger than Mekkar.

Even though Mekkar was born so much earlier than expected, they both grew about the same rate in their early years. Mekkar was for a time there was a little bigger on the more husky side of the two. Mekkar was more physically developed when they were younger but Lasse surpassed him at approximately eleven years old. Mekkar never grew any taller after that age.

Now with this, Mekkar would go on different trips with his papa also. Besides that, every so often he would work in the family restaurant as a waiter serving guests.

After working on the fishing boat, his mama demanded that he learn the English language for the family business because there was a need and she thought that he would be a good candidate. There was also pressure on her due to the increasing number of tourists: Yanks (Americans), Canucks (Canadians), Roos (Aussies), Kiwis (New Zealanders), Springboks (South Africans), and most of all Brits (those from the United Kingdom, specifically Great Britain) that had English as their primary spoken tongue.

Thus, her impatience in this regard was understandable. Mekkar was his mama's choice and she was determined to make him fulfill this role she set out for him even if it killed her. His mama set up home schooling with tutors along with his special foreign language studies. Sirga also felt that this was a good reflection, in one aspect, of her parenting abilities.

When Mekkar's papa Henrik would go to the United States, Britain, or another nation with English as a mother tongue for business, Mekkar's mama made requests of him. It was mainly for Mekkar's benefit in her mind. Sirga would tell Henrik to purchase and bring back English speaking only sports tapes, films, and videos for Mekkar.

She knew that would the best and quickest way Mekkar could grasp the correct phraseology through his passion of sports. Sirga never failed to remind Henrik to tell his translators too. She would do this herself on the rare occasions when she met the go betweens directly that would travel with her husband on those business trips.

It was important due to the fact that Henrik never learned nor spoke English himself. He admitted being taught a few of the swear words as part of the Allied air group during the Korean conflict, but long since forgotten them. Henrik was able to converse fluently in ten other languages, with business vocabulary in German being most important for his employer at that time.

Henrik would buy in North America, at the behest of Sirga; National Football League (NFL), National Basketball Association (NBA), Major League Baseball (MLB), World Hockey Association (WHA), National Hockey League (NHL), & English Futbol (Soccer) items for Mekkar. Henrik would bring back whole boxes of items. This was done to encourage Mekkar to continue on and to help him develop the skills needed as soon as possible. An incentive program!

Sirga had confidence that Mekkar would succeed in the immediate and difficult task she had given him. She had a plan. Sirga held back whipping his rear end and other forms of punishment until the job was done in a satisfactory manner as a last resort. So, when Mekkar's mama felt he was ready enough she put him into the fire by mainly pressing Mekkar into service due to need.

On one of the first days of dealing with the tourists in the family restaurant Mekkar was busing tables and took a couple of orders. One example was some tourists that had just arrived into their small 15 table specialty diner. The visitors from the United Kingdom appeared to be astonished when a boy came over to their order in fairly broken English in their opinion.

It seemed as though both parties understood each other well enough to converse. After his first order was received in the foreign language, Mekkar approached the kitchen. Now he was beaming with confidence, well as much as a little boy could muster. In his eagerness, he took a few more that day.

Later on, another kid in one of the tourist families taught Mekkar a new swear phrase. In a particular instance Mekkar was given inaccurate information as to the meaning of the quip and was told that it meant Hello or referred to it as a type of greeting instead of the phrase's true meaning. Why Mekkar took it at face value from the slightly older visitor we will never know.

Eventually Mekkar used that greeting toward another small group of visitors and received an appalled reaction which caused them to flee out of the restaurant. When Sirga got wind of it she was angry at Mekkar and smacked him upside the head. Mekkar was confused and bewildered to say the least by his mama's response. He thought that he was generally being friendly. Mekkar was unaware that the specific choice of words was a type of curse phrase instead of a friendly introduction.

The lessons learned when his mama explained to him of the true meaning after she was warned by one of her friends who happened to be nearby and spoke English fairly well. Of course, this was before Sirga began her own process of absorbing English for her to be relatable to a host of tourist groups supposedly coming their way in the near future.

This was the only slip up by Mekkar and overall it was considered that he did a good job. Mekkar was rewarded after closing hours with pots, pans, dishes, & cleaning duty. He felt that maybe it was due to his swearing at the tourist earlier. Another possibility might have been because his little brother needed to have an example to follow to be groomed to carry out the same tasks when he got older. It was determined there was just a lack of available bodies to fill all the jobs for now.

Later on the family business expanded into a few other areas and branched out a bit. Sirga also forced Mekkar along with his siblings and friends to expand their foreign speaking skills by hook or by crook for employment requirements. Since, Mekkar didn't go to the formal school and instead had tutors, training aids, etc. he could spend more time working. His extra time was playing sports and just being a kid as much as he could. This was because in this culture children had to grow up more quickly and contribute to the family's welfare. When he got older formal classroom schooling was sacrificed on the altar of sports.

Mekkar was in the process of learning not only his native tongue, but another nearby dialect of it, the national language of the country he lived in, a regional speech, a couple of continental languages, along with communication in English as his mama required. His plate was quite full at this time.

This was all determined by the force of his mama's personality backed by statements of "do it my way or I'll beat your butt!" There was no double standard or dual meaning to interpret regarding Sirga's words or intentions, unlike today's politicians. The goals were made very clear and defined. She meant what she said.

Mekkar's mama also made his brothers, when they reached a certain age; learn other foreign tongues to fulfill various other needs according to her perceptions. Alf would eventually become fluent in easily over twenty languages including Hungarian, which is considered by many to be the hardest language on earth. Eventually Alf could converse in Cantonese Chinese, Japanese, Arabic, Greek, and many of the prominent Finno-Ugric, Germanic, Slavic, & Romance languages. Mekkar, on the other hand, was considered a slacker in his family for speaking less than ten languages himself. However, he spoke English which others in his family did not speak as of yet.

Due to lack of use and practice, in time Mekkar would forget a couple of the tongues he learned when he was a kid. He still remembers odd words however. English was here to stay and would be of more use in the future unbeknownst to Mekkar when he had to flee his home.

Another time Mekkar was outside tending to some of his reindeer to keep them healthy for the tourist business. Then some other visitors were driving by slowly in a vehicle near the area where Mekkar was. The car stopped and a man and what appeared to be his wife along with two children got out. Mekkar recognized them as non locals because of their clothes and he had interacted with some of them in their own language earlier in the day. However, he kept his back turned toward them and continued on his task.

When the man approached Mekkar within speaking distance he said disparagingly, "Hey reindeer boy turn around and look at us, so we can get a picture of you with the animals." Mekkar heard him and thought that maybe the British tourist did not recognize him from earlier. Mekkar surmised that the visitor thought he was speaking to someone else, but he was the only native there at that moment.

Mekkar was perturbed at that condescending comment and responded by turning slowly to his right and giving those arrogant bastards the native version of flipping the bird at them. In case that wasn't enough for them to get the picture, and Mekkar believed that it might not have been, he then proceeded to drop his pants to his ankles and moon the tourists there. While at the same time pat his bare bottom in their direction.

The boy reacted with a flippant attitude in this manner. He did what he thought was an appropriate comeback to combat the snobbish attitude and comments on the part of the out of towners.

Usually Mekkar tolerated a lot due to communication challenges, but when people got rude with him his outgoing friendly demeanor changed. He might say something back that was sharp and blunt in response. "Hey, you don't understand here", he might blurt out. Mekkar never allowed any interaction intimidation by any individual against him. This attitude would also incur Sirga's wrath on occasion also. She didn't want any harm to come to the business.

Some other times Mekkar's buddies would show up at the restaurant to give Mekkar grief and a hard time but it was all in jest. Those, whoever was running the eatery that day whether it was Mekkar's mama, grandmamma, or another family member would proceed to kick the boys out. The aim was to keep Mekkar from being distracted by their behavior and get back to work.

This was part of Mekkar's makeup or maybe just a character flaw. Mekkar had a situation where people came into the diner and tried to get any employee's attention to wait on them. Mekkar came up to their table and was fully confident in his task. He already knew what he was doing and by this time had a lot of experience despite his outward youthful appearance. However, this particular group of tourists did not see it the same way. They tried to chase him off as he was about to take their food order. One of the persons in their party shot out a comment, "Hey, get out of here little kid as we are getting ready to make our selections from the menu."

Mekkar at first thought maybe this was joke on him. Since he was the only one on the small staff who could communicate with these English speakers he felt the need to approach them again. Mekkar perceived the grumpy old man who made the earlier response as another arrogant visitor who thought that they were better than the locals. You know what they say about obnoxious travelers, it fit in this case.

The native youngster once again thought that maybe the man was not too old, but his face made him look older than he probably was. He tried to quickly analyze the visitor by his outward appearance. This way of thinking, was the first instance that Mekkar could recall, where he believed he was being contrary to his own native cultural upbringing.

Unlike, in many other places, observations of people here are usually not based on the first impression or introduction with an individual. The reason is that it is considered a poor indicator and not an accurate measure of a person's character. Mekkar knew that these first interactions should not be relied upon as a true gauge of a person's real personality. Family members and elders in the village had mentioned this in quite a few discussions with Mekkar.

The trouble was Mekkar was beginning to have another standard of which to judge tourists as opposed to other people. An increasing number of visitors seemed to arrive with more superior complexes and this began jade Mekkar's opinion of them a bit.

The customer at the table had a few wrinkles around the eyes and a squint to his facial features. Mekkar, well he tried to copy that as he was taught to carry himself in a mirroring effect with new arrivals when he spoke to them. The issue was that Mekkar, being a boy, did not have a deep voice like the man.

But Mekkar didn't want to show that he might be overwhelmed by anyone. So, Mekkar felt the only way he could be forceful enough to garner any respect was with his bluntness with all people. That was the way Mekkar was and he inherited this trait from his mama's side of the family. His own native language tended toward that straightforwardness also.

Another person in the group spoke up, "Get out here little kid and get someone who will take our order!" Mekkar responded, "I am ready to take your order now." Mekkar guessed that these people still thought this was some kind of prank or something else.

Mekkar suspected that these tourists were from the United Kingdom or thereabouts. He figured that he was the only one able to communicate with them and he was improving his skills and fluency on a daily basis. There was some difficulty comprehending some of the British speech, but this exchange was completely unnecessary in Mekkar's opinion.

There was inferred tone now in his response to the rude travelers, "I know what I am doing. If you want something that is fine, but if you don't there is another long distance up the road, where you can order somewhere else." Mekkar had quite enough of the negative vibe directed at him.

He also perceived that those people in that party looked hungry and tired. They appeared to him to have needed a break. That is one of the reasons why Mekkar took this tact approach. He expected a retreat from confrontation on their part. Plus, Mekkar also knew that he had stretched the truth in his blunt retort. There were other eating places and competition right there in his village and nearby. But, he was not about to give in to anyone's attack against him.

Mekkar had a method to his madness, there was a strategy. He wasn't going to put up with rude attitude nonsense for just doing his job. At the same time hoping that word of his sharp tone, response, and behavior with the guests wouldn't get back to his mama. Sirga is the one who would meter out any punishment or discipline as necessary. Mekkar was determined that no one was going to defeat him with this confrontational strategy of his when he had to rely on it.

The arctic lad noticed the sweat running from their brows and those visitors looked physically exhausted, needing a rest. So, Mekkar reacted with that stance and the gamble paid off and the tourists stayed. They ordered their food and drinks. Unfortunately, for Mekkar they did complain to management, Mekkar's mama, and he did get into trouble for this.

Anyway, it was worth the risk to Mekkar in that he knew if you are stern and stand up for yourself against any type of attack, you will eventually be victorious. This is the way Mekkar thought and he was born a fighter. Even fighting for his own survival at birth. Mekkar is of the opinion that he will always be a fighter throughout his life in some capacity and this would probably never change.

Mekkar once heard from someone close to him that his mama made a dramatic comment regarding him not long after his birth at the hospital. Sirga said, "That boy, if he survives, is going to be feisty because that is what will keep him alive, especially now." Thus, the reason why Mekkar thinks his mama is some kind of prophet or has special powers.

Well, this went on for a couple of years, in between entering into the realm of semi-organized ice hockey and other activities. The hockey was not organized as compared to leagues and teams in the larger town scope some distance away. He just considered it semi structured for the immediate scarcely populated area Mekkar grew up in.

You know, being a kid and even going on special adventures that most children and other people do not normally enjoy. Including going on the reindeer trek. It is well to note once again that Mekkar was brought into this world while a small percentage of his family was fairly nomadic in some respects. That is they used to follow the reindeer in their migratory patterns just as some of his ancestors did.

Some scientists and anthropologists say even as long as more than ten thousand years ago. Carrying out all these various activities in the harsh environment of the Arctic. His native people also existed far below the tundra areas to more southern latitudes. Over time they were pushed northward by other more numerous peoples.

Well, Mekkar and some others in his tribe and village were about to embark on a long round trip trek this time around. Their direction would take them northward to the plateau, swing to the east travelling through some small towns along the way. They were going to go so far east as to almost reach the sea.

However, they didn't want to get so close as to alert the military installations in that region because that would bring a host of other problems the trekkers were looking to avoid. It would be a hard journey through deep snow and the group doesn't want to use up all the food and other resources where they are now and deplete it for future use.

Thus, the reason for the migration and movement for the sake of the animals because they are the lifeblood and identity of the tribe. Some of the members rely on the animals for their main livelihood. If the reindeer can't eat and feel safe from various predators, they will starve and not be strong enough for the journey and won't survive through the season. The result is that the people with the animals will be negatively affected and could starve also.

The reindeer are also valuable commodities as well as, in some cases, good companions like a family pet. They usually listen and don't interrupt you when you speak. Mekkar has this idea that they might have the ability to show some concern and know that you are all in it together. Of course, he hasn't confirmed this theory of his.

However, Mekkar is convinced that these animals are smarter than they are given credit for. On the other hand, some of the beasts can be extremely stubborn and aggressive at times. This is especially true when the antlers are reforming and growing back as well as during round up, rutting time, along with competing for food and treats.

A reindeer is not stupid and can ingenious at times for a pack animal. They have the ability to find food under deep snow because of a keen sense of smell. Mekkar calls it their radar. The animal is very suited and adapted for arctic climates.

The first time Mekkar saw the reindeer stop in its tracks he was amazed as he watched quietly as it located its food source. Mekkar is still amazed regarding that capability even to this day far into the future. Sometimes, he will say to himself, "How did they do that?" Even when Mekkar knows the scientific explanation and answer to his question.

Many people make statements regarding the fact that the human is smarter than an animal because they have the ability to reason. But, Mekkar disagrees with this analysis because he is convinced that in some cases the opposite is true.

As he has gotten older, Mekkar doesn't believe that is the case at all. Through seeing with his own eyes, Mekkar concludes that in a few aspects the animal is much more superior to the human. One reason is that just because humans have common sense doesn't mean many in their species actually use it. Also, human beings have used part of their extraordinary talents to destroy the whole planet instead of nourish it.

Over many years the animals haven't been the ones in command of earth and thus they have not tried everything in their power to destroy it either. Unlike people, the animals have embraced their surroundings, adapted, and furthered the growth of Mother Nature along with native tribes for their own survival.

Whether the non-human species realize it or not, a limited number of people such as native tribes have followed suit in forms of adaptation. Furthermore, they have displayed a caring for the immediate environment around them.

Not forcing or attempting to compel and exploit nature to adapt to people like the modern societies do. This while at the same time the advanced and developed cultures giving lip service regarding the betterment of the planet and their own natural surroundings.

This train of thought is in direct conflict with Mekkar's upbringing and concepts that help shape Mekkar's native people. As stated beforehand, in that cycle of life we are just a small piece in a much larger human puzzle. The people who live in harmony with the land and environment all know that they are all here together.

The whole key is understanding these concepts and the goal of the natives there is to survive and even thrive. If one becomes well off that is even better because it shows that not bleeding the environment dry can be done successfully.

That is successful in whatever endeavor one chooses if they are smart and conduct themselves in an appropriate manner. Of course, there are other factors at play here that many fail to mention that are related to a person being accomplished significantly in life.

One is you have to be lucky; however one defines it, and be at the right place at the right time. Another aspect is that Mekkar like anyone else needs a lot of help from others along the way. Mekkar knows that no individual in existence became super great at anything without some input, guidance, or help. The person who says they did it all by themselves is not telling the truth. Only arrogance and greed proclaim otherwise.

So, connections are extremely important. You know the common saying; It's not what you know but who you know. This is more crucial than ever in today's world. Mekkar likes to add to that well known statement. It maybe more accurate in some cases to say it's who you sleep with takes priority over your brain power and intelligence.

He believes that this rings more true in modern societies if one is wise. This is just some of the thought processes that run through Mekkar's mind. Those ideas have definitely been imparted into his being and influenced him from sources around him especially family members.

Mekkar was still impressed to see these creatures in action even though he had been around them all of his young life so far. The reindeer is not that large or as tall when compared with cattle or a moose. They are shorter but also have a wide body and have lower stature, much smaller than a horse. Very similar to how Mekkar would later turn out to be with a low center of gravity. Others were restricted in their view of him by noticing only his smaller overall stature, but discounted any possible advantages.

Reindeer have hooves that are split and help them to keep from slipping on winter surfaces. They have better traction than people do in regular shoes and boots especially on ice and hard snow. These animals are exceptionally strong for their size, very powerful, and they can sense when something is after them. They can swim too!

Remember, they are still a herd creature by nature and can be, like Mekkar, stubborn to a fault. On an individual basis they make their grunt type, snorting din which can change when being attacked. Mekkar realizes their antlers need to stay strong and sharp. So, they can protect themselves against predators and win tussles to impress others within the herd.

At times, they will use their antlers, along with their feet, for digging into snow to find food sources. Mekkar refers to it as using their radar system, heightened sense of smell, to locate edible nutrition. They are smart enough to rub up against trees and bushes to remove the velvet blood, skin, and fur layer that promote antler growth because they drop them each year. Similar to a snake shedding its skin. Adaptive and creative unlike a sheep but also part of a collective for protection.

Now, the curious thing about starting the trek is not finding the leader of the reindeer. There are a few who will vie for that esteemed function. The key is to recognize the next few animals that follow right up there with or close behind the leader of the pack. The ideal is that the rest of the herd soon begins to follow the clicks of their feet to move the whole group in the same direction.

There are a few reindeer who will do battle for the alpha male leadership role. The baddest, toughest male gets more of the females. Just like it works in the human realm also despite the social engineering that abounds. If Mekkar decided to see things from a reindeer's perspective, he would think why would I want to be the runner up instead of the top "dog".

Reindeer are the only deer species where the females also grow a set of antlers like the male. However, they drop them at different times of the year. Furthermore, the female is required by biology to divert at least some of that calcium to other uses. Purposes such as offspring, production of milk for growing calves, and extraction for dairy products consumed by humans. All this is done without being affected by bone and skeletal cancer like people. Scientists are still trying to gain answers to those questions.

Mekkar still thinks they are amazing animals. While most individuals mistakenly fancy the notion that all they do is fly through the air pulling Father Christmas' sleigh around to help him deliver Christmas presents. Mekkar says hogwash to that impression.

Some of the animals have different colors. They have birth marks and color spots just like people. Their colors can change and vary according to the seasons too! [Wikipedia] There is a tendency to conserve all white reindeer fur a little longer so that the material can be used for more special occasions. Products such as footwear and clothing as used in specialty cultural events such as weddings, etc.

Once upon a time, in many places, the principle was once married one usually stayed together for life. Mekkar suggests that divorce would be almost non-existent on the part of both parties, if there were some type of major price to pay for all involved. A price that involved more than just financial assets. If both persons were to be put to death for this drastic action of separation, then both individuals might think twice and try to work it out. Marriage would also be held in higher esteem than it is today and more like the institution it was in the past. Now, there isn't any place that is not infected by the new divorce trend. To him, it is very unlike the old native customs. In Mekkar's mind, there has been a rapid progression in many areas, especially in the past few generations. He chalks it up as part of a range of negative effects that has affected many native cultures. The dark side influences brought on by modernization and modification. He feels that not all of these changes are good and positive, but instead destroy the old ways. He feels that this is only one element of a larger extensive ongoing agenda. A plan carried out on purpose. One that is predetermined to extinct native peoples by fully and forcibly assimilating them into the overwhelming cultures surrounding them.

Anyway, on the trek the key is to find a few followers among the reindeer to move right along with the leader. The idea is that the rest in the herd will follow suit. A keen herder can soon identify those traits in regard to individual animals and nudge them to the proper locations, if necessary. Those reindeer are harder to find than a number one. There are always a few animals who will battle for the top spot because it gains favor with the females of the herd. Growth and hardening of annual antlers are also used in later dominance sparring sessions around rutting time. Demonstration of individual battle readiness and prowess practice to ward off all foes will be exercised as well. Yes, they make a spectacle of themselves and show off just to impress future potential mating partners, just like people do. Of course, there will be some younger ones, stragglers, and others that are too exhausted for whatever reason to continue onward. In those cases, there are a host of actions taken to transport those animals along the journey.

The trek is an amazing thing. It could involve many reindeer clumped together from different families. To an outsider, it could look like a pure nomadic setting and total chaos, but that observation would be incorrect. There is always a plan and these methods have been used successfully for a long time. The group has chosen a strategy that would take the beasts away from the low lying areas after the long winter. They have been somewhat buffered from the harsh winter weather, now it is time to go. Biology dictates moving the herd to higher ground above the tree line in the spring and summer. All herders desire positive outcomes during the calving phrase. Replenishment is the key to not losing each person's whole collection of animals. A protective and anti-pest rationale is also used to keep everyone on the trek away from predators and nagging insects. This ritual has been practiced for many generations.

Natives joke when giving advice to tourists and others planning to visit the region. If you are arriving here for the nice, sunny weather and the infamous twenty-four hour sun show up in May or June. That is, the sun in the middle of the summer never completely sets below the horizon, even in the middle of the night. They are also told not to come during July or August. Otherwise, the sightseers might become fresh meat and a nice blood supply for the mosquitoes to feed on. As the locals know those insects flourish in the many waters and lakes during the extra sun periods of the year. The vermin can fill the sky when migrating from bush to bush. The local inhabitants of the area then eagerly await bird arrivals, which then gorge on the pests. There is such a plentiful food supply, the fowl get too full to fly. A waiting period is needed before they fly back down south for the winter as part of their yearly migration.

Movement from place to place according to the seasons is based on an old principle. You do not want to have the animals, and for that matter people, use up all the resources that available in a specific area. If a group or individual uses everything up in that small location, there might not be any grow back in a timely manner. That includes limited food supplies also. Like it was mentioned beforehand, it is all part of the cycle of life and taking care of your environment for survival. It is the opposite of the modern concept of always attempting to dominate your surroundings and changing it to suit your needs. Mekkar is of the opinion, those prejudices will eventually come back to bite a person in the rear end, usually at the time when it is least expected.

Outsiders approaching a certain culture always see things from a different point of view. They look at aspects that those who grow up in a society take for granted and never recognize. On the other hand, insiders use metaphors and take stances that outsiders will never understand. It is always a matter of individual perspective and cultural upbringing that shapes a person. Each person is different in how they assimilate the world in their own mind and through their own belief system or bias filters, as Mekkar refers to them. True examples of these different avenues of communication occur specifically in sports locker rooms and companies that have an international flavor. Some of the people who didn't grow up in that particular environment or with a certain language might not understand the banter and jokes among the team or business associates. It takes time to blend in as Mekkar calls it, even more than an individual anticipates.

Okay, so as the crew starts the trek, the members of the herding band have brought a plentiful supply of winter clothing since that season has not completely passed. It is heavier in construction due to an expectation of not so pleasant weather at times on this trip. It is the arctic after all and the climate can do an about-face quickly. On the tunic there are bright colors that stand out and a darker colored background. Some of the older trekkers have black as the background. The young Mekkar sported a blue top with multiple striped colors on the shoulder regions and well as the various edges. The youngster wore the hat that he received, as a gift, from the shaman. In the old days some would use the hat in conjunction with daytime reflection the sun and shadows as a type of compass. Mekkar was hoping for a bonus that included some of the special powers emanating from the shaman himself. He would be disappointed in that regard. The boy wouldn't know how to use those special abilities anyway. Either way, the symbolism is overt and evident. Once in a while, the hat is used for storage for small items or grass can be stuffed in it. The headpiece matched the shoes for insulation. The grass helps with moisture absorption also. The clothing is water-resistant and the boots can be made fairly leak proof depending on the materials used and the amount of effort in the construction. Most outer reindeer fur overcoats are sufficient and thick enough to keep one warm in the frosty elements.

There is also the ventilation feature taken into account. A person doesn't want to have excessive body sweat in the harshest winter cold. The risk of somebody's pores or sweat glands freezing is real. It can result in a slow enough heart rate to possibly stop it and potentially kill you. The worst thing one can do is to fall asleep in extreme cold temperatures. The idea is to keep moving with the blood pumping throughout their body. On television or in photographs, you can see Arctic or Antarctica research explorers cover their face and extremities when outside in the harshest weather conditions. Otherwise, wind burn-marks can result from the pure dry cold. People have lost body parts from severe frostbite of exposed skin areas.

Adaptation to this type of environment, in these areas, has evolved over thousands of years. The norm is a very dry climate with low humidity, however, that depends on the season. The herding party has been fortunate and has encountered snow, on this journey, that is deep and packed down real well so far. In many Arctic societies' native languages there are many more words for snow than let's say, english. Some of the words describe the texture, the type of flake in its shape and size, moistness, and many other aspects of the winter white stuff. Yet, key more precise terminology to keep mere mortals alive in the midst of potentially brutal elements.

Well, as the crew is beginning the trek. Mekkar is feeling prepared and eager to get going. He feels confident in his fairly water resistant wares on his body. Even his shoes are modified to slip on the skis that across his back, if needed. Very similar to the old fashioned methods which his people have been employing for a few millennia. The function of skiing, not just for sport, was invented in the Arctic regions. Mekkar would refer to it as an area north of the Arctic Circle. In modern lingo, it is referred to as a Land of The Midnight Sun. In reality, there are quite a few large territories encompassing this region of the globe.

Past settlers and leaders from outside of the territory have placed their own claims to this land previously inhabited by native tribes. It was common for invading chiefs, kings, and warlords to resort to conquering these vast areas by force. Brutal, forced religious conversions of the local populations were used against the inhabitants already living there. The main goal was to own the area's vast natural resources which included subjecting the native peoples to unconscionable conditions. In some instances, driving them to their death by treating them like worker drones. This was also carried out by newcomers through a method of raping, plundering, pillaging, intimidation, and other means to get what they wanted. Like all so called civilized cultures do, the foreigners' mindset was to act in a manner that imposed their will, military strength, and lifestyle. They have a belief that their actions will automatically bless the hapless and backward natives without consideration to consequences. There is an applicable modern saying that fits the superiority attitude of the invaders, "Might makes right." [The Melian Dialogue by Thucydides, 431 BC; Adin Ballou, 1846] The results have shown that betterment is not the case most of the time. Any benefits afforded the locals are usually negated due to that mistaken ignorance of modern man. Unfortunately, the indigenous people bear the brunt of the suffering.

During this growth period and development children in Mekkar's area of the planet learn to ski, ice skate, and walk at relatively the same time. That is the case for many youngsters in the same age range as him. Exposure to cross country skiing is essential and used as a transportation method during the wintertime. A valuable skill when there is too much snow and one doesn't have the desire or the time to dig out their vehicle. Don't forget the added obstacles of the road conditions.

It is much quicker to slip on your skis and be ready to go. Of course, like anything else a person is unfamiliar with, cross country skiing is harder than it looks. The closest experience most individuals have to it would be the ski motion exercise machines. It is a good workout especially if an individual is not used to it. You work many muscle groups, upper and lower body, all at the same time. That goes for places you didn't realize you had or have neglected for a long time. The next day soreness will definitely be felt by the inexperienced. Mekkar has conducted this activity when it is freezing cold outside. The hazard is one doesn't want to overwork themselves and incur too much exposure to the surroundings. The Arctic boy has learned to first prepare the body for acclimation, similar to a warm up. There is a delicate balance in keeping the body temperature warm and refrain from exhaustion due to amount of effort exerted.

Still, you have all of these reindeer that have been gathered from the various families from the village, including Mekkar's. One question never asked or mentioned would be regarding how many reindeer each family has. A similar scenario would be if a person asked the personal question of, "How much money in the bank do you have?" A real personal and private thing, indeed. On top of that it is also considered rude. The total number of animals in the herd was a fair amount considering the small size of Mekkar's village. Not quite big enough, population-wise, to be considered a town or hamlet by the government far to the south. The number of people in the area would fluctuate during the high point of the peak tourist season. However, it shrinks back down to a certain level of minimal visitors throughout the rest of the year.

Well, this journey began in the late winter and will continue on into springtime. A reindeer round-up area had been previously setup to the north. The goal was to gather the initial herd together for overland travel. This environment is not for the timid and weak. There is a ruggedness of the people that live here and even more so that go on these treks. The problem is there are scarce resources which replenish themselves very slowly or not at all during the winter season. Plus, they get used up quickly by all surrounding them, even by others, who take no precautions toward the delicate environment. It is a necessary concept to trek by moving the animals around from place to place, just as it has been for many years. At least not become stagnant and continue to rotate to higher ground and back down every year. Trekkers benefit as it keeps them regularly in touch with nature. The journey also forces them to learn and remind them of what they need to do to survive. As he got older, Mekkar pondered further on these concepts.

That is the whole key to the Arctic native existence lifestyle. Survival in an area that almost nobody else wants to live in. For the longest time, the regions in the far north were left alone and were basically avoided. Until later, when it was realized that the polar circle territories could be exploited and provide benefits for those far to the south. Vastly outnumbered natives have been pushed further north throughout history. Encroaching populations have advanced up to the point where there is no where else for the natives to go.

Mekkar, in a playful manner, blows air out of his mouth to estimate a guess of the temperature and moisture in the air. He also originally over estimates the number of persons from the village that would be involved on this particular trek. It turns out there would be a little less than fifteen that would accompany the herd. The youngster is raring to go and already had his gear packed along with skis.

Initially, he proceeds to trod through the deep snow among the trees around his house. Mekkar picks up his knees as high as he can in practiced anticipation. The thought runs through his mind that he hasn't done this for awhile. The remembrance reservoir of Mekkar is still so small due to his young age. Not only that, his sense of time is very inaccurate as compared with a grown-up. He regards a week as a long period of time. Oh! The impatience of youth.

The Arctic youth feels like he is ready to get going. However, this will not be a short journey. In addition, this travel route is going to a different place, not their group's usual location at this time of the year. Mekkar has begun to convince himself that this will be a good trip and a positive experience. Mekkar overheard the trek leadership speaking about it and thus assimilated the information into his feelings, his inner being. The boy listened as Ansetti and others were discussing the state of the whole reindeer herd.

The exchange included the last fall selection for edible uses, rutting time, and surviving through the winter season. It was determined by the group that the remaining reindeer will be starting out on this trek as a healthy group. It is important the beasts not resort to laziness either. They also need exercise to increase their strength to fatten up later on in the year. Mekkar listened to the conversations about the parallels of movement increasing stamina. The notion is to fend off exhaustion and disease for the benefit of the upcoming birthing process. Mekkar was being selfish as he heard the dialog by only thinking about himself at this point. He gave no consideration of the trekking hardships and their effects upon the animals.

A small number are included on the journey and traded for other goods or sacrificed for food. Many other parts of the animals' anatomy is consumed in some manner, nothing is wasted. Mekkar has worked out a plan where some of the bones and antlers are grounded up and sold to tourists as an aphrodisiac. It is popular with the Asian visitors, especially the Japanese, because they treated those items as an exotic product. Mekkar was aware that some would pay good money to purchase a small bag of the stuff. He wanted to capitalize on that. Various natives are always searching for ways to supplement their income. German marks, United States dollars, and British pound sterling were the common foreign currencies used in the transactions. Money from the United Kingdom was considered the best, during that time, because it offered the best exchange rate for locals.

Back to the trek, the adolescent Mekkar realized this was the first trek after his family had been fully domesticated with ownership of a permanent home. They were not labeled as semi-nomadic anymore. He knew the conditions outdoors were harsher than normal, but that did not temper his enthusiasm toward the trek that was soon to begin.

Ah! The weather outside was bearable, as they left the comforts of the village, on the first day of the trek. One of the elders made a statement, in a joking tone, that it was a pretty warm day for this time of year. It still was minus 15° Fahrenheit below zero (-26.1° Celsius). There was not too much wind, just pure bitter cold that burned the lungs as it was inhaled. The body clothing was fine and well suited for this. It was made for much chillier maximum conditions than this, even without other additional garments underneath. The outer layer fur coat made it downright toasty for Mekkar's core area and easily kept in his body heat. The boy had his hat too stuffed with the insulation, so he was fine. He was used to being pelted in the face by the cold when frequently playing outdoors. Only in instances when the temperature dropped a lot further than this would he put on protective gear to cover the face. Otherwise, it is too much trouble. Mekkar refused to put on all of his extreme cold season gear for overland travel mobility reasons. Just in case, he kept some of it packed nearby and accessible. Off they went.

The whole crew followed the animals and went about, I don't know, fifteen hours non-stop that day. A few of the straying reindeer and loafers were brought back to the fold by the mixed breed wolf-dogs that assisted the herders. These dogs were kept and trained by Mekkar's family specifically for use on the trek. Their job would be to keep the drifters and slow members of the herd from running off through the action of snipping at their heels.

Those helper dogs were raised from the time they were pups. They were a mix of approximately seven-eighths wolf and one-eighth regional husky dog. Those animals were powerful and feisty too. An inexperienced boy was no match for them. There was a lack of desire to have purebred dogs to accompany the trek. In many cases unmixed pedigrees have certain diseases that have more of a chance to negatively affect them. There is a belief that it considered better to have mixed breeds to better resist potential diseases and they have a stronger immune system. These canines were purchased from a guy down south that Mekkar's papa knew. The hybrid animals were extremely loyal and served the family well. They were still fairly young and had been in service for only a short time before this trek. Yet, they were tough and the reindeer knew it too. The individual members of the herd didn't want the mongrels snapping at their heels. Thus, the reindeer pretty much stayed together as a group.

A few of the hooved animals had encountered live wolves before, so it wasn't unheard of. Those reindeer knew exactly how to react by getting themselves back to the main group. Wild packs do roam the territory and the four legged beasts are acutely aware they could be in for a fight for their lives, if attacked. Mekkar felt the semi-tamed herd animals have some perceptive abilities. To him, the reindeer understood there was no real danger from the dogs keeping the crew together. It seemed that some reindeer also recognized which owners were connected to certain canines. Maybe, the young boy was just dreaming and not being realistic.

Some of the herd that had Mekkar's own ear markings were somewhat comfortable around the youngster. It appeared as though they recognized him and there would be no harm done to them. Mainly because he had a habit of regularly going outside near his house and talk to the animals as they were being fed. On other occasions, Mekkar would give them treats.

Taking a throng of reindeer on a trip is not an easy task. Mekkar relates it to an overseas vacation. There is foresight and logistical coordination involved. Both the breeding and branding processes are a chore too. Most people would be clueless of what to do and the chaos might overwhelm them. In this band of trekkers, there are a small number that previously remembered the last long very difficult trek. It is a numbers game when everyone's animals start off together from the home village with a limited number of human guides to accompany them. The burden is on the individual herder, even little Mekkar. You had to know what you were doing. Competency and skill can not be faked. The risks of a screw up could place everyone on the crew, as well as animals, in great danger. Death is a possibility as a result of a mistake or errors in judgment. Minimum consequences would be a price paid through suffering for all connected with the trek.

It is more beneficial in the native thought process to take your time, do things the right way, and avoid a series of little mistakes that can add up to large ones. Carrying out duties in an inconsiderate, unsafe manner could unsettle and rapidly ruin the expedition. Oh! The pressure. Later on in his life, conflicting cultural differences and similar courses of action would create inner conflicts within Mekkar.

The trek that day toward the west had deeper snow than normal on the ground. It appeared, for now, that the weather was going to stay the same in the direction they were heading. The herd would soon need a fresh plentiful food supply and it was the job of all of the herders to reach that location. This was their quest, for now. For this journey, it was decided that the hooved creatures would benefit by being fattened up at various stages on the trek. The idea was to make them look healthy and increase their survival ability rate as the pilgrimage still had a long way to go. The anticipated added bonus would be a higher value of each animal, when they arrived back home.

After some time along the way the group passed a single, well used cabin. Some of the older, more experienced reindeer trekkers just laughed at the dwelling. Jokes were exchanged between them. Comments such as, "Ha, Ha, Ha. Those are for the tourists and people who really can't handle it out here. They just think they can, but instead are pretenders trying to imitate us." A few other herders joined in with additional amusement and further quips. This experienced crew did not need to stay at a place like that nor desire to use such a poor immobile structure. Plus, it was very inadequate and unsuitable in their eyes Ah! It was sort of an old shelter. Mekkar had not seen one of those small quarters for quite awhile and had been exposed to very few throughout the area. Thankfully, this was the only well-used cabin that they would pass along the way.

It was said that the national government, at one time, built quite a few of these out of the way hovels to serve the travelers that visit this area. The reasoning was it is all in the name of progress. Locals saw them as another item to disturb the land at the expense of the native inhabitants. The usual official rote answer was the project would add money to the official coffers of the various regions. The complete opposite was the reality. Unmentioned was the intentional official lie that this undertaking would help the native areas supplement themselves with badly needed extra revenue. Some have suggested that the whole enterprise stinks of pure exploitation, where only a handful profit from the deal. Mekkar has heard on occasion that there is substantial graft and wasteful taxpayer funds spent by the government which only helps a few individuals. While at the same time, the result is the locals who live in the area are neglected. Many are kept in the dark as to the true purposes. Many are convinced the world over that where there is a government project, a high probability of corruption and foolish spending is involved.

Adults have expressed concerns about outright theft, misappropriated funds, and kick-backs for favors while advantageous for a select few.

As the herd was going by, Mekkar was near the rear of the column. He was one of the trekkers attempting to keep the animals together in an organized way. Against the advice of another, the boy did go up to the cabin and opened the door to get a quick peek. Mekkar heard the creaking noise of door as it swung open. He thought to himself that the place had been isolated for some time. As he looked inside there were a couple of amenities, but on a small scale. Some items were older versions were like home or in other village residences he had previously visited. Of course, he was aware that this spot had not been accessed in a while. There was a little amount of dirt on the floor, small portions of rust on metal objects and that type of thing. The place showed a sense of character, even more so without activity as of late. So, he closed the door and left to catch back up with his group that was still on the move.

Now this trekking party didn't need more restrictions and permanent dwellings, they had that back home in the village. It was better to have transferable, functional pack animals, loaded up with goods, for this journey. Portable tents that could be setup fairly quickly were among the items also. The group had all they needed at the time and still be flexible and mobile too. There is no use for clutter. At this point the day was vanishing fast. Darkness was descending earlier than usual for this time of the year. Thus, the band unpacked to rest for the evening. Only essential and a minimal number of items that was required. At this particular stop, not all the regular materials for a normal full camp were used. This is a key concept, to only get what you need, when you need it. It is a very different mindset from modern consumerist driven societal ideas. There is an overriding consideration as part of the cycle. You don't take more than you require for existence so there will still be provisions for you when you come back at a later time. This way of thinking is fed by the culture itself and dominates the native belief system. This trekking party has bought into that system. They are following patterns used continuously and successfully for generations. All were regional natives from the Arctic, with no contrary foreigners in the group, and thus were in agreement.

The herders followed their animals on the trail to the west for quite a few miles as the time passed. These were ancient migratory routes travelled for many years and well known to the leaders like Ansetti. Not long afterward a horrendous blizzard came upon the group, which changed their direction, before they were supposed to turn northward. It was easy to tell the source of the bad weather. It was coming toward them from a westerly direction off of the sea nearby and over the small mountain range. The Arctic blast built up as it reached over the peaks and the wind gusts swooped down into the valley. They were stuck in the middle of it and were committed to stay on the move to find better shelter. The aggregation of man, equipment, and animals were in an area just north of a designated national forest that they already had bypassed. That particular stretch of tree-filled expanse would have been ideal to stop at. The area was set aside as protected land by the government. Naturally, Juhani asked the question, "But for how long? Only until it can be maximized for exploitation like everywhere else by those who use money to bribe officials to change their minds?"

In this region are some deep valleys and fairly wilderness plains side by side. Yet, going to the north there are another set of height obstacles. There are a handful of the highest points in the territory where the band is headed. However, it is too much to expect this herd will reach any high mountain tops. Natives to this region have seen visitors attempt to climb those cliffs fairly often. The reason these are chosen is they are not too tall like a Mount Everest. Still the elevations are challenging enough in certain places to tease those willing to attempt their ascent. For instance, on the one face of a few of the mountains it is easy just to walk up a path, near the top. Well, if you have experience as a climber. It is not advisable for the average person who might not be in great shape and would have difficulty catching their breath.

On the opposite side might be a whole different story altogether. On the higher fells portions are made up of shoal rock as a friend of Mekkar's described it. That is, after he made the ascent later on. Mekkar's friend climbed some of the more difficult parts here by himself and he said it frightened him at times. It was expressed that shoal rock can disappear underneath you and crumble away when you step on it. He recounted in the beginning, he misinterpreted what was happening on the cliff. An illustration was made to show any hold could fragment in an instant. The enjoyment increased after adjustments were made to combat the hazards encountered and as the approach upward to the peak commenced. A dangerous place indeed, with other risks as well, such as avalanches, etc.

Mekkar, himself, at least tried to stay away from those mountains, and in particular the formidable faces along the range. Since, the arctic boy had no desire to climb hills; those stories slightly freaked Mekkar out. He was not interested in that type of recreational activity. The majority of the herders were not attracted to mountain climbing either. Mekkar liked to keep his feet firmly planted on solid soil, if he could help it.

The problem was the trekking band was in vicinity of the range and had to stop the trek. It was time once again to brace themselves against the onslaught of more nasty weather. Nobody was going anywhere. A couple of reindeer tried to desert them and were brought back. Some others wandered off again to be retrieved once more by their guides.

One positive is the native inhabitants of this area have are some inherited abilities and traits that have adapted over time to help them survive in this environment. The recent settlers and other non-natives do not possess these facets nor come close without specific training. The eyesight is normally better than the average person and in bad weather appear to be closer in regard to birds than people. It is amazing how objects can be spotted in snow areas at great distances. However, not quite like Arctic reindeer that has the ability to see in ultraviolet light. [Wikipedia] The native wisdom says that it is part of adaptation to one's surroundings. Mekkar says it is more individual modifications exercised for use in a unique environment.

For example, some say that moths are a species that have revolutionized their body light and make it able to change colors and blend in. So, no matter where they land or where they hide in the scenery the effect comes from within and displays outwardly on their outer layers. Just one necessity employed for survival and developed through an evolutional process over time. A pattern of genetic alternation through DNA change to aid that continued natural selection on an individual basis. So, the moths do not become extinct and are still here to both people. Many other insects and animals utilize these techniques. [Wikipedia]

Similar to people that live in special climates around the globe, many individuals enjoy specific adaptations to the environment around them. Good sense is also considered necessary. For example, it is better to cover the top of the head where a lot of body heat loss occurs. Thus, the use of head wear in the form of various hats and caps are prevalent during the cooler weather. On the other hand, one can cool off against heat at a faster rate by applying cold items there. Peculiar assets and traits are inherent and learned to give native and isolated peoples a better chance to survive in the remotest regions on the planet. There are assumptions that other Arctic races sport these distinctive features as compared to new arrivals or settlers that now shared the area with them. Some of them are correct and several are inaccurate. A few advantages are quite obvious to all. Trouble is, people usually take them for granted and do not miss them until they are gone.

Observing those staying reindeer detach themselves didn't change the fact that the animals still fled from the main herd. It was extremely difficult to track the wandering beasts through the storm. Mekkar never has understood the stupidity factor that forces something or someone to intentionally harm them through reckless action. The concept itself is very alien to him. When the trekkers found enough cover and a suitable spot they made an early stop, setup camp, and attempted to wait out blizzard. A temporary corral was hastily rigged to keep the rest of reindeer close together and in check. The animals are like the herder's money in the bank. At that time, the animal's worth was not the same as what they are now. That is, in money terms or on the open market. The exchange idea always considers the value of an item is only as much as another will purchase it for. Also, labeling value is seen as continually changing and in a state constant adjustment.

The adolescent Mekkar had help to place his coned tent between two trees. That way it would be better protected from being swept away by accompanying strong wind gusts. The strong weather had brought more than the normal windiness for this particular area. Mekkar was not used to these forceful blasts of air as compared to his home village, where the breezes were a refreshing contrast. Back home was a village and not referred to as a town. This was due to the lack of enough local inhabitants according to the national government standard. Mekkar remembered going outside his house and encountering very little wind as a general rule. The proximity of the high hills nearby and small forests of trees and brush as breaks near the village. The boy attempts to describe a current parallel situation of the Tahoe Lake Valley Airport setting in California. It is a comparable scene in regard to the landscape, but the wind patterns are different and more active there. [flightsafetycounselor.com/Article 04.htm]

It took two days for the nastiest of the bad weather calm somewhat to get started back on the move again. Those delays put kinks in the herder's plans. However, to stop and wait it out for completely ideal conditions was unacceptable. Staying put for longer could mean a possible alternative more reindeer lost from the herd due to various factors. It was a good thing that almost all of animals stayed where they were supposed to be. Mekkar thought that the animals probably knew they might not be any better off by running away into the teeth of the harsh circumstances. Nevertheless, he was unsure if the reindeer were mainly used to more comfortable being exposed to familiarity of their trek guides. In opposition to what was happening around them in the unsettling surroundings.

It made Mekkar, along with a few other attendants; look bad because there were a number of stragglers in the back of the herd. Certain ones took off to follow their own path away from the herd. The youngster was partially responsible like any member of the group. Fortunately, in Mekkar's mind, it was a scattered few so the numbers still looked pretty good. This statistical outlook is a mistaken one and flawed. The positive aspect was there no wolves or other dangerous predators around the area to attack them, so far. Yet, how long would that last? Usually this is an ideal time for aggressors to strike. Right before a storm, during it, or immediately afterward. Raiders seek out situations and instances where they perceive disorganization in the animal or watcher ranks. It sounds very militaristic in a sense. In nature's reality, it is a different type of warfare, a game of survival between man and beast. Outside assailants against the reindeer herders and their group of animals. All over the globe it is truly a balance of an on-going endurance struggle to make it to the next day, month, or season.

Working with the elements and adapt them, as well as yourself, for your advantage instead of fighting against them. Unlike modern man who is, whether they admit it or not, always trying to control all possibilities they can in all situations. The truth is, no one has total control of everything all of the time. It is basically impossible. Mekkar believes that if you oppose nature long enough, you will fail and be overcome. Mother Nature will eventually come out on top and you are kicked down and defeated. Mekkar has grasped this type of thinking by growing up in the native way.

Mekkar was the youngest trekker in this party. Yet, he had other experiences to draw from, despite his youth, due to his travelling around the world with family members. The key was how could the Arctic youngster adapt that to this endeavor and come out ahead.

The boy donned a wonderful hat with individual colored and streaming ribbons flowing from it. Most are identifiers that reveal various skill proficiencies. Mekkar could then fulfill those particular functions on the trek. It would be dangerous to assign a person who lacked competency in certain areas. Yet, businesses and governments do that often. Other symbols worn by any of the trekkers could also show associated training aspects. There was sometimes additional related markings and emblems displayed on the clothing. Those were given for undergoing distinct trials or circumstances. The event experienced did not have to be necessarily related to the trek. Ansetti had so many decorations that he became embarrassed to adorn most of them like military medals earned for valor in battle. He was of the belief that situations are always changing with different factors involved each time. Ansetti acknowledged what you did yesterday or long ago might not be the best course of action to take today. The key, in this case, was could the youthful Mekkar fulfill all of his responsibilities placed upon him? Could he perform them well under pressure situations that his group might encounter on this trek? The youngster's overall exposure was minimal as compared to the vastly experienced reindeer herders on this trek.

Ansetti had an admirer in Mekkar because he chose not to be excessive and fully display the majority of his previously earned wares. The concept was foreign to their culture. There is not an attitude of a single person using their personal awards to show off and lord it over everyone else. A few of the herders find the insane consumer driven modern societies of today laughable. They are unable to comprehend that opposite method of contemporary thought that most people are involved in. The conceit of so called civilized individuals primarily focused to shamefully display of their wealth for all to see. Projection of a certain image toward their peers with an attitude of if you have the bling, exhibit it to have them look at you. It is beyond many of the natives like Mekkar as they cannot internalize that ideology. He says, "Why would an individual target themselves to be stolen from instead?"

People in the trekking party respected Mekkar. At the same time they also had minimum expectations of the youngster to pull his own weight also. He must fulfill his duties as required for a successful journey, otherwise he would have been left back home. There is the adage that as part of the cycle of life, contributions are required by everyone that is able. You are just one part of a team, group, band, or what have you. Yet, one cannot focus on the group only. Neglecting prudent management of their self and family is inadvisable. Taking that approach will eventually catch up to that individual and furthermore affect the whole group.

Okay, as the trek is now moving again with a turn due north. The effect of the surrounding scenery was breathtaking to Mekkar. For a person who grew up in this region and was familiar with the landscape, it painted a picture. However, visitors from elsewhere might have been overwhelmed by the expanse of the isolation.

During this period of travel Mekkar wanted to do something different. He got the chance to ride on the back of a snowmobile during one of the slower movement days. The boy was a passenger as he was too small to reach the guiding mechanisms to actually attempt to drive the machine. This was the beginning that would ultimately get Mekkar hooked on the motorized snow machine. When he grew up Mekkar had no problem taking the snow sled out to play with his friends. He wanted to capture any advantages of independence that he could. Right now, at this point, he was too young and too small to accomplish that by himself.

Near the official border the trekkers passed by a bridge. Mekkar remembered particular photos of this area from back home. He recognized this exact structure. The migrating group had a choice of two different paths, if so desired. Mekkar guessed where Ansetti and the other leaders were directing them, but he wasn't absolutely sure either. The arctic boy still could see some of the tracks left behind. Another party had taken this same route not long before his group. Snowmobiles, helicopters, left their own markings in the snow along the path ahead of them. The trained eye recognizes these indicators and those made by reindeer hooves as well as other animals. Not even a small amount of white powder dusting over the impressions could fool them.

Now, Mekkar conducted some mathematics to estimate how many animals were in the last herd to pass through. It would only be an approximate number as he had no method of finding out the true numbers. Since he was at the rear of the column, providing mop-up duty, he could see other people and animals around a hill that were in the front of his group. At first, he wasn't sure if they were from another herd ahead of theirs or not. He had trouble determining that. Around the bend was a now slightly flowing part of the partially defrosted small river. The large stream appeared to be a crossing for reindeer. Mekkar saw them swimming to the other side. Reindeer are quite good swimmers similar to horses and other animals. Humans as a whole don't realized how adept reindeer are in the water until they are exposed to it and have seen it in action. That is not to say that they can swim as fast as a polar bear, but who can? Not many animals. That is a different discussion altogether due to the size difference.

The crew and herd are going northward where the land is much less disturbed as opposed to major cities …

On the Trek & Environment

For the next week or so it is very warm here for this area. No one living here was used to this, Mekkar recalled. Over the eighty degrees Fahrenheit (26.66° Celsius) was considered hot. This was not normal for this time of the year or this long of a time period. The effects are very noticeable around this area and people get ill if it gets too hot, especially if it stays that way. Mekkar was also affected by these heat issues. His symptoms included not feeling in top peak form and being constantly nauseated. This heat wave seemed to last about a whole week straight. There were no clouds to be seen nor was it overcast in any way.

There are some benefits from uninterrupted heat emanating from the sun that melts the snow and does provide some relief from battles against winter storms. However, that is usually short lived. Mekkar would rather be cold where one can dress for it versus being too warm. His thinking is that he could take off all of his clothing and still feel roasting hot like in an oven. He doesn't think of himself as food to be cooked! Since they were stopped at this point near cover and shade to protect them from the abnormal warmer weather, Mekkar had time to think. He must combat his boredom of just waiting around for the weather to improve. Plus, provide distractions for himself to alleviate his uncomfortableness.

He began to remember the nearby bridge his group had recently passed. Usually, in the early summer those crossings and bridges are above you as you pass. This time, he could only see the girders or the top part of the foundation due to massive accumulated snow of the previous winter. The unexpected and vast differences are regular features one has to face in the Arctic, Mekkar noted.

One advantage reindeer have is in their feet because they have much better traction than people. Sometimes Mekkar wished he was like them in their environmentally adaptation. Especially, when the animals would slip and slide a lot less on the ice and snow than him. The great benefits in speed also fascinated the boy. He fancied having those advantages and having a greater weight for better movement and mobility. But, Mekkar was resigned to the fact that it all comes down to controlling the factors you are able.

At one of the nighttime stops, they unpacked and prepared for a much needed rest period. The teepee was set up with the inner frame as the key. A set of curved ones are used inside to reinforce the teepee and improve its sturdiness against potential winds and storms. A second set of straight outer poles are placed at an angle while meeting at the top. Those outer poles, over the curved ones, that form the teepee shape never seem to exactly be perfect in size and length. Nevertheless, the idea is to use what is available and modify as needed. One would be wise to leave an opening, in the middle of the tent, at the top; otherwise you could get completely smoked out from the fire that usually kept a pot of coffee or some other warm concoction.

Mekkar believed the best materials were used to assemble the more secure sauna tent. To him it was rarely, if ever, empty. It seemed as though there was activity in the hot box all the time. Mekkar needed to go in there himself too. That is, to increase his ability to adapt to the most recent hot spell from above or anytime there were higher temperatures outside. The arctic boy thought that the sauna was also a great place to unwind, absorb, and soak it all in. Some of the head trekkers of the party would use it to plan and discuss matters regarding the trek. Inside they would drink, talk about general subjects, or share old stories in the oral tradition. Mekkar would shut up and listen to those who would reminisce regarding their past personal experiences and many encounters.

The veterans of the treks would also use this area to help them coordinate, adapt, consider various matters, and plan the rest of the journey. Mekkar would at times ponder, think, and come up with some wild ideas while overhearing the adults in the sauna. As a kid he itched to mention some of his thoughts to the trek leaders. However, Mekkar never did voice them out loud and let the leaders do their job without interference from an inexperienced boy.

Quite a few of these trekkers had been over this terrain before, but Mekkar had not. It was all new to him at this point. They knew that they were on solid ground in some areas and avoided the potentially sketchy spots below them. These imbalances and shifts on the surface could happen during any season in many types of scenarios. Mekkar didn't consider those factors at all. It was chalked up as a matter of his inexperience, but there is only one way to truly learn …

Mekkar though of speaking to Aslak the shaman to possibly spur him to take action. He wanted Aslak to reach into his bag of special powers and modify the weather. Mekkar was thinking that it would help the group and animals on the trek. The boy was convinced that providing the most suitable environment for this time of the year would be the most beneficial for all. The shaman was already at work with the others without Mekkar being aware of it. Aslak was making use of his drum, tools, chanting mechanisms, and related symbols that he had at his disposal for this task. Mekkar recognized that Aslak had started his specialized ritual. It went on for quite awhile. Yet, the boy did not understand right then what the outcome might be. Even though he saw it, Mekkar originally thought that he might have been dreaming about the ritual activity occurring around him. Soon enough he fell into a daze and then asleep near the warm fire for a few hours. This was in contrast to the cool night air outside. The next day after the ritual, it seemed to Mekkar that his earlier concerns were not important anymore.

Anyway, the trek continued and weather was much better. It was sort of overcast in the sky. Not too cold or too warm. The temperature was about 7° Celsius (44.6° Fahrenheit). Mekkar reveled in it and thought it was nice, perfect weather. Maybe too good which, in turn, could make them somewhat lax executing their duties? It was now time for a small roundup to take sampling of the whole herd. The reasoning behind it was to separate some animals out that might have issues, etc. Mekkar helped check the reindeer to ward any potential dilemmas before they might arise. The boy even participated in some new functions which increased his confidence a bit.

The trekking party was now ready to send out a forward scouting patrol. They were supposed to check for any recent changes and differences in terrain, fresh tracks of unwelcome predators, and that type of thing. They might go out far ahead of the main group beyond their sight to fulfill their mission. The scouts still must travel that same distance all the way back to meet up with the others again. Antti chose a young Mekkar to be with him in that forward two-person patrol. The wise Antti specifically selected Mekkar to expose him to new activity and further his learning curve. They both would stay in close proximity to each other and be very observant, as well as alert at all times. The object was to seek out any likely hazards, promising advantages, extra sources of food supplies, and many other factors.

Antti and Mekkar headed out much earlier than the rest of the group and were a good distance ahead. They occasionally climbed small hills and reached elevated locations to get a better view. Some of the places had melted snow that saturated the ground to make it wet and a mess. Sometimes the ground had been turned to mud and even the recent heat wave didn't completely dry out the earth. Once in awhile as Mekkar climbed around he would slip. The difference was that most of the trekkers had better footwear for this type of journey. Their hiking boots were constructed with a combination of leather, deer hide, and rubber. They were ideally suited for this environment. On the other hand, the inexperienced Mekkar wore more modern shoes. Despite his reference to his footwear as boots, they were better adapted for moseying around the village playing with his friends. In his stubbornness Mekkar failed to listen to his parents and chose his footwear for his personal comfort instead of function. He was now regretting that decision of ignorance.

In one place ahead of the others, they reached the top of hill and saw a town off into the distance. Mekkar's spirits were raised even if he hid this outwardly. Mekkar thought to himself that it was a good thing that he had brought some personal funds as to remedy his previous mistaken footwear choice. This was his first trek without any member of his immediate family along with him. Of course, there were the elders on trek with little Mekkar and they were all watching over him. Whether he realized or not, his life was in their hands, but he still needed to learn some lessons on the trek.

Mekkar had no idea who resided in that town ahead of them. He questioned whether these were strangers or not. Would the people have an idea of who he was? He could guess, but would it do any good? He resolved this by realizing that the trek leaders knew the territory and probably knew the people they would encounter along the way. Since, it wasn't their first journey of this kind. Determining what type of people in the far off town was not his primary job. His main tasks were to keep his eyes open and stay alert to protect the reindeer. When he was not in a role as a scout, some of his functions included bringing back any stragglers and help those animals in the rear catch up with the rest of the herd. Each trekker, even Mekkar, had to be resourceful and multifunctional with their actions in mind. The main consideration was whatever is needed at that time to make everything move more efficiently. It was time to go back and join the rest of those from the tribe on the trek. Fortunately for him, the herd and crew had been moving toward their advanced position so the distance was closed somewhat. Mekkar was glad and relieved when he and Antti made it back to join the others. Antti is a seasoned individual at this. He has been doing it for at least fifty years and considered to have more experience than any other person in the trekking party.

The scouts gave their observations to the chief of this trip. Ansetti, the chief, took those factors in his overall account regarding this journey.

Ansetti was chosen as the lead because Antti didn't want the job. Antti hated the politics and other aspects of leadership. He preferred to take a more physically active role. Antti actually recommended Ansetti for the position and his judgment had great sway in the younger man's selection as the head of this trek. Ansetti wasn't bothered about any possible extremely bad situations ahead. His mighty experience told him that, at most, they might hit minimal snags in the road. He had a plan and, along with the other leaders, was sticking to it. Since it was working just fine, why change? Mekkar saw that Ansetti beamed fully confident in what he was doing. Mekkar thought there was something of substance behind that assured expression and was ready to follow along, with his fellow trekkers, in support of their leader.

One time during one of the gatherings, Mekkar was advised by an elder to consider a certain observation that was widely believed in his culture. The assertion that ninety five percent of a person's personality was created by the time they are five years old. According to methodology, that means that only five percent is left and no real total change will ever happen to anyone after that age. Mekkar did not grasp much of that statement at the time. He felt it might make more sense to him when he got older, so he brushed aside the concept for now. As a result of hearing and learning from, what he saw as the older and wiser people in his tribe, aspects of Mekkar's character developed rapidly during this time. It cultivated a suspicious element that revealed itself, later on, as part of his personality. Obvious to all around him the tenet became: when in doubt, be suspicious and question everything. Definitely what you think you might accept as fact. Isn't that the underlying basis and true value of experience and education? Mekkar also learned the notion that if there are any positives in your life then, by all means, accept it. It might just be a rare bonus. Plus, life itself can be hard enough as testified by the stories he listened to in the sauna tent.

Maybe that was just a part of the cultural environment Mekkar grew up in. In reality, it can be different from the normally accepted native thought processes. Many attributed it to the boy's exposure to various situations. It was speculated that he might have seen too much at his tender age. Much more in other environments outside his home base than some kids around him and this could have partially warped his thinking in some respects. Mekkar was of the opinion, but didn't say it out loud out of respect for the adults, that his variety of experiences had opened his eyes a bit. He felt that even if was less experienced in reindeer herding and trekking, he was already ahead in some other areas of life, despite his youth. Mekkar got the impression that Ansetti and some of the others had never left this region and visited other places. He was unknowingly mistaken in his assumption. Some of the leaders in the trek unit had been to the capital city and to other large cities far away.

Mekkar was aware that the government seat of the nation was not the center of the world. He had already read about the Middle Ages and understood that the darkest time periods of the past were long gone. Whether they admitted it or not, the natives were well informed of the activity occurring in the big cities closest to them. Internal conflicts arise within each native person as they are torn between their tribal upbringing and the modern world around them. Their very existence also includes non-natives and the dominant cosmopolitan lifestyles which can cause problems. Bad decisions and inconsiderate laws contrary to native survival affect them too! Unfortunately, it is seen as outsiders don't care about the consequences and possible negative outcomes pertaining to them.

Anyway, the scouts reached the group, while the crew made up for lost time by avoiding a very muddy and hilly area. It took about an extra day to bypass those sections down in that valley. The fortunate thing was the more accessible food and berry bushes along this alternative path. Footing was better and there also was a plentiful supply of fresh water for the animals. The stream here had parts that were still running where the ice did not build up to a great amount and freeze down too deep. Powdered snow and the shallower ice would melt away fairly quickly when the weather got warmer and flow into the stream. It helped at this point that the trekkers had not encountered any irregular pattern of weather for about a week and a half straight. Usually the region as a whole had extreme climate fluctuations during this time of the year. Reliable was just fine by Mekkar as long as it is not hot. Others agreed that some consistency made the journey easier. Trouble was, this trend also made all of them just a tad complacent.

The youngster was mindful that circumstances could change at any moment. Weather patterns in that area were very peculiar in their consistency. If it was going to be sunny that particular day it usually blessed the inhabitants with sunshine all day. It was not standard to have ten minutes of good weather and then sudden change to a completely different situation. That rapid switch was almost never the case like in many other parts of the world. An example of this would be the short, powerful, massive monsoon rain bursts from the clouds in the Southern Hemisphere.

Suddenly, the rain would cease but not the flood waters overwhelming the limited infrastructure apparatus. Short ice and hail storms emerge and disappear in this manner as well.

Mekkar, like many in his tribe, preferred consistent benchmarks the group could plan for and hopefully rely upon most of the time. Looking skyward could give away indicators of the opposite situation when a lot of or a little snow would be falling earthward. Any amateur meteorologist could tell when the weather was going to be nasty and warn of a blizzard. It was obvious and easy to predict. Mekkar falsely began to believe he had an additional inherent ability to be able to read the weather. Imaging himself as similar to other special individuals, like Houdini, he had learned about. After this point when Mekkar made a determination, he was normally unwavering and decisive with little doubt in his mind. Only in a rare instance would he change his mind. Some that know him well refer to it as stubbornness.

Being able to count on something for the rest of the day always seemed to reassure Mekkar. The sky, right now, was like a good friend to him in his mind. One present factor regarded by him as unchanging in normally extreme irregular surroundings. In the Arctic inhospitable conditions are usually the rule. Even though he had trouble naming the various types of clouds, Mekkar saw patterns develop. This deciphering talent got better as he got older. He would claim to notice future trends based on past history in almost every area of his life. In some things, these theories have been proven right on the money and in other areas not so much. Of course, the boy had absorbed much of the comparable thinking from his fellow tribal members whether he realized it or not. Mekkar liked regularity, some routine, and predictability in quite a few areas of his life. He felt that it is easier to manage and count on. Chaos, all of the time, to him is stressful and wells up in anger from within him.

Usually that was the case, but not this time. This instance would be the exception. What struck Mekkar as odd is that as they went on a different path to reach the town. You know the one that Antti and Mekkar saw earlier on their scouting venture. As the trekkers got closer and closer to that hamlet, they were at the same time moving away from the originally chosen route. Mekkar looked ahead and thought he perhaps saw a mirage. He thought that maybe his mind was exhausted at this point and it was playing tricks on him. One of the others on the journey pointed out the metal like items strewn over the ground. He accepted that he was not deceived and was blown away by what he saw. He said, "Hey, what is going on here?" This was the first time Mekkar he had been truly exposed by noticing these things. Since this was not his home area, his understanding was lacking, to say the least, regarding these damaged objects. He was unable to identify what he saw and had to ask one of the adults nearby.

Yes, Mekkar heard his mama complain back home about the fact that he would echo modern equipment sounds. All the local kids now did it. She would compare it to the audible noises she would imitate when she was a young girl. Sirga told her son that she used to copy the noises of various animals instead like the reindeer. She criticized the younger generations for not doing the same like in times past. She commented to him many times, "There is something wrong here. You are evolutionizing, but in a way, you are also losing the old (native) way."

Anyway, Mekkar saw one of these flying machines and the items were all scattered about. Everyone in the trekking party saw it. Some tried to pretend not to and turned their gaze away while continuing on. But, Mekkar's curiosity was amazed and his attention was grabbed. He struggled to recall the times when his papa would speak to him about different flying objects. Henrik spoke from his experience as a jet pilot and could fly many different types of equipment. The young boy examined the objects more as he got closer. He made the assumption the wreckage was not from any tool used for reindeer herding.

Later on, Mekkar thought his original analysis was correct as he listened to the main trek leaders speak with each other in the sauna tent. Frequently, he would pretend to be asleep or not appear like he was paying attention. Good thing for him that he kept his mouth shut and was absorbed by the discussion environment going on around him. The boy attempted to recall in his mind any similar past examples as what was broached in the sauna. Unfortunately, Mekkar was unable to find any comparisons. He resolved to ask questions about any concerns he had, the next time he had a chance. However, this was not right time.

Mekkar soon figured out that the leaders of the trek were not referring to this journey, but their own past adventures. Some had involved being in the nation's military. There were no details whether it was related to required regular military service or militia duty, otherwise known as regional home guard. The youngster overheard one of them say the destroyed equipment along the ground over there was not one of theirs. Yet, the boy did not know where that equipment came from and the adults weren't giving up more details. Many in the group wanted to drop the subject altogether as not alarm the others on the trek. A small number of the adults there appeared to have no interest in describing details of past horrors they had seen. They didn't want to be reminded either. Why relive painful memories?

Previously in the village Mekkar has heard the air raid sirens, but he usually ignored them as false warnings and didn't respond with any cautionary measures. Here before him was real evidence and live carnage. He had the realization that sometimes ignoring those alarms can have consequences. It was not pleasant to see and the eyesore of strewn out wreckage penetrating his mind. He detected that there was more than one flying apparatus that had been destroyed, he counted at least three maybe four. Arms, legs, other body parts, plastic, and metal pieces were visible too and the scene him ill with dread. Mekkar thought it looked worse than any trip to the butcher shop he had been to. He was definitely disgusted with the view around him. He had an awful feeling in the pit of his stomach. A sensation of distressful nausea was the result. With that, the group still continued on their way. Mekkar heard somebody make another related comment near him. He decided to seek out answers to calm the anxious state he was now in.

Antti approached Mekkar and replied to the boy feel better, "Yeah, I used to be a scout in a special military unit and these are not ones that we used. These helicopters are deployed for war. Someone else has shot them down. You can tell." Mekkar was wondering why he had not heard any explosions or gunfire near them. Still, the boy did not grasp everything Antti was speaking about. Mekkar was aware, by Antti's speech intonation, that devious intent was carried out through someone else's actions. The young trekker understood those helicopters had been knocked out of the sky, but didn't know why. Being the curious kid that he is Mekkar began to question anyone he could regarding how did it happen?

Those images would haunt and preoccupy Mekkar's thinking for the next few days. The visions haunted Mekkar and kept him up most of each night. He was too worried to close his eyes and go back to sleep. This was not a good thing. Mekkar did not want to be distracted too much. Ansetti pointed out that Mekkar's lack of extended rest could become a concern and possibly affect his performance. He was brought along on this expedition to learn needed skills to use for future treks. Mekkar was required to perform his normal duties like all the herders in the group. There was a codependency within the group that involved each member of the trekking party. Everyone depended on him as he did on them. In fact, due to his youth he relied on his leaders much more than the other way around.

The inexperienced young herder started to let his thoughts wander with fearful questions such as what if those people came back and saw the mess. How would they respond in retaliation? Revenge perhaps? The concerns flood the boy's brain as he listened to Antti speak. Mekkar had to calm himself and ask Antti, "When might they be back? Would they try to get us all? Why? We didn't cause this." The main worry firmly planted in his still developing mind was, why did this occur? The youngster was beyond understanding and comprehension of the situation at this point. He heard the words, but he did not understand. The lack of shuteye was making matters worse for him. Ansetti thought Mekkar was slightly delusional.

Ansetti was a large man, big and strong Mekkar thought to himself. The boy observed that Ansetti is almost as big as my papa. Mekkar always was of the opinion that Henrik was a much bigger than normal individual and was correct about this. Yet, Mekkar had a belief that the person with the most experience, which described Ansetti, had the most answers.

So, Mekkar attempted to ask the mighty Ansetti about these matters, but Ansetti was not in the mood to talk about it at this time. Even Ansetti looked somewhat perplexed and worried about this situation as well. A few of the others tried to unsuccessful hide their anxiety from the boy and Mekkar didn't know what to make of it. It was further reinforced when Mekkar discerned the look on the chief of this trek's face. This made him worry even more. An increase of additional stress Mekkar was already afflicted with and could do without right now.

It was odd that as he heard Antti repeated similar speech to others on the trek. He said that to the effect of surrounding nation's own military aircraft and helicopters don't normally fly in this area unless there is terribly, terribly wrong. So, there has to be a reason they were overhead recently. The band of herders saw other debris as they strode by. More items were scattered along the ground. It was estimated that the items were in the hundreds and that was what could not be identified. Mekkar was still alarmed and this feeling was increasing the more he saw. However, the overriding chore was keep the animals on task and calm as avoid any possibility of a frightened stampede.

Mekkar was now preoccupied with just getting to the town that was not far away now. He thought that would be the best answer and the safest habitat for the trekkers. Others in the group were of the opinion that some protection and cover was better than being out in the open. Mekkar agreed with that opinion. He also thought there might be more overhead activity to be anticipated soon. In either case, their path would bring the group into the town to get needed supplies and replenishment. It seemed to Mekkar that this last part of the trip, before they reached the town, became more difficult. Their arrival could not have come at a better time because they all could use the rest.

The lad's thoughts in his head started flowing as he entered the community. He said to himself silently that there something peculiar about this place. Mekkar wondered if he had been here on a previous occasion. The faces look eerily similar, along with the clothing and its basic colors, and even the décor of the structures as compared to back home. Plus, other features as well. There were some differences also. The town was not only larger than Mekkar's home village, but appeared to be more modern also. On this day, quite a few tourists from the continent were visiting. Mekkar village never has this many visitors at one time. He noticed there was less of an international flavor here, among the travelers, than back home. Animals, mostly reindeer, far exceeded the number of people staying in this place.

The adolescent still stayed on task and his group began to keep track of which reindeer were theirs and which were not. That way there would less hassle and confusion created through mixing of animals and afterward the hectic sorting out process. This is a tough assignment, but Mekkar along with others in his group felt they were up to it. It dawned on Mekkar as he remembered that each herder has their own distinctive branding mark, usually on the ear. No two are alike. This determines whose reindeer belongs to whom. It is extremely helpful, with identification, when moving larger herds.

It was an overwhelming sight to see the sheer numbers of reindeer herders and individual animals they saw in the valley on the other side of the town. There was a overflowing of people as opposed to the relatively small size of the town. At least, the boy thought so. Mekkar speculated after listening to his fellow trekkers that maybe all of these extra groups flocked there because of the situation in the skies up above. Outsiders outnumbered the locals by a great margin. It was a battle for everyone to pickup their supplies and find space to stopover here, due to all of the extra people. Mekkar walked with Antti, Ansetti, and a few of the trek leaders. Most felt that the town was not quite prepared for this onslaught. The trekkers finally found a location just outside of the town to set up the tents for a day or two. Then, they went on their way.

Sunshine was a bright break as the trekkers continued on. By noontime the clouds came rolling in. The mood of Mekkar and some of the others changed just as quickly as the weather. They knew they were about to encounter another fierce storm. This one appeared to be more vicious than the ones they had faced recently. This time it was damp, wet, soft snow that fell down from the sky in torrents and resembled a blizzard. Everyone's ability to carry out their duties was hindered for awhile due to lack of visibility. Interaction by the herders was the least of the problems as the communication methods changed. It was done by only through calls, yells, and other sounds between them. Regular speech was ineffective and normally not loud enough to bridge the distance and the current elements. Unfortunately, this bad weather continued day after day. They bypassed another small town on their journey because there was no good area large enough for them to setup camp. They had plenty of food, yet everybody was weary from the harsh travel conditions.

Mekkar didn't want to fall asleep because realized predators might notice and there would be a greater chance of an attack against him or his group. Speed of movement continued to get slower as the temperature dropped, but the tribe continued on. Even after rationing, this band of trekkers ate all of the food and used up most of the supplies. At that point they had to stop soon to re-energize and formulate a plan. Mekkar put on some clean clothes. Lucky for him he located a pair of high boots that fit him. The winter flakes easily reach a level up to his knees. The youngster overhead another adult saying it was odd and not right for the season to encounter such wet snow in this area.

Nobody anticipated or could have predicted this no one. Mekkar thought to himself, ever since he had seen the strewn out helicopter wreckage, that everything seemed out of order. Events had become very weird and peculiar in his inexperienced mind. Mekkar fired himself up with outward motivation and felt he was ready. His demeanor was if we are going to have to fight, then bring it on! This was Mekkar's attitude; actually more of hostile characteristic exhibited by this situation. A temperament inherited from his mama, Sirga. Definitely, this disposition was not the best mindset necessary to survive in this Arctic environment. Any wrong mental outlook on a trek could kill you, if you are not careful.

Few outsiders know this area and its past history. Some are only aware as far back as the end of World War II. Mekkar was uninformed, but others in the party have known that foreign aircraft roam this area on a regular basis. They have been doing it since the last Great War under the guise of keeping the area free of invaders. Ansetti, Aslak, & the leaders thought that was a ruse to conduct additional not well known activities. In times gone by, other nation's militaries invaded this region and spread far beyond the individual country originally targeted. During that time a few invaders were soundly defeated after quite a bit of damage was done to the territory and environment. Many things were completely obliterated and buildings were burned en masse.

The youthful Mekkar could sense the local's cautious view when any military action was being conducted in this area. Battle exercises were treated with suspicion by those who live in this region as a result of past brutal atrocities. Juhani brought this subject up with Mekkar and asked the boy whether he would be extremely bothered if his home had been destroyed. How about the region decimated by foreigner armies as in the past. Only a handful of nations could relate to that type of carnage. For example, the residents of a couple of Japanese cities that were nuked near the end of World War Two could relate. How about the German metropolitan areas were fire-bombed unmercilessly from the air during the last world war and so on? They persevered on the trek. During the next few days they were exposed to more of the same destroyed objects in the snow. The blizzard could not completely hide them. Mekkar figured that maybe some of the storms must have played a part in the fragments he now witnessed.

Mekkar wondered where the time went as it they prepared the camp of animals and tribal members for the night nearby a different hamlet. This community was much smaller than the town they stopped at previously. Mekkar more accurately described it as a village, with about the same inhabitants as back home. The trekkers labored and at the beginning constructed the temporary sauna tent. It was like a teepee and many of them wanted to enjoy relaxation time in there, after completing their work. It is ironic and contradictory, warm and toasty in the sauna, yet freezing cold outside. There is an opening in the center of the teepee, but the chilliness doesn't seep in because of the flame inside. Since heat rises it forced any smoke from the fire to escape through the cylinder hatch.

Antti and rest of the trek leadership discussed and agreed on a strategy of staying put to outwait the repeating storms they expected to continue for some days. Outside the wind blew and blew. Nevertheless, due to the construction and study design of the native nomadic portable dwelling in use for many years, those inside were unaffected by the conditions around them. Anyway, Mekkar observed these things and listened at the news of Ansetti who said, "They (the group) could be in for a long stretch." Blizzard after blizzard came upon them. There was no letting up. They could tell that some of the trekkers were wondering when a break in the atypical cycle would occur. The hope was for a nice return to normal for this time of year in this district.

A person's natural dangerous tendency is to fall asleep, when outside, during these frosty conditions. It is a battle because that is the last thing you should do. An individual's body might go into shutdown or shock mode the colder it gets. Drinking alcohol deceives the mind into thinking that one is warm and is fully functioning at the correct internal temperature. The reality of physical effects upon the body is still there and real damage cannot be ignored. Fortunately, even the young Mekkar was trained to notice this trend and fight his natural inclination during his guard watch time outdoors. The awful weather partially changed the schedule among the herders. Total neglect of duty was out of the question. Required functions still had to be done with modifications. Survival was always at stake as enemies could show up at any time and cause mayhem.

In spite of the best intentions of the leaders in riding out the storm waves, it was not to be. A new course of action was undertaken to now attempt to resume the trek and optimistically move away from the barrage of strong weather. As they trekked along, more snow accumulated. Snow can fun for some of those who do not see it very often, sort of a novelty. This was no illusion as the struggle on the path continued. Mekkar also went forward despite the bombardment of big flakes and thick snow descending out of the sky. The powder was deep and very soft as his boots planted deeply with each little step. At times, Mekkar felt like he might be swallowed up by all of the whiteness. The youngster himself was exhausted and annoyed by the lack of sunshine. He forgot about the positives aspects. Snow actually provides some brightness and light especially in dark areas and the dead of winter. Yet, this trip was not happening in full winter according to the calendar. The fact was the boy was weary and not enjoying himself as he yelled out loud, "Give us something else besides this!"

Older ones on the journey were used to these extreme changes as they had been on many treks. The problem was Mekkar is still quite young, inexperienced, and new to all of this. Antti told Mekkar that many of them felt the same way about the unpredictability when they were young like him. Now with more experience they are better adjusted to that way of thinking.

Another in the group mentioned to Mekkar that familiarity in a way brings about an ignorance of bliss. Blocking out some of the negatives and just except them because they are there. A realization or discovery materializes that as an individual you are powerless to control certain aspects or unable change them.

Now in this region as one turns and travels further to the north toward the sea they are find themselves near the top of the mainland, the continental shelf. Normally, in this type of arctic area one can find winter huts, winter homes, and additional temporary shelters. Some of them are constructed in a way that is burrowed into the earth like a beavers' residence or manmade caves built into the hillsides with plenty of space. However, in this particular area Mekkar did not notice any of those types of dwellings. This was in the flatland, not a mountainous expanse, what could be considered a valley in the Arctic. Basically, this was the equivalent of a desert and usually described as the tundra with sparse rolling plateaus.

Mekkar estimated after about five days of this same routine, they were approaching another reasonably sized township in the north-country. As they got within about ten kilometers (6.21 miles) away the landscape was sight to behold. The town was very high on the latitude scale and was much further north than some other places Mekkar could think of. Plus, the bad weather started to let up and the morale of the group improved.

Nevertheless, the military air intrusions had come back with a vengeance due to better visibility. Mekkar had heard that the residents here had encountered this for many years. Mekkar thought that they were sort of indifferent to this activity above them as a result of overexposure to this type of activity. As they reached closer to the town, Mekkar saw more debris. More military wreckage than he had ever seen before in his life, worse than earlier on this trek. The whole crew predicted there were more guns here. This information made Mekkar more afraid once again as he didn't who the actual enemy was. Clearly it was decided that weapons would not used here and have their group stuck right in the middle of a skirmish.

Later in the night, Mekkar would hear tales in the sauna about past history. What had happened to this whole region in the days of old. Mekkar didn't think this still existed today. He was under the impression that it was just a myth or only occurred in the past. When Mekkar saw more of these remains, he was disturbed again like before. His belief system was altered and began to think these incidents still happen on a regular basis, even today. His mind refused to fully believe this and accept it, despite the evidence before him. If he admitted that these expeditions were really so frequent and not imaginary, then he would really be increasingly frightened. For practical reasons, Mekkar had to ignore it because paralysis from fear would affect his reindeer herding duties on the trek.

He was still a little guy at best. As Mekkar moved around the town, he noticed other boys his age did not look resemble him at all, at least in his own opinion. His mind flooded with comparisons to and questions about them. Does any of those boys go on long reindeer treks or at least herd the animals? He thought that was kind of strange that some of them wore similar, but different, native clothing like his. Mekkar bombarded some of fellow adult tribesmen with questions and comments as they walked together, "What could they be doing instead? Are we missing out on something? I am helping with reindeer; they are playing in the snow. They don't look tough enough to survive out there with us. Do they even do any work? It looks like there is a lot of work to still be done to me." It got to a point where they stopped listening to Mekkar and finally he shut up. At this point, Mekkar was already in judgment mode. He saw other herders and tribes just outside of the town. However, he didn't see other children as young as his age here working with their animals except himself. This baffled him.

It was not a sense of this is not right, this is not fair, or why can't I be like regular kids my age. It was more like, well am I just different? Why am I doing similar tasks within our group that a few older people I see are conducting elsewhere? Definitely none of them are as youthful as I. Mekkar now had the mindset that he must be special. That is when it dawned on him that he was indeed very different. Mekkar then remembered some of Aslak's past words and predictions in his discussions with him about these matters.

On the other hand, other people there glanced at him in a different manner. He received those gazes as though they felt he should be doing something else until he got older. This began to make Mekkar somewhat self conscious. They didn't know all the details, he thought. After awhile, Mekkar settled down and thought to himself, who cares what they think. Yet, subconsciously his mind was still slightly affected, whether he realized it or not. At this point, Mekkar decided to ignore the stares and enjoy hanging around with older members from his group. The youngster never experienced a wavering in his confidence level and he knew that he was doing exactly what was expected of him.

The young boy was of the impression that the people in this town dressed different. Their native clothing and designs were different from his. The locals there used language terms and some speech inflections that were distinct from where he grew up. He figured that since they were quite a distance from home, this should probably be expected. Many in his trekking group didn't actually get strange looks from the locals that he received. Some of the leaders in his trekking bunch spoke with a few of the inhabitants easily. Ansetti was chattering with a few others he seemed to know there. Mekkar only could understand some of the dialect and words they were using to converse with one another. The youngster could relate to a few similar factors such as tone of speech, intonation, and emphasis some of the time. He interpreted that as Ansetti had been here before on a few occasions. Mekkar took it to mean that some of the locals were known by leaders in his trekking party. The boy also deciphered enough to learn that Ansetti was trying to get the latest news regarding conditions to the east. That way they were more prepared before travelling that direction.

He knew that something was amiss, but he couldn't put his finger on it. Soon Mekkar began to hear the rapid rotation sounds of helicopter blades. These were of similar flying machine noises that Mekkar imitated back home. Next, he heard a whoosh of the supersonic jets zooming by overhead. He was unable to exactly identify them because they went by so quickly. Since Mekkar had seen them on occasion before and his papa Henrik flew all types of aircraft. So, he could roughly identify the objects as planes. Mekkar had even ridden in the helicopters back in the village as they flew at low elevation during herding sessions. The machines were used to keep the reindeer herds together during the seasonal migration. However, he had not been around those aircraft enough to be extremely familiar with them or to distinguish between each one. Thus, whose is whose and which models belong to which side. In time, that would change.

They did continue through the center of town to gather additional provisions for the journey and returned back to their camp, on the west plain, to rest before moving on.

Mekkar thought it seemed darker that night than usual. The moon gave him the impression it was trying to hide. He wondered it this was related to the ominous activity that occurred earlier in the day. Normally, this is the time that some animals in the region come out looking for prey as they are better camouflaged by the dark skies above. This trend of less light provided by the moon stretched on for a number of days as the tribe moved further away from the town. Everyone was required to keep extra vigilant while watching over the herd. Especially Mekkar as he was prone to get bored while on guard duty and sometimes start to daydream as young boys do. Still, the tribe spent the next few days going east while bypassing a scattering of villages here and there.

Now, going this far north and travelling on a long old eastward trail could take them all the way to the sea, if that was the intention. Anyway, along the route going east the weather stayed ideal for about four days. After that, the trekking was tough and the group encountered storm after storm, with each dumping more snow than the last. He felt as if he had not enjoyed a decent night's rest for awhile. His mind couldn't stop recalling the images of the aircraft streaking over the town and this affected him. Young Mekkar began to become weary from the toll it took on him.

There was a lot of deep snow combined with thick patches of frozen earth underneath formed by high winds. Any digging for food by the animals or during camp setup could be a chore. The white powder was very dry there and flakey, at least until it landed on the ground. Dryness of the falling winter layer made sure it didn't stick together very well. It was really hard for Mekkar to even make a solid snowball due to the lack of moisture. To walk on it becomes treacherous because you never know when you might sink. Sort of like a sinkhole on a city street. He figured it would be better and more predictable near the mountainous areas.

One might see some deep crevasse unless a person knows exactly where they are going. It is also key to know the surrounding terrain for all seasons as the drop when the snow is melted could be great. Mekkar was confident in the trek leaders regarding these aspects. The trek always needs excellent path finders and trackers to determine the best routes to travel. At times, the campaign requires them to go over some smaller hills for the best traction. To the uninformed one's footing might collapse at any time. Truly, it is an adventure to watch where you walk with every step.

The hope was to distance themselves from the windy area by moving as close to the chosen route as possible and use the natural terrain as barriers. Strong winds tend to dry out everything and make it seem colder than it really is. That is why the adjusted wind chill temperatures are more extreme than the regular readings.

Anyway, as the itinerary went further east Mekkar was assigned an observation shift one particular evening. On the reindeer trek each individual has to serve and on this occasion it was Mekkar's time for wolf watch. The boy was out under the winter sky performing his wolf watch duties. The lookouts need to observe for any potential predator movement, not just strictly wolves. Yet, wolves in this region are more prominent. The shift lasts about four hours each and they take turns. There is an additional surveillance backup crew also. They might consist of individuals that don't appear to Mekkar as needing as much snooze as he does. He saw a couple of them in a state of superficial rest mode. The others not on duty normally take advantage of this time to catch up on their shuteye.

All of those in second group sleep out in the open, if the weather is not too bad. This was a normal practice of some of the trekking veterans. Mekkar normally wears a hat much of the time. It was easy for him to pull down a flap on the cap to cover his eyes before dozing off. The boy would pick a spot and lay down with his back against a tree or some type of vegetation. Mekkar is unable to get adequate rest until he blocks out light and noise with earplugs. Even the glare from the snow is too much for him and will keep him wide awake. In their wisdom, the trek leaders never assigned Mekkar to the reserve watch for these reasons. They decided that the still growing boy was to be placed in a position to get a full compliment of sleep as to not stunt his mental and physical development. The rest was up to Mekkar.

It wasn't like that he was outside trying to catch a nap in a highly populated town or city. In those cases, there might be traffic at all hours during nightfall or perhaps a drive-by shooting. Here, Mekkar might hear a predatory animal once in awhile, but generally most wild animals stay away due to fear of encountering a large group. However, normally the sounds Mekkar would notice were just part of their own herd, accompanying people, or equipment.

Of course, there are the wolves and less frequent encounters with bears, as they are a different story altogether. Wolves prey on what they think they can get for themselves. As carnivores, they intelligence is underrated. Plus, those creatures hunt in packs. A pack of wolves can even team up with enough numbers to steal from and kill a bear. Not normally a larger polar bear, mind you. Mekkar has seen this firsthand in action where the wild toothed animals have used their advantages to retrieve desired food. Using the various aspects of speed, agility, and teamwork they can succeed in ripping off another beast's edible cuisine and provisions. It is well to note, that all life in the arctic expanse must fight for survival against the seasons and each other. This applies to human beings also because the far north is sometimes an unforgiving place. [Confirmed by Animal Planet TV Channel]

The whole key to dealing with a wolf is to isolate it by itself. In Mekkar's mind, they lose a bit of their aggressiveness until one backs them into a corner where there is no retreat.

To separate one from the pack, an individual has to show courage, confidence, and command because the animal can smell fear. During the dividing out process the individual must always at the ready to take out the potential attacker at any time. You never know as the wolf could respond by taking even more risks or be more cautious. Also, it depends on an animal's personality but Mekkar never wanted to be around a wolf long enough to determine that. A perceptive herder can usually tell in the first few minutes after noticing the untamed beast. The method and manner of stalking its prey and demeanor especially when getting detached from the pack shows tendencies. It is difficult for novices to grasp because experience is the best teacher. Mekkar already knew the first rule of wolf watch. That is, to stay awake and keep his eyes attentive to make sure the herd, as well as accompanying people and resources are not attacked by them.

Mekkar's tribe put him through a few tests related to reindeer herding, but not all. Not even close. Those trials were conducted close by his home village and familiar settings. Before this trek, Mekkar has not been involved in most of the training because he is much too young. That would happen later. Thus, he could not be left alone during the nighttime guard duty in any circumstance or it might put everyone in danger. The youngster never let on if he realized that he was always being shadowed by more experienced tribesmen. Mekkar was actually relieved when he saw others were also alert with him on duty. Looking out with multiple sets of eyes is always a good idea, thought the boy.

The experienced leadership determined the schedule for these tasks and which roles were to be filled at any given time. A minimum of one or two, at different distance intervals, could be the watchman depending on the size of the group, including animals, in their section. There always a few, like Mekkar due to his inexperience, who might be tempted to fall asleep while on active duty.

All members of the tribe understand that their livelihood is out there and protection against danger is paramount. Loss of assets to a roaming wolf is not an ideal scenario. Isolated attackers have a higher possibility to panic and flee or at least hide from view when they see humans. The wild animal understands that they can be killed without their friends around as easily as they can attack. Also, people do carry out preemptive first strikes against predators to gain the upper hand in this struggle.

Pack hunters, such as the wolf, are the reindeer herder's greatest natural enemy, but they are not the only one. Even though they are numerous in the region, wolves are nowhere near as plentiful as reindeer. The hooved creatures are not completely helpless in defending themselves either. Mekkar had been made aware that a lot of the wild animals can be hard to detect in certain environments. Particularly, ones that have a white base color in appearance hidden by the snow.

Native people in this region also have some hereditary traits passed down through the generations to help them adapt to the harsh conditions. One is mainly to help individuals to spot any aggressors at longer distances than would be considered normal elsewhere. Just as many animals use camouflage to blend in with the background to hide their presence. The tribesmen can exert other attributes to discern the predator and counteract them anyway. Ansetti says to Mekkar, "It is a continual, evolving battle and test of wills between man and beast."

This is a major aspect for Mekkar or anyone on the trek to be able to locate the attackers before they descend on the weaker parts of the herd. They always seem to attack where you are weakest. Reducing the amount of opportunities for the opposition to grab fresh meat is just on part of a herder's job. Like anywhere else on the planet, the intention of get it, while you can is prevalent. Mekkar was familiar even at his young age of the survival of the fittest concept. [Principles of Biology by Herbert Spencer, 1864] Yet, the little boy had not grasped the economics regarding the law of supply and demand. [An Inquiry into the <u>Principles of Political Oeconomy</u> by James Denham Steuart, 1767] This would happen in time.

The reindeer can bunch up, while still moving, during one of these surprise encounters. Mekkar says, "It is like slower rush hour traffic on the freeway. The vehicles are still moving, but not at full speed." Wolves, as most predators, like to assail the loners, stragglers, and the young that become separated from the main herd. They are quite aware that full grown reindeer have those large somewhat sharp antlers and can give a devastating kick also. Antlers are useful for other things besides defense and attracting mates. The hoofed animal can employ them to keep from starving to death by prodding for their food. Even more so during the winter, when it is necessary for them to dig under a lot of snow to access nourishment sources. Thus, it is beneficial to keep those antlers in pristine condition.

Overall reindeer are not large animals, well as least size-wise compared to a bear or a horse. Yet, they are stronger and more powerful than they appear. Mekkar knows better than to stand directly behind one and possibly receive a thrust kick to the chin. The compactness of power gives them a good chance of surviving in their environment.

Plus, they can move faster than most expect. Upwards to twenty five miles per hour (40.23 kph) and higher. Their acceleration is more when not weighed down by any objects or pulling a sled like one would see in a race. Reindeer are afraid of being hit in the back of their hind legs because it can throw off their whole balance and stability. Their enemies choose this as a weakness to be exploited while on the offensive. You attack the rear to reduce fleeing speed and running power.

Mekkar uses the analogy of a human playing baseball. When they come up to bat and the hurler is throwing the ball towards the hitter. Most think that the pitching power comes solely from the arm. However, Mekkar knows better and understands that the pitcher actually gets the majority of their power from the legs instead. The boy was aware of this through watching films of Nolan Ryan. As Mekkar has said before, "Boy, that guy can bring it!"

The thing is that in a charge by a pack upon an individual animal is usually done by more than one carrying out a strike. Plus, the target can give a swift kick backwards, but unable to use both legs to deliver blows to aggressors at the same time. If a predator stops their prey in its tracks, overcoming it is more straightforward. A stationary target is much easier to overwhelm and opens up other parts of its body.

In this scenario, a stationary mark then is unable to spin around and exercise its own natural advantages to counterattack the aggressor. One on one, a face off between a healthy reindeer and wolf can be a close battle, especially in an all-out frontal blitz. Mekkar would favor the arctic deer in that case and thinks that many underestimate the reindeer's speed and flexibility. Making use of distractions and conducting a surprise attack from behind normally have quite different results for the antlered animal, but not always.

The hunters are familiar with their quarry and realize that females are attentive to their young and usually have a smaller set of antlers than the male counterparts. Caribou and reindeer are the only deer species that produce a rack, though normally less impressive than the males. A full grown mama can take out a raider just as quickly as any masculine member of the herd. With similar weaponry and quickness too!

These aspects reflect a key part of the native society Mekkar grew up in. The language of the area expresses this as well. The terminology typically lacks a gender distinction in Mekkar's native tongue. Similar words that refer to animals have been modified over time and have been made applicable to humans. Similar to many places, people have continually updated and modernized the vocabulary up to the current day. This is the case in many areas of speech and reveals an always evolving process of adaptation.

Some natives through typology still have the belief that reindeer and a few other animals can survive better in this Arctic environment than humans. Others have the opinion that wild creatures do not need people at all to adapt to these surroundings since they have been doing it for a much longer time. Still, dissenters believe that many individuals are unable to endure the harsh conditions and bitter climate by themselves. In those cases, creatures take precedence over people even in spoken communication. The battle rages and those sentiments are always open to debate among the locals. Still, going back to the source, the cycle of life and existence, the intertwined puzzle – everything stems from that. The view is that all examples emerge from that point or beginning in some respect.

Mekkar was in a state of wonder and also was anxious at the same time because of the helicopters. He knew that those flying vehicles were another thing that could destroy them and the herd also. The youngster overheard conversation about how the field wasn't now limited to only dealing with natural predators in this setting. As a boy, he was still learning about aspects regarding the cycle of life. It was hard to fit those concepts to anything related to the flying enemy overhead. The confusion and lack of understanding greatly increased his stress levels. All the trekkers realized the natural balance between various wild creatures. On the other hand, this way of thinking does create some paradoxes. For example, the number of various enemies against their own herd animals actually creates a sense of evenness to prevent over population of any one species. It would be a bad idea to screw with the natural process by wiping out all of the wolves or bears, for instance. Fortunately, this concept was not the main concern in anyone's mind among the trekking party at that moment. The end result would be some other great enemy would take wolf's place.

Modern society has not learned this lesson. They still have the misguided concept that humans can control the earth and nature to a fairly high degree. History should have taught people that the opposite is in fact the case. When there is too much or too few of a species other issues can arise. Varieties must adapt, become resistant, modify themselves, take on another form, or disappear altogether. Setting artificial limits and restrictions or enhancing over-the-top growth will eventually result in the whole chain of life getting messed up and thrown out of whack to the detriment of all.

Anyway, now these added elements can affect the environment in multiple ways all at the same time. All anyone can do is estimate the damage and effects within the concept of the whole cycle of life. That is truly what Mekkar was bothered by, even if he didn't comprehend all the aspects of its meaning, yet.

Like native children, the animals can get somewhat used to the sound of the helicopter. However, they can also be greatly distracted by the flying machines and panic. The tendency is to flock or huddle together when the flying machine hovers so close to the ground. Ideally, this tactic is done in more wide open areas without vegetation and cover. Hopefully, the herd will be seen from the air, as no threat, and be left alone. The distracted animals feel safer in numbers as to not be fair game for their enemies and invite a ground attack. Stragglers, drifters, and those who stray are the most vulnerable. The point is that one split second can make all the difference between life and death during a raid.

The confusion is somewhat similar, but not completely, to smaller pests like the fly. Mekkar says that when he approaches and surrounds it with both hands, it cannot decide which direction to go. There is a bewilderment and distrust of both directions to flee toward. A reaction is to stop or to run comparable to a fight or flight response that humans exert. [Bodily Changes in Pain, Hunger, Fear and Rage by Walter Bradford Cannon, 1915]

This is all part of the fragile setting, the inter-relatedness of trust and expectation of predicted outcomes. The animals trust the herders only up to a point and usually if there exists some type of familiarity. Mekkar asks this question, "Do you trust anything that you are not familiar with? Probably not." The trouble is, in more modern times, the modified environment have put a wrench into the entire system. It is more so in regard to war machines and combat. Who on the ground can predict what those outside the domain are going to do? This is the kind of stuff Mekkar began to ponder as he grew up and looked back on those situations he was involved in. His youthful captured thoughts were in a very undeveloped, superficial stage and would disappear almost as quickly as they arrived. Yet, these facets of thinking pave the way and frequently evolve into greater depths of research within the mind. Plus, listening to the wise leaders of his tribe didn't hurt either. The young reindeer herder's thought processes would later far expand the present capabilities of his brain. Mekkar required much more learning by him to improve his skills to someday possibly lead a trek of his own.

Following the path the seemingly intrepid party continued on to the east for many miles. Well, it was probably less of a distance than a boy could predict. Mekkar has heard the joke told around the campfire about a relative walked fifty miles through the snow, uphill, and with no shoes. It seems that all cultures have parallel stories used to embarrass and implore a person to carry out an action they want to avoid. Yet, in this habitat and under these conditions, the escapade could be plausible indeed, especially on a trek.

In this case, Mekkar had already travelled many kilometers in deep powder. Some of which had hard crust on top and was soft underneath. Not to forget the blizzards, up and down countless hills, but the Arctic boy had solid footwear. Mekkar had on a pair of fur boots created for the harsh winter environment. Socks were not always needed either just some treated grass inside to absorb the shock and moisture. On their way east to areas Mekkar was not familiar with or didn't remember travelling in. He sensed that he had been on this path before, possibly with his parents. He had been told, by Aslak, about a few of his previous trips in the region with relatives, however he was unable to recall any of those journeys. Either way, Mekkar was looking forward to going there in a more independent capacity.

Mekkar was thinking the settings might be more recognizable to him after the weather had slightly diverted the group from the normal route. He couldn't be certain, though. He anticipated that he might meet a few people that he had a closer common ground with, even in speech. People around the world know everything is all relative to the region one is from. Other places that one cannot readily identify have a whole new set of surroundings and challenges to get acclimated with. Too bad, Mekkar found out that was wrong. As they pushed on, the youngster noticed the people seemed more different than he would have expected. Disappointedly, the boy instead found fewer locals there like himself.

After all, he knew there were other tribes in the vast territory from one perspective, but to run into them gave a different view in person. The people appeared to him as similar to his tribesmen, but not exactly the same. Ansetti explained to Mekkar that the inhabitants here face the very same issues and struggles like him and his kin. It appeared to Mekkar, along the coastal areas in both directions on this journey that more families were dedicated to fishing instead of reindeer herding. These folks work on the boats which he thought was kind of odd. It was a different type of community than his own back home. Then, at that point it struck him that he could relate as he had just completed employment on a boat to begin the working portion of his life. Mekkar next summarized, after conversing with Ansetti, that some exchange of goods might take place. Thus, the reason for stopping here and stocking up with a different variety of goods, some to take with them back home.

However, Mekkar was misguided in his assumption that by this age he would have already explored this whole region in some manner. Of course, if that were to take place Mekkar would have developed a negative trait of cockiness and attitude. He would have also used it as an advantage over his peers at home. Aslak warned him about any potential haughtiness and to use his experiences to enlighten his friends instead. The advice from the spiritual leader was for Mekkar to feel humbled and privileged to be able to share his good fortune with others. Not to lord it over anyone and brag about what he had done because there is always someone who has done and seen much more. Unexpectedly, what was to come was more dynamic than what he had already exposed to, seen, or would have guessed.

The route winded in a southeasterly direction, not far from sea, and continued on for about thirty miles (48.28 kilometers) or so toward the next small town. Unfortunately, before they got there, the trekkers faced another pack of aggressive wild canines. The stalkers were first spotted during Mekkar's shift as a watchman that night. The youngest herder audibly called out to alert the others of potential danger.

Juhani was also on guard with Mekkar tracking the wolves' movements as they sneakily looked to strike. The beasts were ready for action and it was a fairly large wolf pack. The wild creatures suddenly charged the herd seeking to surprise and devour. Wolves are deceptively quick and strong for their size. Yet, humans have a definite weapons advantage if they choose to use it. Guns are useful, but not in all situations due to noise and frightening the herd. One main goal of the herder is to keep their own animals from being spooked for any reason and stampeding away. Hence, knives tend to be more useful and stealthy.

Mekkar swiftly took his blade out from its sheath. Next, he went on the pursuit. Some of the other herders also got the attention of a number of the animals. Well, at least a few of them. Other tribesmen joined Mekkar in the immediate area, at the ready. Juhani later told Mekkar that they didn't want him to be overwhelmed with too many attackers to combat by himself. A part of the attacking pack scrambled a bit. The natives protecting the herd had to be quiet at the same time while counter stalking the enemy. One reason is too not attract the complete bunch and be outnumbered in any individual confrontation. Mekkar says that it is comparable to a military shadow, seek, and, if necessary, destroy mission. The other important aspect is to not spook the reindeer and cause them to run away as a group. No one wanted to watch their valued possessions just vanish from sight.

The strategy chosen was to divide and encounter a few of the adversaries at a time, not all at once. The hope was to split the raiding party up and maybe the majority might scatter after the herders made their move. Mekkar attributes the approach to engaging the leader and defeating that individual first. Then, the rest of the gang tends to voluntarily remove themselves from the battle. Aslak tried to explain to the lad that is an aspect of psychology. Specifically, a theory that after the head is removed as a threat and cannot take an opponent on, the rest of the gang normally loses hope in their chances of victory in the battle. The wise man commented to Mekkar the logic had meaning to people alone. Applying the same to animals without much field examination and evidence was another matter altogether. Not many want to test it out in live situations to avoid injury or death.

Akin to most animals the band of wolves also has a leadership hierarchy. Even observers soon can identify which one is the alpha male or who the boss is. Mekkar has used the New York Yankees baseball franchise as an illustration of this leadership system. Under the operation of George Steinbrenner, there was no dispute or question of who was large and in charge. Mekkar now had the lead animal in his sights and sought out a confrontation to make his mark. On the other hand, Juhani had done these treks for a long time for years and years and first spotted the same one the young herder in training was pursuing. Problem was Juhani had a longer distance to cover. Mekkar's original task description was to help keep the throng bunched together and not let any in the back stray off. Yet, the inexperienced Mekkar let his sight and rush adrenaline overtake him as he broke away from his pre-assigned task. No matter what happened the boy felt that was ready for a strike just in case.

In the nick of time, Juhani arrived on the scene and he faced off with the top dog with his knife already drawn. The wolf rushed as it felt threatened and sprang at the veteran herder. Mekkar saw this happen and thought to himself that this scenario can't be occurring, it was not real. It seemed to the young boy that the animal jumped ten feet through the air like a long jumper in track. The wolf had its teeth bared with a snarl. Mekkar's impression was as if the beast wanted to leap toward Juhani's throat or whatever the animal could grab with its powerful fangs. Still, Juhani was not a small individual and had enormous strength unlike Mekkar. In an instant, Juhani brought up his large knife to the chin of his aggressor. He drove it through the protruding jaw and broke a bone in the assailant's neck as he had been trained so many years ago. The decimated head wolf of the pack was now gone.

Nonetheless, there was a hint that others of the group didn't see their fallen leader as they were occupied in their own pitched skirmishes. After a few more of the attackers had been put down, a couple of gunshots rang out with a pop, pop. Arrows made the ppfft sound as they whizzed past. Bows were repeatedly firing their projectiles off one by one. The scene was unfolding rapidly in front of Mekkar as he observed one of the aggressors nearby tagged right in the head. Finally, the opposition unit started to scatter.

Some of leaders thought it was stupid to bring out the guns and risk the stampede of whole herd. One of them commented toward the boy the necessary additional firepower was needed for that drastic action. Mekkar needed to get back to his responsibilities and contribute his efforts to keep the now frightened herd animals from straying. The mood of the reindeer was on edge right at that time. He along with the other tribesmen knew that if any of their hooved animals had departed during the clash they would have been gone. Most likely killed by the still remaining wolves in the vicinity. The enemies had retreated but were still in the neighborhood simply lying in wait, desperate to fill their bellies.

Little did the adolescent know that two reindeer turned up missing from the herd. As soon as they left not even about one hundred and sixty four yards (150 meters) away Mekkar heard a loud sound. He detected the high pitch and knew one of the stray animals had been attacked. A few of the herders including the boy followed the noise they listened to. Those saw the wolf pack in action. Mekkar said in a low voice as to not be detected, "This is it." The host onslaught was relentless by grabbing the hind legs while the hooved creature was distracted by the adversary in front. Once the aggressors got complete control another jumped for the neck and secured it. Oh, Mekkar secretly wished that he could leap upon prey like that.

The small unit of herders realized it was no use trying to rescue one of the flock now, they all recognized it was a goner. That reindeer was stupid for running away from the bunch and became wolf food because it was too late to be saved, thought Mekkar. Then, Mekkar felt helpless and blamed himself for leaving his post. The young boy did warn the others. At the same time, he was of the opinion that he didn't do anything to save one his tribesmen's animals. The boy's mind told him that he didn't fully carry out his duty. Mekkar technically did not remove not one enemy combatant nor directly save any reindeer himself. The rest of the belligerents had run off. They must have had their fill deemed Mekkar. However, the assailants got theirs. One of them was picked off and later seen with the others of his clan ripping apart that one animal before it soon perished. Not taking it out with the first shot was not a good thing for that one adversary.

After the drama had died down somewhat, it was discovered that seven of the raiders had been dispatched along with two reindeer from the herd. Mekkar considered they had done a pretty good job by only losing two animals to that large of a blitz. Unfortunately, that assumption just showed his inexperience. Seven to two was not considered a good ratio. It was made clear that there should be a twenty to one minimum kill proportion of pack beasts to hooved creatures. The trek leader would not be happy with the outcome. Ansetti was very angry. Possibly it was at the lack of expectation of an assault, defense execution planning, or overall preparation of the crew. Mekkar never received an answer regarding this. Ansetti appraised the situation and was aware that if a party loses two reindeer for every seven wolves you will lose way too many animals. First off, the enemy will gain confidence and this herding group will most likely encounter more packs of potential foes in this area.

They set up the sauna and only a small part of the camp when the activity had died down. All of them appeared ready to relax and took a needed break, except for a few watchmen. Ansetti told them there that the meat eaters would be back on the pursuit. The leaders used the time to conduct more planning to prevent another outcome such as the one they had just endured. "This was only the first meeting," said Ansetti to Mekkar while they were in the hot tent. What was odd to the boy was that all of the tents were speedily dismantled right after the impromptu gathering. The trek leader told Mekkar once again, "The wolves will be back because they see their own. The blood will attract them. They remember their catch from before and that will draw them once again. So, us and the herd should be on the move. Our goal is to finish this journey and get back to our homes safe and sound with our bodies and herds intact."

On the Trek & Surroundings

Ansetti proceeding to tell Mekkar, "Now that I have taken you under my wing, there are a couple of other important things to mention. First, the wolves will be back because the dead animals will attract them. Usually they are not that extremely aggressive when there are so many of us around." The trek chief imparted further insight to Mekkar, "They usually wait to pursue individual animals that wander off, get lost, or are separated from the main herd. The reason for the aggressive action was probably starvation on their part. They seemed to me they have not eaten for quite some time. Thus, the pack became more desperate than usual."

He continued on explaining to the young boy about the event, "The horde knew the risks were high, but sadly carried out their operation fairly effectively against us. We, on the other hand, did not do our jobs as well as I had hoped. Also, the wolves took the chance of a frontal assault because they felt emboldened by the extra help they received. The odds suggested a more favorable outcome on their part, so they acted upon it." It was revealed to Mekkar that wolves are smarter creatures than they are given credit for. They normally attempt to pick the best conditions for them, while at the same time a bad predicament for you as the guardians of the herd, to conduct a raid. In other words, very favorable situations for them to storm, overpower, and extract an easy feast.

"The majority of all in the group seems to believe those same wolves will be back again." Ansetti told the youngest member on this trek. He mentioned this while they were in the sauna tent. It was setup so that the herders could relax from the recent activity. Plus, the leadership could take time to think more clearly and process the plan for the rest of the journey. Mekkar thinks it is ironic that one goes into a restrictive hot area to relax or cool down. Yet, this is a normal daily ritual for his tribe at home or away on a journey. It was only setup for a short while, and then they packed everything up and got ready to go on their way.

Mekkar was confused by the decision to temporarily rest there. He thought to himself we have just been attacked and soon afterward told that the raiders are probably coming back for another round. Why not get out of here and not waste any time in doing so. Responding with irrational thought is not the native way within Mekkar's tribe. The common method is relax, take your time, do things right, and minimize mistakes. Well, at least, not make the same mistakes as before. This is totally the opposite mindset and very different from the hurry, hurry and rush everywhere lifestyle of the average person in other more modern societies.

After the aggressive incident, the herd leaders collectively made the decision to stop and assess, Ansetti lead a more extensive investigation of the collateral damage done. On the other hand, Mekkar was focused solely on when the pack would return. Still Mekkar was a kid and engrossed by his narrow experience and point of view. Many of the adults understood that younger ones, especially ones such as Mekkar, are antsy in certain circumstances. It was normal to have ants in their pants and want to escape the scene as quickly as possible when encountering danger. Their vast experience, as compared to Mekkar, involved seeing the big picture with more factors involved. This is the way the trek leader Ansetti represented the veteran trekkers view. Young Mekkar didn't completely agree with him, but was unable to fully understand why. Mekkar's mind panicked with thoughts of this is ridiculous, why are we waiting around?

The boy's fear of the wolf pack's return grew as time passed. Concerns flooded his youthful intellect. What if they came while they were stopped right now and with a greater number of wolves? In the end, Mekkar kept his lips sealed and did not voice the racing chatter within him. He had to trust that Ansetti and the other leaders had done this for many winters and many summers. A time period that included quite a few full moons and no moons and they knew better of what to expect than a first timer.

When the group finally set off, back on the trail, Mekkar was more relieved than anything. He felt it was good that the raiders did not reappear again in that particular area. But, how could the young boy have predicted a no return engagement, due to the state of mind he was in? The group column shuffled through the night mile after mile. The weather was clear outside and the lack of cloud cover contributed to the brisk cold air. Mekkar fancied the notion that a cloudy sky would have held in some heat to possibly help speed up movement on the ground. Ansetti continued to lead the herders and the flock. Being the smart, wise, and experienced commander that he was, he appeared to accept input from many sources without making rash decisions. The chief even listened to suggestions on occasion made by Mekkar, even though Ansetti realized Mekkar had a kid's limited knowledge. Ansetti was an effective captain without having to be very vocal about it. There were some other rare time times when a point needed to be made and he could be forceful in that manner also, when needed.

He was one of the individuals with the most seasoning on the trek, but Ansetti was not the oldest or the most experienced tribesman on this journey. Not even close. Still, he was uncommon in his wisdom, very wise and consistently level-headed even in the face of danger. The trek skipper seldom got riled up. Mekkar considered that Ansetti's past angered reaction to the earlier loss of animals was very out of character for him.

The adolescent admired these qualities in the overseer of the trek. Mekkar saw the he was unlike Ansetti and also had a different personality compared to a few of the other leaders. Mekkar was not like the very mellow Juhani in his personality, as well. It meant that the boy was developing himself in a unique way and not completely copying someone else. Mekkar felt that he was distinctive from all others, that he was special. The growing boy was convinced that he had features, no one else had. Of course, this was reinforced by his frequent discussions with the tribal spiritual guide, Aslak. The problem was that it might go to Mekkar's head and could give him a complex as he headed toward puberty and later adulthood. To keep the ego in check others around the boy, as well as himself, believed he was still very unaware of many of those special traits. It was only a matter of time before those features would be discovered within him and the subsequent outward rapid growth development. Whether he realized it or not, there were certain expectations of Mekkar fashioned by others around him. Possibly due to the fact that the youngster was a quick learner and had already shown himself to be very resourceful. Unknown to all, except maybe Aslak, there was still more to come.

Anyway, the clan pushed on and continued along the route until they reached another small town. As they got closer Mekkar took a good look at the people there. He was of the opinion; the townspeople here also dress in the same type clothing with similar markings like those in the last town. His little mind churned with more questions than answers. What is so special about this place? Why are we stopping so soon? Let's go further away from where the earlier assault happened. At first, Mekkar didn't notice until he looked at the other herders in his group. Their faces and less spirited movements revealed widespread fatigue. It was pointed out to the young one the reasons why they needed to stop here and set up camp. A distance just far enough away from danger.

Mekkar listened in on the discussion regarding the chosen area's benefits such as a better protective layout and more available people close by to assist them, if necessary. Mekkar began to believe that the decision to stop was not decided by Ansetti alone. Instead, by the head committee of the trek which included Aslak's input. It is true, as in any work environment, politics play a part in determinations regarding managing reindeer, supplies, and personnel during a trek. This was not a dictatorship, but more like a representative republic with consensus being the goal so all will buy in to make the journey less troublesome. This place was selected to assemble camp to take advantage of the terrain with maximum defensive purposes in mind. The hope was to avoid another attack, but if they encountered one they were could be better withstand it with fewer losses. Other positives were brought up by Antti and others regarding the subject about how organized the nearby people were. It was pointed out the town had some hooved creatures of their own and the herders were adept at driving predators away. Mekkar thought, at least visibility would not be an issue here. The camp was organized in such a way to use the increased open area to spot an enemy coming from a greater distance away.

The air was chilly and crisp. They pitched camp about 1 kilometer (0.621 miles) outside of the town. Mekkar saw other tribes and trekkers leading their reindeer herds there also. He figured it must be some type of hub or meeting point of quite a few trekking routes. They began to set up the tents. Some of those in the party commented how this was odd since it was still in the middle of the day to camp. One band from the herd began an inventory of supplies that had run low and confirmed a restocking was in order.

There was another small group, led by Juhani, that went back to cover their tracks to harder for the wolves to follow them. He had a few tricks up his sleeve to distract any potential predators. Sprinkling of blood or food in the snow was used to lead the wolves off the pathway. There are many disguises and materials one can use to prevent getting lost in the middle of nowhere or used for anti-detection purposes. Good use of sights and physical points to mark spots, paths, and locations can be the difference between life and death in this environment. While at the same time, not completely destroying your fragile surroundings as you might need them in the future. This is what Juhani was great at. He and Antti were the best scouts in their group. Both of them had carried out these types of tasks as part of military operations. Mekkar was convinced that Antti and Juhani could survive almost anywhere, against anyone as they had done this so often previously. Only in the field experience develops and adapts these survival skills as needed in each situation.

So, after the camp was in place, Mekkar sat around soaking up the stories in the middle of the camp from Ansetti, Antti, Juhani, and the other veterans. Juhani had almost as much experienced even though he wasn't near the same age as some of the others in the group. Juhani received his wealth of experience by getting an early start and journeying on many treks even with other nearby tribes, not just his own. This time Mekkar didn't hang around as long as usually does but went to lie down and rest in the sauna tent instead. Trouble was Mekkar didn't like coffee, which is considered a staple in his culture, and even detested the aroma of it. Thus, he tolerated it but never immersed himself into the accompanying scene that went along with coffee. To this day, you will almost never see him in any environment where people just sit around and drink the stuff like in your local. That is, unless he has to be there for another reason. As he grew older Mekkar preferred his alcohol straight up on the rocks rather than as a supplement to be added to another liquid. Everyone else in the area seemed to always add a shot of booze to their coffee every time it was consumed. To Mekkar, it appeared as though the whole region had their morning shot of liquor to their caffeine beverage for a daily pick-me-up. It gave Mekkar the impression that there was never an alcohol impaired driving violation given before noon because the entire police force had the same routine also.

Ansetti's tent was another spot in the camp that resembled a happening gathering place that revolved around the pick-me-up drink, especially among the leadership group. The boy wondered if the veteran herders ever slept. If that was the case, he wanted to have that ability for himself. Ansetti's temporary residence, as the trek leader, was the most elaborate one besides the sauna. It stood out with drawings of many reindeers and other auxiliary and appropriate symbols directly woven into the fabric of the deer hides that covered the outer layer of his tent. There was even had a wide strip around near the bottom of the top one third to signify, okay, he is the boss.

The easily transported shelters used toughly treated and formed winter hides. There were additional personal designs that marked each individual tepee also. Since, Ansetti was the leader of the trek he also had the largest quarters because he would need to entertain others. There, or in the sauna, was the place to discuss a specific strategy or change trek tactics if need be.

In desperate conditions, it was required to make major changes to the whole plan. One must adapt and prepare to meet all of the needs of the trekkers and herd to the benefit of all.

Aslak had a different role, than Ansetti, as the spiritual leader. According to public knowledge, outsiders, and non natives these mediators and their practices no longer exist officially. In the current day, there are pretender greedy wannabe neo-pagan shamans that just want to make quick money from unsuspecting tourists. However, those fake individuals have no real power because they are not the real deal.

It is said that this role and belief system died out long ago. Mainly, it was kept hidden and secret below the surface due to persecution, religious witch trails, and gruesome murders. These actions were brought into the region by new "masters" and their sense of justice carried out upon individuals who conducted these shamanistic activities in the old native ways. The foreigners were supported by torturous corrupt authorities along with religious priests too. The native rituals and methods were condemned as what was seen as pagan traditions and a backward people. Aslak told Mekkar he thought the outsiders saw shamans as a possible threat and competitor to the power of the dominant Christianized culture. He went on to comment to the boy that the intruders desired to wipe out all resistance to the forming of a nation-state. Thus, the newcomers respond with forced assimilation of all native peoples to eliminate all that is contrary and make the people easier to control or dominate. Similar to past history and the present time, a common theme is to divide and conquer all that are different.

Aslak had emblems and items such as drums, altars, related utensils, wizardry, magician type stuff, as well as other designs, drawings, and symbols as prominent features on his tepee skins. It was easily distinguished from all the others to identify him and his role. Only he had true extraordinary power as the mediator between the physical and spiritual realms. Both of their quarters were decisively different from the rest of the herder tents. Most of the teepees had more basic images and figures along other less elaborate ancient drawings.

Ansetti and Aslak were both very wise and it was not in their personality to go beyond their official leadership duties and lord it over anyone else. Industrious and led by example, but definitely not control freaks. They sought other opinions and advice among the herd leadership crew. Savvy in their intelligence to know they did not always have all of the answers. Ansetti was chosen as the leader of this trek because of his vast experience in herding reindeer. The final decisions rested with the chief, but Ansetti usually had a committee of individuals there involved in the process. He greatly respected his peer's judgment and alternative perspectives, along with Aslak's input. Before coming to a particular key decision the shaman would be consulted beforehand to look into the future. He could look where no one else had that ability in their tribe. Everyone else relied on the physical world experience which involved trends, predictions, possible outcomes, and current technology. Aslak could perform regular herder tasks as well. He also previously helped perform as a doctor to oversee the birth of Mekkar on an earlier journey. That delivery happened out in the snow. He is the source, where the boy gets part of his full name. It also explains the advisory relationship of Aslak to the boy, where Mekkar could ask him about any subject and if possible went to him first for answers.

Some suspect that Mekkar might have gained a few special powers as a result of the encounters with Aslak or as a factor related to his name. If so, they were are fairly dormant, unexercised, or the boy was not very aware of any unique capabilities within him. No one in the tribe was in the category of Aslak with abilities that appeared to be outside of this realm. Talents that could only be learned through practical experience with specific insights and unreal mental deductions the shaman would share freely with the leaders. Aslak would attempt to teach others to recognize certain things that he could see very clearly. It took other people much training to recognize even a small portion of items or similar situations that could arise. This is where Aslak was very valuable and he was a healer as well.

For example, if one of the wolves directly attacked and injured Juhani, Mekkar, or another herder earlier on the trek that would have been a big deal. Normally the most vulnerable would be one of the individuals far in the rear rounding up stragglers. That is the preferred place packs of wolves usually target their attack. Antagar, his apprentice, would direct the injured person to be cured by Aslak's special powers, whatever that may entail. Aslak was the main medicine man and a constant presence. Despite being truly mysterious, Aslak had an aura of mysticism about him and was still a mellow person, very laid back. Yet, nobody can completely figure out the many facets of the shaman. The spiritual leader sees what others only think about in their conscious mind. The insights and revelations are incredible. The understanding and perception regarding the topics the medicine man speaks about is hard to fathom or comprehend for most. Aslak also gave the impression that he travelled in a different sphere while his physical body was still in the same place. Mekkar describes this trance-like state as fairly spooky and eerie at times and would attempt to avoid Aslak at those particular occasions.

A local slogan says that many opinions and common statements spewed by people are like voices. They are everywhere and everyone has one. The fact is they are usually full of ignorance. Anyone can talk a big game and go on about various things, but unless an individual experiences it or physically goes to that place they have no idea what they are speaking about. It is a matter of having a full knowledge of some aspect. This is the kind of background that the shaman brings to the table with a background in more than one dimension. The medium can never be easily dismissed with regard to any situation the group could face.

Mekkar noticed a couple of things and he had to ask Aslak for answers. They had a discussion. The young boy directed a few comments toward Aslak and remarked that the children here in this small town were not like the kids they saw at another stop in their journey. They are just not the same and don't seem to play as much either even though it is still the same region. Mekkar asks, "Why the great differences?" The interaction between the two included an education about many contrasting locations in the arctic area.

This is in a huge contrast to really big population centers and cities like Las Vegas. These arctic locales would not make a close comparison to even a smaller city like Eugene, Oregon for instance. We are referring to very small places, tiny compared to cities with only twenty five thousand inhabitants. These are modest in size while still currently flooded with all the reindeer herders on trek search to replenish themselves. The old standard normal consideration for a town was one with a population of five thousand of more within its limits.

Regardless, Mekkar calls them towns because they might have special features about them as opposed to vast scarcely populated open spaces. Many of those small communities in this area also know about efficient use of available resources and not use them all up too quickly. Similar to regional natives and nomads who live off the land in a very contrasting manner to modern society. Mekkar has been taught that much of civilized life in many cases just takes over and destroys everything in its path in the name of progress. Other elders have given the boy an image that reveals modern society has its underlying basis built on greed and exploitation of almost everything. This includes all resources, such as people, with very little long term consideration of the surrounding impact.

The curiosity regarding the natives and their past history was the issue of fairly complete homogeneous complexity of the people before the liberal mass immigration of later times. In some of the areas, so far north, a number of communities get to employ a portion of their own local customs as legislation. Some native customs have been in place for a long time, much longer than the national cultures all around them. Those customs are fairly effective in most places and reduce crime on a grand scale. The high crime rates are almost nil and mostly minor offenses such as theft are perpetrated by outsiders. Among the natives most disputes are handled in a quick judicious manner. Very unlike rates in today's large cities where the per capita high crime rates are beyond measure; that is in comparison to these remote areas. In Mekkar's tribe the view is some of the community laws are very harsh, but an effective deterrent factor.

A person cannot function without others in this Arctic environment because sometimes, by working together, is the only thing that keeps you all alive. The harsh environment is the overall main factor that can determine your fate. One individual's selfish ambition and desires, plus rash decision making can bring difficulties for all residing there. One has to be able to trust your neighbor and even more so when you are together on the trek with your fellow tribesmen.

For example, witness the last attack of the wolf pack. If Mekkar neglected to do his job as a watchman or if Juhani did not drive his knife through the mouth and throat of the wolf, a member of the trek might have been lost. Everyone is a key member in this team and dysfunction would have resulted in a lot more lost reindeer too. It was determined the cost of the animals was already too high as it was.

Those reindeer are beings that sustain and provide for needs of the herders also. Some are set out and used for eating, while others to strengthen the herd through organization. This is planned for and set aside by the committee leaders of the trek before it begins. Those particular overseers of the group are chosen by vast past experience and their skill from many odysseys.

As the collection of men and beasts approach the hamlet they load up on supplies. There is a long winded discussion between Mekkar and Aslak. "Aslak," Mekkar asks, "Why are these city people like this? They are so different from us. Have they ever gone on a trek?" Aslak knew that some of the townspeople had not. However, was convinced that many back in their own home village area had not been ever on a long journey similar to this. It saddened Aslak, as an increasing number of natives are losing their in-touchness with nature. Those are developing in the same manner as those in this town. The opinion was that uniqueness is being lost or being forced away by contemporary forces inside and out. Less and less of the natives are herders or work directly with reindeer anymore. Some of these relied on tourism alone instead or have other different occupations as their main sources of income. This can result in ignoring the old native customs of the region and modify their behavior to fit in with progressive societies. Try to blend in and not stand out too much. Aslak reminded Mekkar frequently to not forget where he came from and who he is. The advice always warned the boy that he could lose his personal identity, if he started to forget, whether it was intentional or not. That situation creates another set of issues and problems as a result.

Unbeknownst to Mekkar, his tribesmen have carried out a variety of tasks and functions to provide an income for their families. He thought they only participated in reindeer herding. The different seasons provided different opportunities. In the past, it was due to meeting heavy tax obligations to more than one source. At times obligations were imposed by multiple rulers, governments, and magistrates all at the same time. An emerging boy such as Mekkar still only had a small grasp of the matter. He was not totally informed and thought this could be harmful to his people. Trouble was Mekkar didn't understand why, so he flat out rejected the concept of the whole society for the time being. In time, a few answers would be forthcoming as he listened to the adults discuss matters during stops along the journey.

Aslak mentioned during a conversation that maybe the influxes of modernists into the region were forcing the adaptation of all inhabitants there. The loss of individual indigenous thinking, traditions, and overall cultural identity was too rapid. The danger is that there is no rewind button to take one back to the past like on a video recorder. Once you lose it, those aspects are almost impossible to get back. Antti agreed with Aslak on these points that individual want was a major internal driving force. It normally trended toward thinking on a more selfish and greedily level. The negative end result with that type of attitude would be to use up all of the resources in that spot without time for restoration. That would be disastrous.

Well, Mekkar started to have thoughts on a self-conscious level by seeking further answers to his inquiries, "Why am I so different from these other children that seem to be around my age? They are doing things and seem to be having more fun by playing and having more possessions than me." Aslak was brief, but blunt in his answer he told the young boy, "This experience will stay with you the rest of your life. You will need this because you will need to be hardened against the environment and your circumstances. You will have to work with it, within it, and not be overcome by it. This is the lesson you are learning now because you will be required to call on this experience later on in some other form and in another way."

Mekkar was totally confused by these comments and did not comprehend the meaning of them. He could not grasp their meaning, they sounded like riddles to him. In hindsight, it was seen as a future prediction of a catastrophic calamity that would occur in Mekkar's life. After all, Aslak was a seer. The shaman was to the point, but did not give specific details regarding Mekkar's future even as he saw it unfold. The spiritual leader thought that it might be harmful and told Mekkar so. Aslak said, "I can see that you need this and I know of where and when. Yet, I can't tell you anymore about it. I cannot tell you anymore about it!" he emphasized to Mekkar.

The medicine man continued on, "Trust me, I see this and you do not want to know more about the event later on. However, you need this training for later on. You will draw out the lessons you are learning from this venture a few times in your life because it will be hard." Mekkar, when he heard the phrase that he would have a hard life, his spirits dropped a bit even as he didn't fully digest the meaning. He thought that he already had it much harder than the children he was comparing himself to.

He thought they had more fun, but Mekkar admitted he was enjoying himself too. Actually, he was having a blast and conducting himself like a man as he called it in his time. In the boy's mind he felt that he was doing an adult's work. I'm helping to herd reindeer. How many people can say that! Mekkar knew that this type of job was uncommon. In reality, it is very rare, yet he was unaware of that. He didn't always expect the responses he would receive later as an adult when he mentioned that he herded reindeer. Unfortunately, a lot of stupid quips were directed at him. Even after speaking about working on the boats out at sea. Other reindeer herders know the true article by their speech and how they are dressed. Current day poseurs and charlatans can be exposed very quickly by those who know.

Some of the persons in this area knew his fellow tribesmen and even his papa. His parents took Mekkar to other areas of the globe where it could a different situation altogether. He consistently received a different reaction to his questions from others than he expected. Sometimes it would make him upset as those individuals might be as accommodating as his tribesmen.

On the other hand, he thought that none of those kids in this place could have had this much fun doing what he was doing. Despite the fact Mekkar had to work also. This was the crux of the youngster's interaction with Aslak. Still, Mekkar went on with his queries, "Why do I have to work so much? When these other kids do not? Look, they get to play without working." The reality was that Mekkar was part of a village that had a very different standard of the term "play". Nonetheless, the rewards would be so much more beneficial for him in the long run.

Now that the group was restocked with necessities Ansetti and Antagar led the others in preparing the reindeer to continue the trip. All of the herders on the trek had eaten very well, much better than some past adventures. Rich reindeer meat, cheese, milk, lingonberries, and cloudberries were only a part of their diet. At this point, the tribe took a short break to eat. Aslak told Mekkar not to consume too much. Of course, the little rebel did anyway. Since Mekkar now was full, he sought rest.

The blood was rushing to his stomach from his head to aid digestion left Mekkar tired and ineffective to perform his duties. Regardless, the crew dragged him away and departed. Mekkar was put on a sled so they could travel while he slept. It was not too cold for him to drift into his dreamlike state. It was only about -10° F (-23.3° C) outside and his winter clothing warmed him up just nicely. Mekkar's face was covered somewhat and the exposed parts got slightly flush in color. Fortunately, the native clothing he normally wore could keep a person still operational in much chillier climates. In far below zero degree weather a person definitely does not want to sweat too much. Otherwise the glands can freeze and get clogged. That would create another set of problems toward an individual's health, especially a young boy's. Normally back home in extreme conditions, Mekkar liked to take a cup of water and toss its contents upwards into the air. His favorite part is watching the former liquid quickly turn into powder on its path downward. However, it wasn't cold enough to do that and he was conked out.

Natives long ago adapted themselves in many ways to survive in their unique environments, some of which also includes the clothes they wear. Mekkar's tribesmen modified some of their wares to incorporate ventilation features to prevent great accumulations of perspiration no matter how strenuous the tasks being carried out. This layered winter clothing in theory was designed to keep most of a person's body heat close to the body in environments far below minus 0 degrees Fahrenheit (-17.77° C). However, no one including Mekkar wanted to test those claims and maximum limits. In normal settings, an individual usually didn't wear matching multicolored tunic, pants, and coverings everyday. Unless, it was for special occasions such as a wedding then a coordinated appearance would be important. Plus, there was the aspect of taking time to specially clean them without ruining the handmade material. Even the youngest member of the group knew that many options, not to mention fresh apparel, are limited while on the trek.

A heavy reindeer fur overcoat was only applicable for wintertime use as one would overheat, if worn during the summer. The outfit was toughly constructed with very water resistant skins as the base and the garments were all encompassing. Yet, there was some stretchableness or flexibility to fit the person. In addition to the comfortable boots or shoes without need for socks, unless the individual preferred them. There are also high boots which are used for travelling in deep snow and even whole leg/hip wading boots for fishing in lakes as well as rivers. Mekkar didn't care; he figured he would put prepared dried grass in his regular use boots to keep his feet warm, and cushioned. He next tied them tight so no snow got into his shoes. The grass helped to soak up the foot sweat as well. There is a preparation process as the grass first must be matted, teased carefully, and dried. Not to forget replaced every so often. The process takes time not available on the journey. In previous times this was necessary to preserve footwear. Modernization has changed this somewhat. The boy felt by the time this trek was over his pair of boots would be broken in nicely like well worn hockey skates. By good fortune Mekkar's footwear was used previously and not tattered before this journey began, otherwise he would have some aching feet and possibly blisters.

It had been quite a few miles since they left the town and Mekkar was still conked out on the sled. He slept about five hours on this occasion. For a kid such as him that is a long time. It was concluded he must have eaten way too much. Well, the weather stayed the same and Mekkar finally woke up from his slumber. He looked around and recognized some of these surroundings even though to most it was still another place that was quite unpopulated. This is the arctic, after all.

Much of what grows outside in the wild there is during the spring and fall and buried during the wintertime. Basically you have five main staples while most of the rest is imported from somewhere else outside the region. Mostly from down south and beyond. There are a few types of berries. The natives learn early when they are ripe enough to eat or not by the change of the coloring. Otherwise, there is the high potential to acquire food poisoning or to a lesser extent become really ill. In season, the various favors of budding fruits can tempt a person by their tartness, sweetness, or both.

Potatoes can be creatively grown and harvested with patches of grass or mulch to meet trekkers' needs. Various forms of onions to provide flavor and texture too. Moss and lichen even manifest itself to feed reindeer if they dig deep enough in the winter snows. Oh, my! Reindeer meat is delicious. Fish are available in the clean water streams that are not frozen over. If you are not in hurry, there is the activity of ice fishing. Mekkar would spear fish, during lunchtime, at the river back home but not during the middle of the blizzard season. The point is there are not a lot of options for grub so protecting the delicate balance of nature is tricky at best and can be brutal at worst.

Reindeer is so important to Mekkar's tribe and this area because they can supply milk, as well as make cheese using the ingredients. In theory, a human can use every part of the animal for some edible or functional application. However, one must know the resources that are available and how to make the best use of them. There is no haphazard waste. During the appropriate growing season there are a few farms that grow grains to help make appetizing homemade bread. Supplementary items can be gathered from the various towns and villages they pass on the path. These are the basics of the group's diet at home and especially on the trek. Vegetarians do not thrive well in this environment. Similar to all the children in his village, Mekkar learned these aspects as it was ingrained into him since he could talk and walk.

For the next four or five days the weather stayed consistent and the group covered between thirty and fifty miles (48.28 & 80.467 Kilometers) a day depending on various factors. The texture of the snow, how deep or how hard it was, the hilliness of the terrain, and transport reliability. There were no breakdowns of any equipment, so far. Basically, the expanse of this place is void of people in some areas. Still, the scenery is majestic, if one appreciates it.

Anyway, as the crew approached northward they kept up their pace and chose a certain familiar spot to set up the teepees before the crisp night air swiftly arrived upon them. The group of course set up a sauna tent first because it requires the most work. Almost everyone in the tribe will visit the hot one. Mekkar would go in there himself, yet some adults made it so hot until he could take no more. Anyway, the boy came out refreshed and relaxed from the experience. It is very different from the regular heat generated from the sun. Mekkar has trouble with hot desert-like temperatures outdoors, but the sauna helps him adapt to a certain level. There is a difference between sun driven warmth and hot room heat. If a person went outdoors in 180° F (82.22° C) heat, they might fry like an egg. That definitely goes for the natives from this region as they are not used to a roasting hot outdoor climate. For instance, Southern California during the summer. 200° F (93.33° C) is not uncommon in a real sauna and 212° F (100° C) is the boiling point for water. Mekkar doesn't know how to describe the hot room effect any better for those who are unacquainted with it.

The same setup plan and formalized routine is used to ready the camp in a rapid manner. Mekkar says, "Since it has been effective for hundreds of years why change it?" The little Arctic trekker dozed off as he listened to tales and stories in the tent about locations unknown to him. The adults continued to drink their favorite coffee which Mekkar didn't like anyway. The adults always seemed to follow their normal custom of giving their favorite drink an added spice and zip to it with alcohol. Not long after Mekkar snooze began he was awoken by sounds of howling wolves and reindeer shuffling. At any rate, it was just a false alarm and he went back to sleep.

Mekkar's mood showed that he loved the trek experience, as he was out in the open and felt free. He thought that a lot of people from the southern cities within the country would enjoy this too, only if they knew about it. Due to his youthfulness, Mekkar didn't recognize his own biased outlook. Yet, he still applied his assumptions to people he had come across when he went to work with his mama, down south in the big city. Mekkar deemed that all large city dwellers should experience this natural setting and its wonders at least one time in their life. A beneficial break from the humdrum routine of the average individual's existence. The exhilarating feel of freedom and fresh air in his lungs overwhelmed him more than usual. Nothing significant was occurring when he journeyed outside the teepee. Still, a quiet peace and enjoyment hit him all at once. Even though it had been a long trek so far there was a sense of newness. The young boy, at that moment, was eager to continue back on the journey once again. Aslak inquired of the youngster for a cause for his refreshed vigor, but Mekkar was unable to give him an answer. Nevertheless, Aslak knew and was testing Mekkar for the little trekker's interpretation to determine if it was accurate. The Seer always knew because Aslak could observe from many angles and multiple dimensions.

After packing up the party with their beasts they continued on to the east where there were more flat lands awaiting them. This area seemed more desolate than where the path had taken them beforehand. The folk here seemed to Mekkar to be more cold and distant toward their group also. An aura of distrust appeared to increase when encountering the inhabitants as the herd went further eastward. Mekkar perceived this as the locals might have been even bothered by his group's presence. The boy thought to himself the inhabitants in this place looked even frightened and he didn't know why. Thus, Mekkar went to Aslak and asked him questions regarding this. All of the elders know that kids, similar to the youngster, are curious and seek answers to their questions. Mekkar did not make the connection to the local people's reactions because he blocked out of his mind what he saw earlier on this trip regarding the wreckage. After speaking with Aslak and overhearing a conversation of Ansetti, Ankki, and Juhani is when he began to get some insight that addressed the matter. The residents feared a return of the overhead flights. One comment brought up that maybe the community thought their tribe was a target of a raid of some kind?

It was all too much information for such a young lad to connect the dots and grasp the overall situation. Mekkar listened as he heard comments regarding the locals and their recent encounters with these foreign flying machines and other military equipment. The original plan for this area was an attempt to increase development, yet those goals were never reached. A mention was made about another effort to take control of the area for a hidden purpose, but many in the circle disagreed with that theory. There had to be a reason for the unwanted attention from more powerful surrounding enemies desiring to dominate the area. Mekkar had no clue since he had never travelled to this area before. He became very bothered by the disturbing news. At least he gained a small portion of understanding related to the local's standoffish reactions concerning his group. The deep implications were beyond the boy due to youth and immaturity. It had been ingrained in Mekkar to strive to overcome any deficiencies he had by observing, clearly listen and hear, read if possible, and endeavor through application of all exposed information. Now, The Arctic Warrior is well aware this is a key to development and advancement of the mind.

When the situation was ascertained the group decided to continue on the trek despite that fact there was no town for quite a distance away from their location. After all the dead of winter had already passed, yet spring season had not arrived either. So, the herd with its shepherds was still affected by the frequent, wild fluctuations in the climate. There is always the myth of weather streams keeping certain areas warm. In some cases, it could be true regarding much warmer than expected temperatures at these high latitudes. The perceptions usually applied to the coastal regions, if the jet stream was static in its flow and in continual motion. Further inland, regular weather patterns are the normal tendency and decisions relied upon those characteristics. Actions and labor are determined by an expectation of a much colder environment further away from major bodies of water. Anyone living around mountain ranges is aware that they can provide an effective wind block between the coast and inland areas. Namely, if you are close to them and not in the distance on the valley floor below.

The temperature stayed relatively the same ranging between 25° F (-3.88° C) and 32° F (0° C) with little variation as they travelled eastward for the next few days. At the same time, Mekkar finally started to put that earlier wolf attack out of his awareness, but it was pushed back into his subconscious mind. The party had seen a couple of other wolf groups in the binoculars since then, yet none of those packs had come too close to be a threat. Along with the others, Mekkar remained in his night guard observation duties every third or fourth evening, according to the rotation. In truth, Mekkar basically was a trainee, a minor clog, and just another set of eyes and constantly fought the urge to sleep while on watch.

Nobody truly expected a great deal from him due to his youth and surprised some adults with his diligence by not falling asleep on duty. The young boy didn't neglect the tasks given to him. He expected a lot from himself and always did his best in everything he did or put his mind to. Mekkar held himself up as a special person and sought to apply himself to a higher standard than most. Potentially, it was the workaholic with excellence work ethic influence that was instilled into him by his parents and immediate family members. His parents demonstrated this through their own actions and example unlike a number of modern parents in today's civilized world. Examples of parent neglect and negative child behavior issues are reflected almost everyday in every realm of supposedly advanced society.

Sirga and Henrik never assigned, selected, or predetermined the path of their offspring's' future career or how each would earn a living later on as adults. The fact was they didn't have to because Mekkar and Alf were both internally self driven in their character with the oldest being sort of a perfectionist. The parents wanted their young children to dream and develop their own tastes. Henrik and Sirga felt that there would be plenty of time later on to make life choices as it's a part of life, but not too early. The key was to keep an open mind and not intentionally slam doors that might need to be opened in the future. The parents would not accept disrespectable attitudes and let their sons behave like irresponsible, spoiled, entitlement brats. The concept of real education to them, despite both having advanced degrees, was to question everything. While at the same time, research subjects for yourself to reach your own individual conclusions and belief systems. Henrik and Sirga expected this component to stay with Mekkar the rest of his life as they prepared him. Mekkar would learn what he liked and didn't prefer as opportunities arose. The caveat is when one is young they assume that they have all of the answers, as well as, many years to go to soak up all sorts of knowledge. Unfortunately, that is not always the case.

While they were forging ahead to the east, Mekkar could have sworn that he saw fighter jets after hearing the whoosh sounds overhead. However, he didn't recognize whose aircraft they were. Mekkar was normally spot-on identifying different jets because his uncle used to play recognition games back home with him. The youngster would be quizzed on various local and regional planes that they could see nearby and through binoculars. The game would include automobiles driven on the closest regional highway. The Arctic youngster had another of reference, his papa Henrik who was a pilot that was able to fly any aircraft the national military and airlines had.

Sitting and relaxing around the evening campfire the adolescent heard more stories about old legends and myths while the leaders were gulping down their coffee. Some of the tales and sagas seemed to Mekkar as being a very real part of history. Verbal communication was a normal practice, instead of writing it down, for stories to be passed down from one generation to the next. Long term oral traditions have been a common method of cultural transference for millennia as recorded throughout human history. There are a much smaller number of stories that have been conveyed in written form in comparison. By listening to these conversations in the tent, Mekkar gained an increased understanding of how old his people, native tribe, culture, etc. really was. His people were different from outward perceptions about them. The boy began to understand that many outsiders saw them automatically as lower class because of who they were. Natives were viewed with suspicion and they were considered a people that had lower intelligence.

Mekkar heard one of the leaders in the discussion speak about how scientists were incorrect regarding where his people originally came from and were indecisive concerning their beginnings also. Many of the current accept theories have been debunked in recent years. There are many physical features each individual has and are conducive to the tribes' people in this region that are shared with his own, but no one is exactly alike. A couple of adults there mentioned special attributes and advantages the natives are equipped with naturally in comparison with non-native settlers in the area.

Later during the conversation, the subject matter prompted Mekkar to ask many why questions. Inquiries which are similar to those that all parents are familiar with. Why is that? What for? ... Smartly, the boy continually sought wise sources to find answers. Confusingly, the more replies he received, the more inquiries popped into his immature noggin.

As Mekkar's parents taught him to be open to learning new things, this gave him a false sense that he believed that he was smarter than he actually was. Already, at this young age, signs of cockiness in his personality were bubbling to the surface. Mekkar based his intelligence at the time on having a lot of varied experiences for such a young kid. Also, he already read quite often because it was frequently pointed out to him that reading makes a person smarter.

The native boy heard the reasons related to the differences in the clothing his trek group wore in contrast to the locals in this place. The discourse mentioned the variety in designs, schemes, and color combinations as well as patterns in the tunics and hats. Their teepees were slightly different as well. The adolescent was also unaware of the underlying symbolism and array of emblems until he asked about it. There is a belief that has been instilled into Mekkar's being that states that the only dumb question is one that is never asked. [Albert Einstein] Functions are also alluded to if one is perceptive enough to decipher the codes. Careful detection can identify a tribe's village or clan affiliations. For instance, the shaman's hat could be used as a type of ancient position based directional finder. In other words, a compass based on shadows caused by the sun, the moon, and reflection of light from the snow. Similar to today's GPS navigational tools for land use without the high latitude inference issues that plague many systems in operation now. Of course, use of the antiquated system resulted in some miscalculations as well.

Mekkar never understood why the group rarely strayed far the route even when the herd was forced to deviate from their initial course due to changing conditions. Circumstances such as too much soft ground to trek on and extra stops for food and supplies. Luckily, the trekkers were able to return back on the chosen path. Some of the trekking routes have been used for many years. Long before non-native settlers began moving into the area and claiming some the land as their own. Those deeds permanently changed age-old routes that affected the indigenous people and herds. Mekkar's people have a few concepts that are different from modern society. In Mekkar's culture the land is seen as being for everyone to use and is sort of on loan, in that no one can really own it. Not even the regional chieftains or rulers, the state, nor the governments who control national borders. Thus, none of those parties have any right to take it away or even give the land to someone else like a particular individual, group, company, etc.

Another key point is that in many aboriginal people, like Mekkar's tribe, there is a mindset that all inanimate objects have their own individual life or soul. One must work in cooperation and harmony with those items to benefit. The Native from the North still expresses this habit of speaking to inanimate objects which confounds others to this day. Most people just write it off as craziness, lack of sanity, or senility on his part. A few others think he is just nuts when Mekkar audibly acts in this manner.

The arctic boy overheard several of the trek leaders agree among themselves regarding where the tribe currently was and the course they wished to continue on. Juhani, Ansetti, Antti, and many of the others such as Aslak all had their individual input in the discussion. Aslak later revealed some details of the conversation to Mekkar as a small part of their interaction together. Yet, the youngster did not fully grasp the full meaning behind much of the spiritual leader's explanations to him. Mekkar was experiencing an overload of details, information, and ideas as many of the concepts were new to the boy. However, Aslak sensed this and stopped briefly to let a portion set in. He was wise to proceed on in a slower fashion and reconfigure the important points of his message to Mekkar. Still, the hope was some of the shared knowledge would sink in to expand the boy's brainpower. Long term retention would be a bonus.

Remember, there has always been a connection of the boy with the shaman. One part of Mekkar's name comes from the wizard who helped deliver him from his mother's womb. During that time, Aslak played the role of a delivery doctor. Also, both of them are also related by blood within the tribe itself. Since, Aslak is an extended family member, so he had a stake in Mekkar's fate from the very start. It is well to note, that a high percentage of children usually do not initially survive when faced with such an early birth as Mekkar. If the newborn surprisingly endures, life expectancy is normally very short. Other mitigating circumstances of the event included an outdoor arctic setting and a sizeable trip to the hospital. The odds were stacked against the Arctic Warrior. Some have a suspicion that otherworldly forces protected the newborn. Only one person truly knew the exact sources involved regarding the preservation of Mekkar's life during that dramatic time, but he was very mum with any specifics.

Aslak took time out and gave his best efforts to teach Mekkar many things and insights. This trek provided many opportunities and sources for the boy to accelerate his learning curve. Mekkar's comprehension abilities to intake and process information were also high for individuals his age. Nevertheless, the medicine man also realized there are limits with regard to the mind capacity of a child. There was a risk of too much mental strain upon Mekkar could damage the boy. Outright frustration was potentially high and a possibility as a result. Aslak knew Mekkar got frustrated easily and this deficiency is still evident in Mekkar to this day. Alf would say it has increased in proportionate level to obstacles his older brother has encountered. Mekkar now even quips at times, "Life can be a frustrating experience when an individual has a genius level high IQ as compared to most people." It has never been explained if Mekkar was referring to himself or not. Many assumed that Mekkar was expressing his own belief regarding himself.

Due to his impatience, he wanted answers to his questions like any child his age does, in order develop themselves mentally and plot their way in life. If Mekkar didn't get satisfactory feedback, he would seek out another source. Even more so, the native from the north was extremely diligent than most kids his age. Some would say he was like a pest at times.

Anyway, the trek was constantly moving with time. No one was keeping track and in Mekkar's it seemed to pass by quickly. Later, after a long discussion with Ansetti, Aslak pointed out to Mekkar that this trek was coming to a conclusion real soon. The group had travelled many miles (kilometers) and they were pointed in the direction of home. The reindeer had their needs met and got exercise as well by this movement. When they get home the tribe can fatten the animals up again for the next season's activities. The whole purpose of the trek is so the animal's food supply in one place, their home area, was not all used up. This is a key factor because the ground regenerates new supplies so slowly due to the harsh climate. Mekkar learned this concept from the adults and would later refer to it by his own terminology. That is, a part of the cycle of environments much like three-tier faming and rotation of crops, etc. Sirga noticed that her oldest son, Mekkar, developed a habit of creating his words and phrases. Since he was also learning other languages during this period, she thought it was part of his process and didn't see it as irregular. The habit is still in force to this day.

During this time of year, it was more common for this particular trekking path to have a steady stream of tribes passing by. However, Mekkar's tribe was the only wandering group within sight distance of the closest village. The folks living here didn't seem as uptight to him as some inhabitants of other districts the herders encountered earlier on this journey. Probably because Mekkar saw an increase in the number of helicopters and jet aircraft flying overhead. Some of them he could identify and others he was unfamiliar with. Mekkar thought for a time that his sense of direction was off kilter as he felt they were not in the right area and still further to the east. Yet, Mekkar was a boy on his first long trek away from home without either of his parents, so what did he know? He was attempting to match the flyers in the sky to where he saw them before. Too bad, the anxiety returned and confused the youngster regarding any sense of direction. In his mind, Mekkar tried to match his assumptions with the flight location origins of these flying machines, but he failed miserably. Mekkar inquired a couple of the adults to clarify where the group's whereabouts. Aslak took Mekkar aside and showed him a couple of methods of how to determine where they were. The lesson included instruction of how to draw a bearing on the metal birds in the skies in relation to the sun. Aslak commented to the young herder, "Those aircraft only fly when the weather is good, so they can see where they are going." The shaman even let Mekkar don his special cap for a short time. The boy thought it was so cool and liked it much better than his own hat despite the obvious well-worn material of Aslak's headpiece. Mekkar saw it as a privilege. He next expected some special powers to overtake him while he covered his head with the spiritual leader's cap. Unfortunately, he was disappointed as the expected surge never occurred.

Sometimes during stopovers along the trek, the spiritual leader of the tribe would sometimes play games with Mekkar. Other times, teach him through various means to keep him from getting bored and also develop his mental faculties. Mekkar figured out that Aslak was the person he could learn quickest from, so he spent more time with the seer than anyone else during the trip.

It felt strange to Mekkar as the moving objects in the sky seemed to fly at lower and lower altitudes. Despite the planes flying closer to the ground, the people appeared to continue on with their daily lives and ignored them. Maybe they couldn't do anything about the aircraft anyway so why worry it as it will pass eventually. The youngster gathered some of a conversation when he was with Ansetti as the trek chief spoke to one of the locals about the activity overhead. Mekkar asked if the air forces were friendly or enemy. He received no response. It appeared as though the inhabitants were, in a way, sort of immune or desensitized to the planned patterns above them. Mekkar was told that there was only one way a response would be undertaken or local attitude changed. In other words, if the aircraft went on the attack, the inhabitants would counter attack in kind.

Normally the native population in this region of the world are very much, unlike some other people around the globe, a fairly peace loving people. It is quite a contrast to the frequent warlike mentality that encompasses various regions of the planet. The inhabitants here usually just go about minding their own business. They don't want to be bothered, but to live in freedom. Furthermore, to be left alone to conduct their daily affairs as daily life in the arctic is hard enough. However, anyone is able go into defense mode, if prepared and when they feel threatened by another. Ansetti and the other adult spoke about all the concerns Mekkar had regarding the situation. There was also much more information the boy listened to but didn't anticipate or understand. The man and Ansetti said his piece and the speech went back and forth. Though, Mekkar could gather only some the meaning because the conversation between the two was not in his native dialect.

Mekkar was also present during interactions involving Ansetti and other locals. It seemed the primary purpose was gathering of intelligence. The trouble was Mekkar could understand only bit and pieces of what was being said or none at all. The child definitely didn't gather the gist of the wording of what he could interpret either. He thought to himself those people and we are dressed in comparable ways but not identical due to region and the speech ... Internally, he pondered other ideas such as who are these people? They sort of look like me and kind of sound like me. The people here also carry out functions that we do, but they are not exactly like me. I have encountered this before on this trek. He summed it up with, they are odd in comparison.

With the tools Aslak demonstrated to him, the native runt figured out fairly well regarding where he was now in regard to the herd's location and home. Deceptively, he continued to convey an exterior image of being lost. No matter what he told himself, Mekkar was still worried by the persistent military flurry around him. The boy needed clarification to calm his internal turmoil and sought out the medicine man. Aslak mentioned that this is a regular occurrence because the area is much nearer to a fairly unfriendly national border than Mekkar's village. Although there are more direct line to reach that national dividing line, if one wanted to. It was pointed out to the youngster why the locals appeared unfazed as they must be used to this activity and therefore see this movement all of the time.

These activities remind some older citizens in the area about unforgotten events of how different forces during World War II invaded the region and damaged it severely. Battles raged and explosions were heard right outside their front doors in some cases. Many historical records don't reveal many of the horrors and details involved. Added to the fact, natives are not the only inhabitants that live here, there a few different nationalities. Thus, the number of languages spoken here has not been homogeneous for quite awhile. Not to forget how the indigenous population was employed like slaves by the invaders. A number of those families and individuals were killed in the skirmishes and wars that went on into nineteen forty five and beyond. Even one of Mekkar's own grandmama's was murdered after she poisoned the occupying forces food supply. It was her small contribution to the area defense effort while performing duties as a cook. Territorial disputes and battles between various armed units have occurred in this area for centuries. There have been at least thirty of these unfortunate encounters between rival forces within the last few hundred years. The goal is plentiful, untapped natural resources if one desires to put in some effort to exact them.

There are a number of countries' in the last few centuries where people can relate to this predicament. Many times assorted forces and personnel went back and forth claiming territory for the glory of their national leaders. But, at the same time, with no side being triumphant and having a decisive victory. Yet, the common folk were the real losers through the sacrifice of family members lives, property, homes, livelihoods, etc. These battles also ensued in multiple locations at the same time and on different fronts within the region. Regrettably, the historical lessons are still being neglected to this day with similarly potential ramifications. Applicable in this situation is the conventional wisdom that says those who cannot remember the past are condemned to repeat it. [Reason in Common Sense, volume 1 of <u>The Life of Reason</u> by George Santayana, 1905]

Miscommunication, deception, and outright cruelty were the rule of the day to coincide with political and military aims. It didn't matter if there were blatant lies as long as the particular agenda were successfully executed. Some of false information that was spewed out at the time has now come to light. Very different outcomes could have been attained but the original course was pretty much set and the real goals were predetermined. Governments and populations then put their trust in agreements that were basically unenforceable and easily broken. One enemy came to overrun the area near the border with the premise to supposedly create a buffer for one of their large cities. That was the official line anyway. The truth was that they felt their bullying strategy against those smaller than them would add wealth to the national coffers; for a small cost to increase their domain. Surprisingly, the closest and largest foreign power got what they wanted, but the price was extremely high and probably not worth it.

Unexpectedly, the nasty winter weather along with the rugged terrain played a huge role in the favor of the outnumbered defenders. Fierce local fighting to save their homes and land as well logistical nightmares on the part of the attackers punished the overwhelming invading military. At certain points, the aggressors were stopped cold and ended up retreating. In the end, the dogged resistance was hindered by exhaustion and lack of ammunition on the part of the underdogs. Otherwise, the eventual outcome might have been quite the opposite. In pure numbers on the battlefield the encroaching forces lost big time. However, the underdogs eventually had to surrender. The leadership of the local forces made some mistakes such as awaiting other foreign powers to come help them. Lamentably, those promises were broken often and the relief never arrived. In hindsight, conflict is a dangerous proposition and predicting the future is hard to forecast. Could the whole damaging incident have been avoided? The final peace terms at the end were harsh and wounded the little populated area deeply. It took a long time for a full recovery to be achieved somewhat close to pre-great war levels. On top of that, recognition of local bravery and heroics from that period couldn't be honored until much later. That is, when memories have faded and after the political landscape drastically changed

The powerful neighbor expected it all to be completed and dealt with in a couple of weeks due to having an overwhelming superiority in weapons, soldiers, and supplies. A combination of things helped the regional inhabitants hold much of their territory, unlike some other places. The hindrances included miscommunication and lack of coordination on the part of the invaders. All of these factors together nullified some attacks in their tracks and kept others from deep advancement and total domination of the surrounding countryside. This happened despite the overpowering numbers on the enemy side and the unfulfilled promises of help by quite a few other nations, except for one. Even then, their help arrive with extremely small numbers and many conditions attached. The isolation was repeated in a similar manner of numerous past conflicts. So, it stands to reason why the people in this area have a very guarded attitude and initial lack trust regarding most strangers and their promises. The general feeling is most people from the outside have let them down time and time again. So, why believe them now? Could anyone blame the local residents for their cautious demeanor?

Mekkar had learned a small part of the regional history by listening in at the campfire stories. Accounts told by those who were involved while helping the beleaguered and outnumbered, but game defenders. Antti described seeing and fighting alongside local troops for their homeland and virtual existence. The all white winter uniforms made sure they blended in with the scenery. He spoke about the freezing conditions and not having the correct full seasonal military attire. The individual troops on their side always carried their own portable shelter with them. Also, they were highly mobile on skis that afforded them great maneuverability advantages. Due to the considerable losses, the enemy learned some valuable lessons and later applied similar tactics, which led to victories in other combat theaters.

As the herd ventured toward the national boundary, Ansetti said it was common to see soldiers in this area. He also brought up the point regarding a training area that was located not far away. Ansetti identified, with Mekkar at rapt attention, the soldiers in the all-white clothing as Rangers or Special Forces. He described their provisions and supplies present on each person along with the required advanced tactical training. By the way, skis and sport skiing were invented by the indigenous people in the arctic. Tribes related to Mekkar. Those troops lugged packs and prepared for almost anything they might encounter. Units might be distinguished from the enemy through the use of traditional or formal greetings. Ansetti knew soldiers and said some of the leaders of this trek performed similar duties. Kin that Mekkar looked up to had served in various past military capacities. Mekkar observed that Ansetti seemed to be very friendly with everyone he interacted with in this place. It was, as if, the trek leader had been here many times before. The response to exchanges with Ansetti was positive because many appeared to know him. Later that day, Mekkar was made aware regarding all of this while relaxing in the teepee. He enjoyed the slow paced atmosphere and continued to discover many adventures his fellow herders experienced long ago.

A part of the discussion mentioned how native peoples all over the globe deal with many of the same issues, concerns, and battles to preserve their cultures. The other side in the struggle for self-preservation is the prevailing, dominant civilizations. Problem is, the larger ones make all the rules and continue to spread their reign as the dominant rulers of societies. In a way, similar to an extensive mafia with attitudes and viewpoints that see the natives and their old ways as primitive, backwards, and even retarded. Often times, actions are carried against the indigenous peoples to eliminate them altogether because the view if taken that there is no use for them anymore. Even more so, leaders make straightforward demands that all natives should catch up and adapt to the modern world.

In this area it is normal to have served in the various national military branches for a few reasons: a powerful enemy nearby; this area is sparsely populated; the practice of conscription of all available people for national defense has been conducted for such a long time; and to avoid penalties and punishment for not fulfilling compulsory service. Specific duties depended on each person's talent combined with geographical location. Some towns or areas are split by a national border, thus individuals from the same village or hamlet possibly could represent different armed forces. Hopefully, they do not have to face off against each other. Various types of service included local militia, homefront, or regular duty.

Females were included in the arrangement also since the regional inhabitants were a small number as compared to huge populations and large armies that surrounded them. In this area one has to be fully committed to their assignment. Choices are limited in some respect because there are not enough people, plus you might end up protecting your own family plot. It is important to note that service is not only restricted to able bodied men. No gender distinction is considered when filling needs. Everyone must contribute if needed to protect the land, property, homes, families, etc. Many of the older people are justifiably afraid of the alternative and what could happen. They still vividly remember the World War II time period, when most of the area was burned to the ground. The local thought process is if everybody does not stand up, then everyone here will be defeated, even crushed and conquered by their enemies. The concepts are built on past real life experience and hardship.

Unfortunately, there are conflicts and rivalries between natives themselves, and certain individuals in particular. Plus, indigenous population is not predisposed as a warmongering people. They are a very peaceful society as a whole. Individuals, can be a different matter altogether. Of course, outside enemy attack without provocation can occur. People can respond, in kind, due to the adaptability aspect that consists as part of overall human nature. In the past, this naturally inclined harmonious disposition and neutral stance positioning has resulted in much suffering placed upon Mekkar's people. The perception by others saw this personality trait as weakness and forcibly administered a policy of harsh domination and undeniable cruelty. There was plenty of confusion, due to the multiple layers of taxation, levied by a variety of chief rivals who claimed the area as their own. Locals were expected to pay in money, goods, or services to more than one authority at the same time. Otherwise, violent repercussions could be taken such as a family member being sold as a slave to pay the tax debt.

Mainly as a result of necessity, germinating from past brutal treatment experiences, the last few generations of Mekkar's tribe has acquired an added suspicious defense mechanism. The current age has its dilemmas, but nowhere near the same as in earlier times when the native descendents took a lot of abuse. Massive exploitation of the native people and natural resources by those in authoritative positions was the norm. To some extent the trend still continues, although under the radar and not as blatant. The current laws of the land allow discriminatory practices to transpire at the expense of native interests. Kings, foreign dignitaries, ministers, etc. in former times misused their power in many ways and still do today.

One past example of harsh policy application by invaders was conversion and acceptance of new beliefs. If the aboriginal dwellers didn't convert, through force, to the dominant state accepted religion from the accepted old rituals of the ancient pagan faith, there would be punishment metered out. Sometimes, the choice was convert to our way or be put to death. Many aboriginal people died as a result of their refusal to neither accept nor submit. More than a few overlords demanded that the natives allow their women to be taken away and intermarried with these strange foreigners or make them slaves. Many of the process were part of an overall plan of racial assimilation. Basically, it is culture extinction forced upon the indigenous minorities by government or powerful leaders.

It is well to note that Mekkar's people lived in this region long ago and were even given descriptive terms by ancient foreigners who visited from other lands. Study of the area's languages and dialects have revealed more continuity in the past. Now, there are mostly unintelligible variations mostly due to isolation, locational factors, and national borders. Mekkar thought Ansetti was incredible as he has been able to converse with many different types of people in various dialects of speech. Mekkar admired the trek leader's communicative ability with everyone he encountered and thus looked up to him in that regard. The boy thought Ansetti was special and had a gift given to him from another realm. This talent was something that Ansetti appeared to do better than everyone else in their crew, well at least, in Mekkar's mind. He thought it was so cool and desired to acquire that ability also.

As the youngest person from his tribe on this trek, Mekkar had received wide-ranging special education, whether he realized it or not. Added to the fact, back in the village the wise, medicine man Aslak foretold this would happen. The boy was partially exposed to and being trained in a variety of mental and physical categories, all at the same time. Mekkar still didn't fully grasp many of the concepts due to his youth. The youngest member of the trek was confused regarding some lessons that he was learning on the trek. Later questions and discussion between elders arose as to the boy's education gathered here. Was there high value and how could it be relevant toward the proper direction of the youngster's life purpose. How little did Mekkar truly know that he was being prepared for much more, in the future, than he could ever imagine.

According to the plan, the trekkers never quite reached the other sea that Mekkar thought they might reach. Instead, the group changed to a different direction and progressed toward home. Understandably, it was probably a good thing the boy was not part of the leadership planning committee. Admitting inexperienced children in the decision making of the trek, even one as brilliant as Mekkar, would result in disaster for all of them. One of the tribe elders, Aarro, was a mapmaker and sailor who had spent time in other lands. The world explorer mentioned to Mekkar that the group had a certain number of miles (or kilometers) left to travel. He also told the youngster that the trek would follow a slightly different route on their way back home. Aarro commented that the journey shouldn't be too bad. Along with the herd, they would follow a course which went near a number of a larger lakes and rivers. For Mekkar, there would be more time to progress on to the next level of his development. Aslak and other key players were careful not to overload the growing boy. Information overload avoidance was important. The potential for distraction was great while trying to assimilate everything. Any errors in these environments and situations normally occur due to confusion and lack of coordination among the herders. Potentially costly dangerous mistakes including loss of life was always a real possibility. The idea was to keep Mekkar excited about participating in future treks and not to grow to despise the experience.

There have been great changes for trekkers over time. Groups can now be guided exclusively by modern technology and also aided through the use of machinery with some tasks. Not to forget, the old ways which have been proven effective over hundreds of years. Some tribes, such as Mekkar's, prefer a mixture of the two methods and claim it delivers the best results. Various fairly predicable seasonal weather patterns often determine diverse individual responsibilities, as well as the whole group. Ancient practices followed guidelines by employing features seen in the sky. The March and September equinoxes, June and December solstices, the recognizable four seasons, plus other important points throughout the calendar year could affect the chosen itinerary. It is a common occurrence each year in winter that a person can experience, no true daylight, for weeks on end. Mekkar has overheard older people in the tribe described their depressed state of mind when they observe the dark sky, even in the middle of the day. On the other hand, during the height of the summer, the sun never completely sets even at midnight. The natives see it as more preparation time to ready themselves for the long, harsh cold season. Mekkar's parents, among others, believe the tilt in the Earth's axis plays a role in designating daily weather conditions. In ancient times and similar to an astronomer, a scant number charted these patterns in a manner that was quite different from the current modern day calendar. It was not a complete almanac, but a chronicle to keep track of consistent rhythms and cycles of life unique to this part of the world.

To approach the closest village, the trek was forced to travel around assorted bodies of water. The herders could see, as well as, feel a rush as local military pilots zoomed above their heads. The exhausted and less fearful, young Mekkar accepted this as an indicator of the long final leg of the journey. It was last step toward home or so he thought. They once again set up camp, while a few kept on watch. While listening to the elder's converse in the sauna tent, Mekkar found out that home was not as close as he hoped.

It was about one hundred sixty one and a half miles (260 kilometers) away. Despite the fact the band of herders hadn't technically gotten back to their destination, a small celebration broke out. The trekkers realized what they had endured on this trek, yet they had not been conquered. There was a collective sigh of relief and gratefulness that they were all still alive. Still, as the trek chief Ansetti was the only one not fully content with the results due to the losses incurred earlier during the wolf attack. There was plenty of reindeer meat available to be consumed; Cheese from their last stop was part of the diet also. Ah, this is fun, thought Mekkar. He saw it as a reward for a difficult journey. There were other delicacies to choose from: salmon, cod, pike, trout, char, carp, perch, whitefish, and others. They are readily available in the territory. Mekkar thought to himself, "Where have they been hiding this stuff?" After relaxing an extra day, the crew continued back on the move.

Juhani was the first one to point out their good fortune that this homestretch area normally had relatively few wolves. However, as they have remembered earlier on this trek you never know what might happen. It is always better to be safe than sorry and prepare for the unexpected. Not to forget any number of other possibilities that could arise at any time. The assembly there didn't feel they were in much danger here, but they would stick with the original plan anyway because there were precautions built in.

Overall, most felt the trek had gone well except for that one wolf pack attack. Mekkar felt like it was partly his fault for some of the negative outcome because of failure in the execution of his duties as a watch person. He judged that he could have done a better job and more to prevent any losses in the herd. In reality, an effective response is everyone's responsibility, not Mekkar's alone. The youngster did what he could to the best of his ability by warning the others. Trouble was, he was unable to recognize the dark enemy figures basking in the twilight glow. Only experience could have taught the boy. Usage of terrain as cover for a night assault on a herd has been effectively employed for many centuries. After a day or so, the band reached a plateau in the plain, while at the same time encountering a strong head wind. In this locale the air sweeps over the high hills and small mountains and picks-up momentum on the flat valley floor. The two major villages in the area receive the full brunt of the flow. Amazingly, the gusts appear to direct itself to points further south because there is nothing to hinder their path. When the wanderers reached one of the villages the group took a break for more supplies.

Ansetti, with Mekkar in tow, struck up a conversation with an old man named Jaakka. Aslak joined them as they already knew each other from long ago. Jaakka had lived for a long time in this vicinity. Even before the Great War which involved almost every place on earth. At that time essentially everything in this area was burnt to the ground. Mekkar was surprised that Jaakka could converse with the leaders somewhat in their village dialect since it slightly different. Later, the local man joined them at their camp on the outskirts.

That evening, Mekkar stayed attentive as Jaakka recalled many tales of old. Legends, sagas, and mythos were brought up also. A few local heroes were featured in some of the stories. Yes, the natives have their own mythology just like the Greeks, Romans, Norse, and other native peoples. There are key figures and individuals, like Thor or Zeus as well. The narratives included a history of their tribes too. Jaakka spoke to the group in their home dialect as much as could. He could get by, but he was not completely fluent in Mekkar's dialect of speech. Jaakka had his own regional tongue. Instead he conversed in the main national language for most of the campfire session while most sat around drinking their beloved coffee. Part of the dialogue brought up the point regarding the natives, in most circumstances, are not naturally a warring people. Comparable to most cultures, most people are followers and look to leaders to give them courage, especially in times of adversity. Mekkar's native tribesmen will reluctantly take on a defensive stance if they have to and only as a last resort. To take on a foe in a physical warlike manner is not normally the first course of action.

Yet, the assembly was aware there was still quite a distance to go before they would reach the sanctity of their homes and families. Not long after the small gathering concluded for the night, the wind became heavier and more forceful. The teepees had to be closed more tightly than usual for the next few evenings. It was a good thing the tents are not as tall and wider at the base to make them structurally suited to withstand higher gusts. Mekkar awoke from rest from the noise due to the strong winds. Leaders endured the bursts to gather anything they could to hold down the loose items by staking some of these items into the ground. It was not possible to tie down anything due to a lack of suitable large trees. Many of the trees there were small enough that practically all of the adults could push them over. The problem is the roots are not able to secure themselves deep into the earth due to the permafrost barrier.

End of Trek

The geography has changed back to more familiar settings because the trek is almost over. It is getting closer and closer to home. Mekkar, Ansetti, Juhani, and the rest of the group are returning. Every one of them can sense that another long trek is almost over ...

Some of the older ones, like Ansetti, have recognized the difference between the treks of today and yesteryear which, for the nomads, never ended. The more experienced trekkers recognize the always changing circumstances. They see routes and lands to move herds are increasingly disappearing. Government agencies are continually adding regulations and companies never stop pursuing additional land purchases to exploit remaining natural resources. It seems as though only the inhabitants see the permanent damage to the natural ecosystem. Development projects and construction of large scale undertakings such as hydro dams, etc. gobble up more territory while taking away from animal husbandry activity. Crooked officials use eminent domain and outright, direct government takeover to reclaim the land. Each instance further restricts open grazing and birthing areas that have been used for centuries in these regions. Added to this, encroachment upon ancient native areas, due to enforced new settlement takeover policies, diminish animal movement patterns. Technology has brought great changes to reindeer gathering and management of stock. Reindeer herding is less labor intensive now as a result of modern day equipment being employed in the process. Snowmobiles, trucks, boats, and helicopters are presently adopted to carry out these tasks in opposition to earlier times.

Seasonal Patterns for the herd to follow, while trekking, have been occurring for a long time. In the past, specific reindeer herding villages had their own preset chosen migration routes chosen by the local community. Due to the current ever-changing political atmosphere, natives are in an uproar because they endure the loss of more land for herd movement. Many old pathways are now fenced off for various reasons.

In Mekkar's culture, old native thought practices reign supreme. Everything belongs to the family and the village group as a whole. It is selfish to consider it any other way. Previously, permanent and separate homes or dwellings were constructed without an individualistic viewpoint in mind. Items are not only yours alone but to be shared and enjoyed by all in the tribe. Mutual benefit of the whole group is key. The concept of single person ownership was foreign to the natives here. Sometimes those same materials, which included all supplies and goods, could be needed to ensure the tribe's very survival. If that was ever the case, then so be it. That type of approach, especially on a trek, is executed with maximum efficiency to insure the success of the journey for all involved. It is a long forgotten, nomadic, and tribal approach to ensure continual existence. These thought processes have also been applied and adapted to the modern way of living to a certain degree and with a native flavor. In many cases, far northern latitude small communities experienced forced changes beyond their control.

People are seen as visitors or travelers on this earth; technically you as an individual don't own anything. Not even yourself! Well, maybe just yourself. In some aspects, yes and some ways, no. Everything is only a rental and that perspective benefits the collective unit or group. Extremely selfish people have few, if any, friends in this environment because they refuse to cooperate with anyone else. Those type of people end up having a much lesser chance for survival. In the Arctic people and animals are very connected with a need for each other whether a person admits it or not. Herd mentality is perceived as the best option and has functioned successfully in inhospitable climates for centuries. Uncompromising, solitary folks left to their own devices usually have negative outcomes such as an early death.

This is a concept Mekkar would acquire a better grasp of and expand his learning capability as he grew up. In the cases regarding any type of monument, they are considered to be a tangible gift which belongs to everyone. One's selfish personal desires are disparaged and the objective radiance is meant to serve all who come into contact with the structure. The notion is for greater good encouragement to keep the villagers fighting for survival, one of those of which was Mekkar. A person is looked upon as a grain of sand on the beach and one small piece of the whole, like a puzzle. The native outlook is unchanged for the most part on matters such as these. This is true even as their native world and circumstances get swallowed up by the modern society all around them. Today, Mekkar has recognized a mingling of both belief systems. Yet, each particular piece cannot be discounted and always must fulfill a function or purpose.

Now, since his native people are more settled than they were one hundred years ago, treks can be better contrived due to technological advances in equipment. Trek planning and timetables, in modern times, are less rigid. Nevertheless, some actions must still be carried out on a regular basis during various calendar seasons and animal requirements. Specific flexibility is modified according to the herders and their overall collective mood. In this culture, many tools, accessories, and useful family possessions belong to the whole group. That is, any resource that can be relied upon to meet needs and aid the entire clan. Mekkar sees this as the very antithesis of extreme individualism in various parts the modern world. His upbringing is what is considered as yours is also in many aspects everyone's around you and should be relished in a widespread manner. This applies even to inconsequential personal awards, trophies, and other related items. The truth is, no one ever gets to a high level in any endeavor without help from others along the way. Natives, all around the world, grasp this concept as it has been part of their way of life for a long time. Unfortunately, greedy influences from modern societies have infected change in native cultures more rapidly than anyone cares to admit.

Going on, the trekkers travelled for a few more days and nights and the mood of the group improved along with the weather. There seemed to be less distractions and everything appeared to have become easier during this part of the journey. A few in the party thought it might be a situation of the calm, before a storm. Still, the leader Ansetti had a tough battle to root out any complacency within the party in the homestretch. He knew that any sudden lapse in the attention to detail could result in another attack by wolves or other predators. Experienced outdoor people are well aware how a wolf pack can steal potential food from much larger animals such as bears. They are not afraid to rob from you too! An attack can happen at anytime, especially in the nighttime, even in familiar surroundings.

A number of Arctic animals have adapted eyesight that is superior to big city dwellers, fortunately a balanced number of natives have been blessed with a similar sense. Plus, many animals, in such a harsh environment, are usually visually keen in the dark of night. Populations in snowbelt regions can see how the white snow can illuminate the earth's surface with more light than dark metropolis roads lit by street lamps. That, along with colorful clothing, attempts to make up for some of the darkness and fight off climatic induced depression. This is especially true, when the twenty four hour darkness season arrives.

Anyway, as they reached closer on the path toward home, the leading ones in the tribe told more and more stories about the old ways. Past legends were spoken of during those stops along the trek. There have been films made and books written in other languages about some of the tales and heroes, Mekkar heard in the tent. He listened, absorbed, and learned a lot on this journey. But, he was still young, too young to really understand the whole experience and how it affected him. That would happen in time. As they got nearer and nearer to their destination a few more days had passed. Always at the evening's group gathering was the night coffee. The leaders consumed copious amounts of it. However, Mekkar greatly disliked that drink. It seemed to the boy that definitely the evenings were getting longer as they moved closer to his village. Aslak mentioned to Mekkar, what he was feeling was the anticipation of longing to be back home.

Mekkar's village is divided by a natural water barrier which also functions as a borderline running down the middle of the river. The water flow does become more restricted and narrow when the river winds around, bends, and curves at various points. Some in the village were convinced the map-makers were drunk as they surveyed the area for the national government. It was probably the reason for some of the odd geographical choices that were selected.

There was a celebration when the trekkers arrived in the village. All manner of festivities were involved with singing, dancing, some play fighting with the buddies, spitting of blood, flirting with the girls, and more. Many of these things are a picture relating to symbolism, a symbol of actual experiences that one encounters and actual desired results of making it back safely. The trek chief Ansetti, well, was not so happy because there was lost reindeer and he felt responsible. Some of the trekkers felt that they did better than they should have in that instance due to its suddenness and large number of assailants. However, that was of no consolation to Ansetti. Overall, that was the only major attack on this trip. Young Mekkar was pleased and he felt proud. He was the youngest person in the herding group on this trek. Yet, there was no reason for him to brag to his friends about being chosen for this completed trip. Another youngster, male or female, from the village would be chosen to participate in the next travelling party with the reindeer. Of course, after the young member of the tribe was somewhat trained and "prepared" first. The boy made it through and there was also a sense of relief on the part of his parents. Mekkar made it back from his long reindeer trek without his parents accompanying him on the journey. There was also a surprise in store for him as his own family was now settled in their new, larger permanent home. Mekkar felt that he had come back to an existence more planted after this trip. This meant no more wandering for awhile. Now was the time for Mekkar to carry on with his free will and be less limited by his surroundings and as many predators. The boy would later see that his assumption was mistaken.

Expanding His Vision

Early on Sirga would make Mekkar work in the family restaurant by serving customers and carrying out tasks behind the scenes. Mekkar would do as Sirga commanded to avoid any possible repercussions. Some travelers visiting the area made comments to staff members after seeing young children employed at local businesses. Those individuals didn't realize that was the normal practice of the regional culture. If a person observed closely, they would notice that Mekkar was not alone in that regard.

Mekkar did a lot of odd jobs as he progressed along his employment path. It was fortunate that he benefitted from a varying hourly schedule in most of his positions up to that point. Thus, the youngster from the Arctic was able to travel, all around the globe, with his papa and mama. Mekkar's papa gradually climbed the corporate ladder of a conglomerate from his teen years on. With each step, as Henrik advanced upward, the perks became better. Travel was more extensive to additional different locales on this spinning orb. Mekkar did not get a free ride when he went along with his papa; the boy had to carry out various tasks assigned by Henrik or his office secretary. His duties involved having Mekkar sort things like paperwork and figure out some simple issues through analysis. As Mekkar got older and better at testing the data, his papa would entrust even more responsibility to a smart boy like him.

First, would fulfill their business requirements and then have time to experience some fun activities afterwards. Mekkar, of course, preferred the latter. Mekkar thought it was so cool to observe and experience many things on these trips that many people only read about. When he returned back home, while being questioned by his friends, others began to identify a different mindset of haughtiness regarding the overseas travel. After some time had passed Mekkar took to another reindeer trek. A long one, similar in distance to the last journey alongside the animals. It was not the same route as the last major journey, but more to the south in a westwardly direction

The emerging lad also participated in common pursuits along with the other boys his age. The harsh winter season restricted many outdoor activities, yet they adjusted and came up with new ones to entertain themselves. Mekkar spent the majority of his free time alongside his best friend Lasse and that included causing mischief together as well. Not to discount the fact, it seemed relatives always seemed to show up frequently. Mekkar always wondered why his residence, despite not located in the middle of the village, buzzed with liveliness on a regular basis. Probably, he figured it was the attraction of their multiple enterprises such as the small restaurant.

One example arranged by his mama forced Mekkar to work in a travel agency assisting one of Sirga's friends. He didn't have a choice in this matter. In the period before personal computer usage in this particular office, Mekkar would constantly be on the phone. Sometimes, simultaneously one phone with the car rental company on the line and the second phone in his hand with the customer. If both sides actually knew how young the person on his end truly was, they might have expressed great anger. However, Mekkar quickly became adept in his assignments, which belied his age. He also went beyond and familiarized himself with supplementary helpful information. For instance, airline schedules through an extensive timetable catalog called the Official Airline Guide (OAG). The positive gained from working there was exposure to travel industry and airline business. Plus, previous travels were another resource that he could draw upon and this would be useful in later endeavors.

Southeast Asia was an odyssey utterly different from anything Mekkar had encountered before. The area could be dangerous due to the conflict raging in some of those nations. He went with his papa and the experience was eye opening to say the least. Due to his background, age, and origin of his passport it was much easier to move around freely than some others. The corporation that Henrik worked for never chose sides in any active war zone. It was perceived as an opportunity for profit and many times business was conducted with both sides in any struggle. Who was on the right or wrong side was considered of no consequence with regard to business. Mekkar's papa was brought in to setup the lengthy process of negotiation before any physical construction would begin. Arrangements, interaction, and on occasion bribery, with the correct important people in the area were necessary to set the operation in motion. Before building anything one must overcome required building codes, etc. in most places. The standards and methods followed are very different around the world. Henrik's employer had one overriding rule: Each of the projects must be constructed for the benefit of people in some manner. Those same ventures were never war related and designed to make them difficult to convert for armed conflict purposes. The structure could function as a pharmaceutical plant, hospital, manufacturing factory, as well as similar type businesses. Henrik laid the initial groundwork because he was excellent at doing so. When actual construction began, Mekkar's papa would move onto another assignment. Sadly, some those projects later became casualties of war or misidentified collateral damage through bombing raids.

Mekkar's papa wanted to expose him to new things and expand his vision of the world around him. The goal was to increase his learning far from his native vision and upbringing alone. The idea was to increase Mekkar's ability to adapt to changing circumstances. Reminding Mekkar the same level of tranquility doesn't exist in other areas of the globe, as compared to back home in the village. Yet, Mekkar's papa did not explain these reasons to him because Henrik felt his son was too young to grasp the concepts and reasoning. Henrik went on to quiz him about some events and things he saw previously on the past extensive reindeer trek. Specifically, about the downed helicopters, the damage done to them, and weapons that he might recognize. Mekkar told his papa that he overhead Ansetti told stories of past events and spoke about other connected subjects in the trek tent. Henrik inquired if he was okay with this because he might see worse there. His papa also asked him many questions to determine if he understood what items were used and each one's purpose. Henrik would then fill in the blanks for his son. Henrik was blunt and described the true situations they might encounter where the trio was travelling to. Contrary to what information could be gathered through the news and reading books, Mekkar's papa would expose the environments and living conditions in other locales, especially ones away from home. This was the majority of the conversations between them on the travel itinerary. The result was Mekkar's young mind was overtaxed and flooded by all of the information he attempted to digest as his papa communicated with him.

After leaving home, the trip took them through parts of India and Singapore onto their destination in Vietnam. Mekkar saw a flurry of activity on the ground on their final approach. The boy's conscious mind became overwhelmed and he only remembered a small amount of what he saw by the time they finally arrived. Fortunately for him, fear was almost non-existent due to the presence of his papa. Saigon or Ho Chi Minh City was the destination on the agenda. Mekkar had never been in this part of the world before and hence, it was a culture shock for him. The reality of being accompanied by his papa and the additional company representative on this trip saved Mekkar from total unsettlement. At the time, Mekkar could not identify this lady who went along with them. The youngster was only aware that she was a person who worked with his papa. Later on, Mekkar found out that she was related to both of them was there to keep a close eye of him, specifically.

There was an abundance of soldiers moving to and fro. The boy observed they were not dressed like the ones back home. Mekkar thought their military fatigues were in an irregular arrangement of design and colors. There was a mixture of black, brown, and the base was green. It was in contrast to the soldiers' attire back at home during the wintertime which was all white. Mekkar discerned that these troops all over the city didn't have skis' with them because they probably didn't know how. His previous geographical studies fostered the question, how much snow could a place like this have? These troops had much larger packs on their backs and were normally either on foot or in a mechanized vehicle of some sort. Mekkar surveyed the surrounding area and discovered no snow anywhere to be found. Brave and bold boy that he was, Mekkar approached one of the troops and asked him how he was able to ski with all of his gear on. The warrior just kind of peered at him strangely and pushed him away. Mekkar thought maybe there was a communication gap. He did try to choose a soldier that had the appearance and insignia of a European that could speak a common tongue with him, that is English. Truly, how hard could that be? Eva explained to Mekkar, "Perhaps, the gun toting individual felt he was as out of place here as you do? The main difference is he is much larger and has a weapon."

In this case Henrik, Mekkar, and his attendant were still tourists in this land. Quite a few inhabitants appeared to be scrambling around them, while at the same time, columns were on the march. A lot of hustle and bustle was taking place among the people along with a scattering of a few very poor residents. The extent between the rich and the poor was extremely evident; there was no way to hide it. Mekkar detected this but he did not understand its meaning until after they had left. Questions ran through his limited mind, what is my papa doing? He sends me to this place, but I don't understand why. Even though, Eva did her best to explain it partially to him, the comprehension of it all still didn't make sense. Later that day his papa tried to answer any questions Mekkar had, but he sensed much of the message wasn't sinking in.

If he just kept a watchful eye out, some answers would come to him, thought Mekkar. Despite a very high intelligence, Mekkar still needed interpretation and portrayal along with what he saw. Two aspects were conspiring against Mekkar's situational understanding: One was his relative youth and inexperience and the second, was the cultural influence and background. Mekkar grew up in a place with a language and customs that were to the point and very blunt. Back in his village, everyone was straightforward with "no beating around the bush" in any circumstance or situation. Definitely, recognition or ability to look beyond one's vision or "read between the lines" was absent in his young mind. That comes with maturity.

Anyway, they were only in that city for a couple of days. One of the nights there in Saigon, Mekkar thought he had explosions way out in the distance. At that particular time, Henrik had gone off somewhere for a meeting. Mekkar had no clue as to his papa's whereabouts. He figured the other side didn't want any children around to distract them.

One of the times Mekkar, with Eva his chaperon, went walking down one of the streets in the urban area. They approached an open market, which resembled a small flea market. One booth had hanging pots and that type of thing. It was fairly crowded which indicated a demand for the items being sold. Mekkar assumed that people needed these goods due to the ongoing military activity around them. The little Arctic Warrior based this opinion upon the visual images of military wreckage on the reindeer trek. Eva and Mekkar were among the throng that viewed the different wares and food offered by the street vendors there. One stand caught Mekkar's eye. He was still a kid after all. He was fascinated by the intricate paper machete items that looked like dragons to him. Maybe, not exactly like the medieval creatures, but had similarities in design. Some of the objects were in the form of flying kites and other household ornaments. Eva mentioned to Mekkar about an upcoming celebration or a holiday time related to the inhabitants of this area. The boy thought it would be hard to for the people to rejoice with all of these soldiers here. Yet, they are selling kites! Mekkar even blurted out to Eva and said, "Somebody is going to shoot at one of these kites. What a silly thing to have here." Mekkar was too immature to understand the concept of people trying to find meaning and normalcy in the midst of chaos. When an individual, family, or group lives in a war zone environment, they need to find or do anything they could to help them forget about it. In a matter of speaking, escape from where an individual is, as well as, not focus on the misery and destruction around you. The view is that any type of distraction is a good thing. If a person gains a little bit of pleasure and mental healing, at the same time, regardless of…

Well, Mekkar fixated at this and then shuffled on to the next booth which sold meat and other food items. Next to it was a cigarette and tobacco kiosk. A considerable number of soldiers were there purchasing those products. Top of the line smoking items were in great demand, while at the same time, there was little quality product available to the public in that area for purchase. Mekkar observed long lines to that booth. He stayed some distance away due to the smell and negative tobacco effects to his still developing body filtering system. The pair continued wandering slowly along the street with Mekkar intrigued by the activity. This was the most frantic exchange activity he had seen in such a small area. Mekkar thought he had observed a lot of indiscriminate movement in his previous travels. Places like India with his papa, a couple of times to Brazil, and a few other venues. Still the ambience and resulting commotion were at a higher level here.

Anyway, they were only in that city for a couple of days. On one of the nights there in Saigon, Mekkar commented that he had heard a few noises that made a boom sound in the distance. Those events continued to bother Mekkar as he stayed up most of the night while sitting by the open window as if he were on wolf watch on the trek. Added to his concern was that his papa, Henrik, had gone off somewhere unknown to Mekkar for a late night meeting.

The next day Mekkar and Eva, his chaperon, were walking down one of the streets not far from their hotel. They surveyed the open market to kill time and soak in the urban flavor. One booth had hanging pots and similar wares for sale. The stand was swamped with many customers, so the boy assumed the demand for those items was really high. By the crowd behavior he observed there, Mekkar believed that people greatly needed these goods because their homes were being destroyed by the ongoing warfare.

Eva and Mekkar strolled on and examined the different wares and food offered by the street vendors. Paper machete items caught Mekkar's eye at one stand. In his mind, some of the featured articles appeared to be dragons and totally out of place here. Sure, maybe not exactly like the medieval creatures, but there were some similarities. There were plenty of objects that resembled monsters or displayed supernatural beings on them. Mekkar decided that he couldn't leave until he purchased one that was made in the form of a flying kite. The Arctic boy figured the local people must be having a celebration or a holiday, just like back home. What seemed out of place to Mekkar was the number of soldiers here. Right then, he remembered his papa's warning - that wherever there are troops, there is trouble and battles nearby. Mekkar even blurted out his thoughts to Eva and said, "Soldiers don't buy kites. They shoot at things. I think those kites are going to be destroyed. What a silly thing to have here." Mekkar was not grown up enough to understand the concept that often people use coping mechanisms to try to find meaning in the midst of chaos. For example, if a person lived in a war zone environment, one might attempt to find or do anything they could to forget about it. In a matter of speaking, escape from where an individual is and not focus on the hell and destruction around you. Any type of distraction could be a good thing for mental health. If that same individual is rewarded with a little bit of pleasure at the same time – that is an added bonus.

Well, Mekkar progressed onto the next booth that had meats and other food items available. Next to it was a cigarette and tobacco kiosk. Quite a few soldiers surrounded that particular stand and purchased those products. Smoking supplies were in great demand, while at the same time little product for purchase was available in that marketplace. Mekkar observed the continuing to grow long lines to that booth. The smell drove Mekkar to begin stepping away and attempt to stay some distance away due to the negative tobacco effects to his still developing body filtering system. Mekkar was intrigued by the increased frenzied activity as he and Eva wandered slowly along the street. The boy from the far north had never seen this much hustle and bustle in such a small area before. Mekkar had plenty of experience to compare it with and thought he had observed a lot of chaotic movement in his previous travels. Places like India with his papa, a couple of times to Brazil, a few places like that. However, those exhibited goods were far different from the novelties offered in this place. The Arctic youngster had traveled quite a bit in his young life, but had mostly spent the majority of his travel time on the same continent. So, this was a new region of the globe for him. Henrik was aware of this and wanted to expand his worldwide exposure to diverse places and people.

On one occasion in the outdoor bazaar, Mekkar and his chaperone Eva were stopped and questioned by the soldiers there. One of them asked him, "What are you doing here?" and went onto say, "You are too young, you don't need to be in a place like this". Mekkar didn't fully comprehend the true meaning of that comment. Even though Mekkar was already learning the language and knew many of the words spoken to them, there was a lack of grasping the meaning behind the phrases. Mekkar was unable to distinguish the subtle messages as part of what was being said. The soldier's real directive to him was get out of here before you get hurt or get killed. It appeared to Mekkar as though the infantryman looked at him with confusion. The serviceman assumed that Eva was a newspaper or media reporter instead of Mekkar's guide. Anyone could easily see the young boy was out of his element and not a native. The other concern also expressed by the servicemen was why Eva would bring a child along with her to a war zone. Plus, expose the child to gruesome and dangerous visual images. Eva, on the other hand, nodded her head in the affirmative as Mekkar saw it. The boy believed she knew the purpose for both of them being here. In this situation, she acted demure as if she didn't fully understand what the soldiers were saying or what was happening around her. However, Mekkar noticed the opposite was actually the case.

Anyway, both of them continued walking along down the street. All of a sudden, Mekkar and Eva heard some potshots. A couple of the gunfire rounds were fairly close too! Mekkar, crazy soul that he was, did not immediately duck behind cover. Instead, he just stood in the same spot on the sidewalk of the street they were previously strolling on and surveyed the surrounding area. He mistakenly figured since he was small enough that he would be hard to aim at and hit. Of course, it was not the smartest course of action and Eva told him so. Still, he did not seek protective cover for himself. He stayed right where he was while everyone else around him was scurrying to hide. Despite hearing the shots ring out Mekkar didn't move. If he was an esteemed adult, it would have appeared as though he was posing in a majestic movie scene, but this was real. In this instance, other people sensed the boy was frozen, stiff, and scared. Soon, everyone's attention was grabbed by the large flames shooting high into air. Then, a loud explosion happened with a resounding boom! Mekkar saw the flash and items flying, it seemed, everywhere. The soldier was right, some gruesome stuff. A collection of arms, hands, legs, an eyeball, and other debris were spread out along the ground. If it wasn't the case before, Mekkar was in shock and definitely frozen in his tracks now.

Another couple of shots could be heard by the nearby corner. At that moment, a second explosion rang out. After this, Mekkar was absolutely unmoving as if he was frozen solid as ice. Mekkar was a brave boy, yet his mind was racing. He thought to himself, why can't I move? It appeared the boy lost many of his senses and didn't grasp the environment he was in. Mekkar was concerned that he might a target. Mekkar asked more questions in his mind whether he was next. His body still did not respond with any movement. Fight or flight syndrome had failed him.

Mekkar was made aware that the soldiers were powerless to protect him and Eva from harm. He had no idea which side the troops were on either. These were things that Mekkar's papa had been speaking to him prior to this journey. Henrik wanted Mekkar to learn specific lessons. Henrik also wanted Mekkar to be able to use his mind and reason under duress. Very heady stuff for a young boy to experience in an unfamiliar environment. Instruction in life survival skills that would be necessary later on. The experience would be invaluable because everyone in the area Mekkar comes from has to fight for survival. Most definitely during the long winters. Not only that, they have to serve in their own country's military for a time as well. There are not enough people for any healthy individual to get out of that type of service to their nation.

The authority's even use physically challenged people in various tasks to fulfill their military obligations. They will find a person to meet a need or place them in tasks despite the disability. The idea is to maximize the abilities and blend them with the resources that are available. It is a necessary strategy because there are just not enough people to meet all the gaping holes in the region's defense system, while still providing a perceived deterrent to any possible enemy. Women, along children that can stand up and walk, also have to serve in some capacity, even if is just to provide support to the soldiers.

Up to this point, Mekkar did not grasp what was materializing in front of him, although he saw it with his own eyes. Stupidly, Mekkar was fixated on the second explosion undeterred by flying objects from the wall of the affected building landing nearby. The burning building and spreading fire fully consumed all of his attention. People all around him were as if mad in a flurry of activity. Yet, he was still in a trance-like state. The Arctic boy wasn't taking a step or going anywhere on his own. It was Eva's responsibility to pull him away from danger. Mekkar gazed at the folks littering the street; they were like blurs at this point. He was mesmerized and distracted by the unwelcome sight that had unfolded before him. After what it seemed like forever, but actually was a short time, Eva grabbed him by the hand and they rushed for cover. This action finally snapped Mekkar out of the haze he was in. She told Mekkar, "There might be more to come. We have to protect ourselves just in case." Mekkar was not feeling very brave anymore. Nonetheless, he tried to not show outwardly. Mekkar didn't how to neither deal with nor react in this type of situation. The little Arctic Warrior started to think of how he could show more bravery in the face of another situation such as this. Trouble was, there might not be a next time.

Cautiously tracing their steps, Eva and Mekkar made it back to the hotel, which wasn't far away from the damage zone. The day's activities the young boy witnessed kept him frightened throughout the whole night and affected his sleep. The non-stop thoughts ran through his brain wondering if he was safe in defiance of the many soldiers currently patrolling this neighborhood. He remembered when there were a lot of troops in close proximity back at home, he felt much safer against harm. Mainly, Mekkar felt comfort in the fact the enemy that could be identified easily and early in the wide open Arctic region. Although opposing forces might be well above us dominating the air space, while at the same time, exposing home guard troops on the ground. These are concerns that northern hemisphere individuals, such as Mekkar, were not occupied with all that often. In contrast, these were daily worries that directly affected the local populations and mentality of many soldiers in Vietnam. If ignored, the alternative was to not adequately protect one's self and ending up returning home in a body bag.

One of the soldiers told him and Eva, "We can't have you walking around anywhere you want freely anymore because we fear for your safety. We are unable to guarantee your personal safety anymore". The mood became tense, uptight, and restless. It seemed the explosions, accomplished their goal by creating a more restrictive and hostile environment for everyone in that area of the city. By this time, quite a few people had heard about the explosions and subsequent fire. Unfortunately, Mekkar got to see it with his own eyes. He had no idea regarding who did it or why. The little one from the far north was ignorant as to the combatants on each side and who opposed who in this conflict. He could only judge by his sight alone and attempt to mirror the locals who lived there as best as he could. This was still a large metropolis where most of the inhabitants were not dressed in military uniforms. The perceptive boy that Mekkar was, he decided that he would observe the city dwellers to determine when something was wrong. The indifferent conscripts appeared to keep any developments or news to themselves. In his mind, the troops only seemed to bark out warnings or orders in a heartless manner.

It is well to note, that Mekkar already had started playing sports by this time, so he was aware about being on the same team with other people. Working together toward a common goal was not foreign to him, despite the fact that the extremely stubborn Mekkar is not the most agreeable or cooperative individual. In the far north, Mekkar learned how to ski, skate, and walk all at the same time which provided early advantages for him and many in his age range.

The two of them left the scene and scurried back to their hotel on foot. Soon afterward, Henrik arrived back from his meeting. Well, Mekkar assumed that his father came straight back from the important appointment. However, the boy did wonder why it was so long considering the events that recently had taken place. Mekkar's questioning was never voiced because he trusted his papa. Eva was very stoic, as was her normal disposition, and unlike her vocal exhortations during the explosions earlier in the day.

Early the next morning, Mekkar, Henrik, and Eva left their temporary quarters while being escorted by armed solders in a small convoy to the airport. They went through all of the many checkpoints with no hassles. Along the way, the Arctic youngster thought to himself - that his papa must know some important people in this place. From Saigon, they boarded a commercial jet and flew non-stop to Bangkok, Thailand. When they were out of range of the fighting on the ground below, Mekkar finally breathed a sigh of relief. After their arrival in the Thailandese capital, the wait for their connecting flight out was long. Mekkar became irritable, restless, and uncomfortable while stuck in the airport. On the occasions when he did not take naps, Mekkar noticed the harried and crowded environment. In and around the airport was quite similar to where they had left. The major difference he observed was the lack of large number of troops everywhere. This one factor provided some solace to Mekkar as he grew more impatient.

A few people were bold enough to approach and discuss with Henrik and his secretary regarding their situation. Some would pat Mekkar on the top of his head or rub it, in front of them, and boy did he hate that. Others would ask the adults to describe what transpired in the war zone of Saigon. Many were stranded while waiting to leave Bangkok. Mekkar was too young and didn't understand the concept of delayed flights and what that entailed. Well, for now at least. During this time period, Henrik left Eva and his son at the airport for another business engagement. Mekkar's papa assured the boy that he would return in plenty of time for the next journey on their itinerary. Mekkar believed him, yet still missed his papa and felt assured that he was going to see him again soon. Mekkar just figured that the next trip would be a return back home. Contrary to the impression Mekkar had, this was not to be the case. Henrik had more adventure in mind for his son.

After what seemed to take forever, Eva and Mekkar saw his papa rush and arrive out of breath to meet them again. Approximately ten minutes later the overhead speaker blared out the correct flight information and passenger loading gate number. Mekkar was still in the dark regarding the next stop. If Eva knew, she wasn't telling the boy anything about it while all three of their small group proceeded to the proper boarding location. The next flight immediately became a very rocky adventure, soon after takeoff, in the commuter plane. One time, Mekkar looked out the window where he was sitting, then pulled the window covering down quickly. He didn't like what he saw outside. Since the plane's elevation appeared to lower below the clouds than he was used to, Mekkar thought he saw small objects on the ground as they reached the next city of their expedition. It was quite obvious to anyone who had military training that some of those popping sounds outside the aircraft sounded like anti-aircraft gun fire rounds. The little Arctic Warrior had questions that couldn't be answered such as why would anyone be shooting at us?

All of the passengers and crew could hear the rumbling of explosions that were taking place which grew louder upon their arrival. The boy was lost and had no idea where he was, the only thing he could do was trust his papa's judgement. Mekkar voiced his concerns to his papa sitting next to him. The son asked, "Why are we are getting closer to the military action again?" The dangerous environment was obvious even to a young person such as Mekkar as the activity was more frequent. Henrik told them, "Hang on because it is going to be a bumpy ride before they land." When Mekkar looked at Eva, he saw her apprehension and concluded that something was definitely not right. Mekkar's mind raced and he didn't know how to stop it. The boy thought to himself – here we go again. The last part of this flight circled a few times while the boy from the Far North was stricken by inner turbulence. It was almost with a sense of comfort when the flight touched down on the landing strip in Hanoi.

The three of them rode a shuttle near the center of the city. Henrik explained to his son while they motored together. Thus was exactly what Henrik wanted him to see. Both sides of the conflict from two different viewpoints. Henrik wanted to drive the point home that war is hell and it is not a pretty sight. The lesson that his papa wanted Mekkar to learn was that many things are not as they seem in the media and very divergent from real life. Additionally, the intention was for Mekkar not to lose his compassion for others due to becoming desensitized as a result. Suddenly, Henrik had to go to a separate area for another briefing. It was just the two of them now in an unfamiliar city.

Then, a stranger to Mekkar approached Eva and gave her some local currency. Mekkar never did figure out why. The boy began to have directed conclusions that his papa arranged everything and had it taken care of. Mekkar glanced at Eva and she looked more relaxed than on the plane. He figured that his brain was telling him that some rest was in order after the recent tense experiences. Mekkar let it slip out loud from his lips, "Where is this unlimited energy that all children are presumed to have because it was non existent right now". Eva reassured him and tracked down the next mode of transportation. They gave the driver money and off they went back out of the main part of the capital city. The youngster didn't recognize this type of transportation vehicle and thought it was distinct, but cool. At first, Mekkar thought it was a motorcycle, but it really wasn't. The transport was similar to a bike where you have the peddler guide in front and the passengers sit in the back. The closest object Mekkar could compare it to a desert three wheeler machine. On the other hand, since the mode of transport was not motorized like a snowmobile back home, Mekkar thought it looked real flimsy and not sturdy at all. He compared the vehicle's construction to the paper machete kites he saw previously. The Arctic lad squirmed and was not comfortable during the ride either. Still, he hoped this vehicle could take him where he needed to go, despite not knowing where they were being led. At least, the both of them were away from the utter confusion they had witnessed down south. The boy from the Arctic knew that he was special and extremely intelligent for someone his age. The problem was the youngster was not as smart as he thought was and was in unfamiliar territory to boot. Mekkar would soon find out that he was sorely mistaken in his assumptions and more would be in store for each one of them.

Their destination took on a lonely path some distance to the city. Mekkar missing his papa and was hoping to see him again. They youngster had that inner sense that he was going to reunite with Henrik at the end of this jaunt. About 5 minutes after disembarking from the transport and seeing his papa, the air raid sirens blared to warn the surrounding people. Mekkar wondered what was happening. Henrik said to Mekkar and Eva that a bombing sortie from sky was about to transpire soon. All of them followed other residents into the entrance of a make-shift underground bomb shelter, where they would be safe. Before long, the blasts began to pepper the area. The people in the temporary quarters below ground could feel reverberations and shock waves from bombs that exploded nearby. The lights in the dwelling flickered on and off continuously.

At that moment, Henrik began to explain to Mekkar what was happening, why, and the various parties involved. Part of the intent of Mekkar's papa was to reassure him, so he would not be scared to death. Henrik described the reasons behind the air bombing campaign. He said to Mekkar, "As in other wars in this century, one side is using this type of strategy to break the local population's morale and willingness to continue to fight this war. There are only two possible outcomes against an enemy through the adoption of these tactics of total conflict. You either drive the people to be more dug-in and strengthen their resolve to outlast your forces. In other words, the side that carrying out the air raid is attempting to force the opposition, on the receiving end, to crack. If it is not successful, the tenacious spirit of the defenders counts on securing eventual victory. Their goal is to employ any means to hang on until the attacker's will to fight achieve victory in the conflict has waned. Past history has shown that air campaign bombings alone never win wars. Instead, public resolve among the targeted population usually increases exponentially and resistance becomes stronger the longer the methods are employed against them. The stubborn will of some people is ingrained in different cultures to overcome and never surrender." Mekkar's papa spoke additional wise words to his son until the bombing had stopped. In single file, the people emerged from the shelter in a single file line. All three in their small group survived the chaos to continue on. Now, it was time to go home.

Around the Village

Not long after Mekkar started working, more expectations & increased responsibilities were placed upon him. Mama would tell Mekkar that if he wanted clean clothes, he would now have to wash them himself since now he was old enough to start helping out the family around the house too! So, at his young age, little Mekkar would go collect the washboard along with his dirty clothes and cleaning supplies and head down to the calmer, but still flowing part of the river to wash his clothes by scrubbing them on the board that was propped up against him and in an up and down motion. Mekkar had selected a location of the river that was not the same area where he and his friends would catch fish. After all, he didn't want to get swept away by the river's current but needed enough flow to send the soapiness down the river. Mekkar's mind was very focused on his task at hand, because one slip-up and he or one of the items he was washing might be gone for good by floating down the river. He would be expected to go through his whole basket of clothes, however, there were some delicate items that needed to be specially cleaned, but not dry cleaned, and that were exempt from the board less they be ruined.

Sometimes, his mama would blurt out as a reminder to him that "the washer and dryer is not for your personal use, their operation had a priority that was for the business. You could use it for items related to the family restaurant and tourist businesses and usually when you were working only. It's for the tourists and those working in the business, not for you and your friends," his mama bellowed. These privileges were extended only when functions related to the family and work were involved. Mekkar's mama would also rebuke him, when he would share reindeer meat that was drying on the line with his friends, saying "leave some for the rest of us, the ones who worked through the process from raising the animals to drying/curing the meat to make it edible for human consumption, otherwise it will all be gone!" Part of the reasoning was that it was a management of the reindeer meat resources, so there was an account of where it was all going. Some to the tourists that ate in the restaurant, some for family enjoyment, and then have a bit to share with a few others. But, she knew that if the decision was left up to Mekkar the meat would have been all gone quickly with a very limited number of people enjoying the rich and tasty morsels of this delicacy.

Even when Mekkar's family stopped being nomadic on a greater basis and became more permanent with a family home, things were still highly organized. The main meal of the day, was usually in the middle of the afternoon, about 2pm or so, and the preparation of the dinner table was important. No, the people do eat buffet style meals on a daily basis, just on a few specific holiday occasions and that is only a few times per year. This tradition is even more pronounced normally down in the south part of the country where the national culture reigns supreme, because if the natives ate like that every day they would be way too overweight, 600 lbs each, and would never get any work done. The preparation work for wintertime is always part of the life cycle that is a part of life in the Arctic environment. Each of the children was expected to clean and set up the family table, specifically their own items required to consume food with. Each kid, in Mekkar's family, had their own plate, bowl, cup, fork, spoon, and knife individually engraved, marked, or labeled with their initials or something similar in regard to marking. If the utensils were not cleaned or setup ready for and prior to dinner time then they didn't get to eat dinner. Mekkar had to learn this lesson the hard way a few times at first, but because he didn't relish missing the best and most abundant meal of the day, he wised up fast. It was no fun to miss meals, especially good and tasty ones, and watch his family munch away without him. It wasn't like Mekkar could order pizza with a few toppings down the street, from the local eatery, and then be able to sneak it by his mama without her knowing. His mama would remind him, once in awhile, with statements such as "I am a mother and that means that I am All-Knowing and All-Seeing." She inferred this comment in regards to him on a personal level. Mekkar would respond in his mind like Oh! I can't do anything without getting caught. Thus, Mekkar started to suspect that maybe his mama had special powers like Aslak the shaman. Mekkar already knew Aslak pretty well, due to quite a bit of interaction with him in the village, so Mekkar thought that he knew that his mama was not a shaman or one with that type of ability herself, but maybe he was wrong.

Mekkar just thought that she was a bit cocky and now knew where he received this character trait from. Mekkar's mama, Sirga, didn't put up with any grief from anybody and had a no nonsense personality, another trait that he acquired from his mama. The Native from the North knew that as a boy, he would be a person that would push the limits of his mama's patience. It was kind of a game with him, in his subconscious mind that he wasn't always aware of. However, Mekkar always knew when he crossed the line and Sirga's wrath would be exposed in regard to him. When she would yell out first the dog's name, his bother's full name, and then his full name, all 6 of them, in a strong, ticked off manner; He knew that his rear end was cooked and he was in real trouble. Sometimes, his reaction to his short tempered mama's fierce anger was to get as far away as possible and go down to the river. Another option was to go to a friend's house for awhile, even at times for days. While leaving to avoid his mama's wrath, he would respond with an unwise comment or a distaining gesture. Sirga would yell once in a while, "If you go to your best friend Lasse's house I will have his mother beat your butt for me". In that small town or village, Mekkar felt that he never could escape his mother's punishment whether it was warranted or not. Maybe, this was the beginning of the worldwide adventure streak developing within Mekkar.

In another instance, Mekkar would at times leave his toys around the house and scattered throughout his room after playing with them and his mama would bark at him to "pick up your toys or I will throw them out". On a few occasions, Mekkar would ignore the bark from his mama. Unfortunately, the bite was worse because his mama would carry out her threat and throw the toys away in the trash. Then, Mekkar would get spanked and his mama would sometimes use anything she could grab close by to do it with, a large kitchen spoon, a book, a wooden piece, etc. Other times, she would force Mekkar to go get a tree branch or a stick for his own butt whipping and if the stick or branch was too small or not strong enough, she would keep sending him back out until she was satisfied. Mainly, the punishment would occur for not obeying her and Mekkar would receive another round of the spanking from his papa with his extremely large hands that would resonate with a loud crack on Mekkar's behind. The second punishment was due to Henrik, Mekkar's papa, being upset because he would to reconstruct and recreate some of the freshly discarded toys. Mainly, because Mekkar's papa would make some of the toys by hand-crafting, carving, & cutting them from wood. Plus, that would Henrik's time away from other needed to completed projects, whether they related to his papa's work or not. Projects such as various to-do tasks around the property because there seems to always be something that requires fixing, it is never all finished.

At times, when playing outside when the northern lights were at their most active the kids would be more subdued than usual. Even the adults didn't want to yell or exhibited an extra aura of fear in their speech. They didn't want to say anything negative nor tick off the old religion ancient native deities while they were doing their thing and going about their usual daily life routine. Being under the amazing display in the heavens was now not regarded as special anymore to the locals who live in that area since they have seen it so many times each year, every year just like a holiday season. It was just part of the routine in contrast to the tourists who were fascinated by its newness. An apt description by the elders would be like an animal's tail whipping against the sky while creating sparks at the same time. Mekkar has never bothered to research what the Northern Lights phenomenon really is in its true scientific state. The reason could be possibly to native superstitions or a set of beliefs in legends passed down to him from a few adults in the village. [nordicway.com; Aurora hunters - ft.com; Aurorafires. ie; Wikipedia; bestnorwegian.com; hellomagazine.com]

However, Mekkar could never completely discount and shun the old ways because they had been ingrained internally into the very fabric of his being. Plus, when Mekkar was younger during times on the reindeer trek, he spent much time with Aslak, and they would together ponder the mysteries of the universe. However, Mekkar at other times would try to avoid Aslak when the elder would be in his trance-like state or conducting his medicine man duties. Mekkar would get spooked and creeped out by the unfamiliar other realm spiritual stuff the boy saw and referred to it as such. The Native from the North could sense, even though he couldn't always describe it, the power Aslak had during some of their verbal interaction sessions. Other times, Mekkar would sneakily or stealthily so he thought, observe various leader meeting of the minds sessions during the animal migrations. No matter if whether he comprehended it or not, Mekkar realized that there was a whole other unseen realm/dimension that he didn't understand. Even after being around Aslak for so long in the small village and seeing some of these activities, Mekkar wanted to stay away. Especially from some of the deeper aspects which he felt would impact him. He felt getting involved with those aspects was playing with fire and Mekkar didn't want to get burned. At this point, the Arctic boy still didn't comprehend what was really taking place at these sessions and scared at the possible effects upon him.

Alf called it by what he thought it was, Mekkar's insolence, and Alf didn't feel that Mekkar cared one bit about the old ways and mannerisms of their native culture. Even though Alf shied away from admitting that he was a native altogether. Alf felt that Mekkar also was not concerned about ticking off the old native religious deities. Alf, Mekkar's younger brother, had even said this a few times previously by describing Mekkar as having a smart mouth and manner of speech. The sibling stated that it was also getting worse by the day as Mekkar got older. Mekkar thought this was an unjustified perception of him by his sibling considering that Alf rarely admitted his native status to avoid persecution and negative judgment by others. Mekkar commented that his brother could get away with this due to his non-native appearance. Alf would go on to describe that his older sibling as showing early hints of a screw you attitude towards the world in some aspects of Mekkar's character. Mekkar thought Alf was sort of judgmental against him when he was attempting to avoid that very thing from outsiders. Alf had pointed out, what he thought was the recognition of these flaws regarding Mekkar to his face. Still, Mekkar just brushed them aside and attributed those comments as just part of sibling rivalry issues.

Mekkar feels that no being, high or low, or person should receive automatic respect from him because of one's position in life or occupation, no matter who they are. He knows that his belief in that area is extremely contrary to most people. To Mekkar, one has to earn his respect on an individual case by case basis. Mekkar also has this concept, that he is so well adjusted enough and has a fairly good level of knowledge of the world, as a result of his travels, reading, and through other methods of learning. Mekkar reveals this attitude and point in one of many blunt statements, "If I don't know who you are, then you are not a star. It doesn't matter who or how big or famous you think you are." Mekkar knows this is a cocky stance and refuses to back down from it and this thinking has never wavered in Mekkar's mind even to this very day and it will definitely never change with him.

On the other hand, Alf and Lasse both are of the opinion that there is just a little too much cockiness on the part of Mekkar. When they noticed that trend, they increased the amount of pranks they would play on him. The idea was to try to temper that big ego they feel is growing too quickly and put him in his place. Basically, Mekkar's younger brother and best friend think Mekkar is full of himself most of the time and just likes to run his mouth. Other adults regard it as a matter of a teenager who thinks that they know everything and are always right about everything. But, adults usually know that is not the case and have learned from experience that the opposite is true. If a person is honest, what parent hasn't encountered that in their children, especially teenagers, anywhere on the planet?

More Around the Village

After being forced, by his mama, to watch and learn English from the sports tapes and films sometimes. Mekkar would put some of those new skills that he had learned into practice. For example, he would go outside afterward to play, but he had to use many words that he heard in the English language so far. That is, from the teaching materials his parents had acquired just for him. Sometimes going to great lengths to get them for him, while they were on their travels around the world. Later on, when he got older Mekkar would be required to gather these materials for himself.

At other times, his mama would bark at Mekkar that he could only speak in the english language and no other, just after his lessons and while playing with the dogs. The reasons for this were that not only to force Mekkar to quickly learn english as an asset for the family businesses but also because his godparents dog understood english along with 9 other languages. Attu has escorted Mekkar's godparents around the world to more places than many people on their globe trotting adventures. So, Mekkar would be found practicing his new found lingual skills would not be too much of a foreign thing to Attu. Now, Attu was not a small dog when Mekkar's godparents purchased him, when he was young, under mysterious circumstances in Siberia, Russia. Attu was a half Siberian husky/Malamute mix with black, gray, and white colors in his thick coat of hair. Attu's weight fluctuated between 160 to 180 pounds as an adult and he ate a lot. As Mekkar's god mama would say, "Eat her out of house and home".

Attu was a very playful dog especially with little Mekkar. One time when an excited Native from the North brought outside a football, they got on a journey to America, to play with the dog. In Mekkar's mind, playing with the dog this time was seen as a relief that the language study time required by mama was over and he wanted to get as far away from it as possible. This is a strategy that many kids use around the world to get away from unpleasant situations and things or so Mekkar thought. Right off the bat Mekkar threw the football up in the air and as its flight downward back to earth was commencing Attu caught the football out of the air and at the same time bit all of the helium out of the football. While still in his mouth the dog would run around the yard in sort of a daring manner challenging Mekkar to not only catch him but also take the football from his mouth. Sometimes, since Attu was so large and agile for his size he would run over Mekkar in a playful manner, not in a vicious way. The dog still dared Mekkar to remove the football from his mouth. It was actually pretty difficult for Mekkar to catch Attu and he was big enough that Mekkar couldn't even put his arms around the dog when giving him a hug.

That was one example of their relationship that they would enjoy for many years while Mekkar and Attu grew up together. That continued until Attu's legs could not support his weight anymore and the pain became too great for the dog. Attu lived for 24 years, way beyond his expected lifespan and then was sadly put to sleep. Attu was always protective of Mekkar, especially when he was younger, against other unknown dogs, wolves, and other non-family critters. One time, Mekkar tried to outfit Attu with warmers and such but since nothing fit, Mekkar quickly gave up those ideas regarding his boyhood buddy. Attu, due to his playful soul, was very popular with the kids around the neighborhood. All the children seemed to love him and the family did too! Attu was much more popular than Mekkar dog, Laka and Laka comes from a pretty playful dog breed himself. However, both Attu & Laka did dislike cats very much and would chase them and never would back down from them, not even larger animal from the cat family like lynxes, etc. At the same time, Attu and Laka got more spoiled the older they got, especially Attu.

Sometimes, Attu would catch birds and other small creatures and bring them to the dinner table, not to eat them, but as a gift. Attu would then give that look at the table like here's my gift, now I want my steak and red wine because Mekkar's god mama gave him that as treat at least three times per week as a normal ritual for most of Attu's life, besides other treats. Attu was always trying to catch birds, and Mekkar would see this alot. At times, the dog would stand up on his hind legs next to the house. Since Mekkar's god mama was a bird photographer and had bird feeders filled with seed and red colored liquid also. At first, the feeders were on the one edge of the outdoor house roof, but since that part was lower than the rest and Attu, when he stood up, could capture the birds there when they landed at the various food sources there resulted in some damage to that edge of the roof.

So, eventually Mekkar's god mama had to set up the bird feeding stations much higher up on the roof. She would now have to go through the attic to get to them and take the close-up pictures of these creatures in feeding mode with her fancy camera. Mekkar thought it was pretty cool to see hummingbirds captured in full flight and hovering in slow motion suspension. His god mama took pictures at home and at different locations all over the world, once in awhile Attu would be in some of those photos. Even though it was her hobby she did make some money for those efforts.

Even with his main source of bird caught gifts removed, the number that Attu brought to the table during dinnertime never really decreased. Attu was found to be a very resourceful animal that, in Mekkar's opinion, adapted and found other strategies to get what he wanted. It didn't matter whether it was love, approval, or acceptance. However, Attu was never used around reindeer or on the trek and he didn't mind because the dog didn't have that desire to go on those journeys.

One time Mekkar's papa made him a skateboard, well it was for Mekkar, the kid. Some of the materials used were metal wheels with steel ball bearings because composite wheels were not available to the public. At least not in this part of the world; and Mekkar's papa modified used cross country skis. Fiberglass was added to make the skis wider than a regular ski, like snowboards today but not as wide. Since the ski board was longer than a normal skate board, there were additional sets of wheels added to the underside of the board at evenly spaced intervals. They were added so it would not bow in the middle and drag around the ground in the middle and possibly snap the board. The problem was that Mekkar rarely got to use the ski skateboard. Even though his papa made it specifically for him and was individually tailored to Mekkar's weight, foot step patterns, etc. It seemed to him that kids that he knew were always coming over the borrow it. Mekkar lamented one time that even his younger brother got to use the ski skateboard way more than he did.

One of the few times Mekkar had a chance to use his before its time toy, a tourist operating a rent-a-car almost ran him over. It was right in the street despite the clear weather, sunny day, and few people or animals alongside the road. There weren't a lot of obstacles there that day except for the crazy motorist. Mekkar surmised that the driver must have been distracted somehow, by what he had no idea. He thought to himself, at least I didn't get hit by the car and blurted out "dumb tourist, who doesn't even know how to drive". Especially, since Mekkar was only riding his board on the side of the road and not in the middle of the street. After that incident, he was not so keen on using his created toy as much as before, mainly because he was not a fan of being a road target or street pizza. From then on, he preferred to use his kick sled instead but it was only useful in snowy and icy conditions. Mekkar even commented, "At least, we don't play as much road/street hockey as much as we used to because of outrageous and dangerous motorists who visit the area. Well soon, we can go out on the frozen lakes to play."

There were games Mekkar and the kids around the neighborhood would play that sometimes included all the children, with boys and girls of all ages. At other times, a few of the games involved just the older kids or the more athletically gifted ones of which Mekkar was usually included even when he a bit younger. This was because Mekkar was one tough son of a gun; some of his friends thought it was because his parents conformed him that way. Some of the ice hockey related games, on the frozen lake, were what they call shinny, pond, or pickup hockey in other places around the globe. At first, when Mekkar was included into some of these play activities and was treated like he was entering into an initiation and introduction process conducted by the older kids and there was some physical damage metered out at Mekkar.

Since, there was relatively no protective equipment being worn, by the participants. That is, except the padding provided by the cold weather layered clothing his mama or another family member dressed him in. Plus, there were no boards set up around the small lake where the children played there which included little body checking, at that time. That would change not long afterward when portable rink accessories were created by a few people in the village. Sometimes, Mekkar would encounter a hip-check in the middle of the ice surface, especially since he was a newcomer. In addition, there was very little roofing of the puck towards a person's head because that showed direct intent to injure other kids there. People forget a direct shot to various parts of the human body can kill a person.

Anyway, some of the older boys still wanted to test Mekkar's mettle and the initiation into their activities would include cheap shots at times such as elbows to the head, mouth, and specifically his nose where his eyes would water up and his vision would be temporarily blurred. Slashes to the back of the non padded parts of the legs, arms, and hands would result in cuts, bruises, and some swelling at times. But, Mekkar took it all like a man, even though he was still a boy, and eventually as he got older he started to give some of that right back too! Unknown to Mekkar, it would help prepare him for the future. Once in awhile, Mekkar would come back home after these episodes a bloody mess.

His papa recognized the signs and started to take him aside to teach him how to really defend and protect himself. First through boxing, hockey fighting, and later on put Mekkar into martial arts training. Mekkar's papa showed him different techniques such as pulling the jersey over an opponent's head, as tie up your challenger's arms while in a fight on the ice. Henrik taught Mekkar that the first key is balance in any hockey fist fight for two reasons: you are on thin, sharp blades instead of own feet, which are much wider. The second key is not to fall to avoid hitting you head on the ice, because ice always wins and you can get knocked out or worse. Mekkar understood this through actual events and in those days most players performed without a helmet and that ones that did were usually considered the kooks. Plus, those that did don the head gear still lacked a half or full face shield like many players use today at all levels.

During this protective training process arranged by his papa Mekkar would come more bloodied and bruised. One time he got frustrated while punching the heavy boxing bag and ripped off the gloves, went over to retrieve the axe, took it and swung it really cutting a huge hole into the bag. The sand inside quickly ran out onto the floor. Henrik made Mekkar buy another heavy bag to replace the one he intentionally damaged and it was not cheap! Mekkar's mama would sometimes yell at Mekkar, "Don't bleed all over the carpets and the house". She eventually got Henrik to build a clean up area with a shower, a storage area, racks and hooks for gear, etc. and a bench as an addition to the main house near the back entrance so the kids wouldn't make a mess of the polar white colored carpet that covered the whole of the house.

Mekkar always grumbled that everyone had to remove their shoes before entering the house but realized this was a normal tradition throughout the whole nation and even more prominent down south. Mekkar always wondered why he, his friends, family members, and other locals they knew seemed to only approach the house at the back door. So, one day Mekkar asked his mama why this was the case and she responded that, "Only strangers come to the front door because of World War Two, when the enemy would kick in the front door of each household during each of their different invasions.

This was the beginning of other atrocities against the local populations of this area such as the burning of almost everything as they were leaving.

That is the reason why most of the older people in our area here still know how to handle and operate a multitude of weapons. They had to shoot some of those guys back in the day to protect themselves. You have noticed a few of the old small and now rusting anti-aircraft and ground rocket firing machines from that time period hidden in the trees and bushes around, haven't you?" Mekkar still to this day, even while living in a different part of the world, always announces himself with his first name when coming into the front door of where he lives. It is either a cultural installed reaction or a force of habit created within him. Perhaps, it is a subconscious response as to not get shot. Mekkar still does this, even when he lived by himself because some childhood developed habits are extremely hard to break.

Even though where Mekkar lived was not officially considered a town by designation of the national government, he still referred to it as his home town. The country standard for a town was 5,000 or more inhabitants and it wasn't the case unless you included all the people in the adjoining village across the river and tourists that seemed to Mekkar to visit at all times of the year. Mekkar's village still had a special significance as a reindeer herding district and gave the natives who lived there, like Mekkar's family, a few special privileges since they were nomadic in earlier times. Mekkar thought about this and as he got older, he grew more aware about what he called "the guilt makeup" for past poor treatment of natives and exploitation of the native area use lands by some in authority on behalf of the nation.

Mekkar wondered why various distinctions were made regarding minority peoples within a country by the government overlords posing as beneficiaries on their behalf and rights; Plus, Mekkar noticed that his neighbors didn't trust these outsiders. He felt it was only a matter of time before those same nation-state overlords would start to take away those native rights little-by-little until they were all gone in the future. Even though those individuals and their representatives in charge of the nation had never understood nor lived in the far north, they also had no concept of how their decisions affected how to make a living in that environment. Yet, they passed rules, regulations, and laws that favored everyone else in the region except the natives. In Mekkar's mind, it seemed that those officials wanted to totally destroy the native way of life while at the same time force the native peoples there to give up their cultural identity on an individual and collective basis. Mekkar saw it as an agenda to setup the circumstances to force them to leave the area also. Then, the overlords and their captains of industry could ramp up their ultimate plan to take over everything there and greatly increase natural resource exploitation like they have done to other native peoples around the globe. [Wikipedia; utexas.edu – gaski-newera.htm]

Even though, from an outsider's point of view, there seems to be limitations on the number of fun activities available to arctic children. Especially during wintertime, there is more than meets the eye. Fun, recreation, and activity was not restricted to usual associated pursuits such as reindeer herding, skiing, skating, and fishing. Mainly because of the creativity and ingenuity of the natives themselves, modification and invention was rampant for playtime. For instance, there were games out of the frozen lake ice such as King of the Ice, where everyone would be pitted against everyone else. If any part of the body was pushed off the ice surface onto the snow, in any manner, that participant would be out of the game until the group had a winner and began another new round of the game. This game taught speed, agility, maneuverability, dodging, and avoidance skills.

What would tick Mekkar off would be when a small group would attempt to remove him from the ice because he got pretty good at sticking around toward the end most of the time. He had a knack for being crowned King of the Ice on a regular basis. His competitiveness meant he just hated to lose at anything and helped him in these children's games. To keep all of the children involved, every so often the group leaders, some of the older kids, would decide that every one, especially the less athletic kids, would be victorious and let them win at this game in rotating intervals. In the long run, everyone would continue in the activity and it made it more fun for everyone. However, this still frustrated Mekkar because of his super competitiveness and he always liked to win.

The added benefit was that the winner gained a prize which was provided by the rest of the losing group. The reward was a treat like ice cream or pizza or could be a service rendered such as doing the winner's chores for a day. Mekkar knew it was beneficial to give everyone an opportunity to taste victory in the overall scope of things; however he really hated to lose at anything, anytime, or to anyone. Mekkar was not a person to just let you win because he felt that if you beat him in any manner you should have to earn it. Otherwise, it gives a person a false sense of confidence as well as hinders a person's character development because in his mind you cheat yourself. He knows that the world outside doesn't just let people win. Mekkar has done his share of travelling to come to this conclusion, and in his opinion, through a lot of observation of other people on his part.

Mekkar believes to defeat him meant that his opponent was better prepared that time and in that instance than he was. Mekkar was rare, in the fact, that he outright disregarded the new modern world court of opinion aspect until he was forced to accept it, in some form, by the majority. Suffering defeat would make Mekkar even more determined; some would classify it as plain old stubbornness, than before to win the next time. This did show up as a type of ruthlessness in Mekkar's character. To Mekkar, losing is worse than dying and to him winning is everything and defeat should be eliminated. Maybe it was a survival mechanism for Mekkar instilled at birth or a trait that would be needed for later in life. Either way, he was unsure why this very different mindset existed.

To the Native from the North, every little thing added together are examples of past, ongoing, and future trends in his life. Like a person forecasting the weather or a particular stock from the market and then basing a specific future outcome from those indicators. That is how Mekkar determined some certainty in his mind from the environment around him. That is partially how Mekkar looked at the world and that would help develop his beliefs and convictions. Deep determination is a very strong internal trait that has always driven Mekkar to excel in his life.

The Far North Native knows that he is a take charge, leader type personality. He is definitely not a person to always be one to follow the crowd when he feels the path requires him to stand alone and against all when necessary. He was a leader, even if he was somewhat reluctant in certain situations due to a benefit analysis conducted for himself. This mentality also shapes his no nonsense attitude to boot. Like all children, Mekkar would try to test the limits of his parents' instructions and their resolve for correction of his unacceptable behavior.

One time, Mekkar's mama instructed him not to run fast and stop suddenly on the ice with the particular shoes he had on because she warned him sternly, "You could fall and get hurt". Well, the rebellious Mekkar ignored the warning as he many times did. Next, after going outside and arriving at the frozen lake he took off running full speed to play with his friends and just then he stopped suddenly near them. Unlike his normal tennis shoes that he regularly wore these heavy soled rubber bottomed shoes were created to slide very little on icy surfaces for good traction. So, when Mekkar stopped abruptly, he fell down and landed the left-side of his face directly on the ice and broke his cheekbone. There was instant pain felt by Mekkar. Despite the cold there was still a worse nagging feeling inside because he now had to face his mama after not listening to her earlier stern advice.

When he got back to the house, his mama was there waiting for him, because she knew sensed something was not right and another kid had already notified her about Mekkar's misfortune. Due to Mekkar's moaning and groaning she would have surmised anyway what had happened, but Sirga also wanted to teach him a lesson. So, she scolded him and then told him that she was "going to make him wait before she called the doctor because she wanted him to suffer a little bit to remind him of this moment. Maybe next time you will listen to me, huh!" Sirga knew that the local physician couldn't do much about an injury such as the one Mekkar had except to give him pain medication and advise him to rest to let it heal up. She wasn't about to tell Mekkar this and what she had learned about a similar cheekbone fracture that happened to herself from her earlier days.

Sirga felt that if Mekkar encountered pain as a result of his direct disobedience then bad behaviors on his part would be more likely avoided, like burning a finger on a hot stove. This is what her advanced education had taught her through various psychology classes. However, she seemed to understand that bullheaded Mekkar had to learn many lessons the hard way and from his own errored ways.

Other games were created or adapted according to the conditions by the participants such as 15-on-15 ice basketball; sometimes there were more than 15 kids on each side but still with pretty many evenly matched teams according to their individual athletic abilities. Unlike King of the Ice where all the players involved could use regular shoes or skates, ice basketball was played exclusively on ice skates as dictated by the group leaders. The baskets were 5 meters (16.4 feet) high on a pole setup at opposite ends of a smaller frozen pond or lake. The baskets were constructed by some of the more mechanical men in the village. These baskets also had a small white backboard like one a person would find in an elementary school yard and they could be set up and taken down easily by the older kids among the players.

The rule was the first team to score 10 baskets, with each basket being counted as 1 point, through the 5 meter (16.4 feet) tall hoop was declared as the winner or when visibility became too dark or foggy to see well anymore. At that point, whatever the current score was would be the victor. Trouble was scoring a basket was much more difficult than it looked with a rim higher than in pro basketball with children trying to throw up a regulation sized basketball through the high hoop. At times, games could go on for hours and since a player is unable to dibble a basketball on ice, they can only advance the ball, by skating, up to 3 meters (9.8 feet) until required to pass the ball. Mekkar never wanted to jump while taking a shot at the basket because one of the first things he learned when beginning to play ice hockey is to not leave your feet! If you jump into the air, in hockey and in ice basketball, you are asking to get tagged and will probably get hurt. Mekkar didn't want that!

Any of the players, whether they are in possession of the ball or not are subject to get body checked and tagged hard. Thus, Mekkar and all of the others always had to keep their head on a swivel and be aware of everyone and everything around them. At any time Mekkar could get knocked on his rear end. This activity was also beneficial to improve Mekkar's defensive hockey skills, whether he realized it or not at the time.

Mekkar would also for amusement play an army men battle game with his younger brother Alf, when his younger brother got older. The rules were fairly simple as there were the same exact number of plastic toy soldiers, tanks, and artillery on each side, but no aircraft was used. Mekkar, being the older sibling, always got the first choice of sides and he always chose the blue colored soldiers and equipment. Mekkar seemed to always pick a western nation as his side and he declared Alf's opposition black colored soldiers and equipment as the communist Russians. Mainly due to historical distain for the big bear frequently trying to conquer neighboring lands. Mekkar thought that this is ironic since the Rus were Swedish Vikings and Russians, even if they don't admit it, are their descendents. [Wikipedia; dur. ac.uk - origirus.html; users.mildura.net.au - vikrusia.htm]

Anyway, they would have anywhere between 15 to 30 minutes, as determined beforehand, to setup their sides in a predefined territory with snow ridges, bunkers, etc. They could only use items in that particular territory, nothing from another area was to be brought into the game. The battle would begin with Alf rolling, tossing, shot-putting, or pushing from the air or ground a bowling ball from two thirds of a meter (2.16 feet) away from the others' battlefront lines. Whatever the ball hit directly or if it made any type of contact through rolling after hitting the ground afterward was considered dead. They removed the ones hit from the battle front, and put into a dead items graveyard pile off to the side next to but outside the battlefield zone. This back and forth by each side could go on for awhile as each of the brothers would eventually get tired of tossing the heavy bowling ball and they would take short breaks. However, there were no modifications, readjustments, or realignments of their forces allowed after the game had begun. One side would be victorious when the other's military was ultimately depleted or the captain announced surrender. Well, Mekkar was always too obstinate to ever surrender.

The kids in the neighborhood would play other modified games that they had heard of, seen elsewhere, or were introduced by Mekkar, Lasse, and others as a result of their overseas travels. Foreign activities such as Truth or Dare and Kick the Can, which is just a version similar to Hide and Seek, were done by as many participants as could have been persuaded to play. The youngsters would also play army too knowing that it was a precursor for real military training and service that would be required of them later on. So, the kids would try to make it as fun as possible.

There was one infrequent activity that Mekkar was involved in and he referred to it as "the dog bowl". Only a few of the older kids, along with Mekkar, were included in this devious behavior because if they got caught the police would probably show up and possible incarceration could be a consequence. So, the rebellious Mekkar was definitely game! This gathering acquired from one of the regional hospitals: Four flexible 3 meter (9.84 feet) long sections of stretchable rubber tubing, each piece looked like a small clear colored hose, and a large yellow heavy plastic, later on a metal one when it became available, dog bowl. This dog bowl could hold six good sized snowballs. Sometimes they would become an ice ball when it was much colder outside or formed and left overnight to harden. One of the boys cut, or drilled with the metal bowl, holes in the sides of the bowl to put the tubing through. There were two tubes on each side of the bowl.

After that they would pick a launching location by a nearby road or highway. If there was no cover to hide their activity, the small group with Mekkar in tow, would build a snow wall or use some equipment to make a good sized snow mound. The wall or mound had to be at least about 1.85 meters (6.06 feet) high at a minimum to cover them. After completing that task they took a break and drank enough to get buzzed and to summon up some liquid courage to go ahead with their planned activity. The boys would then form about 50 or more snowballs for their ammunition. For the first firing session the four biggest and strongest of them, with two on each side one individual holding each tube, would wrap the end of the clear tube around their hands and put it over their inside shoulder while facing forward toward the target. The tube was wrapped around the hands for grip and to prevent slippage. Mekkar then filled up the dog bowl with six large snowballs that had now become a little harder and icier.

He pulled the bowl back and the tubing stretched, like it was supposed to, a couple of extra feet or more and then when they had reached their limit, Mekkar let his hands go from each side of the bowl. It was just like a big slingshot effect and the snowballs flew a few football field's distance over a moving automobile on the road. This unidentified flying object appeared to startle the driver of the car, but they didn't stop. So, the boys had to recalculate their position to get a better fields of fire range for their next target. Fortunately, for the passing motorists that day the boys' aim was slightly off. Mekkar figured it was due to the effects of the alcohol they had consumed. But, they figured there would be other days to perfect their contraption and hit to miss ratio.

Mekkar also played imaginary games that he designed for him and to serve two purposes, relieve some boredom and to keep his mama off of his back because she would frequently ask if he was exercising his newly learned English language skills. It all stemmed from a practical family business need. After watching the mama forcibly required english language sports films, tapes, or reels that could be run on either a 8 or 16 millimeter or reel-to-reel projector; or a European beta-type early version equivalent of a vhs machine. This equipment was acquired by his mama somehow but Mekkar didn't ask her where or how she got them for him. Mekkar would then go off by himself and create his own little world.

For example, after watching a baseball game on tape, he would go outside and painted on an adult sized armpits to knees strike zone box on a nearby cement wall and made a line about 12.19 meters (40 feet) away. The MLB standard of 18.44 meters (60 feet 6 inches) pitching mound was a little too far for Mekkar at that time. Then, Mekkar being ambidextrous and able to throw the ball with both his left and right hands, he would choose pitching matchups. He would pretend to be a real pitcher, sometimes it is one that he had just watched for his language lesson, and then tries to mimic that pitcher's stance and movements. At first, he used a tennis ball, and then much later on as he got older he used a hard baseball.

He would attempt to throw only the pitches that he found out or observed a particular ballplayer possessed and Mekkar was able to copy. The game was based on strikes and balls. There would be a hit when Mekkar made an error or missed the ball as it was coming back off the wall. Since, the game would go a full (home and visitor alternating sides of the order) nine innings or extras if tied after nine. More hits would result from his increased amount of errors as Mekkar became fatigued towards the end of the game.

By watching the videos, tapes, etc. beforehand, Mekkar began to learn batting lineups, pitching staffs, and full roster names and eventually his game became a little more sophisticated as time went along. Plus, his pitching, baseball fielding skills, and stamina also improved. Mekkar also was creative enough to invent his own games to play by himself, if so desired, in other sports fields as well such as soccer, football, and basketball. This was not necessary for hockey because Mekkar already played ice, pond, lake hockey or shinny with the other children in the area. Girls would be included and play on the frozen ground along with the boys in the games, mainly because there wouldn't be enough kids otherwise. There was not any favoritism for the females either; they were treated exactly like the boys during the games.

However, the sides were fairly evenly distributed talent wise or either alternatively drafted or picked with two of the oldest kids being captains and doing the choosing for the teams. Depending on the available time, sometimes small sectional and portable boards could be setup prior to playing but not everywhere because the frozen surface was too big and they didn't have enough boards to cover it all. There was checking with the hip, body, and the stick, but carrying out a check on such a large area could put Mekkar way out of position so it was not smart to try to run someone. The girls were pretty tough too and would also throw checks on other players. At times, Mekkar and other boys would receive a stick spear from the girls in the heat of battle because there was little favoritism among those kids that were about the same relative age or size. The difference is that some of those females who just dished out a cheap shot at them were still cute enough to date later on, as they grew older, in Mekkar's mind.

There were times when Mekkar and his brother were able to put their work clothes in the restricted washer and dryer because they had worked in one of the family businesses that day. Otherwise, clean clothes for the boys had to be achieved in some different manner. Their grandmamma would check their clothes to see if anything was left in the pockets, etc. to teach the boys some responsibility and attentiveness. If there was anything there, along with clothes, she would claim any of the items left behind with the clothes as her own. The brothers knew this, so they remembered to check most of the time but once in awhile forgot and lost out.

One cold and chilly Christmas Eve Mekkar put his shoes outside on the front porch. It was after the majority of Jule traditions for that day had been completed, such as decorating the tree, singing songs, and even drinking a bit with the family after the eve dinner. He put his specially made shoes outside right next to his brother's. It would be hard to tell the difference between the pairs of shoes because they both had been made out of reindeer hide with fur on the top. Plus, Mekkar's younger brother Alf had big feet for his age and at this point, they both pretty much wore the same size shoes, actually Alf's were larger.

The children who were good throughout that year would have their shoes filled with candy; bad kids would get sand in their shoes instead. It was considered that the elves, Father Christmas' (Santa Claus') helpers, would carry out this activity along with a few others' on the Eve of Jule. It was thought that some magic was required on the elves part since Mekkar's village was nowhere near beach sand. When the boys woke up the next morning on Christmas, they went to retrieve their shoes from the porch. Mekkar was not as eager to check as Alf because Mekkar usually got sand in his shoes while Alf always seemed to get candy in his. Mekkar even snorted sarcastically "Alf is such a kiss butt"!

Sure enough, Mekkar's brother's shoes were overflowing with goodies, but to Mekkar's surprise and astonishment there was candy and treats in his shoes also! The problem was that the shoes and their contents were still frozen solid from being outside all night. They looked like a small statue and needed to be brought inside to warm up, so the boys could retrieve the goodies from them. It would only take a bit of time to thaw the shoes. However, Mekkar unknowing to him, he put his pair of shoes much too close to the fireplace, even closer than Alf did, because he was impatient due to his glee over finally receiving a prize for being a good boy, for a change. After leaving the shoes there near the fireplace, Mekkar went upstairs and put on another pair of shoes and went outside to play. He forgot about the candy filled shoes. A few hours later Mekkar went to get his shoes, but the goodies inside of them had melted which ruined the shoes completely. His brother had a jolly old time by laughing at him and even taunted him about it.

When Alf had come earlier to retrieve his own shoes filled with candy and treats away from the fireplace, he purposely neglected to remind or warn Mekkar at that time. Mekkar called his brother a devious individual and he knew Alf was relishing this misfortune of his. Mekkar then proceeded to get into trouble for his forgetfulness and the ruining of the specially made shoes. He also received a second punishment because a family member would have to create a new pair of those same hand crafted shoes for him from scratch. It was not planned for yet because the shoes wouldn't have worn out by this time and should be still useable, but now weren't due to special circumstances. It is well to point out that Mekkar never again got candy or goodies in his shoes when left outside on Christmas Eve, just sand. Eventually, Mekkar just stopped leaving his shoes outside on the porch hoping for extra Christmas treats, so he wouldn't have to clean the sand out. Fortunately, sand was easy to remove and clean out of the footwear.

Like his papa intended Mekkar was finally enrolled in the local martial arts class, where his younger brother had begun a few years earlier. Mekkar was hesitant, but his papa required him to do it and Mekkar was not going to tell his large papa, No! Plus, Henrik told Mekkar that martial arts are very beneficial for improving his sports footwork and protective skills.

When Mekkar first started out in the martial arts training class, he felt stupid, clumsy, uncoordinated, embarrassed, and out of his element while he was getting his rear end kicked, punched, thrown, and flipped a lot! Mekkar figured that everyone has to start somewhere and some point, so why not now and here. At first, he was humbled big time because he thought that he had gained some toughness playing hockey and other games with the older kids on the lake. However, this martial arts activity was a different ballgame and coming in with a toughie attitude was a mistake and it changed quickly, since he was in actuality, a beginner. Mekkar, after some time, began to put some more time into it as he started to see improvement in his skills. As he worked hard at it, he got to a level of brown belt in karate and noticed that others that had this bad boy newcomer disposition, would in time, be knocked of you by those instructors and higher level students with more experience. Mekkar observed this and had learned from his previously errored ways.

Mekkar, from then on, would attempt to advise some of the others that were beginners in the martial arts endeavors to leave their egos at the door but many ignored his heed and suffered the same indignation that he did at the very beginning. So, Mekkar just focused on his own martial arts development and later on earned a red belt in Aikido. The techniques he learned here would help avoid some more serious injuries later on and one day Mekkar realized his papa did know what he was talking about and not feeding him a line of bull to get him to participate.

There was one time at home when a very frustrated Mekkar was punching and kicking at the large heavy canvas colored 1.21 meters (4 feet) tall hanging from a hook and a rope from a large beam. But, Mekkar had a nasty temper also and on this occasion had an overwhelming need to win. So, he went over and grabbed an axe and swung it in a chopping motion cutting a big hole on the side of the bag near the bottom. As the sand inside started running out onto the floor, Mekkar tried to gather his wits about him and attempted everything he could to stem the flow of the sand because he then realized the consequences of his actions and dread set in. When his papa came home, Mekkar got into trouble again, because it seemed Mekkar was always in trouble. Not only did he have to clean up the mess he made but also had to fork out a good chunk of change to buy a new heavy punching bag and it had to be exactly like the old one. Mekkar had to replace this bag that he just destroyed because his papa had bought the previous one for everyone in the family to use. It wasn't cheap and had to be shipped in because you couldn't just go and pick one up at the local store, here in the arctic.

Since Mekkar had no drawing talent whatsoever, he had his friend Iilvas create a caricature of the national government assigned overseer of this area. The kids would jokingly refer to him as the imbecile mayor. Mekkar seemed to think that nobody in the area liked this person, as they thought of him as a state sponsored arrogant spy who was there to tattle on the natives, back to officials in the halls of the capital buildings down south. The locals also saw him as an observer of how to rip-off more of the natural resources there, as well as get rid of the rest of the remaining native culture like they having been trying to do for hundreds of years. This, all on behalf of the state and big business.

Mekkar was correct in thinking that most of his contemporaries also hated the governor, who was not a native minority and was unable to speak neither the native language nor the local dialect of this region. They thought that he was a city slicker and noticed that most of the adults had little interaction with him and avoided him if they were able due to a lack of trust of this outsider among the locals.

Well, being kids pranksters to boot, Mekkar and his buddies decided they would give the governor a little gift. Iilvas drew a picture of the regal mayor with his head between his legs and up his butt. The locals would recognize the person who the drawing represented. The special artwork was then cut out and glued onto the cover of a 1,001 Jokes about ... book and translated into a language so the governor could understand it. Mekkar, along some others, went up to the mayor's front door as he was unaware of most of the local customs, and they left the book in a package box next to the door. Then, they rang the door bell and ran. Then, they hid themselves nearby so the boys could observe. They saw him open the door and pickup the package and take it inside the house. Next, they heard a loud voice ring out a long string of obscenities from the house.

It took all of their strength to keep the boys bursting out laughing right then and there. Eventually, when Mekkar and his friends got far enough away from the house, as to not be discovered, they heartily cracked up. Supposedly, none of the boys in the posse told anyone else about the prank. However, the next day in the village the story spread like wildfire in the sparsely populated area they lived in. Even though it was not a crime, the boys didn't want to be revealed and prank perpetrators were never found out. So, they celebrated among themselves by getting drunk on one of the hills overlooking the village.

Mekkar lived in a nice house that his parents bought not long after he was born, but after awhile it required expanding to meet the families' needs. Mekkar's family grew in size after his younger brothers were born and then the home actually became a real settled permanent dwelling for them. For larger scale additions and projects related to the house that his papa didn't have time to do himself would require some materials and needed labor from further down south. Henrik would make all the arrangements for this, which included some input from his mama. Some of these house projects were carried out in parts over a period of years. Some bribery, also known as locality charges and fees, was in order to get the job done.

The house had a large underground basement area built that was more than just a cellar. It always seemed to Mekkar to be cold down there because it part of it was built into the permafrost, which is only a short distance below ground. The cellar and the ground floor are not considered by the national standard as stories, only the levels above ground. Mekkar's parents had a whole extra story, which spanned the length of the home, added to the top of the house along with an upstairs attic for bedrooms and activity rooms for the boys.

For a long time before, Mekkar had pestered his mama and papa about having his own room, especially for being the oldest child in his immediate family. Yet, Mekkar was not successful in his avocation for a Jacuzzi. Mekkar felt that being the oldest should count for something since he had much more responsibility than his younger siblings combined or so he reasoned with his parents. At the same time, since Alf grew up very fast and was already taller than Mekkar in no time at all, Mekkar got sick and tired of having to share a room and sleeping in an oversized king sized bed along with his younger brother.

Alf drove Mekkar crazy with his continual tossing and turning and swinging his arms in his sleep. Even though Mekkar would sleep near the far edge of his side of the large bed, once in awhile he might receive an elbow in the back or side. Mekkar, would then get ticked off and return the favor back. It was so difficult for Mekkar to get some shut eye because of Alf's crazy sleep habits that Mekkar would grab some pillows and other blankets and go to sleep in a different room of the house.

Finally, after a few construction projects were completed and built each of the three boys had their own bedroom, a hang out room with a pool table and a big television, and a trophy room in which each sibling had their own wall for jerseys, etc. Outside a cool club fort was constructed with seating for about ten kids. Also, Mekkar could never forget about the sauna too! The sauna was one of those special projects added to Mekkar's family home for a variety of reasons.

Many homes in the area had home saunas, either attached to the main dwelling or as a separate small building. Those that have the saunas could be invite others over or go to one of the community ones available for public use, since this was normal daily custom for many in the area. Mekkar understood that these hot rooms were invented, in this area of the planet, to provide personal relaxation and a few health benefits for the residents. It was also a place of interaction also.

Many business deals are arranged and conducted while taking a sauna together. For example, heads of state and big time corporate executives have negotiated some business matters there. This is true especially in larger cities down south similar to head honchos who wheel and deal on gold courses in other parts of the world. This activity could be participated in chilly weather outside during wintertime and it is very adaptable too! Some individuals, like Mekkar's parents, would go to the sauna for a bit of solitude and what they called "self peace time".

Boy, it would get hot in there with temperatures high enough to make Mekkar feel like his hair was on fire. Even though he would pour water on the treated rocks in the sauna to get it nice and toasty, it was still more comfortable to him compared to a Turkish steam bath. The steam bath air was so thick with steam that Mekkar could hardly breathe in it. Mekkar went to the sauna almost every day when he was home and there was still room for more people. Some people using the sauna would tap or lightly whip themselves to stimulate and improve blood circulation and get a person's skin pores to open up. Some in the hot room quickly drink a beer or two to prevent such quick dehydration, but would get someone buzzed twice as fast. Afterward they might go outside to roll in the cold winter snow or jump into the shallow unfrozen part of the river. Rolling in the powder gave Mekkar a numbing sensation, and he was certain that after drinking in the sauna that was the only reason for the odd feeling.

Mekkar preferred to air dry by walking around outside after exciting a hot room to let the pores close on their own instead of using other methods to shock them closed. The shock the pores closed process could be through coming into contact with extreme cold or heat. However, Mekkar preferred his way because he felt that his body had been cleansed and refreshed. At times, Mekkar would invite a few of his closest friends over to the sauna in his house. He figured it was being used for its intended purpose, to entertain guests. Of course, Mekkar would also go to the community saunas, with his friends, to meet girls.

However, Mekkar's papa had constructed this particular sauna with other additional functions in mind such as heating up the water to provide more hot water showers, etc... This hot room was always turned on and kept in a warm state because you never knew who or when some guest might drop by the house. Thus, an all inclusive practicality was a requirement for the original building and the presence of the hot room along with the usual benefits for those who enjoyed its medicine.

The Far North Native thought that Alf always wanted to test the limits of the sauna's added hot water production. Alf would proceed to let the upstairs bathroom fog up something fierce, even with the powerful vent fan running, because Mekkar's brother would turn the shower knob all the way to the hottest setting. Alf then would fall asleep on the large bathmat in the middle of the bathroom floor, while letting the hot water flow from the shower head. Mekkar suspected that Alf would just pass out from the hot steam. Since this was a frequent occurrence Mekkar would then after a certain amount of time have his youngest brother Niillas or another family member pick the lock and open the bathroom door.

However, Mekkar was not good at that type of thing. Mekkar knew that he would never be a good thief because he wasn't that mechanical and was unable to jimmy or pick locks. So much for being like one of his heroes, James Bond! Mekkar then would then drag Alf's body into the shower, soap, scrub, and rinse him off. Then, Mekkar would attempt to dry him off with a towel as much as he could and next set him back out of the shower stall on the floor mat. Mekkar eventually got an extra bathroom door lock keys made for future use. Each time Mekkar hated to go into the bathroom in that situation because it felt like a Turkish steam bath to him and it was hard on his lungs, very much unlike the sauna. But, he was the oldest ...

The Far North Native would then take his own shower since he was already there, after taking care of his brother. The problem was that most of the hot water was nearly gone and needed time to be replenished. So, poor Mekkar had to gotten used to taking quick lukewarm water showers and is still his habit to this day. Mekkar feels scalded or burned by any very hot water now since he was not used to it, thanks to his younger brother's actions.

Mekkar's papa, Henrik, was kind of an inventor and very much a handyman and had the ability to create or fix a lot of different items, when he had the chance and time. Mekkar did not inherit Henrik's mechanical ability while his younger brother Alf did. Mekkar's papa attempted to create a smaller food cooking device for their kitchen and that would also be used at times for the family restaurant. It had to be much smaller and cook quicker than a stove or oven and hopefully use less energy because there would not be a need to preheat it beforehand. One time, Mekkar had a sneak peak at their home's power bill and it was astronomical.

It was an experimental process done for family need reasons and not financial gains sake. But, the process had to be tried out in a true living situation, but Henrik used too strong and powerful waves for his built-in prototype microwave cooking machine that he had constructed. This was a few years before nuke machines were ever massively sold to the public. The result from the first attempt was that it melted down part of the kitchen counter area. The machine sat nearby the large refrigerator, but thankfully not right next to it. Sirga was ticked off about this development because she knew there would some time delays to correct the issue and there was the need to repair the damage the machine created. The house kitchen was in fact used as the overflow preparation and cooking area for all of the family businesses including the restaurant since the diner kitchen was much smaller. The early version microwave's issues were soon fixed and corrected after the previous minor contamination and reconstruction of the damaged area were solved. Mekkar thought that his papa made it much better this time with more features added to the kitchen itself.

Henrik had built some things himself with his own hands or on bigger projects arranged for other special tasks around the family lot with the goal to improve their quality of life. Mekkar's papa constructed from scratch and from his knowledge a large round TV satellite dish. Mekkar describes it as like one you might see at a television broadcast station. It was built to greatly expand the available channels they could get on their television. An example of this was that they could television signals and shortwave radio signals from various parts of the globe. It made Mekkar's house the place to hang out. Both parents thought that was a good thing since Mekkar had a penchant for finding trouble. Sirga mentioned to a family member, that the dish also helped keep Mekkar from taking off to who knows where and creating mischief. But, no matter what it seemed to find him.

Sirga and Henrik felt the more Mekkar was around and nearby the better they could influence him and watch over the sly Mekkar more often.. Mekkar had noticed throughout his travels around the world that parents, in general, have the same worries about their children and express it in similar ways. However he didn't learn this until much later after he had moved away from home for sports. Mekkar thought his parents were pretty much the same as others as he only had Lasse's parents and some others in the village to use as a real comparison. They were pretty much alike except for the fact that his mama was much more feisty, blunt, and would assert this attitude when necessary. But, he knew the whole local culture was like that too! It was just that Sirga was the most strong about it.

Mekkar really knew when he was in deep trouble for something especially when Sirga would call, mainly yell at him by his full complete name, all six of them. This, after she would first shout out the dog's name or one of his brother's full name. Mekkar would respond with a statement, "wrong child!" This would incur an increasing fury from his mama. Mekkar's next natural reaction was to flee and to not be seen or heard by his mama, but where could he go? Not very far, as it turns out, since she knew or was acquainted with a lot of people in the area. Mekkar knew that she had her long arm of the law and she was the sheriff and his arrest and punishment would be coming soon.

Sirga thought that she was all knowing and she wouldn't hesitate to tell Mekkar that fact on occasion. Her reason she stated was because she was a mother and they know all. Mekkar believed her because she seemed to always find out the details, even when he would keep quiet, it baffled Mekkar. That perception kept Mekkar more in line and in reasonably good behavior than he would have otherwise because Sirga usually didn't have to tell Mekkar what to do in most situations, he already had a fairly good idea what was expected. Sirga almost never had to get Mekkar to follow her commands and do her bidding more than once. Mekkar thought many times that she was like an military officer barking out orders and you better follow them or else. Later on during his military service boot camp, the drill sergeants were a breeze as compared to his mama Sirga, Mekkar recalled.

Very infrequently, some of the people in the village had a pancake eating contest and Mekkar was feeling confident, so he entered and was determined to win. The first place winner would claim a prize equivalent to $500 dollars. Now Mekkar didn't need the money because he was working, but he was so hyper competitive he just had to be victorious and win big! Mekkar knew that many activities that happen in the village are gambled upon, even the kids do it. Betting on different things was just part of the local culture. However, it didn't always involve money, but could include purchased or bartered items or even services provided by the losers of the bet.

Anyway, Mekkar had seen this contest awhile ago when Paalii was victorious and set the record of twenty nine pancakes completely eaten. The flapjacks were fluffy, made with sourdough mix to get that rising effect. Each one was big enough to stretch to the outer rim of a regular sized dinner plate. They were not tiny! When Mekkar overheard a week beforehand, that the next contest would take place at his families' restaurant because of the home backup kitchen would be used also, he was gleeful. Mekkar thought he would have home field advantage for the event. While most of the others who would observe the event felt that this home kitchen location selection would be of no help to Mekkar.

Well, Mekkar had very little body fat content, which by the way was inherited from his papa, along with a high metabolism rate. So, these factors made it so he could eat massive amounts of food for his age and burn the calories right off too! This was the case with all the three boys in the family at the time, too bad it doesn't always stay that way. But, Mekkar went into food consumption training mode during that week prior to the pancake eating contest and continually increased the amount gradually. He knew that to break the old record of twenty nine it would be a stretch for his tummy and Paalii, the current champ, would show up and be competing in this event. Even though many tried to keep this fact hush, hush, Mekkar had his ways of finding out not so well known inside information.

Each day prior to the contest Mekkar consumed any sourdough related items, like bread and pancakes more and more. By the time the contest rolled around, he felt that he was ready to kick some butt and did not drink any liquids the day of the event because Mekkar was convinced that any fluids in his stomach would expand the sourdough foods and lessen the amount he could take. The contest began promptly at twelve o'clock noon with ten competitors and after a fairly short period of time only Paalii and Mekkar were the only individuals left in the contest still munching away. Both were near the old record and soon they broke the previous standard of twenty nine pancakes eaten.

After about thirty five or so Paalii began to slow down his pace at this point and he was now some distance behind Mekkar. Mekkar was still chomping away quickly. Paalii finished with forty, but Mekkar was on a mission and did not stop until he set the new record of sixty five. A few minutes later both of them could be heard hurling like mad outside in the woods. At the same time, some of Mekkar's friends were collecting their winnings from their wagers. Sirga refused to let Paalii and Mekkar make a mess of the restaurant restrooms for their barfing session, otherwise she would have kicked the stuffing out of both of them. Mekkar's brother, Alf collected Mekkar's funds from the bet he had placed upon himself. It was important to note that many of the contest participants would need some time to recover including Mekkar who required at least a couple of days, where the sight of any food made him ill.

Since, Mekkar lacked the mechanical aptitude of his brother Alf; he was not subject to specific special tasks given to Alf by Henrik. At first it started with a small project where Mekkar's younger brother was required to take apart a radio. In some instances, Henrik did the dismantling of the object beforehand. The idea was to have Alf spread out all of the pieces on the ground or on top of the snow during wintertime, then put the object back together again. The kicker was that it better work great, just like it did before the radio was torn apart, or trouble would be at hand from the taskmaster papa Henrik.

Once in awhile, Mekkar would observe this and glad that he wasn't involved because Mekkar had to carry out his own tasks assigned to him by his papa. This destruction and rebuilding process that Alf was required to carry out had no written documentation or manuals included, there was no public web he could search for and download. Mekkar's papa was thoroughly confident that Alf could complete these tasks with flying colors. This perception was based on how much time Henrik had spent together with Alf, while teaching him at the same time, on various projects. They even coexisted on some high tech electronic ones related to Henrik's work.

Thus, the boy's papa got to see his son Alf in action and felt that he could do the job with possibly a little guidance from him. Each special task became more difficult, larger, and more extensive than the previous ones. Another example had Alf conduct the same process with a large home television set. Alf finally graduated Henrik's special schooling class after completing his last project. That was dismantling and full reconstruction of a 1960's rounded top body design race car. This all seemed excessive in Mekkar's eyes. But, after Alf finished that project, they went for a joyride to test it out and push it to its limits. Mekkar drove it and said afterward that vehicle handled great and was fast too!

Alf had finished the entire list assignments setup by his papa by the time he was just thirteen years old. Mekkar thought that Alf had a pretty good handle on it and demonstrated a competent ability in these areas. Alf was relieved that he never received punishment for a lack of functioning success of the finished items. Mekkar was a little bit older and felt lucky that his interests resulted in him getting to travel to far away places with his parents instead. However, travelling with papa was not always fun and games, there was some work to be done too!

Once in a blue moon, North American college scouts, coaches, and other representatives would arrive in the area to try to recruit and get future ice hockey commitments from a few local players. Mekkar, Lasse, and a couple of others were targeted due to their international experience and to familiarize them with these various squads. This type of activity was still a fairly new practice started by some World Hockey Association (WHA) teams in this era to discover untapped sources of talent. The idea was to gain exclusivity and a foothold in those areas of the world that other hockey leagues had previously ignored. Since the WHA was considered by many as the outrageous pro circuit [Ed Willes, The Rebel League] as they were breaking down all barriers, changing all norms, and were doing things in a new and exciting ways.

Now these other hockey leagues, professional and otherwise would beginning to follow those same discovery paths. Mekkar saw this as a positive change. This development was crucial especially for him since his essential on ice contributions to any potential team was less noticed on many score sheets. However, he had skills and heart that any franchise would deem necessary.

In one humorous instance, a famous college coach from across the pond came to Mekkar's family home to offer him a future based scholarship to play hockey in North America. The coach had seen him play during a match against his team on a previous travelling tour. The pitch was that Mekkar could play the game he loved and gain a college degree at the same time, along with minimal cost to his family due to the sports scholarship. Some in the village, along with Mekkar, thought it was maybe just to make contact with him and get a solid future commitment and signed on the dotted line from him for later on. Mekkar was still a teenager at this point.

Mekkar was back visiting his home village for a couple of those days but he was over at his best friend Lasse's house. Fortunately, Mekkar's mama Sirga had a friend of hers, who spoke good english, over at the house at that time when the coach arrived. (Mekkar would be filled in as the details of this exchange later on). Anyway, the coach knocked on the front door along with another individual who showed him where the house was. Sirga immediately knew it must have been a stranger because they approached the front door which wasn't the norm here because of past episodes. The door bell chimed. Sirga answered the door with her friend and translator next to her since Sirga hadn't learned english yet. The coach asked if Mekkar was home.

Sirga was now on the offensive and asked to see some type of identification. She bluntly stated back through translation, "What do you want?" in a suspicious tone of voice. After this question was relayed back to the school representative, the coach was taken aback, visibly frustrated, and turned around to walk away. Then, Sirga taunted audibly in her native tongue at the departing school official, "This guy came half way around the world to not even spend thirty seconds, how stupid. Well, I don't want my child to go to that school because they are too easily intimidated". The coach couldn't comprehend a word that Sirga had said. Sirga and her friend laughed out loud regarding this whole encounter. Just like that, this brief multi lingual exchange was over.

Later on, when Mekkar heard about this, he felt that someone had led the coach there and were hot on the trail and there might be more on the way. The rub is that if Mekkar would have been home during the coach's visit, he would have rejected the offer anyway. His focus instead was to play professional hockey as soon as possible. It would take a lot of convincing on the part of some of his own coaches, parents, friends, and teammates to have Mekkar wait to perform at the higher echelons of the sport until later on. Especially if he were to make an Olympic or National team or travel internationally on an All-Star squad. Those advising Mekkar told him to enjoy the experience and not to rush it because these situations do not come around very often. They said to him that if it ever happens, it was meant to be.

In hindsight, this focus was a short term viewpoint on the part of Mekkar and later turned out to be a big mistake. What he failed to see, due to his youthful desires and dreams dancing around in his skull, is that an athlete's sport career is only just a short part of one's overall life span. That is based on a seventy year or more span of an individual's potential lifetime. But, Mekkar had doubts and conflicting thoughts just like everyone else. Mekkar felt that maybe he grew up way too fast, in comparison to others, and didn't get to be a kid long enough during his formative years. Mekkar entertained this thought circling his brain at intervals, Hey I am going to be a child as much as possible, for as long as I can, because I have experienced the other. Maybe it was some type of syndrome to delay adulthood, perhaps?

Flash and Harnessing Up the Skis

In Mekkar's culture even young kids bet on almost anything, sort of like their own version of Las Vegas. They traded stuff all of the time after becoming bored with those items. Constant trading and bartering of goods between them was normal. Very similar to how kids used to swap baseball cards once upon a time. The kids had created their own little item swap meet. Yet, very little money exchanged hands. This was one reflection of a culture that avoids unnecessary waste if possible. It is better than throwing it away when someone else can use it for awhile longer, Mekkar reasoned.

One amusement involving Mekkar that he liked to participate in was referred to as the flash item memorization game. It was definitely another contest for money. Plus, he engaged in it with only his closest friends and on occasion his younger brother, Alf. Involvement included only individuals that he could trust. Only those he knew that would not cheat him or try to rip him off could participate. It consisted of one person who would flash a card, sticker, box, or another object for a specific amount of time. Sometimes, witnessing the article for as long as thirty seconds. The goal was to memorize as much as possible about the temporary flashed item.

After the object was taken away, the idea was to correctly recall the most information about that item. Identifying features were audibly spoken back toward the group. Even words, marks, scratches, and other detailed information would be described. Usually it was one individual against one other. Once in a while they might add a second or a few more to make it more interesting and compete for a larger prize amount. The others there not guessing acted as the judges. Some of the individuals there had photographic memory capabilities, so it was not as easy as it sounds. Competition became fierce because Mekkar always had the desire to conquer and win in every endeavor he partook in. The winner was determined by relaying the most details about the targeted item toward all that were there. The format was always winner take all in regards to the victor's spoils, as many of these small contests were. The game was simple but challenging. Mekkar was pretty good at it when he was younger. But as he got older and received a few head blows from sports, he was less adept at it and never won that contest again.

Another time when the boys were figuring out a new activity to begin, they came up with this one, a race. Mekkar put on his skis, harnessed up his chosen reindeer, and took the reins. Next, he headed out to meet a few of his friends at their rough version of a race track set into the snow. Basically, it was just a fairly large open, flat area set in a small valley between the hills. The boys raced for money. At the same time, it was a dare and a challenge. Mekkar knew that rejecting a challenge was socially unwise among his peers. Activities like this are just what boys do. In this instance he was pitted against his older best friend Lasse. This time they all decided on the large, sort of oval shaped, open course about five kilometers (3.1 miles) in size. The group began clearing away as many small potential obstructions as they could from the track

The race began and the animal was soon pulling the racers behind them up to 48.28 Kilometers per hour (30 miles per hour). The speed could have been faster in Mekkar's estimation. At top speeds, it was a matter of just holding on and hoping not to crash or wipe out. Mekkar was ahead in the two lap race and as he was on the last lap in sight of the finish line, he looked back at Lasse. Outwardly when he peered at Lasse, it was a glance of I am kicking your butt. In reality, Mekkar was just holding on for dear life and didn't feel that he was in complete control of the situation. Of course, he wasn't going to let everyone there know that.

Trouble was his glance caused a shift where he slightly leaned too much to his right and forced him to lose control. All of a sudden, Mekkar flipped, then rolled and rolled finally coming to a stop. He landed with a thud in the bushes and small trees off to the side of race course. During his tumble, Mekkar had heard the sounds of branches breaking off as he furled past. One of the twigs had penetrated and partially broke off in his wrist. Mekkar felt that he also did more damage to his wrist as it might be broken too. He felt the physical pain. However, he was more embarrassed because he had bit the dust in front of his friends. He was also ticked off over losing a race when he was in the lead and felt the win was in the bag. Plus, no cash prize for him further irritated Mekkar. All competitors contributed their share toward the grand prize. Especially, when there were multiple people racing or a series of races consisting of one-on-one. The award for finishing first was winner take all and the losers go back home empty handed with less pride.

At that point, Mekkar wasn't thinking straight. He wished there was more than two people in that last race and thought it would be best having a different payout system. Comparable to a horse or dog race have Win, Place, and Show payouts with everyone contributing. Contrary to his desire, it was always winner takes all and the losers go home with no cash and no pride. Mekkar knew this, but he just didn't want to accept it at that point. Plus, the injury pain started to get worse and wake him up to the reality of his situation.

Reindeer Bones

During the tourist season Mekkar would encounter tourists at his families' restaurant that catered to them. It seemed to Mekkar that the travelers were always clamoring for native knickknacks and objects to take back home with them. So Mekkar decided to be entrepreneurial and capitalize on this.

Even when he was working while waiting and bussing tables at the diner, he would bring up passing conversation with some of those visitors. Mekkar would work it by telling them how to get unique native items for gifts. Especially with Asian tourists, who seem to have always bought everything they could get their hands on. Mekkar had previously done some research. He had also heard from others that tourists from that part of the world greatly desired ground up reindeer bones for use as an aphrodisiac. So, Mekkar saw an opportunity and arranged for a cut of the profits with another person in the village who would grind up antlers for him. Another slice of the money made went to his mama. Otherwise she would be ticked off that he used the tourist business eatery and its customers as a pitch place for his little cash operation. Plus, Mekkar had an excess of supply, little storage space, and knew where to get more. It was helpful that both the male and female species of reindeer grow antlers every year and also drop them annually.

Another factor was the great amount of reindeer in the area, thus a bountiful supply to meet Mekkar's need, and most of the natives had little use for the bones, especially the antlers. Only the people who made local native goods such as knives, etc. used some of the bones for the handles, utensils, and other such trinkets. For those items the stronger preferred internal bones were extracted after a separation process for the rich, tasty meat was completed.

It was a good thing for Mekkar that the antlers were replaced every year so they were plentiful. Mekkar would then guide these tourists to the appropriate person that he previously arranged business connections with. It was a specific individual in the village of his choosing to sell the ground up bones and antlers. The travelers' desires were met and everyone benefitted. So, why shouldn't Mekkar wanted to make a little money for his efforts! It wasn't like there was a ready made market for a lemonade stand and something like that. Mekkar made it very clear regarding purchases. He would tell the buyers something to effect that we only accept cash and only certain types of money: U.S. Dollars, British Pounds Sterling, German Marks, Swiss Francs, & a few other stronger currencies. Mekkar would go on to mention that No Japanese Yen, Russian Rubles, nor other weak currencies would be accepted as payment for the products due to their lesser values in exchange. There was a lack of getting any fair conversion rate for those involved regarding those less valuable monies. Plus, few of the area banks would even bother to handle those other mediums of exchange at all.

Remember, Mekkar lived in the country not the big city where there is plenty more options. The native boy was just trying to put his creative native brain power and capabilities in action as he knew that adaptation is key to survival. This applied to many realms in such an isolated environment. The ability to use what is easily accessible to forge out a reasonable existence there.

First Time Heard Anything Like This

Mekkar was getting older, but was still young enough to hang out together with his mama on one of her modeling trips. During a break from a modeling photo shoot they went walking together outside. They needed to get some fresh air because it gets stuffy in those studios. The suffocating tension among the crew and models continued to accelerate also. Plus, Sirga wanted to get away for a bit from the constant motion and craziness, which is normally inherent on many assignments in the industry. She definitely needed to lower her stress level as much as she was able. The question was would she would be able to accomplish that with Mekkar around. Usually her oldest son caused her stress levels to rise instead of decrease. Mekkar had that knack and affect on her.

They had only journeyed, for a few blocks away from the building that housed the photo studio, along the streets of New York. As they passed by a number of small businesses, Sirga and her son heard a noise above them blearing through a speaker. This little record shop there grabbed their attention, especially Mekkar's. The boutique seemed out of place in this stretch of blocks. A short distance further away had a good number of small music shops located together in their own section.

Instantly, the boy heard a totally different sound was from anything else he had listened to before. Mekkar looked up and determined it was undeniably coming from the electronic systems. With his curiosity peaked, he had to check it out. He begged his mama to enter the store with him. Mekkar boldly went directly to the person at the counter and inquired as to who were the featured sounds he heard outside. "It is Cheech and Chong, a different kind of comedy duo", was the response.

The native youngster normally carried his own cash with him when travelling with either of his parents. The audible interplay was so different and sounded so cool to him. The lad was frequently drawn to many things that were considered different from the usual. He thought that his friends at home would like it too! His peers in the village welcomed Mekkar's visits to the four corners of the earth. They always anticipated Mekkar would bring back home odd stuff from other parts of the world. More so, it was even expected that he would share his new prizes with his buddies. He just had to buy it. So, it was good planning that both he and his mama had gone out earlier to convert their money into the local currency. That way purchases could be conducted with no major problems.

Mekkar knew there were no issues with his mama regarding this purchase. Especially, since he paid for the item with his own money gained from working. Sirga was glad that she was not on the hook to buy it. Added to the fact, that Sirga would have refused any purchase by her son if she thought it was harmful. Mekkar couldn't wait to bring these records back home. On the recommendation of the shop counter person, he purchased multiple albums put out by those guys. "Wait until my friends hear this, it will blow their mind!" Mekkar quipped. Altogether it would be another new experience to enjoy with his friends. It was a bonus that he knew that no one around him had heard anything like this before in its entirety.

Driving with Mama

Mekkar first learned how to drive when he was twelve years old. His mama felt that maybe she had waited a bit too long to teach him a little bit. It was common in the region for kids, Mekkar's age, to drive any number of motorized vehicles. The main exception was the highways away from a person's village. Few really worried about whether one had the proper national driver's licenses or not at that time. It was not a big concern as long as an individual could operate the vehicles and machinery in a safe and proper manner. Plus, there were not many traffic police wandering through the area either.

The sticklers for obeying all the national driving laws were always individuals who were employed by some money-grubbing government agency. Way down south the minimum age limits for obtaining the correct driving documents are much higher. This stuff was for the big city folk not us country people, thought Mekkar.

Mekkar and his mama were about to begin his first driving lesson together. He thought, in his mind, that it was an unfortunate thing that his mama was his driving instructor. He preferred to take these lessons from his papa instead because Henrik was calmer and laid back. His mama was too feisty and not patient in his opinion. Mekkar's papa was less likely to react in a manner that would result in him getting frustrated and distracted. Especially, if Mekkar made any inexperienced driving mistakes and a possible argument might occur. Mekkar right then thought that Sirga might be just a little too crazy to teach him how to drive a car.

However, the boy realized that he needed to make the best of it and appreciate the opportunity to learn offered to him at this time of how to drive a vehicle. Another benefit was he also got to spend time with his mama. More experiences to develop his own growing independence streak were important issues with him too. It was a stage that Mekkar was going through as he was getting older. Becoming more self-sufficient would only be a larger concern to him in his teenage years. Sirga said that many people her son's age have those same attitudes. Many emerging young people gain the mindset of wanting to show themselves as capable people before they reach adulthood. This is reflected by not having the desire to be constantly around their parents and pursue other interests. Mekkar's mama admitted that she was like that also, but commented that the circumstances were very different in the post World War II era.

Sirga's backed her nicely kept cherry red 1972 Porsche 911 Carrera sports car from the garage. Mekkar excitedly opened the door so he could hop in behind the wheel and his mama moved over to the passengers' side. She reminded her son that this two-seat prime machine came right off the line, brand new, from the factory. The boy was trying to get the clutch and shifter timing down as they drove away from the house. After about twenty minutes they reached a flat stretch of highway. There were few cars on the road where they at during this part of the day. It was a very flat terrain with little overwhelming visible scenery for Mekkar to be distracted by. This was not a major highway like an Interstate freeway in America or the multi lanes of the German autobahn. In this section, it is primarily one lane going each way side by side with large center divider. Every so often there would an extra lane so slower vehicles could be easily passed. The average driving speed was fast, higher than the posted limits. The season didn't matter either even when the road was like an ice sheet during wintertime.

The weather was a nice sunny day and not too hot for Mekkar's liking. They were cruising along at about one hundred miles per hour (160.93 kilometers per hour). Mekkar was now feeling confident as a driver. However, his mama wanted to give him a surprise test. So, without slowing down Sirga reached over from the passenger's side with her leg and her foot slammed on the brake. Well, Mekkar had to react quickly to get out of the slide they were now in. When he regained control of the vehicle, he lost his cool and yelled at his mama, "What are you doing? Are you crazy?"

Sirga's reaction was not what he expected at all due to her usual straightforward intense demeanor. This time she was sort of calm which surprised him. It was the total opposite from her normal personality. Before long, Mekkar's mama did return to her usual character and snapped at him, "First of all, don't you talk to me like that!" The car was still moving as he was attempting to gather his wits. She then slapped Mekkar across the face with a whap and it stung. Mekkar replied back in a sharp tone, but he was focusing on steering the car as it slid off to the side of the road into an open field.

As they came to a stop, Mekkar was glad that he didn't roll the car. He repeated again, "What did you do that for?" He added, "Why did you slam on the brake while I was driving your car at that speed? You do know this is my first driving lesson." Mekkar's mama responded, "I chose this area because the ground is relatively flat here. I felt that there was little chance of rolling the car over here. If you slide off the road, no big deal!" She continued on, "I have driven this road many times, so I knew what to expect. Also, it is easy to get back on the road again after going off the highway". Sirga went on further, "I started to see that you were confident in your ability to handle the car. You know how long winter is and it's coming soon. You should already know this through previous experience." Mekkar took this as a backhanded compliment from his mama. The motor was never shut off throughout this ordeal. The youngster next put the car in the right gear, got back onto the road and the driving lesson continued. At this point, the flustered Mekkar just wanted to have this training time over with and get home as soon as possible.

Wolf Test

At fourteen years old, Mekkar would have to prove himself once again. Successful completion of the wolf test would be important in regard to more important reindeer herding assignments. The whole idea is to show that the individual can protect the herd at all times and under duress.

He was no different from others who trekked with the herds as they had to go through the event as well. With greater trust in Mekkar's abilities in handling and protection of animals resulted in more responsibility given to him, especially on the trek. Parents in modern societies would have a hard time letting their teenagers be involved in such a dangerous ceremony. The natives knew that it was necessary to test one under extreme pressure, in case that same scenario happened in the wild. Failure to pass resulted in death for the teen. It was very different from flunking a class in school. There was very little margin for error.

The teenager had recognized the reason behind why veteran herders in his village had colored ribbons streaming their hat. One part was to indicate what type of functions each could perform. Herders in other places might not have any of these indicators as they do not care about this. Despite this there are many that are also well experienced in many facets regarding reindeer herding.

On the hat there could be a spectrum of colors like red, yellow, blue, green, and a few others to show adeptness and proficiency in various areas of how to protect the herd. It could range from whether a person gets to use the snowmobiles, those who specialize with operation and coordination with animals to move the herd along. Other symbols can identify which individuals are able carry out other difficult tasks. The toughest is building and removing fences, as well other temporary structures, for roundup and more. Mekkar thought it was because those people had to do it despite the conditions, including in deep snow.

Despite the youthfulness of those who get initiated through this ritual, the only defensive and offensive weapon the participant gets to use is a knife.

No guns are allowed. The reasons are very clear in the field. The teenager has take on a live wild wolf one on one with only a knife. In some cases out on the tundra, shooting a firearm could spook and stampede the herd. The herders would be fairly helpless as their animals ran away. That would be similar to waving your bank account, goodbye. Reindeer have some worth and value in monetary terms.

Unknown to many outsiders of the area, it's rude to ask how many reindeer a person or family owns. Usually there would be no response at all or some type of general response is given to distract from the question altogether. It would be like if one person asked another, who they didn't know very well, how much money do they have in the bank. A true response would be "None of your business."

There are usually more than a couple of teens that are the main focus of this ritual. Usually, the wolves are expected to leap up and attack the individual's throat region. Part of the preparation is that one wolf is separated out and enticed to attack. This becomes a one on one battle between prospective full responsibility herder and the predator. After the initial aggressive stage has begun, no party from the outside can interfere. That is, until either the kid or attacking animal dies. One has to prove their mettle under extreme pressure. What was worse, just prior to Mekkar's turn, was that boy did not overcome and was defeated. The wolf jumped up and bit him in the throat, which took out the boy.

It was time for the young man to have a go at it and justify himself. He already knew to outwardly show any fear would benefit his opponent. Inwardly he was apprehensive, but this quickly turned to anger and a different mindset. The change in Mekkar's demeanor became one of Come on, let's see what you have and you will not defeat me.

Mekkar, being brave and a quick thinker in his mind, stuck his left hand into the attacker's mouth. Next, he retrieved his knife from its sheath. It didn't have a small blade but nowhere near as large as a crocodile hunter's either, but somewhere in between. Then, the animal chomped down hard and almost bit all the way through his hand. One can still see the bite mark scars to this day. It was excruciating is how Mekkar later described it. He took this action because he figured the challenger can't go for his throat, if it is already occupied with the hand.

The Arctic Warrior then drove the knife up through the aggressor's jaws while his own hand was still stuck in there. Mekkar came very close to piercing his own limb. Fortunately for him, the extended dagger went right between Mekkar's middle and ring fingers. This did not mean the action did not result in consequences for Mekkar as he growled in pain. After that, Mekkar twisted the knife back and forth and with his other extremity struck a bone in the neck of the wolf. This basically broke the bone and killed the attacker. Finally, Mekkar was able to remove his injured hand from the animal's grasp in this dual to the death. He thought to himself what a stupid thing to do. However, it was another instance where Mekkar prevailed to live another day.

Moving Away from the Village

Unknown to him and because Sirga just didn't tell Mekkar why she chose that particular time to teach him how to drive. It would be revealed very soon afterward. Mekkar would have his revelation of this when he needed to move away from his village area. It would be a permanent move, even though the village would always be home to him. It was required for him to relocate to the closest city to further his hockey skills and a possible future in that sport.

Fortunately, it was only a little more than one hundred miles away and he could come back on a regular basis. Whether he knew it or not, Mekkar would learn and use more life skills than he ever imagined by being away from his original home. The main reason for the move was that it too difficult to deal with the frequent and long travel distances required getting him where he needed to be.

It was especially true of transportation during the winter time when the highway would become a mess at times and an adventure at others. A snow-plowed road does make for more accidents, slow down issues, and greatly lengthened travel time.

Henrik and Sirga, Mekkar's parents, based their decision for him to relocate because they felt that Mekkar was mature enough to be able to handle living by himself at twelve years old. Other factors also played a part in the move. It wasn't as though Mekkar was moving to a small city that he was not already somewhat familiar with.

Since, Mekkar was currently being taught through individual studies; in other words, being tutored as well as not attending the local village school, education was not a consideration in the movement decision process. Mekkar had been working for some time now, so money was not an issue and of no concern in this matter.

Mekkar's papa agreed to help him arrange suitable living quarters and sought out some of his own contacts in regards to this situation. Henrik knew a lot of people due to his employment in a multinational corporation. Henrik also laid out some grounds rules for his son regarding the arrangements. He located a place in the northwest part of town near the old arena.

The city council was already in the preparation stages for the construction of a new ice hall on the opposite side of town. It was a strategy taught to Mekkar, by his papa, to live as close as possible to his workplace, if possible. The new arena in the south east corner of town near the railroad line wouldn't be finished for at least a couple of years, reasoned Mekkar and his papa.

They decided together that they would come to that bridge when they get to it and work on that issue when it came about. Mekkar figured he would be much more familiar with his small city by then and they might build new housing too closer to the new arena when it was completed.

It is well to note that this is not referring to a large city like some of them much further to the south. So, transportation and traffic should not ever be a problem. But, as Mekkar likes to say, "You never know what will happen!" Plus, the weather could be nasty at times during the arctic winter season.

The Native from the North thought that if it was close enough to walk where he needed to go, he could handle any trouble. Mekkar had been on reindeer treks before, so he was used to carrying his gear with him in any weather. He was proficient enough to use his kick sled with a good sized basket to haul around town what he needed. It was also a good exercise warm up for him on the way to the ice house. Pushing a kick sled is kind of like propelling and riding a skate board on hard pack ice or snow, especially if Mekkar wanted to arrive in a more rapid manner than walking.

Mekkar wanted to get a feel for his adjusted surroundings because that was just the way he was and he knew that it took time to do so. After a while though, Mekkar realized he needed a more stable mode of transportation, a vehicle, and that his papa could hook him up on that front too as long as Mekkar had the cash. Mekkar had already stashed some money away for a car and the search for the right one was the next step.

There was a James Dean club down south in a nearby big city that had a few thousand members. Those individuals in that club tried their best to emulate the now deceased American actor James Dean. They adopted images from Dean's time period such as the hairstyle, sleeveless jeans jacket with a sewn-on Confederate rebel flag patch on the chest, & other aspects. It was similar how people today imitate Elvis Presley's features and mannerisms. Many in the club drove American made vehicles from the 1950's and early to mid 1960's that matched the image from that era.

It seemed to Mekkar that there were quite a few white 1960's Chevrolet Impalas with what he described as having the rear fender wings. Mekkar spotted the make and model he wanted and proceeded to show his papa what the car looked like. Henrik began to make some more contacts with a few of the club participants. Mekkar was alongside of his papa and was learning wheeling and dealing strategy as Henrik went into his business mode of interacting with people, speaking, and negotiating.

Mekkar thought that they had picked a good day to be there since some of these vintage cars were being bought and sold there. Henrik hoped to cut a deal before the auctions were to begin. The whole scene was just like muscle and antique car shows that people go to see all over North America.

Due to the continual flux of incoming new and outgoing club members, it seemed there was a lot of activity and buzz. Mekkar figured some were selling their vehicles due to various factors. Maybe because their interest in the club had waned, they need the money from the sale, or possibly a member recently became deceased.

Henrik wanted Mekkar's first car purchase to be a fairly reliable, sturdy, good quality, old steel, tough vehicle that ran well. Vintage American cars had that positive reputation in this part of the world. Since Henrik was an extremely hands on and mechanical person, he thoroughly inspected the potential vehicles himself on Mekkar's behalf. Henrik considered the amount of slip and sliding that could occur, especially with a inexperienced driver like Mekkar, in winter weather in the far north. The reasoning was valid due to the increased number of accidents that happen during wintertime on an annual basis.

The thoughts ran through Mekkar's mind regarding the oddness that these club participants appeared to partially worship a figure who most of them had never met. Now they would never get the chance either because Dean died at such a young age, before really establishing himself as a star, and long ago ironically in an automobile accident halfway around the world.

Eventually, when Mekkar's papa made the vehicle selection for his son, they paid out the cash, and set up all the arrangements for the transport of the vehicle to Mekkar in his newly adopted hometown. The arrangements included details such as registration, insurance, and other stuff like that. All the paperwork and documents had to be in Mekkar's parents name because technically, according to the national government, Mekkar was too young to operate a motor vehicle. However, that wasn't going to stop him!

It would be another day or so for the vehicle, Henrik had just purchased with Mekkar's money, to make it legal. The next step was to transport the vehicle to Mekkar's new dwelling place in the small city that is named after a regional bird species located in these parts. The Arctic Warrior became very familiar with the vehicle during the long drive back home.

When, Mekkar and Henrik arrived back, Henrik proceed to go instead to their hometown village to get some rest. Mekkar needed to conduct some preparations to get him settled into his new home. First Mekkar collected a set of keys to his apartment and mailbox from the property management. He had not seen the inside prior to his moving in because his papa took care of all of the arrangements including packing, moving, and unpacking of a few of his personal items. Mekkar just gave Henrik a chunk of cash to cover the moving costs, initial expenses like utilities and phone, plus deposit, first and last months' rent.

When Mekkar unlocked the front door and looked around inside he was pleasantly surprised and stated, "I can always count on my mama and papa to get the job done right."

Mekkar was unaware that his papa gave an additional set of his apartment keys to an assistant coach of the ice hockey team. This was done to make sure that Mekkar got his butt up, with some help, early in the morning for his training. Henrik was wise and knew that his son was not a morning person, and still isn't. Henrik gave instructions to the coach to dump Mekkar on the floor, if required, to wake Mekkar up in the morning to begin his daily routine.

The awakening started everyday at four o'clock am sharp and started the very next day after Mekkar had moved in. He had not even gotten a chance to get situated and comfortable yet and unfortunately that still would take some more time. There were still a few boxes strewn out all over the flat even a week later because he was thrown immediately into the fire in preparation for the upcoming season.

Mekkar thought that the solid wood floors of the flat was pretty neat considering the bargain cost he felt he receiving for renting this place. However, he would find out that he was mistaken because the floors could get chilly and held less heat inside. Moreso, the wood floor in the bedroom was a hard surface to land on when being dumped onto in the early mornings to start his day. The daily routine always seemed to Mekkar to begin when it was still dark outside and sunlight in the arctic was becoming less and less as winter was coming soon.

The Native from the North had been saving a good portion of his money from working for a few years already, so he knew he could afford the apartment with no problem. He just wished that his papa would have warned him of the morning issue situation and the extra key ring given to the coach beforehand. Mekkar just wanted to be prepared because he very much disliked being left in the dark about certain things. Mekkar thought that sometimes his papa would leave some details out in different situations that Henrik put Mekkar in. He was unable to determine if this was an intentional tactic or not. Maybe, Mekkar thought, that his papa was continually attempting to stimulate Mekkar and have his son think on his feet. Mekkar knew that his mama used the same strategy on him, but she was more straight forward about it. Sirga would tell Mekkar to his face that she was not going to let know everything needed for his own good so that he would learn some things for himself and become self reliant.

Anyway, Mekkar lands on the hard wood floor with a thud because the coach tugged on and flipped over the mattress. This was unexpected and Mekkar would eventually let his papa know about his displeasure about this morning episode.

Mekkar seethed with anger regarding this matter and wanted to light up Henrik verbally the next time he went back to the village. It wasn't as though Mekkar was never going back to visit the village he spent his early years in. He could catch a bus going toward that direction almost every of the week in the city. So, it was possible for him to go back often during breaks in his current schedule.

Not only that, sometimes his parents would come see Mekkar when they would need to fly down south from the local city airport. The airport was only one of two places nearest to the village to have regularly scheduled flights to points southward.

Continuing on, Mekkar was only half awake, cranky, and in a ticked off mood. After the coach quickly left, Mekkar wanted to whip someone's rear end, anyone's right then would do. His emotional state and mindset was that whoever was on his bad side in practice the rest of the day would pay the price as retaliation for this. Mekkar definitely thought this to himself and might have let it slip out of his mouth, "Too bad there isn't a game today to exact some punishment".

Mekkar was fully aware of the regimen for this day's activities and the one thing that helped him through it was the surprise visit of his best friend. Lasse knew Mekkar better than anyone else here and was also his teammate now. Lasse had also moved into a flat next door and had to participate in the same training regimen as Mekkar. Mekkar later found out that Lasse's mama had conversed and planned this move together with Henrik for the both of the boys. Similar arrangements were made for the both of them by their parents because Lasse spilled the beans regarding this matter. Lasse had mentioned it while they were performing the early morning five o'clock five mile run as part of their hockey training.

They would start off together but Lasse was a faster runner and more of an early bird morning person than Mekkar, but not by much! Lasse almost always finished the five mile jog in the required time of thirty five minutes. While Mekkar almost never met the time requirement set by the team coaching staff. He would normally complete the task a minute or two slower because he sometimes wouldn't be at full capacity and totally awake until some distance into the run.

If Mekkar failed to cover the course in thirty five minutes he would have to run an additional five untimed miles as discipline. Fortunately, there was another teammate that was in the same predicament as Mekkar, as he wasn't too much of an early bird also.

The benefits would be evident later on. As a result of running ten miles almost everyday instead of the regular five miles like their teammates, on top of the other training, those two slacker joggers would rarely get tired in the latter part of games. They both were in better overall physical shape especially near the end of the season when all players are nursing bumps and bruises.

Thus, in an odd way it turned out to be a benefit for Mekkar. He could still consume enormous amounts of food and still keep his very low body fat physical structure. Mekkar was thankful that he had a natural muscular extremely minimal body fat solid body thanks to great genetics from his parents. Plus, it helps to be young and highly active.

There was one instance later on when Mekkar went to bed late the night before or into the next early morning, he was hazy on the details. Anyway, he went to bed in a foul mood. The next morning when Mekkar was dumped out of his bed and onto the floor he was ticked off at the coach. Next, Mekkar proceeded to get up and punched the team official right in the middle of the coaches face breaking his nose.

This action resulted in a suspension from the team for Mekkar. The small victory in all of this is that at least none of the coaches ever came back to his apartment and do that again. The team staff changed their tactics and would resort to early morning phone calls or having teammates drop by instead. Since, Mekkar lacked an answering machine, because they were not that common in those days, sometimes the phone would ring and ring incessantly and continuously until it was answered. That way a team official was sure that Mekkar was up and beginning his morning preparation process, in other words get dressed, eat breakfast, etc.

Snowmobile

From time to time Mekkar would go back home from the smaller city where he now resided. Sometimes he would return with Lasse and other times alone by himself on the bus. Well, Mekkar and his best friend were still teenagers and still country boys at heart. They were both used to doing insane things without, as of yet, too many repercussions as a result of their actions. It was said that due to their youth and immaturity, Mekkar and Lasse were shielded from drastic consequences. The two developing young men were relishing in their newly found independence of living on their own at such a young age. They needed to grow up quickly as individuals away from their home village. However, boys will always be boys and when those two get together sparks can fly.

The small city Mekkar and Lasse now lived in had a greater number of fun activities to be involved in, but in some areas it could not ever match back home. Activities like ski racing while holding the reins as a reindeer pulls them around real quickly. The whole betting culture, among even the kids, which encouraged wagering to pick the winners in most everything they could think of. Plus, other enterprising undertakings that could be engaged in and possibly dangerous if it got out of hand.

This was also the beginning when Mekkar wanted to test the limits of his need for speed in various realms. He would have ample opportunities for this too. Mekkar thought that it was a good thing that he was still young enough that his hockey agreements didn't have extremely restrictive clauses. It was not common to limit off ice antics and potentially self damaging physical activities away from the main sport or occupation. Well, at least pursuits that could possibly effect Mekkar's needed contributions and performance related to his team. What if he got injured in these outside enterprises?

However, as Mekkar progressed up the ladder these aspects would soon change to protect both the individual and the franchise. The team already had some investment in him, through coaching and training. They desired

Mekkar to develop as a player in a manner that would best benefit the team itself. Public image and perception also plays a part because positives sell tickets. Mekkar was well aware that he was not untouchable, but expendable like any other team member. Still, his philosophy became why not have some fun while you still can and try to keep it a secret from the club, if possible.

On one of these visits back to the village, the restless Mekkar and Lasse sought out the expensive first generation, prototype turbo engine snowmobiles in the barn. They both checked to see if they had enough fuel for their adventure. The problem was that these machines were only supposed to be primarily used on reindeer treks. The idea was to chase down stray animals and guide them back to the herd. Otherwise, those wandering animals might become a feast for another predator. Emergency applications were additional functions for the machines such as if someone gets lost during a blizzard, etc.

Both Mekkar and Lasse were fully aware that these machines were a newer supped up and custom modification version of snowmobiles. They could easily travel twice as fast as or more than the normal machines available for sale. Mekkar had been with both Henrik and Lasse's papa when they acquired these special machines for village needs. On that particular journey Mekkar saw, with his own eyes, these snowmobiles in action and knew they were fast. He felt that might be the reason for restrictions regarding personal use.

This got their blood boiling with excitement and daring. Curiosity got the better of both Mekkar and Lasse and they took the machines out of the storage building. Without attracting too much attention they proceeded toward a makeshift 3.1 mile (5 Kilometers) snow covered racing track nearby. Mekkar called it their track, but basically it was a fairly flat open area which was normally cleared of any big trees. Mekkar likes to point out that the tree roots encounter permafrost below the soil at about 6 feet (1.82 meters) or less. So, it is fairly easy to remove any obstacles when they appear. Next, they scanned the area to check if most of the brush was removed, skipping an odd branch or two here and there.

There were only a couple of other buddies there beside themselves and they would be the judges of the race. Mekkar knew that they would be fair with no bias because there would be hell to pay otherwise. Plus, being dishonest, cheating, and playing favorites would mean losing friends. Since there is not a large selection of buddies to choose from that would be social suicide. If any of his peers wanted to be flat out crooked, like a politician, from that point on would forevermore result in a lack of trust of that individual. The first action taken would be a severe butt kicking while attempting to beat the corruption out of that character. The hope was to bring that one back to the fold as soon as possible.

So, after Mekkar and Lasse checked their machines again, they got back onto their vehicles. Mekkar's heart was beating fast and he had beads of sweat running down his brow even though it was cold outside. Still, it was a little warmer than usual. Janne jogged out to the starting area and raised his arms above his head. The signal was given when Janne dropped those arms and they were off in a rush.

The race was supposed to be a minimum of 3 laps around the so called track. Mekkar was ahead the whole race. The ice sleds created a small cloud of snow dust due to the friction from the skis on the bottom, as well as, the rate of speed emanating from the machine which creates heat. It was fortunate for the trailing Lasse that this was not a pure ice track or his visibility would have been much worse.

On the homestretch Mekkar looked back at Lasse to see where he was. However, Lasse was not that far behind. Yet, Mekkar began to laugh at his best friend and even shout out cocky statements in Lasse's direction. This caused Mekkar to lose focus. Just then, Mekkar slightly swerved a bit which forced him off the main part of the large oval shaped track they were on. This caused Mekkar to collide with a small tree. It was afterward described as just a large branch standing straight up out of the ground.

At the speed Mekkar and Lasse were racing, a collision with any object could result in some damage to the machine. There was contact with the front of the snowmobile and Mekkar flew forward in the air of the suddenly stopped machine. He landed on a small bank of soft snow right on his rear end in a prone position. The problem was that a small wooden object penetrated the side of his right wrist, past the skin into the muscle near the joint. It was the same arm and wrist that was injured before in a previous ski race.

Because of the adrenaline rush the injury was not Mekkar's first concern. The physical pain to him was much less than the fear of damaging the front of the snowmobile. The psychological torment in Mekkar's mind was worse right then. The teens knew specifically that these machines were not to be used for play or their own private purposes, but for work only.

Mekkar yelled out loudly, "My papa's going to kill me for this!" He realized right then and there how much he screwed up through his devious actions. Before long, the injury pain was triggered and those messages travelled to his brain. In Mekkar's mind, the actual damage to the snowmobile could have been worse. Nevertheless, it was enough to render it unusable for its full capability and intended purpose.

His cockiness caused Mekkar to lose big time. Let's see, he didn't win the race, lost all his money bet on it and had to fork over cash to Lasse. Not only that, Mekkar suffered an injury and would have to face the music from his family's wrath for damaging the ice sled. In addition, Mekkar would be on the hook financially to have the mobile machine repaired to make it fully operational again.

This all happened because Mekkar acted stupid, cocky, and arrogant for just a moment. The teenager thought to himself what a terrible day, but it was an expensive lesson learned! Time will only tell. These thoughts went through his mind while getting back onto his feet. From there, they had to first go back to the village to retrieve a vehicle to pickup the now not running and noticeably damaged machine. Somehow, he hoped to haul it in for repairs before being noticed. All in the group knew what Mekkar's fate was if he did not succeed.

Nervous Biscuit Errors

In an exhibition hockey game against the Northland Aces all-star squad, Mekkar was fortunate to play alongside one of his heroes. The matchup this day was in his heroes' hometown. Mekkar was part of a youth team program there also. So, Mekkar was on the local side that had a mix of professionals and a few younger athletes which included him. The Arctic Warrior even stated, "Wow, I am playing with a superstar!"

Mekkar's nervousness was evident when the game began. His teammates saw that he was overwhelmed by the situation at first. Early in the game, Mekkar gave the puck away on foolish turnovers. It happened not once, but twice in a row and deep in his own zone. Those turnovers resulted in two quick goals by the opposition and the netminders was not too happy with the young defenseman.

The superstar tried to calm Mekkar down and told him, "Don't worry about it. You need to relax and we will get those back. Play your game in the manner you usually do and everything will be fine. I have seen you perform before and know what you can do. I will be there to back you up."

On the bench in between shifts, one of the pro's on his squad told Mekkar, "You are not the second coming of Booby Orr. It would be foolish for anyone to compare themselves with him. Mainly because nobody does everything Orr can do. A player just needs to work hard to improve their skills, especially their weaknesses, and try to everything well. Be your own person! Don't try to copy someone else." Another pro seated next to Mekkar on the pine chimed in, "If it wasn't for all of Orr's knee injuries, we would have thought that he wasn't human. You are still a kid; just learn from your mistakes."

Those were the magic words, because suddenly Mekkar found his groove. His normal method to get rid of game environment jitters was to bodycheck opponents and throw around his body. Sometimes, it also resulted in getting hit by someone on the other team. It took awhile for Mekkar's side to come back and make up for his early mistakes. Yet, they did and were victorious with a late goal in the third period by his hero.

Netminders

Most netminders, even in very different sports, have similar traits and quirks. The position tended to attract those types of personalities. It was even more so for old time hockey goalies. There were a few exceptions but it was a small number in comparison.

Guardians of the goal spend way too much time alone in Mekkar's opinion. He mentions that many have more superstitions than wizards or witches. The Arctic Warrior comments that an individual must have some mental issues and be a little crazy to be shot at over and over by a frozen, hard vulcanized rubber disc. In the old days, goalies risked their very lives to stop pucks and played the game without facial protection.

One thing the forwards and defensemen didn't want was to be caught on a bad line change, especially in the second stanza, when the bench is further away. Leaving your own goalie deserted on the ice usually results in the unpleasant scenario of you getting the business later on.

Mekkar could somewhat relate to a netminders' mindset since he was used at times as an emergency third goalie during practice. He was glad that he never had to play the position in a real game. Thus, Mekkar feels that many people do not fully appreciate goaltenders enough. This goes for him also, as he would sometimes forget, with his non-traditional almost always attacking style of play. That is, instead of cutting off the passing lanes during odd-man rushes by the opposition. Mekkar's style was big risk, big reward. He wanted to mainly close the gaps of space and speed up reaction time of other players to force them into turnovers.

This meant leaving the far side of the net vulnerable by not cutting off those potential back door plays. Also, unaccounted for were open opponents trailing the play into the center of the ice for prime scoring chances on net. His mindset always expected to arrive at the right time and keep the puck from getting behind him toward the goal. There were many times that his own netminders and teammates bailed him out when he didn't get there for the hit in time.

The young man from the Far North was fortunate to play with and against some fantastic big name goalies in his time. At times they were very displeased with his style and would later chew him out for leaving them "out to dry" by themselves for a breakaway against. Mekkar frustrated fellow teammates with style of attack which could often take make him positionally vulnerable. In Mekkar's opinion, he would have been less successful if he adopted a more passive method of playing defense. He would tweak and modify his style a bit but decided to never completely change it altogether.

Despite the flaws in his game, many appreciated his extremely hard driving effort. No one ever criticized his no quit demeanor, no matter what the scoreboard said. The knock against Mekkar, by his detractors, was his on-ice decision making, even though he had a high hockey IQ. It appeared to some observers as though Mekkar would selfishly disregard the safe play on a too frequent basis.

World Wide Hockey Tour - Pre Tour

The exclusive upbringing in a sparsely populated area, the time period, and cultural background Mekkar grew up in dictates his views. He looks at many things from a very different perspective than most other individuals. It is not saying whether one way is better or not as good as the other; it's just from a different cultural inclination.

For one thing, Mekkar doesn't compare himself in a physical sense in either size or stature to other people. It wouldn't make any difference anyway. The contrast he makes is to bears, even polar bears and other wild animals in nature. Mekkar does that with all people, no matter how large or small they are. To Mekkar, everything in life is a matter of perspective and affects their individual outlook. Plus, Mekkar already takes the position that most people are taller than him anyway, so it rarely crosses his mind and is a non issue to him. Thus, he is not intimidated by humans and has regularly throughout his life dated women much taller than himself.

Sometimes players on other teams, as well as, their more vocal fans would taunt him. A few of those shouted out statements were in a derogatory sense. Some of those words directed at him were regarding his statue and native background. Mekkar figured it was the case because he has some native traits compared to most of the people he encounters.

Comments would come down from the stands like fireballs from a magician. A few signs with cutout pictures of The Arctic Warrior in compromising positions, swear words, and worse were aimed specifically at the teenager. It would sometimes make Mekkar seethe with anger and want to go into the crowd and kick some butt. At the same time, Mekkar would also use those negative darts as motivation to heighten his intensity on the ice. It meant that Mekkar would amplify his in-game nastiness far beyond his usual feisty disposition. This could be problematic for him due to the fact his attitude change would cause Mekkar to take more penalties and leave his team shorthanded more often. Goalies and coaches were not always happy with him crossing over that fine line between effectiveness and disruption to the overall game plan.

Mekkar would moreover use any cheering and support for the home team's exploits as fuel for him. On the road he would accept actual crowd applause and make his own. A sort of deceptive mind game, if you will. In any case, Mekkar tried to apply any whistling or booing directed at him as targeted toward another player. It was not always a successful endeavor because Mekkar has incurred a variety of food and liquids dumped on him while spending time for his actions in the sin bin. These mind tricks eventually made forays on the road more bearable for Mekkar. Even so, Mekkar can't stand to lose and it is much more difficult to be victorious in games away from the comforts of home.

Later on, The Arctic Warrior was given a piece of advice in a meaningless exhibition match by one of his hockey heroes that was a well-known defenseman. His idol told him, "Just let it (the statements) go, don't worry about it, you can't change or fight everyone." Sirga, his mama, repeatedly gave Mekkar the same advice. Still, the native from the far north brushed aside the advice and continued to do things his own way. Outwardly, Mekkar still continued to play effectively on the ice. Inwardly, the comments continued to bother Mekkar enough to make him want explode with fury. Added to that, it stewed a desire to inflict retribution against all who crossed his path. Once in a while, after incurring objects tossed at him from the stands, Mekkar would boil over. Then, he and other teammates would climb over the glass or metal gates (which he referred to as chicken wire) above the dasher boards. They would seek out those responsible for starting the melee and pay them back with a physical beatdown. Players venturing into the stands and having altercations with fans was not uncommon in that era. The most well-known example was the Philadelphia Flyers, who were also dubbed the Broad Street Bullies. Still, there was a risk for all parties involved. Unfortunately, Mekkar's angry behavior forced the squad to frequently play shorthanded, while he spent time in the sin bin.

Trouble was, Mekkar was extremely headstrong and received that trait from his mama and grandmama. He was young, dumb, and full of ... [John C. McGinley as Ben Harp character in Point Break, 1991] Mekkar even replied back to his idol's wise advice that was given to him by muttering under his breath, "Wanna bet, I will kick all of their butts, all that taunt me, those stupid morons." Oh! The wisdom and sage counsel wasted on the young. [Kurt Vonnegut, 1997 MIT graduation ceremony speech]

However, that freely given advice turned out to be absolutely correct as Mekkar matured, got older, and became more aware of his ever changing surroundings.

The fledgling young man had heard all kinds of crass remarks and jokes directed his way regarding reindeer. Alf, on the other hand and most probably because he did not resemble any outward native characteristics, avoided this abuse on purpose. The younger sibling of Mekkar hid any aspect of his native status or background including using a different last name than Mekkar from the legal birth choices available.

These factors eliminated negative preconceived ideas, perceptions, and bias towards Alf. Mekkar embraced his uniqueness and would on occasion correct others as to their misconceptions. At other times, he would outwardly brush off ignorant statements of the unknowing. That depended on his mood at that time.

Taunts showered upon The Arctic Warrior throughout the season and multiplied as the Christmas season approached. Fables such as Rudolf the red nosed reindeer and more direct personal attacks heightened for the duration of the winter. Mekkar knew better and was intimately aware that reindeer drop their antlers on a yearly basis. This normally occurs with males after the rutting or mating season in the late fall/early wintertime. Yet, it is not unheard of still having them later on in the calendar year. Remember, there are always exceptions to every rule. [Marcus Tullius Cicero's defense of L. Cornelius Balbo in 56 BC; alt-usage-english.org/exception_proves.html]

He had also been present during many instances when the female reindeer drop their antlers earlier in the year. Females normally grow them back after calving time in the very late winter/early spring. Mekkar got sick of the constant barrage of those stupid myths retorted over and over from many directions. Mekkar would comeback with sharp remarks such as, "If a reindeer has a red nose it probably came about from either being attacked by predators or in the process of being slaughtered." Sometimes, Mekkar would get the business from fellow teammates as well. Usually, in a jovial setting. Mekkar says that he has heard it all, especially the wisecracks regarding herder occupations and native stereotypes.

When it came to dishing out the physical punishment Mekkar never held back. He should have played smarter earlier in his hockey career, but Mekkar was too young to realize it at the time. In other words, letting his frustrations out by dishing out vicious bodychecks at every opponent as retaliation for the abuse he received. Sirga warned her many occasions by telling him that he is one person and can carry out a limited number of actions. While, there are more individuals who can avenge in return. Mekkar surely does understand his folly now, in the distant future, as his body is crippled and falling apart. Some days it is a chore just to get out of bed for the day. However, The Arctic Warrior was aware of the potential risks and accepted them willingly to play a game he loved. Mekkar to this blames no one else but himself for the results. He just wishes the miniscule salaries of his time would have been comparable to the current era.

It is too bad the bullheaded Mekkar didn't listen to others who had counseled him through their own past experiences about the prospective physical results. Mekkar now wishes he could have looked in the future and observe the consequences. Yet, he had to learn his lessons the hard way. He now attributes it as being juvenile with the thought that it will not happen to him. As the paraphrased saying goes, "Those who do not learn from past history are doomed to repeat it (and its past mistakes)." [Edmund Burke, 1729-1797] or something to that effect according to Mekkar.

Sirga told Mekkar flat to his face on more than one occasion, "No matter how much you give, you always receive more in return. That is because there is only one of you and so many more of them ready to return the favor." This statement or a variety of it had been passed down to Sirga by her mama and through their family lineage. Sirga also related this piece of wisdom to her oldest son regard to a physical health. But, of course the young Mekkar did not take it to heart nor apply the message into his play on the ice.

There is an adage used frequently during the Christmas season – It is better to give than to receive. Mekkar preferred this application instead. It showed itself to be especially true when he would throw his body around on the ice. From time to time, Mekkar would wipe opposing players out with hard body checks of all types. Some might have been crossed the line of fair play.

Yet, Mekkar like most other teenagers are prone to blow off much of the advice and sage wisdom given to him by adults. Mainly because he thought it was so old school thinking and the times had changed. Mekkar was growing up into adulthood, so he thought he knew better. Young people in this stage of life tend to think they know it all and much more than anyone else. Mekkar felt that no parent or relative could relate to him during this stage of his own life, as well as, his own chosen direction. There is the tendency, for young people, to forget that all adults have already gone through those experiences beforehand. They have made it past that age.

The result usually is that each individual, as Mekkar eventually did, has to stubbornly learn the grim realism of various lessons in life. Yes, Mekkar would find out that when he thinks he knows it all, that attitude will soon make him look foolish. Life has tested him and humbled him through trying circumstances. Trials and tests would materialize sooner than he ever imagined. It was destined that the boy would become a man by gaining the necessary life instruction and attributes to journey on to the next phrase.

It was beneficial that Mekkar had been previously prepared for this upcoming hockey tour. Even the right wrist and hand that had been injured earlier in the year in the snowmobile race was fully healed. Mekkar was unaware that he was a cog in the wheel and part of an overall evolution process in life and sports. His own native culture emphasizes this belief of individuals are part of a larger design in the world itself. Fortunately, the extremely tough training regimen helped shape Mekkar into the player and person he would become.

This was a period of time where he would normally play for various clubs throughout the year and then take a five week hiatus. The break from hockey would occur during part of the summer. Mekkar would participate in other sports to still keep in shape. Many players in those days took a true off season break from athletics in general or work more hours at their place of employment. Very few superstars could claim sports as their fulltime employment. Lower pay dictated that Mekkar had to work for a living like everyone else. The idea was to get as far away as possible from their primary sport endeavor to avoid complete burnout.

Some players like Mekkar would increase their daily alcohol intake during this time. It was more for enjoyment and pleasure. Sometimes it appeared as if he were deprived of it and trying to make up for lost time. When in reality Mekkar drank quite a bit during the season. Many players used booze as a pain killer to numb the senses along with medications. That is, when he wasn't partying with his buddies. After the sabbatical, many players like Mekkar would return with a fresh attitude and a renewed appreciation for the game. Training camp was primarily used to get back into hockey game shape. Mekkar loved the games themselves, not the daily grind.

Very different from today where year round sport specific training and tailor made workouts are the norm for athletes. Numerous individuals hire instructors to have them come into pre-season camp already in fantastic shape. Mekkar refers to it as a refining process into full sport and specific preparedness. This is not to say that all dry land exercise was avoided altogether back in the day. However, it was nowhere near as prevalent as in current times. It was a different mentality than because the majority of hockey players and professional athletes in general received a small salary in comparison. Most had to work at jobs during the off-season just like the rest of society.

Mekkar is of the opinion that some of those factors made pro athletes more in-touch and relatable to their fans of yesteryear. It was an environment that is very dissimilar to many detached athletes of today who can afford to take off-seasons to sculpt their bodies on a full time basis.

The young man himself played other sports during his time away from ice hockey. He would play some soccer (futbol) even though he was not nearly as good at it. His hockey defenseman mindset compelled Mekkar to position himself as a defender on the pitch, as well.

Alf has said that Mekkar was also a decent tennis player who could easily move around the court and chase down shots in an efficient manner. Plus, he had a wicked first serve that more than one hundred twenty miles per hour {193.12 kph) at times. The problem was that the serve was erratic at best and fantastic when he got it in. Mekkar would mess around with inconsistent second serve. Occasionally, he could put an outrageous chop spin that would sometimes barely cross over the net and die inside the service court on the other side. It didn't happen often. Plus, Mekkar double faulted frequently due to his unwillingness to adapt his serve. He would try to his the ball as hard as he could. It didn't always matter where the ball landed. Mekkar used the notion that force is everything revealing his feisty nature on the court. He did not apply himself with the same drive in tennis, as ice hockey. Alf commented that his older brother only used racquet sports as a distraction from his main sport. At times, his competitive nature and fiery disposition would take over and express themselves in a variety of ways.

The adolescent had observed a bit of live match play and many games. Mekkar also watched some tape and films featuring top notch professional tennis players. Bjorn Borg, Rod Laver, Jimmy Connors, Roscoe Tanner with that fast serve, and more were present as visual tutors to help improve his game, if he so desired. Mekkar attempted to incorporate what he could and modify it to his own game abilities.

Mekkar was a poor volleyer at the net. His reaction time was fine, but racquet control to keep the ball in the court was an issue. At first he followed the mainstream use of the smaller head wood frame. Then, later to the newly introduced oversized metal rackets. [Wikipedia] They both contributed to many tennis balls flying out of bounds on Mekkar's part.

He was basically a baseliner and learned the extreme top spin forehand shot by watching Borg. Since Mekkar had very strong wrists developed in ice hockey timing of the ball meeting the racket strings at the correct point was the goal to get the desired effect. Bjorn was at the top of his game during that period. Mekkar was unable to copy Borg's two handed backhand. Instead, he would try to emulate Connors left hand cross court deep returns, especially when receiving serves.

To cover more ground on the tennis court Mekkar might receive a serve from his opponent with the racquet in his left hand and switch the racket from one hand to the other. This had to be done quickly and frequently depending on the situation during a point rally. He got good enough to do this during individual points without looking and still have the proper grips on the tennis twig.

This was effective for Mekkar. At first, some others watching this thought it was a very odd technique, but Mekkar used anything that most useful and adaptable for him. By watching Rod Laver on film, he learned better footwork for efficient movement around the court. The Arctic teenager also had hockey quickness in his arsenal. Even though Mekkar was at the time slightly more dominantly right handed he was basically ambidextrous in many areas. It would freak out people on the opposite side of the tennis surface when Mekkar would return serves with the racquet in his left hand. His groundstrokes were better and reached closer to the back line from the left side.

Previous injuries had forced Mekkar to be able to use both arms and hands more evenly. One side would be enhanced while the injured part is recovering back to full strength and use. This was helpful for the advancement of his hockey career. Mekkar customized these additional developed abilities into his imaginary games like throwing a ball from both sides of the body. Due to more serious physical setbacks later on, those formerly developed skills have all been negated.

The adolescent's understanding of the game and fairly competent tennis ability helped him get a job for a short time. The place of employment was at one of the premier sports clubs after he moved to down south to the big city to play hockey for one of the local teams. Mekkar considered the possibly of forming important contacts, at this exclusive place. Anything to help Mekkar reach his goal of playing pro hockey.

He has developed a philosophy that eventually you might need a skill or something facet you have learned for a particular future instance in your life. Akin to a reindeer no part is wasted. The trouble is Mekkar never knows when or where it might be required or exercised. The hope was Mekkar retained some of instruction previously given by Aslak, back in the village or while on the reindeer trek.

Mekkar is a very rhythmatic person. He feels like he is at his best when he is in the rhythm of something. This applies to all areas of his life. Thus, being in rhythm is quite key to him and central to his way of thinking. Mekkar understands that most people are unable to relate to that because it is an ingrained native aspect to his character.

Anyone who knows Mekkar personally can see that his survivor fighter type personality is not an act. It has stemmed from the far north native environment and upbringing he grew up in. This was easily assessed by Mekkar's quips and retorts on the ice toward other players. Especially ones who wanted to do combat with him or those who desired to ramp up their roughness against him. "Hey, where I come from we have big bears and you are much smaller than a bear. So, how are you going to scare me?" Mekkar would snap back at times.

It seemed that every time Mekkar participated in any games against North Americans, exhibition or otherwise, they all wanted to test him. Since he felt that his size, or lack thereof, was like a greeting card advertising an invitation to start the rough stuff with him. Many times the cheap shots and extra aggressiveness would take place, even before the youngster would open his mouth to show that he was an accommodating adversary. It wasn't like Mekkar was unwilling to oblige either. Mekkar sought an answer that maybe it was something in his countenance on his face or an aspect in his appearance perhaps. However, he never received a satisfactory response to these questions. Ultimately Mekkar discarded that notion due to a lack of useful information gathered on the subject. He was forced to accept things as another part of hockey environment.

The Arctic Warrior was a product of an era and time that had a different mentality. Many of the most famous big name hockey stars would fight back to defend themselves. The list included the biggest names in the sport - Gordie Howe, Bobby Orr, Bobby Hull, etc. The current specialization of athletes has removed the need for this because there are enforcers who defend their team's star players. Rarely, if ever, did anyone see Mekkar back down from a direct challenge. The native from the far north figured if the superstars can protect themselves on their own and fight back, why can't he?

Not to mention many aspects were different in those days along with unwritten rules and conduct that applied as well. Mekkar understood this and still his on-ice demeanor crossed the line of breaking those rules on many occasions while performing for various squads. As for the whole hockey industry, Mekkar refuses to speak for it because maybe many aspects he believed were universal. In his mind, people in all fields take some things for granted whether conscious or not.

For instance, the head injury issues that many have now become aware of were as common as today. Mekkar suspects it was more so at the peak of his athletic career. However, scientific discovery and advancement in technology were not as advanced as today. Concussions were only considered as headaches and, Mekkar knows about this firsthand, some were worse than others.

There are times where Mekkar was incapable of recalling from his memory banks whole days, weeks, and matches that he was involved in. On some of those occasions he would have a portion of the info filled in by his brother, friends, and others that were present. Since they all pretty much played the sport too, Mekkar would do the same for them in return. There was an agreement that if one of the teammates had a blank bout due to head trauma the other players would collectively take care of each other by filling in the missing details.

Mekkar now experiences a consistent level of headache, along with their varying degree throughout everyday of his life due to the frequent rattling of the head. He understands that he took the risks and fully accepts the consequences. Thus, he sucks it up and deals with it in his own way. His ingrained mentality is that he is a hockey player, long after his playing days were over. Thus, don't be a baby about it and keep your complaints to yourself – despite the deterioration of the physical issues. Everyone around The Arctic Warrior sees this outward expression and attitude including his doctors and neurologist. Yet, no one wants to trade places and endure the daily challenging circumstances that have risen as a result.

Fortunately, Mekkar was always glad that he wasn't suited up as the backup goaltender for a live game. The backup was usually positioned, closest to the puck bucket, at one end of the bench. The pail was used for the nauseating excretion that could occur as a result of a heavy hit to the head and other reasons. Normally, the second goalie that occupied that spot on the bench rapidly adapted and later became immune to that foul smell. Similar to the garbage man around stinky trash or a plumber who unclogs pipes of human waste. Still, that scent always affected Mekkar and made him want to puke so he would try to sit as far away as possible because he never got used to it.

There were many instances, which involved Mekkar, that would be labelled as concussions today. Little was known about those issues back then as compared to now. For example, Mekkar would suffer a firm blow through contact of his head with an opposing fist, elbow, the ice surface, boards, etc. Team officials or trainers would arrive with smelling salt packets to wake him up if he was completely knocked out. A few times, according to Alf and Lasse, Mekkar didn't even know who he was and answered all of the questions directed at him incorrectly.

On a number of occasions after regaining his senses Mekkar would then be helped to the bench. Next, vomit into the bucket and go to the dressing room to be given pain pills and commonly alcohol for the numbing effect. He would then hear, "Hurry up; you only have a few minutes for your next shift so be ready." Ah! The good old days.

Mekkar has experienced times where he was in a blackout, non-remembrance frame of mind for awhile afterward. This happened more often than he would care to admit but the response was suck it up you're a hockey player. Unfortunately, it also became his normal point of view by not considering the future adverse effects.

It was amazing that Mekkar didn't miss more time by playing through it all. He rarely missed games and almost never did for an assortment of minor injuries. He feared that he could be replaced if he was out too long. All he wanted to do was play the game. The matches were rewards to him for being diligent in practice, going through the training regimes, and the other preparation activities.

In addition, there is the matter of gaining the respect of your peers, fellow players, coaches, fans, etc. Mekkar didn't desire to be labeled a wimp, chicken, or one who couldn't handle the roughness of the game. So, Mekkar soldiered on without consideration of any possible long term negative affects. He didn't want to disturb his confidence level and that is such a fragile thing at times for most athletes.

That period was very much unlike today where the big money invested in athletes is so much greater and the overall physical contact less. Now, whole careers are taken into account and the athletes can retire on the salaries earned nowadays. Mekkar has mentioned it before that he felt that most athletes back during the duration of his career and before were treated many times like a piece of meat. He has even quipped, "The help was cheaper to replace when the meat was not so delicious anymore."

Another aspect was the attitude exhibited by a few of the clubs Mekkar played for. If you are injured in any way just get back to the bench. The players were told flatly, "If you are not dead or unconscious we will not come and help you off of the ice. At the very least, be tough and get to the bench under your own power, somehow!" It was a different era. That is the reason why in one game during his playing days Mekkar broke his leg. He was unable to stand up or put any weight onto that limb. He then proceeded to crawl on his hands and knees along part of the defensive blue line while the puck was up ice. Mekkar struggled to get back to his team's side and only then was helped to the locker room for further analysis.

Due to this inserted conviction, Mekkar feels that many individuals went beyond the call of duty. Some performed with injuries back then that wouldn't be considered according to the current standard. He attributes it to the expendability factor of yesteryear as the Native from the Far North refers to it.

It was a good thing Mekkar was blessed with a measure of natural athletic ability but quite a few specific skills had to be learned, developed, and ingrained over time. Mekkar was in top physical condition due to the excruciating and demanding training program. Plus, he had such a low center of gravity that made it hard to knock him off of his feet. On the other hand, the lack of height made Mekkar very susceptible to opposition elbows and cheap shots to his upper body especially the head.

Mekkar has affirmed many times that fighting in hockey is preferable than the alternative, more dangerous stick work. Mainly, because there are those individuals that are reserved for that role of policeman for your team. It is a matter of being a deterrent like nuclear arsenals during the Cold War. He has asserted that if there was no fighting allowed at all the abuse suffered could be much worse.

Cheap shots to the club stars and main goal scores would increase dramatically. Injuries from evil stick work would be out of this world. Mekkar knows about these nasty tactics because he has been the target of it himself. He has suffered a host of various induced maladies as a result of opposing maltreatment from vicious hidden uncalled penalty stick infractions. Bad intentioned twig-work has caused Mekkar more trouble to his body than anything he has suffered in any tangle or fighting escapades involving one's fists. There have been some hockey leagues around the world with the bad-stick label attached to them. Thus, top players avoid those locations like the plague.

The native young man has never lacked internal drive; some others would call it passion or refer to it with other terminology. That resilient fire is sometimes the very thing that kept him going through the bog and the mire. A toughness trait that keeps him upright and still looking forward to make a positive play or set up a prime scoring chance during a game. This all while being checked and possibly crunched into the boards by the opposition like any good hockey player, performing their duty, would do.

Ice Hockey is considered one of the fastest team sports in the world along with Jai Alai, Badminton, Bobsledding, and others. The difference is the added physical element that also makes hockey a violent game and a collision/contact sport. The players are quite aware of the speed that takes place within a game. Most fans will never be able to conceive of it without direct participation. Watching the game on television doesn't come close to revealing to the non-player how quickly it all moves or how fluid the sport is.

Even now though he prefers listening to a match on the radio to keep his mind sharp, when Mekkar watches a game he sees it from a much different perspective. Friends of his notices when going to a live hockey game with him that Mekkar still actually shouts instructions toward the ice. On other occasions Mekkar becomes very quiet and extremely analytical of the play on the ice. Others can vouch that Mekkar even voices instructions and tactics toward the players during a game – whether live or on TV.

It is not surprising considering Mekkar did later coach a younger championship squad, while he was still playing himself. That team roster had a couple of future pro stars, but Mekkar's implemented system and training was considered too exhausting for all involved. However, he liked the teaching aspect but not the overall aspect of coaching too much. The main reason is that you can do everything to prepare your team but there is only so much control the coaches can exert in regards to the execution of the game plan.

After all of this time, when Mekkar views a match live, or on television if the cameras are in the correct places, it is in an unequal manner to those around him. Despite all of the head trauma, he presently sees the play in, what he describes as kind of slow motion. He scopes the activity as it develops on the ice, through recognizable patterns, particularly around the net area. There is his early distinguishment of possible scoring chances and resulting goals as they happen in real time. Those observing the match right next to him might only hear an oh! Sound from Mekkar before a goal is scored. Yet, there are other occasions where he has trouble remembering who he is – all inside the same skull.

Parts of the processing center inside Mekkar's head are much quicker than he could ever describe with his mouth and his trap is pretty fast. Mekkar has what Alf and Lasse describe as an almost non-stop motor mouth with constant yammering. Part of Mekkar's was being a disturber, or a pest, and he was good at it by chirping away at opposing players. In many cases, he would descend into the realm of uttering similar comments at teammates as well.

References to a player's error-prone mistakes, how they looked, odd individual traits, regarding their talent level or lack thereof would be capitalized upon. Nothing was sacred and no topic or subject was out of bounds or off limits for use by Mekkar when he was in the provoking mode. Sometimes he was assigned by the coaching staff the purpose of getting inside a specific player's head so they might take a stupid penalty. This ploy was applied to throw the opposition player off of their game, well at least for that particular tilt. The idea was to positively affect the results in the rink for his own team. Of course, Mekkar was not an expert at this technique or in the same high trash talking stratosphere level as some other players. There are masters of confusion that came along later such as Finn Esa Tikkanen who even invented his own language Tiki-Talk. [Wikipedia; Livestrong.com]

Mekkar has heard the following statement a few times and from a variety of sources in the form of, "Eventually you will get knocked on your backside and it will happen a lot. If it hasn't happened yet, it is because you are not playing hard enough or not at a high enough level of play." This was a positive aspect for Mekkar as he saw it. Plus, the Northern Native already had a never give up philosophy and never surrender character no matter what the circumstances he faced or what the scoreboard read. In addition, Mekkar had an extreme level of mental fortitude and toughness. All hockey athletes are aware, as Mekkar was, they could suffer a crushing blow or a career ending injury at any time. Yet, at the same time have a high pain tolerance or be able to bear a continuous level of great discomfort; to a degree that most individuals can never relate to and possibly would drive many to constant wailing. Mekkar just accepted it as part of the sacrifice for the love of the game.

The emerging young man had exceptional hand-eye coordination and instantaneous mental faculties working at top speed together. It was required for Mekkar to endure the rigors of his position such as throwing his body in front of a 90 mile per hour + (144.84 kph) slap shot to block it. [Livestrong.com] Mekkar thought that a person had to be a little bit crazy to do that without hesitation. Certainly, he qualified in that psychological aspect. Even more so, in an era where the protective equipment was nowhere near as good as today. Mekkar would make jokes about this saying that he should be committed to a nuthouse for these types of reactions and on-ice behaviors.

The teenager always tried to give his best effort every day and night, during practices and live games. He is aware that is how you win the respect of your team and the fans. Mekkar accepted the fact that anybody could be observing him at any time. The realization of being in a fishbowl where everything is visible and out in the open. When he could not do anything without an entirety of people seeing it placed added pressure on Mekkar. Eerie similar to some of the lyrics in the song Somebody's Watching Me. [by Rockwell, 1984]

Mekkar discerned that there were other off-ice areas he needed to markedly improve upon such as humility, approachableness, and conducting himself appropriately when engaging the media. He had a plan of good intentions in not swearing too often (which is common with hockey players) around reporters. Not only that, the Native From The North attempted to show respect to various team officials, along with on-ice officials. The results did not quite pan out as well as he hoped. Mekkar tried to keep, his displeasure at times, inside. However, it was difficult because of his growing lack of trust in any authority figures in general.

Fortunately, scouts and other hockey people saw this as a trait of youth that could be corrected easily with proper teaching and more exposure to a variety of environments. Those in charge focused on Mekkar's physical abilities such as being a strong skater and his fearlessness. Also, those same individuals admired his ability to maneuver his way through tight windows on the ice due to his compact, low-centre of gravity, stature. Not to forget Mekkar was normally prepared to take a hit, just to make a good play with the puck. [Livestrong]

Any player who is focused on their feet or frequently looks down at them negates many facets of their game. The issue is that your attention is solely on yourself not on what is going on around you on the ice. Mekkar states, "That if a player cannot skate well then you will not get very far. It won't matter how good that player's other skills and abilities are."

This manner of adaptive thinking Mekkar also exhibits into other areas such as board games like Stratego. Mekkar normally kicks rear ends in the game because it appears that his thought process is a few steps ahead of everyone else. He tries to consider multiple possible scenarios or outcomes that could be sprung upon him, at any time, by his opponent. It's too bad, that The Native from the North cannot transfer this same forward thinking before opening his mouth.

In Mekkar's mind, playing a sport on a couple of thin blades is not a natural act for a human being. The difference of not using one's own, more stable and much wider, two feet is what separates hockey players from other collision and contact sport athletes. Most others are barely adequate at the skating part, and much less adept at the other skills required for hockey to perform well. The Arctic Warrior feels that he can emphatically make this statement since he has participated in quite a few other sports as well.

The dedication of Mekkar, towards sports that he enjoyed participating in, was not without its hazards. It's well to note, that he spent a lot of time rehabbing many injuries common to athletes, especially hockey players, on a frequent basis. This included foot, ankle, leg, knee, hip, groin, and many other wounds. There was also time spent in a swimming pool with water playing the part of resistance to help him get back to full health. Mekkar seemed to Alf to be habitual water visitor. Alf observed his older brother using the sessions to go through various range of motion exercises, as part of his overall physical recovery routine. When you play the type of games that Mekkar did – it was a constant fight against ailments. Even to this day, when Mekkar is in a pool he unconsciously still performs some of these exercises. Nobody seems to ask why. Many assume that the Native from the North has a desire to check his current flexibility. To this day he has never given an adequate answer.

The international system, mainly developed in Europe, is the type of hockey environment Mekkar was also trained in. The premise is with more practices and increased practice time to develop personal skills and fewer games on the schedule. This is the reverse from the scheme in North America where it was based more so on instinct. There were more live matches to apply those learned abilities at game speed and less practice time.

Mekkar always felt that the smaller ice surfaces in the United States and Canada better fit his play the body, not the puck, style. It did help that he was very good in his positioning toward the play happening around him. In Mekkar's mind the extra dimensional space of an international ice surface made a big difference.

He felt it was harder on the big ice to play a neutral zone defensive strategy like the trap, wing-lock, or similar system. It was easier to advance the puck and maneuver around it. If a defense first dominated game plan was implemented it was typically a retreat further back closer to one's own net. This fleeing and clogging up a team's own the zone with all five skaters reduces offense and play making flair from the game. Fans are not as entertained by that method.

To Mekkar some of these blueprints are similar to a press defense in hoops. The idea is to force the opposition with the puck to areas where the defense dictates. As contrary to where the offensive team in possession of the biscuit controls the flow. On the smaller rinks these trap and lock systems are easier to implement and would make Mekkar's tasks much easier. Not only that the center red line, like the fifty yard center line in American football, helps defensemen from being burned by the long homerun breakaway passes. Well, that was the case before leagues began to change the rules negating the two line offside infractions.

The current Kontinental Hockey League (KHL) in Russia is throwing a wrench in all those previously accepted defense theories due to the focus of skill versus mucking and grinding. How that circuit also has some less talented squads invoking "clogging defense" strategies at their own blue line. Mekkar is waiting to see how it turns out as he watches hockey matches from all over the world on the internet in the twenty-first century.

Another thing, Mekkar is a great fan of contact sports and has played many of them. He is aware that "American" gridiron football (not futbol or soccer) was actually born in Canada by British soldiers against civilians in a game in Toronto on November 9, 1861. [cflhq.ca/articles/gridiron-football-the-evolution-2; ezinearticles.com/?Who-Invented-Football?&id=1364334; Wikipedia]

Unknown to many people, there are many nations with professional or semi-professional gridiron football leagues and those with organized leagues and championships. In fact, there are more than 700 American football clubs in Europe alone: USA, Canada, Mexico, Japan, Ireland, Great Britain, France, Spain, Holland, Belgium, Germany, Austria, Switzerland, Italy, Norway, Denmark, Sweden, Finland, Poland, Luxembourg, Czech Republic, Slovenia, Slovakia, Russia, Hungary, Ukraine, Turkey, Greece, and Israel. 48 nations on 5 Continents and it is spreading out to other places. [International Federation of American Football (IFAF) - ifaf. org]. Around the world, the game is gaining ground with a future goal of becoming prevalent like ice hockey. There are hockey squads right now in places, one would not normally think of - such as parts of Africa, South America, Mexico, etc.

Mekkar is convinced that fans in certain areas of the planet are different from the rest of the world in their preferences of many sports. He feels that in North America some are more drawn to games as spectators with higher scoring like indoor soccer, arena or indoor football, etc. in addition to their natural counterparts. In many other places, those modified athletic events wouldn't fly or draw well. He attributes it to having less appreciation for exceptional defense with the exception of ice hockey in Canada.

The Native from the Far North routinely points out that all sports for viewers are another form of entertainment, a distraction to venture out to the movie theatre. The Romans and many cultures of the past have used diversions to subtlety make their population more docile and easier to control. Mekkar believes that if an individual's fanaticism becomes an overwhelming distraction to their life survival occupation; then, other additional healthy alternatives are needed.

In lower scoring sports turnovers and mistakes by participants are much more magnified. Even more so, in instances that can lead to an opposition score. Mekkar wisely chose not to focus on those negative aspects. Otherwise, he felt those potential outcomes might occur more frequently due to increased attention to them. That was something he wished to avoid. He did not want to become ridiculously superstitious like many athletes, especially with regard to hockey netminders.

He felt fortunate to have played, in his judgment, as part of the golden age of hockey. Mekkar narrowed the time frame to the mid nineteen sixties to the early part of the nineteen eighties. The minor believes it was a time when there was more experimentation in sports, individuals, cultures, and life itself throughout the world. To him it just seemed like it was more real with more human interaction. In the nineteen fifties fans could still meet the favorite major league athletes face to face, and without as much obstruction, before a game or match. But, the times were changing in rapid order. This has now transitioned into something altogether different in our own individually isolated current time. Maybe, Mekkar is being nostalgic or reflective of an era that is gone, forever.

Free agency in pro sports had its beginnings in the nineteen-seventies. In Mekkar's own sport hockey, there was time lag before it was swamped by the big money machine and corporate influence we see today. Before all era of great change, most athletes just appeared to Mekkar as more genuine & friendly in those days gone by. The Native from the North considers there were more changes during that time period than any twenty-year period in history. Innovation was not restricted to technology alone. He speculated that people were more in touch with their environment around them. Well, except for politicians and bureaucrats - who are always out of touch with all reality. Now people just don't care, because they are so wrapped up in their own little world more than ever before. It doesn't matter if it is a right or wrong, it matters only how Mekkar sees it.

Top-notch athletic pursuits & leagues, with radical adjustments, grew at unprecedented levels from nineteen-sixty to nineteen eighty. A stodgy, rigid atmosphere that was screaming for transformation. The old way was dead and the stranglehold of the status quo was bursting at the seams. Convinced by these signs, the Arctic Warrior feels that current twenty first century life is just a shadow of its former self. The one big question Mekkar asks is, "Where is the loyalty?" His answer is, "There is none anymore, anywhere."

Mekkar realizes the settings are not the same anymore. Unfortunately, the hands of time cannot be turned back. In his self-absorbed mind, all things appear to be tainted in today's world. However, he is unsure to what degree. Mekkar, now places most present professional athletes on comparable ground with politicians. The overwhelming attitude of give me what is mine and unrelatability to their supporters. It actually ticks him off and teases him with the desire to punch them, one-by-one, in the snout. The same maniacal reaction as when encountering a bear at the backdoor steps back home. Mekkar does not think the information age, advanced civilization as a whole. At least, nowhere near as much as the mainstream media wants the people to believe. His conviction is that in many areas society has actually regressed since nineteen eighty. The underbelly of hate and distrust had bubbled over into all areas of society. Sometimes used, by those in charge, to sway public opinion.

The lad from the Far North has a sense that today the essence is different; a needed element is definitely missing. Yet, he is can't put his finger on what it exactly is. His interpretation is it could many things but people seemed to be more real and less pretentious to him back then. It is possible that Mekkar's influenced viewpoints were instilled by elders and adults that grew up in a different time. A very unimaginative, predicable surroundings of the post World War II time period. In some ways, a hidden innocence existed, very much unlike today. The native blood flowing through Mekkar determined that he was too close lineage-wise to the old way. In contrast, he was currently in the growth process of forming his character in what he calls, "The Breakout Age".

Back then, most of the time an individual normally was on a first name basis with most of their neighbors', where they lived. In Mekkar's twisted observation, today's neighborhood community interaction has changed immensely. Nowadays, Mekkar's main question is, "Who can you trust?" His answer is a select few individuals and they could fall away from being a priority in his book.

He examines whether this state of affairs could be the result of the super disinteraction and depersonalization of further advancing high technology. Mekkar is under the impression that all forms of communication attempt to belittle people. A dumbing-down of society, if you will [Many Books & Sources]. Through convincing them to individually concentrate on more superficial and disengaging pursuits; while missing out on the true enjoyments of life. The young native analyzes it as an underhanded plot carried out through the methodical use of isolate, divide, and conquer. He has stated out loud that he is convinced the activity is for the purpose of complete control of the masses. Perhaps these beliefs are due to Mekkar's young age at this point and his view of the world at large during his teenage years. There might be something to an alternative perspective. Still, what teen doesn't have an aversion to all types of authority and authority figures? Think of who makes the rules!

Currently, Mekkar concludes that everything, everywhere is so over the top and in your face all of the time. There is no sense of mystery regarding much anymore. Mekkar, as he normally does, has termed it as, "We live in The Age of Hype and Drama." He believes there is an intentional directive carried out by a controlled media, with an agenda, to shape perceptions in young people's minds like his. Those with dominion and clout portray many things as glamorous and attainable for anyone regardless of social status. The truth realized by Mekkar is that the reverse is the case. Many matters are not nearly as enchanting for a great majority of the population but only for a select few of the silver spooners as Mekkar calls them. Another inquiry of his - is who does the selecting?

Often, Mekkar has a definite reaction when sees or hears any advertisement for any product or service. He will usually flip a vulgar gesture and audibly call out the lies, as he hears them, while directing his comments toward the intended target. Mekkar has not been blind to the growth disparity between the common individual and the super wealthy. The Arctic Warrior notices the ongoing robbery prevalent in cultures worldwide and the continuing increase in the wealth gap on a daily basis. Mekkar notices a prevailing trend in his time that matches what has occurred throughout the history of mankind. The scale is clearly unmistakable and the gulfs of social class, as well as status are growing more divided as time goes on. [Nineteen Eighty-Four by George Orwell, 1949]

Due to his native status and appearance, Mekkar is considered to be from a lower echelon on the social caste ladder system. This is even more so, in the larger cities down south, where he is considered similar to a country bumpkin. The daily struggle within Mekkar affects every part of his being. Still, he is aware of the interconnectedness of it all despite living in a contrary manner. Society and life as Mekkar knew it has changed far too much, as well as modifying his own personal nature, and it will never be the same again. He is quite aware that the clock of time can never be turned back.

Yet, as he has hopefully grown up somewhat to discourage reverting back to his more childish viewpoints. The wide array of exposure to many things seen and done, in his young life, has altered him much more than he believes. Not to forget, it is assumed that people will live longer than ever before. Thus, more time to affect more change. In some instances this is considered as progression, more mature, and beneficial. At other times, it creates a raging situation of inner conflict that is difficult to resolve and a potential identity crisis that could affect Mekkar forever.

World Wide Hockey Tour – Houston

The upcoming hockey tour marked the first time Mekkar and his younger brother Alf got to play together on the same team. That is, on a national level and in a formal manner outside of the village setting. It was mainly because of the age gap because Alf was about three and a half years younger than his older sibling.

Since Alf was large enough size-wise and skilled enough talent-wise he was an exception. Thus, the reason why he also usually participated with the older kids, along with Mekkar's group, back home. Alf was very used to being one of the youngest, if not the most youthful, on any team he played for. Mekkar joked that his brother was just following in his footsteps in that regard, but it was far from the truth.

Now, Mekkar would get the chance along with some of his teammates to haze the rookie Alf in a team environment to introduce him to the fold. One of the tasks was that the younger players and definitely first year rookies on the squad had to load and unload as well as carry hockey equipment bags of teammates. To and from the buses, trains, autos, hotel rooms, and arenas on behalf of veteran players. It was all part of the initiation process and must be done to be one of the guys. All players have had to go through this process and it was easier than on some other squads.

To avoid or not participate in it was career suicide and the individual would be labeled as not a team player or worse, a troublemaker. Those unagreeable individuals would be ostracized and end up mostly by themselves. Few other players would want to interact with them or be associated with the extreme rebellious ones.

Some coaches would go even further and reduce that particular athletes' playing time. Many would cut them outright, remove them, or attempted to remove that person altogether, through a trade if possible. It was like dealing with a cancer in the skipper's mind and they want to use a proverbial scalpel to cut it out and remove it. Remember, most bench generals at that time were former players too! All respect for the unwilling participant to go along with the program would also be lost for good. Normally, that player would "hit the glass" (ceiling) and fail to move further upward to a higher level as a player. To avoid any issues, Alf chose to conform to the peer pressure and go along with the prescribed plan. Plus, he has an easy going disposition anyway.

It is important to note that Mekkar was not stupid and would use his intelligence to take advantage of this hierarchy of duty assignments. Even better still, The Arctic native would always have Alf sharpen his skates. The blades of Mekkar' two fighting sticks also. Mekkar figured why should his younger brother's talents be wasted. Plus, Alf was much better, in comparison, at this task than the Arctic Warrior. Alf was mechanical at his core and had a lot of practice at developing these particular skills back in the village. Requirements, such as these, were even placed upon Alf by his older brother. It was seen as a privilege to hang out and play games with the older gang, Mekkar's buddies.

In attending to his role as the older guardian brother, Mekkar felt that Alf was getting an easy time of it on this squad. Well, as compared to some of the hazing rituals Mekkar had to endure in other locales and teams. Mekkar pondered back on some clubs' past initiation customs. One started with being overpowered by a number of his new teammates. Then, being held down and tied to one of the locker room benches. Next, the Native from the North had all of the hair on his body completely shaved off. Boy, Mekkar flashed back in his mind, and remembered that he itched like crazy all over for awhile. At least, until all of the hair grew back. It was a good thing; at that time that Mekkar was younger then and had a lot less body hair. Either way he felt it grew back way too slowly, especially down below. Yet, right before being held down Mekkar got in some good shots of his own and a few teammates sported black eyes. It was no big deal because facial cuts and wounds are considered as normal to most hockey players. Injuries are seen as positive injuries to be bragged about and also receive sympathy from admiring girls.

Some past personal ordeals and experiences were the reason Mekkar refused to engage in many actual initial physical trials with regard to newcomers. Instead in his cockiness, the Arctic Warrior thought he was too smart to occupy himself in the physical side. Alf and Lasse have a term for it – arrogance. As a substitute, Mekkar would conduct mental and psychological warfare with the rookies because he enjoyed it.

The Native Son from the North wanted to save his brand of dishing out physical damage to be directed at opponents during games. Mekkar's thinking was that you don't hurt your own side, but unleash in all ways possible send the nastiness towards your real enemy - the opposition. He decided that the other side should always be the ultimate objects of his wrath. In furious tirades of berserker-like rage, at times Mekkar would forget this self made rule and directed his rage at fellow cohorts as well. It is often called - Passion for the Game - as he referred to it. However, many times on the ice, Mekkar crossed the fine line between madness and the usual routine.

Mekkar was always of the mindset that if you do not like the other team's excessive and over the top glory performances after scoring, then do something about it. Take matters into your own hands and stop them. Leave them defeated them on the scoreboard too! Mekkar is of the belief that only losers and the double-edged sword media complain about trivial matters such as these. The Arctic Warrior has said on a few occasions, "If you want to shut someone up, kick their butt during the game, but in a much harsher tone. If you get to physically punish your opponent, even better. But, no whining about it!" Otherwise, Mekkar is convinced that the winners should get to celebrate their success and victories anyway they want.

Unlike most people, he admires the nineteen eighties and nineteen nineties Miami Hurricanes football team celebrations and on the field end zone touchdown antics. The accomplishments were earned during the game. They deserve to celebrate them. Added to that, Mekkar knew some individuals who attended Miami school during that run. He asserts, "Forget cultural norms of not being offensive. If you don't like it, do something about it or shut your trap and go away!" Mekkar's attitude is diametrically opposed to today's cultural environment of not offending anyone. The Far North Native believes Political Correctness has a damaging effect on the culture. Also, he is diametrically opposed to that way of thinking because it restricts freedom. Games on the ice were one place where Mekkar experienced a degree of independence. He is of the opinion that this PC issue is used for control of the people, by certain interests.

The minor grew up and played sports in an era where there was little buddying up or friendly interaction with the opposition. That applied during a game or at the playing venue and to relatives as well. The discussions in those cases could begin at home or in a different location away from where the match was played. Yet, chirping and ribbing was allowed between them.

Mekkar has seen changes which are due to constant athlete movement in all sports. In his opinion, these practices, in conjunction with the media, have fostered an environment of false solidarity. It has been forwarded through the use of selected images and projected a certain picture to the masses. All forms of the communication industry have developed a fractious opposition struggle and climate of ideals; In Mekkar's inclination, that is of the worker athlete versus management and still another group - sports fans. He feels this is deceptive and done on purpose to create an illusion for a hidden purpose and agenda. Only, Mekkar is unaware of the who is behind it and what is the payoff for them.

Along with some of his Selects teammates, Mekkar was pumped up and raring to go after they got some rest on the long flight. Yet, as they would discover it wasn't nearly enough recovery time from the jet lag. Sleeping on an airplane is not the same. Plus, it wasn't even a charter flight this time. Due to previously working some in the travel industry, Mekkar knew that general rule for body adjustment purposes was a day of rest for every three time zones travelled. The team had crossed quite a few time zones on this journey. On the other hand, many know how boys are, restless!

The team had arrived a couple of days early for the scheduled game. Johan mentioned that he saw a movie house nearby as their bus approached their hotel from the airport. Since it was still early enough in the daylight the coaches ordered all players to rest for a specific amount of time before the team meal.

Some of them began to make plans to circumvent the evening curfew and escape in the evening. They want to get out and get away even if it was just to watch a movie at the little theatre that Johan spoke about on the bus. Mekkar was definitely part of the plotting group. He thought what harm could it be to go see a film. It's not like they were going to cause a raucous or any trouble, right?

After the required team imposed rest period and function Mekkar, Lasse, Alf, and Johan all sneaked out and walked a short distance to the cinema house. Mekkar had learned from his earlier research prior to the trip that Houston had questionable areas. He remembered statements made by former heavyweight boxing champion George Foreman about rough neighborhoods there. [Sports Illustrated; various TV interviews] Fortunately for these four newcomers to this area this was not one of the places to avoid. Even when they heard an ambulance siren on their foot travel, they were not worried at all.

As they approached the theatre they all noticed on the offerings board the martial arts movie Enter The Dragon starring Bruce Lee would start in about ten minutes. This movie house was kind of older and appeared to Mekkar to run aged movies at a lesser ticket cost. It definitely wasn't one of those monster sized eighteen theatre complexes they have in the suburbs today. All four members of the team bought their tickets and went inside to purchase the goodies that one consumes at the movies – popcorn, drinks, etc.

Mekkar noticed thing that was radically different from home. At the snack bar, popcorn at home has choices with additional toppings offered such as various grated cheeses that they could not get here. Oh, well the joys of travelling Mekkar thought to himself.

The four young men chose and were glad to watch this movie selection. There was also an unhappiness that no other teammates came along with them on this excursion. Mekkar guessed the no shows might have gotten bored with the lack of selections and would have made it harder to have a good time out together. "Their loss," quipped Mekkar.

Mekkar, Lasse, Alf, and Johan were the only members on The Selects roster to be involved in any martial arts as actual students. Plus, each of them were already big Bruce Lee fans and had seen some of his other films back home. Some that were made in China and displayed the subtitles across the bottom of the screen so the people could understand the dialog. They all loved the butt kicking action. Mekkar was aware that the plots were not the greatest, but he didn't care. He had a feeling that he might hand out some butt whipping of his own during games on this tour. Thus, the influences for their film choice.

Alf was the exception among them as he had an advantage of understanding a portion of the dialog in those foreign martial arts movies from Asia when they played at home. Mekkar's younger brother had already learned Japanese and was learning Cantonese Chinese in which he would later become fluent in. At this point it was as a result of Sirga's accelerated language learning program for him. As with each of the boys it was done for the benefit of the family business. This was just a small part of Alf's eventual impressive array of languages topping the twenty five tongue plateau. Alf would just pick them up like he had a knack for it comparable to his mechanical ability. Mekkar said, "Alf absorbs languages like we drink water."

While waiting in line near the snack bar counter to get treats for the movie, they were commenting and debating amongst themselves. The topic was Who was The Man. The other patrons there were unable to decipher what each were saying because they were not conversing in English. Mekkar switched to English as he reached the counter as to be understood for the order of the items desired. He was chosen because his English speaking skills were better than anyone else in their group as well as having the most confidence in those skills. After receiving and paying for the items the conversion hovered back to the subject in their own tongue.

"Bruce is the man," one of them would say. Mekkar pointed out that back in the village James Bond was the man all the boys wanted to be when they grew up. For Mekkar it was the 007 character played by Sean Connery. All four of them distinguished that Bond was still a fictional film icon while Lee was at one time live in the flesh.

Lasse, Mekkar, and Alf were all involved in the same local dojo back home, while Johan was part of a small city club much further south. As students of the defense and combat arts the four hockey players could really appreciate the athleticism, fluidity, lightning fast speed, and power generated by Bruce Lee. Alf was the youngest of their group but was by far the better martial artist among them. Alf spent the most time honing his skills in the various disciplines and the craft. Mekkar's younger brother liked Lee's training and method of using the best of many styles to mix and adapt them to his strengths. This was similar to Mekkar's view that there were team benefits to the mixing of hockey players, multiple styles, and systems of that time.

It encouraged Mekkar as he felt emboldened like hey, if a little guy like Lee could take on larger people and kick their rear ends when necessary, why couldn't he? Of course, Mekkar realized that Bruce was in a class all by himself. Lee was an innovator and might never be matched in the combat arts realm.

Nonetheless, Bruce in his films provided some additional inspiration to Mekkar in regard to overcoming his lack of imposing physical structure and size to make great impact anyway. Mekkar also referred to him as, "The Bruce man," as he called him admiringly, "Probably hasn't encountered a pack of wolves or a polar bear too close for safety's sake." Well, in this one area, Mekkar thought in a humorous way, that he an advantage over the out of this world Lee in his realm. Each of the four in that crew at the movie house continues to love and enjoy good action martial arts films ever since, plots and speaking be damned.

During next day and in the span before The Selects match against the home team at the Summit arena, the Aeros has a surprise activity awaiting their tour guests. The hosts invited The Selects team members to join them to attend a major league baseball game at the Astrodome.

The Astrodome was the first multi-purpose dome stadium in existence when it opened in nineteen sixty five. Approximately a decade before other early domed facilities such as the Superdome in New Orleans or the Kingdome in Seattle. The Astrodome was nicknamed The Eighth Wonder of the World as it was one of a kind at the time it was built. Now, it is empty and houses almost no sports - probably just rats, Mekkar figured. [Wikipedia]

Mekkar was familiar with baseball because he had been forced to watch many tapes and films. He did this along with other sports as part of his mama's plan for him to learn the english language. Plus, Mekkar had previously played similar games like pesäpallo, rounders, and over-the-line. So, attending this game would not be a total foreign experience to him.

The Aeros and Selects players sat in a section designated for them down near the field level. Undoubtedly, the Selects players enjoyed the various snacks and beverages mobile vendors would bring by during the game. Unknown to Mekkar, many of his teammates had never been to a live baseball game before.

As Mekkar was trying to find his seat he blurted out the comment to one of the home team players, "You know that this doesn't change the fact that you are still the enemy come game time tomorrow." On of the Houston players' responded back, "That is tomorrow, just sit back and relax and enjoy today's game as our guest." That particular home team player was there with other members of their family to enjoy the day off. Since, it is a rarity during the long season.

Native from north Mekkar was enthralled by the indoor playing area and soaked up the atmosphere of the place along with the game as well. It was good thing that Mekkar had brought his binoculars, as he usually does, to see things more close up. He just thought that the hometown Houston Astros Rainbow, Tequila Sunrise uniforms with the multi-colored stripes were the coolest things. [Wikipedia]

He is a sports fan in general and welcomed colorful items and clothing. Mekkar has the concept of if you just want just black without color in everything, like the trend is going in today's sports world, just revert yourself back to the nineteen fifties and before. Similar to the period before the advent of color television.

The visiting teen hockey player doesn't remember who won the baseball game or even who the opponent was and didn't care. He did get to have some interaction and converse with each of the Howe's - Mark, Marty, and Mr. Hockey Gordie. That itself was the highlight of Mekkar's day. Mekkar had got wind that there was supposed to be an evening meal with both teams together later that day, but it never materialized. That was okay because some of the Selects' team members had consumed too much of the ballpark goodies. A copious amount beyond what was beneficial for their own good. Those same individuals paid for it later.

Suspicious in his nature as he was, Mekkar thought that maybe the whole thing might be a tactic used by their opponent. Not only to soften the Selects' players up but also to distract them. This in turn, would affect the upcoming match. Mekkar unwittingly made his thoughts regarding this matter audibly known to others around him. This was by the way a regular unconscious habit of his.

Some of the squad hung out together in one of the hotel rooms that evening after arriving back from the ballpark. During the banter when Alf heard his older brother's incredulous comments, he rebuked Mekkar. The reply was, "We are not in Eastern Europe behind the Iron Curtain you paranoid, unappreciative oaf!" Mekkar gathered Alf was probably right. Yet, he wouldn't admit it outwardly as to not lose face. Definitely not in front of the team.

On the bus ride from the hotel to the arena a couple of hours prior to faceoff, Mekkar noticed that a couple of his teammates looked lethargic. It seemed to him like they had the flu or something related. So, Mekkar decided to move over to sit by the goalies as they might be more alert. Mekkar figured that they would need to be more awake if a lot of high speed vulcanized rubber was about to be blasted at them. Since netminders are normally so superstitious, he calculated their other worldly aura might separate him. That is, whatever was affecting the sluggish ones he saw on the bus.

Mekkar went through his common pre game routine and it was not long to game time. He started to get revved up. He also grasped that the Aeros were a veteran team with a championship pedigree. Early in the match he foresaw that this was going to be game involving a lot of speed and skating along with quick puck movement. He also supposed there was to be minimal plodding, grinding, bulliness, and thuggery on the ice that night. Some of the Selects' players had pre-notions, expectations, and assumptions of a North American goonish style they would face before the game began. The Aeros could bring the wood or the pummeling if they had to but it was not necessary for this matchup. This was a definite relief to Mekkar.

In the beginning, the pace of the game turned out faster than what a few of the Selects' team members were used to. The smaller rink dimensions, as compared to an international ice surface, also added to early perceptions that made it seem quicker. Not only that, there were fewer stoppages in the action. Mekkar discovered his pre-tour research that Houston was probably one of the top squads the Selects would encounter on this schedule.

Every time Mekkar kept chipping the puck off of the wall out of his own zone, it seemed to come back almost as rapidly. No matter how often he would head-man the puck forward or sent a crisp tape-to-tape pass ahead to a teammate, the biscuit repeatedly returned. Out to center ice and further just to withstand another onslaught.

He was busy in his defensive responsibilities inside the Selects' own blue all night. The only breaks he received was during the shift changes that brought him to the bench then back out again for some more. Mekkar was feeling frustrated at this situation because he sensed the pace of the game was picking up at an increasing rate. The native boy asked himself a question, "Do these guys ever get tired? They appear to get stronger as the game has gone along." Mekkar was beginning to believe that this is how it is with the top pros in the world. He identified the standards required to be consistent at this high level, up close and personal.

The Aeros were dominant in the face off circle in this game. It also appeared to Mekkar that the Selects were out there chasing them and the puck everywhere on the ice all night long. The Native from the North instinctively knew that when he is behind trying to catch up to an opponent there are certain infractions referees are looking for. Thus, he wants to use other ways to slow them down such as body checks or better positioning.

Mekkar has a philosophy regarding when a team wins draws in their offensive end of the rink. It is much easier to set up plays. Yes, they do have set plays in hockey just like basketball, indoor soccer, and other sports. This makes it possible for better scoring chances and quick shots on a rival's net. However, when a squad loses face-offs in your own zone these same factors work against you. It is all a matter of controlling the puck and possession, which means you direct and dictate the action during the game. The club that keeps the puck the most normally is the winner.

For comparisons sake, as in soccer the team that has the most possession of the ball usually wins the game. That is unless your team's defense and goaltending really stinks. These strategies and styles are what make the Soviet and some club teams in Europe so successful and dangerous. When a squad or anything has mastery over another they typically mandate many variables to the other side.

During a forwards only, not the whole five man unit (excluding the goalie) line change on the fly, Mekkar followed the play and charged straight ahead. He continued despite his warped sense of timing was off by a second or more. Mekkar was in attack mode like a heat seeking missile searching for its target. He went much further deep into the offense zone than he should have and now the defenseman became a forechecker. He chugged along and had picked up his pace. The Arctic Warrior Mekkar saw a Houston player along the boards behind the backline still with the rubber disc at their feet. Mekkar thought he would be tenacious and take this opportunity to try to check that player hard into the wall. It was in retaliation from an earlier hit where the hometown athlete said, "You set your sights on our players, and you will pay the price." Mekkar was focused on making his opponent feel the crunch of glass. What happened instead was that the Aeros' player raised his elbow and The Arctic Warrior received a collision of his own. He ended up leading with his face into the elbow bone breaking his nose instantly.

With blood streaming out of his nose and mouth as well as his blackened eyes watering up Mekkar skated back to his side's bench area in shame. Alf then blasted his older sibling with a number of comments. One of them that Mekkar's little brother fired off and many Selects players heard was, "You are an idiot. You have watched the films a number of times and you forgot about the prominent elbows? Since you didn't seem to pay attention and learn your lesson, you got exactly what you deserve."

The home crowd fans heard the comments also but they probably were unable to decipher the meaning since the words in the Selects' team speech and not in english. Many on the team there just cracked up laughing until the coaches admonished them, "That is enough. Keep your mind in the game." A few of them on the bench figured that the crowd would be laughing with them, if they could understand.

After Alf's criticism Mekkar went to the dressing room to have treatment on his upper body injury. When he came back to his team's side not long afterward, Mekkar remained incensed at Alf. Now Mekkar was looking a chance at payback or redemption of any kind.

Some shifts later, Mekkar was back on the ice at the same time as the Houston player that had broken his nose. Mekkar caught him unaware this time and got his retribution with a downward chopping motion hard slash of the ankle with his stick. That retaliation on Mekkar's part not surprisingly got him sent to the sin bin and he received a game misconduct penalty. Thus, his night was over and Mekkar concluded with a trip back to the locker room. The target of Mekkar's nasty display of frustration was now extra motivated and hurt the Selects where it counted most, on the scoreboard. The Aeros' team member potted two goals himself after Mekkar had been ejected from the match.

What saved the Selects from great embarrassment of being blown out that evening was the travelling team's goalie made fifty six saves. However, Mekkar's team was still on the wrong end of a four-two score in favor of the home side. Some nights you have it and some you don't! Well, Mekkar knew it was not the thrill of victory, but the agony of defeat. [Jim McKay; Stanley Ralph Ross, ABC's Wide World of Sports! 1970] What a way to start this tour thought Mekkar. He just hoped the rest of this slate of games was different or he was in for a long trip.

World Wide Hockey Tour - Saint Paul

Before this matchup against the Fighting Saints, the Selects had participated in a few other games such as a 5-2 victory over the Birmingham Bulls. That game gave Mekkar some fisticuff headaches for defending his teammates. The next one was a 4-3 score, in the Selects favor, against the Cincinnati Stingers. In that tilt, The Native from the North won a tussle against a now well-known TV hockey analyst – who has a far different image today. Of course, the self claimed World-Wide Leader in Sports Television neglects to mention anything regarding hockey player service in the World Hockey Association. Today, NHL avoids anything WHA like the plague, even to the point of stripping all in their 1979 merger. All despite, the WHA teams won the series vs. NHL teams 34-22-7. [whahockey.com/whavsnhl.html] Hey, the NBA accepts ABA stats and experience.

In Mekkar's different from the norm thinking, the National Hockey League should be ashamed of their bad behavior. But, who is the Arctic Warrior to judge. However, Mekkar highly dislikes any double-standards of any kind. In addition, no one was eager to get Mekkar going regarding the Hockey Hall of Fame selection process. The last undertaking before arriving in Minnesota, the travelling team lost an uneventful game versus the Indianapolis Racers & their boisterous crowd 2-5. The Selects were looking tired and were thoroughly outskated that evening.

As per his normal routine on a game day, Mekkar usually like to ponder the opponent. Their strengths, weaknesses, and possible strategy for a bit. After the last few matches on this journey of the North American continent facing off against a host of widely different squads, Mekkar routine would be interrupted. The ritual would have to be changed on this particular day since he just wanted to enjoy some extra rest instead.

The teenager was young and in tip-top physical condition with about three and a half percent body fat content just like his papa. But, he was playing for his fourth different team within the last eighteen months or so combined with a full slate of games for each squad. It was an equivalent of two full seasons worth of matches along with the maximum compliment of playoff tilts crammed into that time frame. Mekkar had gone non-stop for that whole time with no break from injuries either. At this point during games, the Arctic Warrior's mind began to wander more often due to fatigue. Sometimes, it became noticeable especially in the third period.

A state of fatigue can result in more mental and positioning awareness mistakes on the ice. Which contributes to more physical affliction and errors that could cost his team victories at the same time. Maybe it was that brutally, punishing match against Birmingham that occurred earlier on this tour, Mekkar thought to himself. Mekkar was trying as hard as he could to rationalize his tiredness away, but he knew the truth. He could just not accept the fact the real reason why exhaustion was setting in but it was obvious to others on the team. However, stubborn to a fault Mekkar still refused to admit it. After all he was a hockey player and nearly indestructible as his deceived mind told him.

Later on, when the Selects exited the transport that brought them from their lodging to the rink, Mekkar went straight away to check out the ice surface. It was his general custom upon arriving at an arena, especially ones he had never visited before, prior to a match. It was then that he remembered his inquiry that he conducted back home poring over various written materials such as The Hockey News, etc. Prior to this barn-storming tour his study and research included any information that he could gather. It included anything odd or peculiar about the opponents he would encounter on this trip – teams, arenas, leagues, fans, and more.

All of sudden there was a sense of dread on the part of Mekkar about this evening. He thought back to the ancient Romans and how his team could be more meat fed to the hungry lions. Mekkar thought silently, here we go again. He speculated that he, along with his team were in for another long night.

A few games before, the Selects team had been terrorized by a virtual goon squad as one of Mekkar's teammates put it. Mekkar recalled that the home fans of the (Birmingham) Bulls loved every minute of it. That earlier opponent tried every tactic in the book to intimidate Mekkar's squad and they pretty much accomplished that goal. It was a style adopted with other teams in their own league as well, plus it helped to fill the stands. In the past that approach was used against other touring international touring clubs, like the Selects, that previously visited North America. Despite the scoreboard, the Bulls conducted themselves in the same manner when they went overseas too!

The Selects' earlier adversaries in Birmingham had been designed and built for their fans' tastes. The paying customers in football country loved the violence and quickly adopted the team and ventured to the rink there to get their evenings fill. [billsportsmaps.com; hockeyfights.com] Mekkar felt that was probably an indicator of a similar scenario waiting here in the capital of Minnesota, as well. [Wikipedia; billsportsmaps.com]

After the required morning skate by the coaching staff, Mekkar wanted to get his midday meal finished quickly. His plan was to get back to the hotel a little bit earlier and catch up on some extra quick recharging rest. He wanted to be on his A-game both physically and mentally, but even more so pugilistically this night. Just in case it would be needed come game time that evening.

Mekkar was one of the players expected to help prevent manhandling of his more highly skilled teammates. Even due to his lack of size he could fight like a beast. The Arctic Warrior has whipped adversaries in scraps three times his size, when necessary. A test as part of the regimen for Mekkar was putting his fist through various objects like bone. Lasse, Alf, and some other buddies and fellow teammates back home were witnesses to this display. However, the punching prowess paled in comparison to the non-stop, unforgiving flow from Mekkar's mouth.

So, Mekkar had the ability to defend those Selects team members from paying the price toll that could be extracted from them during a game. However, the question was regarding desire of whether The Native from The North wanted to accept physical punishment on his part. Mekkar was aware of this too when he stated prior to the match that night, "Guess who's going to get stuck with the bill of sticking up for these guys?" Mekkar knew that part of the fighting currency would be paid by him and few others on the squad. Thus, Mekkar resigned himself to prepare for the upcoming pugilistics, he saw in his mind.

There was an odd observation by Mekkar upon seeing the rink despite reading about it before. It now dawned on him right there. There were see-through clear glass dasher boards around the rink all the way down to the ice surface. Well, there was a white stripe around the outside of each piece. It was one of a kind and it made it easier for those fans to follow the play close up. The boards were designed to help visualize the puck in play due to the arena's roundish structure. [Wikipedia; thirdstringgoalie.blogspot.com] Well, that is how Mekkar interpretated in his mind after curiously asking one of the individuals employed there.

During his previous reading beforehand, he had seen some photos of this unique aspect of the place. By what he heard and investigated the constructed clear boards did not exist anywhere else in the world.

Later on that night Mekkar would get a firsthand connection with those one-of-a-kind rink boards by having his head driven into them on a number of occasions. Of course, no boarding penalty was called during the matchup. It was a case of the parable if you live by the sword you die by it also. Mekkar was very familiar with that.

During the game day walk-through, Mekkar anticipated two potential problems due to this particular feature. One that he never encountered before. Mekkar would eventually play hockey in some weird environments around the globe on this journey. One issue he considered was that if the fans in the first rows wore dark colored pants, shoes, and socks in some combination the clear boards might create slight visual issues. Potential depth perception problems in conjunction with a dark color puck. Especially if Mekkar was across the ice and moving toward it.

Added to the fact that Mekkar had inherited partial color blindness from his father Henrik. His papa was completely color blind. Mekkar only had trouble distinguishing between black and dark navy blue or something close with very dark aspects as part of the color spectrum. The slight shades in differences reflected in clothing are the most difficult for him. Fortunately, his mama Sirga was a model and was extremely fashion conscious.

Mekkar was surprised that she didn't play pranks on either him or Henrik regarding this. But she was not the mischievous type; she was too straight forward for that. Mekkar did try to hide this flaw from his own teammates, but Lasse & Alf knew better. So, Mekkar bribed both of them to not make light of his somewhat color blindness. Mekkar feared that it might cut into his playing time determined by the coaches for matches. This was especially true in the case of tonight in a rink of clear glass.

Then, Mekkar remembered the World Hockey Association's innovation in the use of a blue colored puck. [whahockey.com] He was hoping for this night's game they would insert it because it would help the vision problem and make it easier to deal with. The youngster still felt this whole issue would be difficult to deal with during the game.

The second potential problem that Mekkar noticed was the clear boards could give the perception to players on his team that the ice surface was smaller than it really was. He felt it appeared smaller than the normal standard in North America which was already dimension-wise more cramped than rinks back home. The common international ice surface, and also used in the Olympic Games, was about 20 feet wider. Mekkar had distinguished the positioning required for each set of circumstances.

To double-check his perception Mekkar spoke to a couple of the arena maintenance employees. He asked if the rink was actual regulation size for the continent and each responded that it was.

However, he was not convinced and his suspicious nature wasn't buying it. This questioning everything aspect of his personality would continue to grow more prevalent as he got older. Now he trusts his own instincts and gut feeling over anyone's claims, opinions, and so called expertise regarding just about everything. It is even more skeptical when he is familiar with a particular subject or issue. There are very few examples where his opinions can be greatly changed by another person; But, only unless he knew that individual very well and trusted them, which is a rare thing for him. Mekkar's attitude in the current day is I am wrong when I change my mind. [John Maynard Keynes, 1945; Paul Samuelson, 1970]

Since Mekkar has seen and participated in quote a lot of hockey so far in his young life, he was sticking with his initial instinct that had served him well up to this point. A couple of things contributed to this contrary perception by Mekkar about this rink. Today, the St. Paul Civic Center currently no longer exists. It was torn down and replaced by the newer fancier digs that are the current home of an NHL team residing there. [Wikipedia] Mekkar later on did see a part of that demolition and reconstruction process in person.

Anyway, Mekkar noticed the odd seating arrangement for improved fan viewership and enjoyment of the game. It is well to note that Mekkar already had some experience in club and facility management while at the same time as a player. This would expand in related enterprises in the future. So, he had a slight insight advantages regarding hockey and sports variances as he called it.

He was hopeful about the upcoming game in one area. The home side might act like this game was just an exhibition. However, the club struggled financially just like their counterparts across the Mississippi River in the south of the Twin Cities. Based on recent past experience with Birmingham, other drawbacks were possible. Mekkar thought that were was a much higher potential for increased goonery to draw in and please the paying customers. [whahockey.com; Wikipedia; Local media sources]

Mekkar was optimistic that this matchup wouldn't turn into the debacle that occurred in Birmingham, but realism got the best of him. He was aware that many teams are formed and built talent-wise to be ideally suited for their home arena and fan base. Mekkar would learn that like the Bulls, these fans didn't really care as much about wins as much as being entertained by the fights. Yet, the Saints usually had a winning record. [whahockey.com]

The Native from the True Far North was wishing that the home team was drawing fewer fans to their homes games, especially this one. To Mekkar it equated to a less fan based rowdiness and abuse of the visiting squad to deal with. He figured the less boisterous the fans, the less chance of becoming a pugilistic affair on the ice. Mekkar was wrong about this however because the crowd that did show up was the most hardcore of them. Added to fact that this matchup was a novelty game which usually meant that more patrons pass through the turnstiles. Larger attendance draws are normally recorded when tilts against international squads are on the docket.

During this era it was common for many professional hockey and sports clubs to rely on just there presence to bring in the fans to home matchups. It was nowhere like today with the hype and drama sports climate and unprecedented marketing campaigns. The old attitude resulted in a terrible local marketing strategy of throwing open the doors and expect the flock to just show up. A mistake of a high reliance of advertising and promotion was placed at the league level. This theme was even more acute in this grassroots hockey region. [Local media; The Hockey News]

Later hockey history of the area proved that was a flawed strategy and culminated in utter failure a few times. One example was the cheap ownership of the Minnesota North Stars who ended up leaving town. Just because a city, region, or nation has a strong support base at the lower echelons in any sport doesn't equal automatic success at the pro level. That is without an extreme amount of effort. Mekkar knows about this firsthand.

The emerging young man was informed enough to know that even many large corporations in many fields have declined in a big way or have lost market share. Some of those companies completely crashed outright or were taken over by rivals because the organization got fat, lazy, and happy. Mekkar was mindful that getting complacent and staying in one's own secure place by becoming very set in their ways of doing things is a dangerous place to be. Mekkar is of the belief that if you not going forward you are going backward, you just don't stay at a plateau for very long. [Confucius; Yo-Yo Ma]

Awhile ago one example would be International Business Machines (IBM or nicknamed Big Blue) comes to mind. It was well publicized that the corporate culture and behavior was in a manner of assured continued dominance in a particular industry. Being convinced that your business product or service will always be wanted by the public at the same level as before is not wise. The world expects some change and improvement. An environment that dismisses or does not consider any new ideas, possible positive changes are always stymied and make it very vulnerable.

A lack of forward-looking strategy results in inertia, which sets in so that anything different becomes almost non-existent there. By the time a wake up call is needed or when innovation or change is later required to still be profitable and thus stay on top of the market it might be too late. Action decisions are very slow or lacking altogether and any positive future outcome to change it is too little too late. Next step, an undesirable fall or decline begins.

On the highest level of the professional hockey industry the NHL dominated the scene. They suffered the same malaise prior to this era that the NFL and NBA did and a sports revolution emerged with challenges to the establishment. It would not be possible in today's climate. [Michael Murphy of the Houston Chronicle – The ABA Way; remembertheaba. com – Steve "Snapper" Jones comment] The National Hockey League never expected the WHA to be a threat or get started at all in the first place. They relied on their stranglehold and control of the major pro hockey field. They had always triumphantly beaten off all previous adversaries to its lofty heightened place atop the hockey realm in the past. [Wikipedia]

Like mighty empires and businesses that have long since past. The NHL ignored many of the trends of the upstart league at the time. The big boys on the block had become arrogant and suffered from Mekkar called cockiness disease. Most of the earlier contestants attempted little that was refreshing and new in comparison until the WHA came along. Very little seemed to have been learned from a recent threat from the Western Hockey League (1952–1974) in the late nineteen sixties that caused expansion into new markets as a response. [Wikipedia; Official Says Hockey Would Go Big Here aticle by Charles Curtis - Los Angeles Times, 1959]

Even though the young league (WHA) lasted less than a decade, the game of hockey and sports world in general was changed forever. Some rules and ideas that originated from these rival circuits during this period are still in use today in the big leagues many years later. [billsportsmap.com; Wikipedia; hockeyfights. com; whahockey.com; Playing Hockey the World Over - ... wha.htm]

After doing his homework before the tour and reading local media sources on the road, he would try to compare and confirm statements.

Mekkar was becoming educated by adopting a method of checking out multiple sources and making up his own mind. He was not just going to accept what one person said as fact. His parents installed into him the premise that reading and always learning something new make you smarter. The teen thought to himself when the new outfit attempted to put any of their franchises where there was already an established presence they failed miserably. The big brother in a particular city had it in its grasp already. The Minnesota capital was the only exception for a period of time but it did not last.

Big boy circuit (NHL) reaction to market penetration by the new guys through the granting and acceptance of expansion teams are not enough to ensure a viable product. Use of lawsuits by way of the crooked justice system failed. A tactic of hastily awarded expansion clubs in some cities to stem the tide did drive the rivals out of certain territories. It only flourished temporarily and rarely an advantageous long term solution. Mekkar thinks that doing things reactively because you have to instead of being proactive - never works in the long run.

The World Hockey Association (WHA) was determined to change the old way of conducting business and be progressive as well as innovative. The same people who were first behind this project were the same individuals that began another pro rival league (the American Basketball Association) a few years before. Eventually some of those clubs were merged into the well rooted loop. [Wikipedia] It was not all rosy because those individuals were less fortunate in a few other sports endeavors.

This duration in time was an era of cultural experimentation and the desire to try new avenues for most people. The exceptions to the forward moving mood were the firmly planted and entrenched big businesses and industries. Plus, government entities who are always resistant to change of any kind. The status quo always looks good to them if there is continual growth in their influence, scope, and power. The rebel league [Rebel League by Ed Willes] did much better and experienced more success as a crowd draw than expected. Especially in cities where there was no current, at that time, major league pro hockey franchises. In some cases no higher level pro clubs had existed for quite a while. Plus, the NHL itself was not planning on serving those markets either. [billsportsmaps.com; whahockey. com; Wikipedia]

Mekkar has a sports and other realm philosophy that is contrary to conventional wisdom. It is also in the spirit of American military general

George S. Patton. Mekkar states matter of factly, "Don't take what the defense gives you, and instead take what you want! How you want! Then, take it all on to victory!" Added to that concept he is also convinced that Sun Tzu's strategies are vastly overrated and out of touch with the modern world.

Anyway, that evening's match got underway and by its conclusion The Selects were handedly defeated six to three. Unfortunately, the Selects as a team failed to follow Mekkar's advice to dictate the temp of this game and lost. Afterwards, Mekkar felt like he was in a fog resulting from, what he believed was a continual slug fest. Him and Lasse were the only ones seeming to be always in the mix of combative battle scraps during the match against the likes of Jack and Steve Carlson, Dave Hanson, Gordie "Machine Gun" Gallant, Curt Brackenbury, Bill Butters, etc.

Even what Mekkar lacked in size in comparison to most players, he was a gamer and his heart was not ever questioned. His sanity was a different matter altogether. Mekkar concluded he held his own on a few occasions in the night's encounters and refused to be intimidated by any man unlike most of the Selects roster. Plus, he always felt that he had a punchers' chance because his paws could exert great force and do serious damage due to past training by him.

However, Mekkar took the worst of it in his last fight of the game for him. He got bloodied for his efforts on that one. By that time the score was pretty much decided in favor of the home side. Mainly because most of the Mekkar's team was thoroughly dispirited by the WHA's version of the Board Street Bullies - the Fighting Saints (Of course not including Birmingham), and the opponent's moniker fit perfectly. [Wikipedia; billsportsmaps.com; whahockey.com; markwilland.typepad.com/whablog/fights_and_brawls/index.html; hockey.ballparks.com/WHA/MinnesotaSaints/index.htm] Mekkar was of the opinion that the nasty nature of this game is the reason why the Selects got whipped as a team on this night.

In his last tussle Mekkar after wrestling for position while standing upright on his skates was unable to tie-up his fellow combatant's jersey or arms. The native youngster was slightly being pushed off-balance with the grab hand. In that instance, Gallant hit The Arctic Warrior so many times in rapid succession that it resembled a machine gun. Yes, it takes more energy and is harder than it looks to fight for prime position, balance, and throw fists at the same time. Plus, Mekkar was worn down near the end of the third period. This could be readily seen by some wild punches thrown by him that uncharacteristically missed the mark – the head of the opponent.

After the fracas was broken up on the ice by the linesman and referee, Mekkar struggled to get to his feet. Alf described it as kind of a wobbled or staggered stance as his older brother skated back to the bench with help. Then, The Native from The North also needed his teammates to help him to the Locker Room. Notwithstanding, even in the punch-drunk state he was in, Mekkar was still wanting to tango again, if necessary. He usually always was ready to go, that is to fight, brawl, etc. with anyone anywhere at a moments notice. A couple of his Selects' teammates and staff advised the stubborn Mekkar not to go back out and engage in another round of fista-cuffs. Expressly, since he got his butt handed to him in the last go around and hit the back of his helmeted head as both belligerents fell to the ice at the end of the scuffle. Mekkar's night was over as time soon ran out while he was in the locker room.

Maybe it was a good thing that the Selects mandated all of their non-goaltending skaters on this journey to wear helmets or the damage would have been much worse. Netminders have their own special equipment. The teenager normally played without a lid back home. Until later on when he finally got used to wearing it. His issue was that wearing a helmet could affect or even cut off one's peripheral vision on the ice.

Mekkar didn't remember much of the next couple of days until the next stop on the tour as his noggin throbbed non-stop. The teen was kept awake also even when he desired sleep. Alf, Lasse, and Johan tried to fill in most of the daily details until the Mekkar got many of his wits back.

The Far North Native would never admit to suffering concussions during his career and now pays the piper for that past attitude. Players in those days never told the coaches or management about head injuries that occurred. The athletes just wanted to play and anything that kept that from happening was not acceptable. Players even made swear packs between them, especially in the cases of Alf, Lasse, Mekkar, and Johan. None of them were to ever tattle on any of them or vice-versa. It didn't matter if one of the group recognized that something was definitely wrong and just not right mentally.

Concussions were only considered as just headaches back then. Their was a belief at the time that they were nothing that pain pills and alcohol couldn't cure. Mekkar says, "Or you just didn't care about it because you were buzzed." It was fitting the Fighting Saints were battling to stay alive. Their club eventually folded due to a lack of funds. [billsportsmaps.com; whahockey.com; Wikipedia]

World Wide Hockey Tour – Winnipeg

The Selects came into this game against the talent loaded WHA Winnipeg Jets on a two game losing streak. That put the travelling squad's record of two victories and three losses so far on this tour with a long way still to go. Anyway, it was still a better record than some hockey people, not associated with the Selects, expected. Most expected the barn-storming team to lose and lose badly all of their games up to this point. Plus, it is expected that Mekkar's team would pile up more defeats for their remaining matches versus the North American professional clubs they still would face.

Mekkar also noticed that when his team first arrived in the Manitoba province his team was pretty beat up physically. It was from the mugging they received in a couple of past matches so far. Mekkar suffered more during that last contest than most of his teammates.

However, he had been looking forward to being a part of this matchup. Mekkar was not about to miss his expected shift responsibilities in this game. Even despite the Selects' staff's desire to keep him from the lineup because of prior head trauma. As a result of having his head driven into the boards and punched repeatedly before this game.

The young arctic man wanted to observe the blending, as he called it, firsthand with his own eyes. He was there to judge for himself if this was the wave of the future and his own place in it. That is, facing off against a truly international team with players from a host of different nations. Mekkar had heard about its success in winning with this strategy. Still he alone in his mind could really determine if this mixing did work well in the real world. [Wikipedia; billsportsmaps.com; Playing Hockey The World Over... - wha.htm; whahockey.com] He was about to receive a definite answer to his questions that resounded inside his head. Yet, it would not be anything like he anticipated.

Due to late collapse in the second match before this one and the intimidating thrashing put on the Selects in the last one, the whole squad got blistered and reamed out by the head coach. He was merciless too, even including the netminders recent lacking performances. Mekkar disagreed with part of it and was of the opinion that the goalies had played much better than the rest of the squad as a whole. He just thought that they were under siege throughout and kept the games from being embarrassing blowouts as forecasted.

Mekkar deems that it is a good thing every so often for players to get called out by the coaching staff. Especially if the individuals are not executing up to par. Despite the common practice of carrying out criticism behind closed doors; Mekkar feels that if it has to be done in a public forum, so be it. To him this tactic should be done judiciously and should give incentives to strive for improved performance. Not only that, be a motivating factor to drive him and others to produce better on the ice in whatever area is needed.

That doesn't mean to say that he enjoys the method and does not guarantee he will not get ticked off about it. Usually to him, the normal procedure with the first step of handling the issue internally and at the team level has already been passed at that point. The public rebuke is the next level in the inducement progression because the previous strategy did not produce the tangible results desired.

He feels that the current coddling of these million dollar plus salaried athletes, excluding the money made from endorsements, wouldn't fly back in his day. There were only a few making a million dollars then. That would be Bobby Hull. He doesn't count the Derek Sanderson Philadelphia Blazers situation because it didn't last long enough. Mekkar was now trying to prepare to face The Golden Jet (Bobby Hull) in the next matchup.

The youngster is of the opinion that many of today's spoiled, wealthier, and increasing out of touch from the fans athletes have become softer mentally and psychologically. Don't forget the way too sensitivity to any criticism aimed at them. He deems it is part of a reflection of a degradation of society in these areas. In Mekkar's mind the media is so much more prevalent today and in everyone's business especially with regard to public figures. He is including paparazzi in that assessment.

There are trade offs. Mekkar has thought the athletes of the current time couldn't handle the all gloves treatment of star players from yesteryear. Most of them had to defend themselves also well maybe excluding Wayne Gretzky and very few others. Mekkar says, "The protected superstars of today could flee to the area that seems to have more months of winter than any other season to be safer but the pay would be a lot less."

This brings about another quandary of Mekkar's beliefs. He states bluntly, "Anyone who advocates taking fighting out of pro or junior ice hockey does not know the game all that well. It doesn't matter where those people reside. Those players who had protectors on the ice to fight on your behalf for the majority of your battles know who they are. Their opinions and statements in the press on this issue do not count and should be ignored." Mekkar goes on to say directly, "That they should shut their trap because they are too breakable!"

Furthermore he goes on to mention that most current fans and current athletes are unaware of the history of their sport. There is not a consideration and a lack of knowledge of various innovations and equipment advances made thus affecting main contributor's production. Fans compare statistics of athletes from clashing eras with little, if any, examination of different rule changes to enhance scoring and reduce physicality. The historical environment influences and contrasting field conditions of those matches were important too. Various athletes were considered stars in their own time for reasons that cannot be described enough to others who only watch the games. One had to play during that time to really understand.

It ticks people off when Mekkar states unapologetically, "That athletes had to be much more resolute in the past. Frankly, because they were considered more easily replaceable. The majority of people currently are totally unable to relate to this concept. There was the absence for the most part of the big money too!" He continues on, "Dick Butkus would be considered too mean and intimidating to play in the NFL of 2016. His ferociousness would not even be allowed on the field now." [youtube.com/watch?v=ywLftmEtOsY; bleacherreport.com/articles/188642-nfl-legends-dick-butkus]

Anyway, Mekkar has determined that eliminating fighting altogether from the game of hockey at the professional level endangers the player. Specifically the stars who people buy tickets to see. By taking away the fist-cuffs completely would result in more injuries to them. Plus, add a watered-down product which could affect the number of fans thus the amount Continued of gate receipts. Since hockey is so much more dependant on fans attending games than the other big sports. The financial health of teams and leagues would be severely hindered.

The instigator rule already is detrimental and curtails the ability to combat cheap shots against the star players that puts fans' butts in the stands. Mekkar reasons that designated policemen also free up space on the ice and create for more unobstructed movement and offensive flow during the game. However, those fighters must have other skills to contribute to the rest of the club.

The Northern Native further comments, "Fighting in our sport is a preferable alternative to other adverse effects from vicious surgical-like stickwork and nasty elbows." [cbc.ca; Wikipedia.com; Livestrong.com; bleacherreport.com; thepolitic.com/archives/2006/11/09/why-fighting-is-good-for-hockey] He knows this from experience and the number of scars from the evil stick tactics and cheap shots on his body. Even in some non-descript places. Mekkar's advice is check with some individuals who participate in pro hockey leagues in other locations of the planet that have banned fighting. Those people will tell you stories and give a very different picture regarding that dispute.

He doesn't want the want the sport to adjust its core self to win over fringe fans in locations that reject the game of hockey. Mekkar nails it in a off the cuff manner, "If they don't like it, forget them!" He also quips, "The largest gridiron football players don't scare me, and I have never met one that I couldn't handle. That goes for most sports athletes including fighters. Remember, I rapped a (non-polar) bear in the nose and told it to leave or it would lose its life!" Mekkar has victoriously tangled with a few of those from other endeavors before. He is afraid of no human, just the trepidation of not succeeding.

As he was watching a hockey game on one of the local channels in the hotel his team was staying at, Mekkar became bothered. One of the hockey commentators, he doesn't remember which, made a statement that set Mekkar off shouting, "That is such a crock!" at the television. The person on the tube was mentioning something about taking shots on net from sharp angles on the ice. The announcer commented about this factor normally results in a higher percentage of initial goalie saves and rebounds back out in the slot area. That is, in front of the net from the face circle on in to the net. Mekkar notes his disagreement because netminders are getting better at redirecting the puck over toward the corners and boards away from the net to remove second chance opportunities. He says that opinion is old and changing much quicker than anticipated. At least that was the case with goalies Mekkar has played alongside and against.

Mekkar has the mindset of why should an attacking offensive player intentionally limit themselves and their options for potential goals. Especially by swinging out wide and taking the shots from there only. There are more options and holes to score a goal when shooting on net when an offensive player is directly in the center of the ice in the slot and goal crease areas. The netminder is unable to cover all of the net no matter how large they are and they have to be nimble as well. Well, there is more logic to this train of thought Mekkar asserted. When a goaltender stands in the net in the ready position, there are seven open areas that the goalie must cover: Glove side – high and low, Stick side – high and low, between the pads or legs, and added later between the goalie's glove or blocker and rib cage. [en.wikipedia.org/wiki/Five-hole; hockeygoalies.org/resources/glossary.html; schoolyardpuck.com/2010/10/why-it-called-five-hole-in-hockey.html] Why shoot where it is easiest to stop?

Then there is matter of goaltenders playing and cutting off the angels to dramatically increase their ability to stop pucks. [hockeygoalies.org/advice/rule5.html; ehow.com/how_2294079_improve-angles-playing-goalie-hockey.html] This was even more helpful to Mekkar due to his frequent riverboat gambling and aggressive style in relation to checking attacking opposition forwards. Don't forget about the amount of communication on the ice needed between teammates. Most definitely between goalies and defensemen like Mekkar. These are nuances that are only acquired through familiarity and pre-arrangement between team members. [hockeygoalies.org/advice/rule4.html]

The burgeoning young man has seen many instances of hockey matches at many levels where one team has vastly outshot their opposition. Yet, that team lost the game anyway because that squad had the majority of their shots on net from the sides instead of directly out front. To Mekkar, it is the matter of prime scoring chances right out front of the net and in the middle of the ice that means more than the shots on goal statistic.

Yet, the Youngster from the Arctic felt that the goaltending on the Selects squad had to be absolutely superb - very similar to the early part of this tour, to have any chance of winning this game. It could not be lackluster as in the last couple of matches. Mekkar has seen the Jets play some exhibitions against various teams outside of North America. He had even seen others on film as well. So, he guessed that he was familiar with their style of play. The fact of the matter was that Mekkar was wrong and way off base.

Winnipeg had added a few members on their roster recently and were about to show why the Jets were considered one of the most talented hockey clubs on the planet. The skill level was beyond Mekkar's expectations and he would get a close up view this night at the Winnipeg Arena.

[billsportsmaps.com; Wikipedia; whahockey.com; Playing Hockey The World Over … - wha.htm] A butt kicking was about to begin at Mekkar's expense. Fortunately, the whipping was only going to be on the scoreboard and not smacks to the head.

This match was not a goon-fest unlike some of the others. Part of it was the difficulty for the Selects to keep up and catch those in the Jets' uniforms on this night. Thus, there was an absence of challenge them to a few bouts of let's go or do the tango – aka fighting. Otherwise, the lopsided score probably would have been worse than the nine to one embarrassing defeat Mekkar's squad suffered.

During the second period of this ongoing debacle, the Selects received a few too many men on the ice bench minor penalties. Normally in most rinks both team benches are roughly the same size and on the same side of the ice surface. There usually are the sin bins and possibly a scorer's box or something similar in between them. Each team switches sides of the ice for each period, thus creating a rotational change for a team but keeping the same bench. In this scenario, the second frame results in the team's bench being further away from a particular club's defensive zone. This makes on the fly line changes, without the benefits of a stoppage in play, more problematic. Due to the fact that your team's bench is now further away.

Overtime play is harder because of the matter of player fatigue. The smooth and fluid Jets took advantage of those infractions and capitalized on those man advantage power play situations. One thing Mekkar did notice while skating near the home Winnipeg bench to arrive at his own was difference between the two. It dawned on Mekkar that the hometown club had a quicker change of players between shifts. Maybe, he thought, it was because their area was a lot larger and was more spacious than the one available to the visitor's.

Mekkar thought to himself then no wonder the Selects were receiving all these were due to a lack of space. It felt kind of cramped on his side and he wanted to find out who was going to makeup for the disparity or receive punishment from him. He later found out, from an arena worker who admitted the discrepancy, that the visitor's bench is quite a bit shorter than the homeside area. Mekkar quipped distastefully, "Another home ice advantage in their favor as if they needed it." It made a difference when a player coming off of the ice approaches the bench within five foot range. A player outside of that limit cannot replace the one coming off of the ice and join the play. Otherwise it is a penalty for too many men on the ice for your team. Once a player removes themselves from the activity from the frozen surface there is a shifting and readjusting process on the pine.

Usually offensive trios and defense pairs on a squad sit together on the bench and converse with each other about the game. Sometimes, it is instruction by a veteran to a younger member of the club. There are questions regarding assessment of the play, recognition, anticipation during action, a quick breather, and much more. This all happens until you are re-inserted back into the fray. The intense adolescent wasn't about to let easier line changes, homeside differences and preferences, and awe of his opponent effect his performance on the frozen slab of water.

The last period of this game still gave Mekkar incentive that with a few breaks here and there the Selects could still be competitive in this match. Well, if Mekkar or someone else on his team could draw some man advantage opportunities by way of penalties on the Jets. However, Winnipeg was loaded with talent such as Bobby Hull, Anders Hedberg, Ulf Nilsson – the Hot Line (Mekkar instead called it the International Line), Willy Lindstrom, Veli-Pekka Ketola, Lars-Erik Sjoberg, Heikki Riihiranta, and more. During this third period the Jets got hot & lit up the scoreboard like a pinball machine. There was a hope in his brain of an outside possibility to win this matchup. It was not to be however. A Break was the correct term, but not in a manner that Mekkar expected.

Some minutes later in the final stanza and toward the latter part of the game, Mekkar was on another man-down situation because of a stupid penalty on the part of a teammate. He was just glad it finally wasn't him this time since he was so well adapted to the confines of the sin bin. Mekkar became fatigued and this started to affect his judgment during play. Unfortunately, it was not quite time for him to be replaced either.

As he was drawing near to the shooter at an angle, Mekkar slightly lost his balance during a sharp turn. This while chasing the movement of the puck on the Winnipeg player's stick. The Jets' player was winding up to take a slap shot. Mekkar began falling at an odd angle and going down to the ice quicker than he normally did to half-heartedly attempt to block a shot from that point (Problem was, shot blocking was much less common in those days). He thought that he might have hit a rut in the ice or something similar. Yet, he discounted that thought because the ice here is known as pretty good for the most part and there was still too much time to go for that.

Anyway, he was more concerned about hindering the potential shot on goal. As Mekkar was going down he put his one hand up to protect his face, jaw, and neck region. Problem was that it was turned palm side open towards the shooter. On this occasion, Mekkar forgot to turn his hand the opposite way so that the back of his hand with all the padding was facing forward instead. He was tired and not thinking straight out there and probably should have been already off the ice.

The hard shot was taken and the rubber disc hit the unpadded palm at full bore. Instantly, the cracking and crunching sound of bone being broken was heard by anyone nearby the bench. Some of his teammates that close by at the bench heard it too and cringed. There was also damage to the ligaments and tendons, as well as the wrist area. Mekkar knew it was bad right then and just tried to tough it out and finish his shift, which still had about twenty more seconds to go. At this point, those twenty seconds seemed like an eternity to The Arctic Warrior.

Soon after the puck was successfully whisked out of the Selects own zone. The Native from the North finished his shift and went directly to the dressing room area. He heard the news about his injury and found out after the x-rays about a number of broken bones in his hand and wrist from that episode.

Mekkar received treatment and showed his toughness by having his hand heavily taped to get back out there to help his team. Of course, the medications and alcohol helped a bit. He ended up only missing a total of two shifts on this tour. Both were during this time as he was being tended to in the locker room for this particular injury. Mekkar's hand was badly impaired. He was unable to even hold a pen to sign his name. The teenager would now have to wear a removable soft cast or brace when not playing. The brace was not allowed to be used during matches, so the continued practice of heavy taping would be required if he wanted to soldier on.

Fortunately, he could eat and carry out some functions with his healthy left hand. The rub was that his minutes per game went significantly southward as determined by the coaching staff. Mekkar was a right side defenseman with a right hand shot. Now the injury affected his grip on the stick in his fingers and in turn greatly reduced the effectiveness to shoot the puck with his stick in the desired direction. Mekkar's wrist shot was in effect fairly negated at that point. The key was not letting the opposition know to avoid exploiting that shortcoming. After the match, he was really starting to feel the effects of the all the things he was given.

Alf's older brother began to be a wise guy and tried to conceal the seriousness of his injury to his teammates. Mekkar came back with the comment to Alf and Lasse, "Do you know who broke my hand with his famous slapshot? At least, my hand was shattered by a wicked shot by the great Golden Jet, Bobby Hull!" Alf spoke up again to his older sibling, "Everyone, who is familiar with the game, knows who he is! You are at fault because you were star gazing instead of being in the correct position." Lasse and Alf and a few others on the squad then just shook their heads in mock disbelief at the jest. They thought it was the mix of medication and alcohol doing the talking.

This incident changed the tour for Mekkar and made it less enjoyable. The main reason was it limited his peak performance for awhile until the affliction fully healed. Even to this day one can still hear the cracking and popping sounds from numerous movements by Mekkar's right hand and wrist. He describes it as if there is a spring or something resembling that in there.

World Wide Hockey Tour - San Diego

Mekkar had been to San Diego a couple of times before, once with his papa, but he was too fairly young to remember much of those trips. Travelling to different places wasn't such a big deal to him either since he has been many places. People are normally surprised The Arctic Native has journeyed all around the world at such a young age.

This jaunt was different because this time it was to play hockey. He felt there was a lack of quality ice rinks in the area. Even back home someone seems to know something about always sunny California, especially the southern part of the state. It was an image created by marketing campaigns to draw foreign tourists. Part of that was the surfer music of the Beach Boys, Jan and Dean, The Ventures, and more that perpetrated those myths about Southern California throughout the whole world.

The youngster listened to some of that music and had even heard statements such as it is the land of the beautiful people. He didn't believe it because he was there right now and was not the recipient of his mama's model looks. Mekkar thought that the city seemed like a nice to be, perhaps a little on the warm side for his taste. After all the area is a desert, just not an arctic one.

Adolescent Mekkar loved playing on the smaller ice surfaces in North America as compared to the standard twenty foot wider ones back home. Plus, some here in The States and Canada were even smaller than norm regulation size which even more suited Mekkar's hitting style game. The more dinky, the better in his mind because he regarded the boards as his friends. He also used them to angle opposing forwards in his defensive zone to crush those who venture there with devastating hits. Mekkar employed his powerful legs, lower body core, and very low center of gravity to play the body on enemy players. That meant all types of hits were dished out in many forms, even open-ice hip checks too!

He figured if there is less ice for speedy opponents, then it is easier to track them down. Hopefully, he is not chasing them. In that scenario, it would mean that Mekkar is already behind the play. The Arctic Warrior loved to hand out to other players a hard body check that hopefully would create a turnover. The lack of rink size equals more restricted maneuverability of the opposition's part. Also, a turnover can start the transition to offense for Mekkar's squad.

The concept of Mekkar was that, if he could apply more energy to the actual hit itself, it would zap some energy from his enemy. Additionally, Mekkar felt confident that he could use less physical exertion to get to the spot and make it happen in the first place. The benefits would show later on in the game when fatigue on both sides set in. Towards the end of a match when more frequent positional mistakes happen, especially in overtime. Not to forget, Mekkar had other distractions as result of his hand injury.

Mekkar was not a respecter of persons when he reached the ice. He just didn't have any fear or concern about any individual opponents' size or the name on the back of their jersey. It didn't matter to him if that player was popular or not. He did not care in the least bit. Everyone was fair game to be hit by him. In other words, Mekkar considered himself to be an equal opportunity punisher or body checker. That was part of his job on the ice and he did it as best as he could.

The Arctic Native was an original that is for sure. Mekkar was also a pain in the rear end. Even his own mother would describe him that way and took the opportunity to tell him on a not so infrequent basis. Mekkar had another role to play and that was to be a pest on the ice and possibly, or at least willing to, brawl too if needed. He used all of these factors together to get into other competitor's heads and mess with them. The goal with these tactics was to throw the opposition, especially the stars, off of their top game. That might make the difference between victory or defeat. Later on, Esa "Super Pest" Tikkanen used this same strategy to accomplish the same result, but Tikkanen had much more offensive upside than Mekkar. [hockeyfights.com; The Hockey News]

It is a risk using these types of tactics because the potential to receive a great amount of bodily harm is high. These schemes worked more often than not for Mekkar. The Native from the Far North's reasoning was if it works, even most of the time, keep doing it. Thus, he continued to follow that same course of activity. Mekkar attempts to use the principle of: If it isn't broken, don't (try to) fix it. [T. Bert Lance, 1977; Ann Landers; & possibly before]

Alf's described his older brother as being an absolute ruthless, mean individual on the ice. The Far North Native could be one at times outside of hockey as well, depending on his mood. The best way to describe Mekkar's playing style was that it was quite similar to another undersized individual of more recent times. That person was still larger in statue than Mekkar. Mekkar is reminded of himself when he has observed the play of Darius "Kaspar The Unfriendly Ghost" Kasparaitis. Plus, Darius had more offensive prowess than Mekkar. The ice cold young man Mekkar was meaner than Kasparaitis and chose to focus more on his defensive responsibilities. Mekkar did this at some expense and sacrifice in the offensive end. Both players were however unflinching in their own zone on defense and suffered for it. Even though Darius' last name sounded like some kind of ailment or disease, the only cure was to try to remove him from the game somehow. The same as Mekkar. [hockeyfights.com; The Hockey News]

Some of Mekkar's teammates described his metamorphosis as he transformed into like a werewolf or similar type creature right when the match began. Mekkar's brother Alf said that his sibling turned into a super-jerk at game time. Alf one time explained it as, "Being sometimes more than just a jerk in any competitive atmosphere to everyone around him. This included coaches, teammates, and fans also. He (Mekkar) makes no apologies or excuses and carries out this attitude without any apprehension or hesitation whatsoever. It is like there is no doubt in his deranged mind that what he is doing is correct and proper." Alf went on to say, "Mekkar is not one to consider one bit about the effects or consequences of his outward actions regarding others around him. He doesn't seem to care either. Like a type of narcissistic selfishness on my older brother's part. I don't think Mekkar totally realizes the complete change going on. Similar to an old time berserker warrior in a trance state." Alf continued, "Mekkar would then revert to his usual inconsistent moody or at times outgoing self afterwards when the match was over. Trouble is, you never knew which one it was going to be."

Mekkar's best friend Lasse would refer to The Arctic Warrior's personality change on the ice as one (Mekkar) who goes to his deep, dark place inside of himself. Lasse describes it as an area that sometimes Mekkar himself does not want to visit. The hulking Lasse should know too. Since many have said outwardly, and Lasse agreed with affirmation, that he has almost the same exact nasty on ice disposition as Mekkar. The difference is Mekkar's best friend is physically much bigger, stronger, meaner, and nastier of the two. Lasse is always on the lookout to carry out his brand of bad intentions than Mekkar ever could, at his worst. Added to the fact, that Lasse had less control and it was hard for him to turn off the nastiness switch in other parts of his life. This is possibly the main reason they got along so well with each other because they could relate to each others' inner demons, just waiting to come out.

Lasse and Mekkar both had a similar character and they had an almost exact upbringing by growing up together in the same village. Mekkar's best friend recognized that he will always need some type of physical or creative outlet to combat that internal tug-of-war and subsequent outward mean streak manifestation. This will be especially true when his competitive athletic days are completed. Otherwise, there will be episodes of lashing out or blowing off steam. Lasse joked many times about the fact that Mekkar will never get married due to the fact that he is extremely uncompromising, unlike politicians. He is very consistent in his stances and unwavering in those areas of his nature.

Like or not, these behaviors are an ongoing struggle for many athletes in violent contact and collision sports. These matters become worse for athletes as they approach the end of their chosen profession with diminishing skills or after career ending injuries or forced retirement. The issue is that the particular individual loses their outlet or expression that was the focus of their inner drive. After the active sports career is over there is no way to get out that built-up inward conflict out of themself. In other words, the release mechanism is now absent and something else must fill the void. The associated problems with lack of aggressive expression require a permanent resolution or it never gets solved without an extreme amount of help from others.

Most ex or former athletes are taught to push it down deep inside or to ignore these issues. They are told it will take care of itself, but in reality that usually is not the case only the exception. That is only one factor that was mentioned above as related to the psyche of an individual. There are other considerations as well such as the loss of higher income in most respects. Those accomplishments and blessings which normally are perceived as being at the top rungs of society at large disappear. Don't forget the loss of adulation from fans and no more attention from the crowds. Even temporary glory, fame, and other post endeavor lost benefits like daily life structure for the most part of a professional athletic career is suddenly gone. The great upheaval and understanding is lost on those people who have never experienced these factors. Thus, depression can set in big time.

If there is a lack of post career preparation the questions come like a flood, what do I do now?

The cold weather young man would describe his central condition by using an external example such as like the horn type sound that is made during a heavy London fog. If no sound is made or the noise is ignored most likely bad things can occur. A ship or boat loses its sense of direction and runs into another object or aground. Mekkar would at other times express the continuous resident turmoil as boiling to the surface. Another indication was small tremors released to hold off and avoid a large earthquake.

He always felt he needed that abrasive edge in his game because of his smaller stature for his position. Some would say Mekkar went over the edge on many occasions. Mekkar went out of his way to get respect. He also knew that by carrying himself in this manner, he was playing with fire and could get burned. Even go over the edge or just snap on a mental level and become a basket case. Yet, those risks Mekkar was willing to take in the short term without assessing long term ramifications.

At times Mekkar would do this to kick-start and motivate himself. The idea was to knock any listlessness out of him through the dishing out of taking a hit to make a beneficial play. If there was any lethargy left in him, he was determined to removal it all any way he could. Many times after games Mekkar felt more relief than joy in this frame of mind, even if his squad was victorious. It was physically exhausting and mentally draining to play the style he did. Then, normally he would revert back to his regular frame of mind. The dilemma was that, not even Mekkar could predict the tone and expression of his own character. The Far North Native has some major questions regarding the realm of his daily existence outside of participating in active sports. Would he be a personal, but guarded individual when he was away from all sports or games? Or would he be a total jerk and have an explosive personality toward everyone around him? This is how Mekkar imagined himself and his outward demeanor. Of course, others around him saw Mekkar in different light, which included those closest to him on this trip such as Alf and Lasse.

In Mekkar's mind, he was glad that some of the more physical teams and good squads at the beginning of the tour. He was hoping this would result in his team playing some better hockey when the fear factor was removed. The benefit of that schedule for him is that it got Mekkar's competitive juices flowing in those early matches. The downside was that it could wear him down rapidly, if he wasn't careful despite anything to the contrary that his mind told him.

There was the belief of Mekkar that the Selects as a team had been fairly fortunate to achieve a couple of victories so far on this ice hockey expedition. Well, considering the high level of opponents the Selects had encountered. Any early success by Mekkar's squad was mainly due to an increased effectiveness on the man advantage power play unit. It seemed to start to click and produce more timely goals. A good power play is an effective weapon to punish opposing teams for undisciplined play and taking stupid penalties. The travelling team's power play became more dangerous and was operating at a higher clip with each successive outing. Ever since the recent surge of the Selects man advantage unit, the competition began to think twice before taking unnecessary liberties with Selects players. Careless play and the parade to the sin bin was greatly reduced. Too bad the lesson was lost on Mekkar because he mainly lived in the short term..

Even though this aspect of Mekkar's team gave them more confidence, the Selects' as a club needed a lot of improvement of their own regarding their penalty killing. The short handed specialty outfits probably would get better if players like Mekkar would use his own good sense. For example, decrease his own retaliatory infractions. He is acutely aware that referees almost never notice the initial rule violation, but almost always catch the response. Mekkar needed to get his pest shots in first to have a better chance of not getting caught and thus would pay less visits to his home away from home, the penalty box.

A true assessment of the Selects performance on this tour was that they were still getting dominated at full strength five-on-five play. The coaches were not happy about the squad getting their rear ends handed to them during these points in the earlier scheduled games. If the Selects found a way to get better in this area there was the assumption by the staff that most, if not all, of the goonery might cease. Most athletes want to avoid a wounding of their pride when performing in front of their own fan base.

To Mekkar, it still was a good thing to take advantage of any opportunity the Selects' could get. Some of the earlier opposition thought that they could intimidate Mekkar and the whole Selects squad through the use of rough and tumble tactics, while employing a more physical style. Just like some of these same clubs had employed with other previously visiting international squads. Since it worked before for the most part, continue to use those nasty tactics. However, the young barnstorming team was catching on. [Playing

Hockey The World Over…wha.htm; whahockey.com; hockeyfights.com; Wikipedia; billsportsmaps.com; The Hockey News]

Unfortunately for The Native from The Far North, most of his teammates on the Selects squad were learning these lessons much too slowly. They were effectively bullied by some of the more pugilistic home sides on this far flung schedule, but not Mekkar or Lasse.

Though after suffering a serious injury prior to this matchup, the teenager promised to be ready for anything. That is despite being hampered in his effectiveness to carry out all of his on ice responsibilities, in full measure. Of course, Mekkar's cockiness wanted to write checks his body couldn't deliver at this time. Mekkar just wanted to enjoy and participate in as much as he could during this perceived once in a lifetime journey or so he thought at the time.

The arctic boy was of the view that some of these teams that would brawl first to open up space for offensive opportunities and scoring goals later. For example, like the Bulls and Fighting Saints had not learned any lessons from their earlier employed stupid strategy. These errored ways lead to the use of similar undisciplined, bully-style hockey now - during matches here at their home rinks. It was also the case when back when they were visiting Mekkar's own area of the world on quite a few instances throughout the preceding years. [whahockey.com; Playing Hockey The World Over… wha.htm; The Hockey News; billsportsmaps.com; hockeyfights.com]

Mekkar's response was quite predictable for anyone who really knew him because he was so bad at hiding his true feelings. His thought process was always to get mad and get even or try his hardest to proceed on this course of action. Not only would Mekkar fight with his enemy opponents, he would also return the cheap shots and uncalled for stickwork of his own, if necessary. At the same time he and his team would attempt to punish them for their stupidity and arrogance on the scoreboard by converting more often on the power play as a result. "Kick their butts in both ways", as Mekkar put it.

The adolescent saw an example of this, of which he was present at, as a younger spectator with Alf, Lasse, and his papa at a match back in his home area. During that tilt the squad from North America was being completely outplayed early in the game and could not match the skill level to keep up with the local club, as Mekkar described this scenario. So, the visitors got crazy and became more of a thug squad on ice and started to really goon it up. It was a nasty brawl-fest. Thus, they dug themselves a deeper hole.

That visiting team was eventually spanked and humiliated by looking at the score. [Playing Hockey The World Over…wha.htm; whahockey.com; The Hockey News]

On this particular trip, Mekkar figured if these teams wanted to conduct themselves in the same manner of thuggery on the ice as before, punishment would ensue. He knew that he would have to be one of the players on his team to help beat the lessons from those earlier episodes into the thick skulls of his opponents. Mekkar hoped there would be increased scoring for his side due to more power play chances acquired by his team from the enemy tactics. "Go ahead and continue this undisciplined moronic strategy and we will embarrass you!", he snapped. Mekkar would repeat a saying that he learned from a previous coach on a team he played for not long ago back home. He quipped, "If you want to play like a clown, we send you back to the circus with your tail between your legs, so you can hide from your shame."

Plus, Mekkar wanted to retaliate too, if needed. He was not one to just stand there take abuse like a fool and a victim without doing anything in response. He also desired to kick some butt because that was in his personal nature. It did not matter to him that he wasn't the biggest person in statue. The Arctic Warrior was the shortest person in his immediate family, by far. Still he had to heart, training, and skill to brawl. Mekkar would take no grief from anyone and unlike some famous fighters, take on all comers who challenged him. No person on this planet scared him at all. Mekkar termed it as just a matter of relative perspective considering where he grew up. He has observed aggressive action of wild and sometimes large animals such as various types of bears, moose, etc. on a regular basis in the arctic. Plus, Mekkar has encountered on occasion some of the beasts himself. It is a fine line between bravery and stupidity. After those experiences, even the largest human beings look kind of small in his eyes. The problem is he is not afraid to tell them that fact to potential combatants faces either.

This squad, the Selects that Mekkar was a part of and representing his nation for on this tour was not considered the real, true, or top level national team. Yes, they wore a similar version of the national team jerseys with the same color scheme. There were slight visual differences to the trained eye from the top level national squad, which was also on their own scheduled jaunt through different nations. The Selects were considered as a young second tier or even less a C-level squad similar to a high junior in age or lower rung minor league pro team. Mekkar was of the opinion that they had been hastily thrown together without a whole lot of time beforehand to jell their individual talents together as a unit. The original idea was to expose and prepare these young athletes to other surroundings for future matches, so there would be less chance of being overwhelmed when appearing overseas for games.

Any all-star team that is made up of a collection of stars has issues. It is even more true in ice hockey where timing and positioning is crucial due to the extreme speed of the sport. The executives who assembled the squad planned on the players becoming a cohesive team as a result of all the players being together on such an extended long, long road trip. This same journey that would take them through the North American continent and later beyond to other regions around the globe.

Trouble was, the erratic schedule along with the individuals not meshing together as well as management hoped showed in the Selects play on the ice. It was especially true in the early portion of the trip. In addition to the fact, the competition they were facing was getting stronger as the matches progressed. Mekkar felt that the team executives should have known better of what to expect since most of them were former players themselves. He chalked it up as either one or two reasons for this oversight. The first was the lack of time to assemble a decent squad and let them learn how to play together to take advantage of their individual strengths. Nobody wanted the Selects to embarrass the powers in charge that put together this journey.

Most of the team management time was spent on the logistics of the tour itself due to ever changing scheduled matches in the various locales. Mekkar thought those in charge of the team did a bad job with poor planning. The other reason that was plagued this trip was that possibly the executives had forgotten, similar to many bosses in the workplace and all politicians, about the resources needed to complete the work at hand. In this case supplying the players who perform their duties on the ice with all they need to succeed, just like other entertainers such as movie and television actors and actresses. This is how the inquisitive mind of Mekkar operates!

The Selects were a fairly young team with the oldest player being almost twenty-one years old. Everyone else on the squad was younger. That maturity was the reason the oldest member of the club was also chosen as the captain of this Selects team. Alf was the most youthful of all the players, even though his outward appearance and size reflected an opposite image. The Selects wished that their squad could have been designated as the junior national team. Unfortunately, that was impossible because the rules state that all individual players on the team, except a few, must be eighteen years old or younger depending on the time of the actual tournament being participated in.

Despite their relative youthful ages individual members on the team had varying levels of experience against international competition. Thus, not all of them were completely green in lacking true big stage game experience as a group. It was a good thing for the Selects that the statistics and results of these exhibition matches would not count in the standings of the home teams. Unlike a few other touring international game tilts during the decade. Nor would these games versus the Selects effect any of the host clubs' playoff aspirations. The hosts clubs only focused on things which would affect the bottom line in regard to gate receipts and potential profits. [Playing Hockey The World Over…wha.htm; whahockey.com]

If these matches had counted in the standings, increased nastiness probably would have the order of the day in Mekkar's mind. The Far North Native was also glad there was no radio or television broadcasts of any of these matches back home just in case of possible blowouts in favor of the home sides as previously predicted against the Selects.

So, it seemed to Mekkar that some of the professional North American squad's older veteran players lacked full fledged efforts in a few of these exhibition matches. They appeared to be going through the motions as much as possible in a collision sport such as ice hockey. The lights may have been on but it was questionable if somebody was home in the head. At the same time the home clubs' younger members and non-superstars were bearing the brunt of responsibility for their team's on-ice performance. Mekkar surmised it was either to keep those individuals on the big league team and out of the minor circuits. If it took using their fists to gain themselves a roster spot, so be it. Also, to preserve the pride by showing that the North American style of hockey was superior to the international norm. [Playing Hockey The World Over…wha.htm; whahockey.com]

Mekkar thought this helped his touring squad, even if he didn't mention it outwardly. It was a rare thing for The Arctic Warrior since he keeps very little bottled-up inside of him. He is the complete opposite of his brother Alf. Mekkar felt that might be part of the reason for the Selects having more success against their rivals on this tour than expected. Even more than Mekkar had anticipated after noticing the North American pros, at times, had much stronger performances against top tier travelling competition on other jaunts. "Maybe, some of the squads over here have begun to wake up and are gaining understanding from the error of their ways," reasoned Mekkar, "But, not all of them."

By this time the WHA was the most successful challenger and rival of the big boys on the block, the National Hockey League. The overall quality of play in the World Hockey Association circuit might have been slightly less than the totality of the whole NHL. Some of the teams in the upstart league consisted of a few established stars who jumped to the newer, more fragile and unstable circuit. For, in some cases, much higher promised salaries than they earned before. In other instances, it was about more opportunity to exhibit one's skills or gain more playing time. Another reason was that some players were just more suited to the run and gun, up-tempo different WHA style of hockey and those stats reflect this.

Usually the rest of the team rosters had a less talented, but nonetheless needed supporting cast to aid the stars. An assortment of mid-level career pro players; Plus, those recently graduated from the college ranks, and like. The majority of which would have been overlooked or never have gotten a sniff of time in the NHL. [Wikipedia; whahockey.com; billsportsmaps. com] Supplementary players that didn't get a shot in The Show (the NHL) now had a chance to impress and become integral parts of a top club, not just stuck in the minor leagues. Teams that are made up of all the same type of players very rarely are successful and not effective long term. There are various roles to be filled on a squad to provide balance such as pluggers, checkers, defense-first forwards and defensemen, offensive defensemen, power-play and penalty killing specialists and more. Not to discount the very backline of a team, the goaltenders. It is well known in hockey that a hot goalie can make up for a host of mistakes by their team. [Goalie Quotes - msu.edu/user/baujason/quote.html; hfboards.hockeysfuture. com/showthread.php?t=1267123]

The big leaguers', as well as, individual NHL team owners attempted to react and combat the new league through many methods. Plus, there was the painful matter of the rival circuit's somewhat successful raiding of talent from National Hockey League squads. Quick action was taken to the assignment of new expansion franchises in key metropolitan markets to shut out the upstarts. Cut off the places where the new guys hoped to succeed and prosper and hopefully they will go away. For instance, the NHL granting an immediate new entry in the New York City area, which is considered by many to be the media capital of the world. The idea was to squeeze out any potential rival from setting up a flagship club there in the most influential press market in the world.

Other owners made life difficult for the upstarts by playing nit-picking games, adding ridiculous fee charges for basic necessities and amenities, etc. Specifically in cities where the WHA teams needed to share fan bases and already established facilities for home matches until the new clubs could secure their own home digs. {Wikipedia; billsportsmaps.com; The Hockey News; whahockey.com; Sports Illustrated]

The rapidly maturing young man thought, by way of his pre-tour research, about some possible reasons for the two top North American hockey leagues' turf war tactics, counter strategies, & subsequent actions taken. Mekkar did gain some business sense from the many trips by being involved with both his mama and papa in various settings. It is well to note that any business, especially large ones always want to have and keep a dominant share of the marketplace for their particular industry. In this case for a sports franchise to monopolize the fan base in their sphere of influence. It is considered to be paramount for any company or team to be both profitable and have long-term stability.

Even a young Mekkar, who was now a teenager, understood that the old guard, the already entrenched circuit had to execute their plan to force the upstart league out of the larger media markets altogether. That tactic alone could pretty much minimize the threat to the status quo and keep their dominance in the professional hockey industry on the continent. These actions had the effect of pushing the newcomer (WHA) clubs away to the fringes. At the same time, punishing the other league, as well as, new team owners in a variety of ways for even having the audacity to invade the NHL's so called turf. The wish was that the newer coalition might disappear sooner than later as a result of these many actions taken against them. It is well to note, the National Hockey League never expected any threat to their domain. They believed the WHA would not get started or get off of the ground nor any playing games, in the first place.

This was excluding the on-going, continuous legal battles conducted through the corrupt court system. Contradictory as it is in administering real justice to aggrieved parties to right wrongs. Not to forget the double standard decision making process normally based on a concept of who is supplying the legal industry members with the most favors and outright financial bribes. The court oligarchy created backroom deals and behind the scenes buddy-ship which protects each other and the status quo. Ruled by the premise of you scratch my back and I will scratch yours. Mekkar sees this pattern as a double dealing downward slope to becoming much worse in the future with very little possibility of ever being fixed.

However, the dominant league miscalculated the resolve of a few individuals involved against them, as well as, the future effects that would ensue. The main rival was dismissed with all of its faults including being new and fairly unstable, but the impact was far reaching upon the hockey landscape.

Mekkar learned from his business savvy parents early on, to have any chance of success at all, the newer and smaller business has to do it differently. Especially in an established business environment or in this situation, leagues must look for ways to make positive modifications or tweaks while still being innovative and fresh. Yet, not totally destroy the integrity of the sport itself. Mekkar says, "Throw the standard means of carrying out the old status quo and the rulebook right out the door." That is, like in battle planning, attack areas where you think the big guys are weakest. Also, like in warfare, strike at positions the stronger group either ignores by choice, arrogance, or complacency. This is a phenomenon used in the business world since the beginning of time itself.

In a historic manner the World Hockey Association did that and went far beyond expectations. The era resulted in some changes for the good of many affiliated with the game. Well, maybe except for the old, big league club owners like the Toronto Maple Leafs Harold Ballard who lost a bit of control over player personnel. Soon the fervor increased and everyone was looking for talents in greater numbers all over the globe. This included the virtually untapped United States hockey pool. The prior trend was forever reduced of purposely restricting the searches in Canada alone for able athletes. It was now time to widen the scope to recruit talent.

The experts were now realizing that players from all over could adapt, with time, to the North American brand of ice hockey. Possibly, at least blend that style with each individual skill set. For the longest extent the neglect of broadening the horizons for new proficient players was controlled by many doubters. There were the restrictive beliefs that talent from locations outside of The Great White North (Canada) & a slightly south of the border were incapable of successfully adapting in North American pro leagues. This mistaken idea was proven to be false and even more so as the years have passed. [Wikipedia; billsportsmaps.com; whahockey.com; hockeyfights.com]

Instead the new circuit had a philosophy of more offense or a faster paced, more offensive game which is better for the fans. Mekkar called it "A different, rarely seen approach in the Western Hemisphere at that time, up-tempo mode of play on the ice." He, along with others, mainly saw it as due to the infusion of extensive outside talent from overseas and the States. That is, outside the confines of the Canadian border.

Mekkar liked the WHA for the main reason was that it created more opportunities to make a potential career out of hockey for him. If, he ended up getting that far. It wasn't just some type of pipe dream for him as some scouts had told Mekkar that he had the potential to reach that level. The P-word. Potential, what? He hates that term. To Mekkar saying a person has potential in an area is like a person has the promising capability to intake air. To him, everyone has potential to accomplish great things in their life. The issue is whether an individual gets a chance to use that potential to succeed in a particular endeavor, is a different matter altogether. It is rarely what you know, but more so who you know that truly counts on advancing upward on the social scale.

Lasse's best friend, Mekkar welcomed more position openings for hockey players to further pursue their craft and stick it - to the man. In the manner of breaking down the draconian stranglehold of recent earlier times and limits for athletes. Mekkar felt that the upward glass ceiling was being smashed through during this era. Restrictions were readily unlocked much quicker on player compensation and the negation of the minimum age limits. Also, successful legal destruction of the modern slavery inducing reserve clause which automatically tied an individual to a specific club indefinitely. It was previously renewed when a player's contract ran out. Particular wording in the document didn't matter; standard practice was just instituted as before. The times were changin' baby! Player movement was now in full swing. On one hand it was positive, but it did also create instability for teams in some cases. Pro baseball was at the forefront in its free agency infancy stage, which affected the whole realm of the sports marketplace too! [Wikipedia; whahockey.com; billsportsmaps.com; Playing Hockey The World Over… wha.htm]

He thought it was cool to change things up a bit in relation to items that are really in essence for the fans. For example, the all-star game formats. In most of the years these special activities were anything but set in stone. Mekkar was glad that the WHA was willing to put some pizzazz into those matchups to keep the league followers always guessing as to What comes next? [whahockey.com] In Mekkar's mind, this shows bravery and a creative out of the box mentality. On the other hand, that type of thinking can also be a pain to prepare and plan for, as well as, setup the final details.

Some change is beneficial and reasonable to Mekkar as to prevent staleness and inertia. However, constant change on a day-to-day basis with no structure or consistency-base whatsoever creates a dilemma for Mekkar. He is like most people in that he also likes to get settled into his environment, at least for a bit. To him variety is good as long as he is not always in the middle of it and the ever changing eye of the storm. Thus, gradual change stance creates a direct inner conflict for Mekkar. Maybe in spite of himself, like most individuals Mekkar is, at the same time, a creature of habit and routine whether he admits it or not.

Moreover in his native culture and reflective upbringing one had to be always aware of surprises and sudden change. Those situations could be very dangerous and life threatening. They could easily get out of hand resulting in a negative outcome, such as costing a person their life. Mekkar often repeats a certain quip, "You don't get a second chance to make a first impression with a polar bear because he might look at you as a snack!" In reality, bear attacks upon people are not as common as many believe, but who would want to take that chance?

This new brand of hockey brought about a more wide open game and higher scores which, let's face it, fans in North America seem to prefer. Possibly, that is only Mekkar's conviction with regard to people's sport choices. That is why he believes basketball is so popular due to the increased numbers on the scoreboard.

Since Mekkar is a defenseman, he understands and appreciates good defensive play in many sports. Plus, to him higher scoring matches show weaker protection of your own goal capability. Mekkar has participated in basketball, but it was not his cup of tea. So, he feels that he can authoritatively speak with regard to issues such as this.

Alf's older sibling, Mekkar gravitated to and engaged in more of the physical contact or collision athletic pursuits. Undertakings such as Rugby, Australian Rules Football (Footy), American (Gridiron) Football – which by the way was introduced in 1861 in Toronto, Canada, Hockey of course, Boxing, Lacrosse – which has more battles than most conclude, and others. Not only that, Mekkar has also dabbled in additional sports like Wrestling, Soccer, Volleyball, Surfing, Sailing, etc.

It makes sense to Mekkar that if a side controls the ball, puck, and tempo of a match that squad should have more turns to notch scores or points.

This faster paced keep control of the puck as much as you can style of ice hockey was based on the Soviet five-man unit and Nordic models that are ingrained through the youth ranks there. It is a free flowing game in the words of former Edmonton Oilers coach and general manager Glen Sather who was part of the last National Hockey League dynasty in the nineteen eighties and nineteen ninety. Sather said that he borrowed and modified a system of hockey, to his roster of players that he learned through direct observation. It was rarely used during Sather's playing career except when his squads faced off against opponents such as the WHA Winnipeg Jets. Also trips with his WHA Oilers overseas gave him much material for him to install and help insure Sather's own team's success. Of course, it is a boost to gather all the proper talent to execute the plan.

Some of the strategies used in Europe and other places were that young goalies and position players played multiple positions. They went through the skills, development, and training for everywhere on the ice, plus a lot to improve skating growing up. This meant, in some cases, filling in at other positions to help their squad in other areas - if needed due to a rash of injuries, etc. Understanding and appreciation was gained and respect was earned because each player could relate to all of the others on the club. Learning to speak english was huge during this time if an individual wanted to expand their horizons internationally and play in other circuits. For a long time goaltenders were just an afterthought in youth leagues because most kids wanted to be the main goal scorers and almost none would volunteer to be the netminder. This early version of hockey related cross position training put all through the same stuff and a minimum standard had to be met when they reached a certain age and level. There was no favoritism either, if you couldn't cut it, there were limits at the next stage in the chain.

Sather instituted his fun and gun offense which was perfectly suited to the up-temp World Hockey Association. [Playing Hockey The World Over... wha.htm; whahockey.com; hockeyfights.com; Wikipedia; billsportsmaps. com; The Hockey News] Mekkar compares Sather's approach to a few clubs and the wide open American Basketball Association. More specifically to the late nineteen eighties Loyola-Maramount Lions basketball team philosophy under coach Paul Westhead. There are other later examples of similar offense-first schemes such as Doug Moe's Denver Nuggets and

Phoenix Suns under Mike D'Antoni of the NBA. No matter what system is instituted it always takes awhile to put all of the right pieces in place. Glen also made maximum use of what hockey insiders consider as the fastest, as well as, best ice surface for hockey in the world at the Northlands Coliseum in Edmonton, Alberta.

The arena has a different corporate sponsor and a thus is known by another name nowadays because that is the current trend in the professional sports realm. A sense of tradition and history is no longer considered as important when there is money to be made. Mekkar is of the opinion it is one more indicator of the increased decline in society that has sold out to greed.

This hybrid style took off and took over the National Hockey League after the addition of four WHA teams to start the 1979-80 season. In truth, it was a mini-merger but the WHA clubs got the shaft and basically buildup their rosters from scratch. This afforded Sather with the opportunity to shape the Oilers in his image. Edmonton ended up obliterating the offensive record book with much success and championships. The next decade helped, along with the Eskimos, Drillers, etc. to turn the northern Alberta metropolis into the City of Champions.

There were clubs awarded in locations by the WHA that the NHL never even considered before and probably never would have. Some of these places included cities in the hotbed of hockey (Canada). Mekkar loves to read about history, especially sports history because he feels it is a partial reflection of society at large. He knows that a person can learn from study of the past and has heard the mantra many times, one who doesn't learn from past history tend to repeat its mistakes over and over again. [Reason in Common Sense, volume 1 of <u>The Life of Reason</u> by George Santayana, 1905]

One of Mekkar's favorite aspects regarding the upstart pro league (WHA) was the addition of sudden death overtime to determine victory in outcomes during the regular season. This greatly reduced the stranglehold in the amount of tie game results. Mekkar hated no clear winner and regarded them as worse than kissing your ugly sister. Who wants to do that?

Another trend and impetus happened during this period of time due to the rebel league's influence. Individual players broke the mold and began to wear higher uniform numbers. In the past, especially if one was a rookie or young player trying to establish themselves in pre-season training camp. You didn't want high jersey numbers unlike today. Otherwise it usually meant that player probably would not make the big club and would either be cut outright or demoted to the minors for seasoning. Thus, Mekkar donned low uniform numbers his whole hockey career depending on availability. Phil Esposito changed his uniform number to seventy-seven after his trade to the New York Rangers around this time. Even Wayne Gretzky didn't always sport his now famous ninety-nine sweater. There are videos, photographs, roster lists, etc. of Gretzky wearing pro jerseys with the numbers nine, fifteen, seventeen, twenty before his well known standard ninety-nine. [whahockey.com; jerseydatabase.com; thirdstringgoalie.blogspot.com; youtube.com; wharacers.com; whahof.com]

Mekkar examines these factors as part of a cultural shift and people's desire to get noticed. Everyone is aware of how an individual seeks to transcend all in many aspects of society today. He believes that if something gets mentioned frequently, it is because that concept or commodity stands out from the norm during its time. For example, Ground Chuck (Knox) football offense scheme was primarily run oriented. While at the same time, the National Football League was beginning its transition to a more pass-happy circuit with rule changes, etc. in that new direction. [Wikipedia]

It was a good thing Mekkar didn't have any sisters. Mekkar also loved the fact that the rebel league squads had an overall winning record versus NHL clubs in head-to-head exhibition competition. Whoever said the upstarts couldn't hang with the established major leaguers? This mark ticked off the big boys (NHL) which Mekkar thinks resulted in the harsh surrender and absorption terms for the Québec Nordiques, New England (Hartford) Whalers, Winnipeg Jets, & Edmonton Oilers in the eventual merger. The longer the negotiations dragged on between the WHA and NHL the more screwed over the WHA squads were. That is, if the rival league hoped to have any of their teams be accepted into the fold later on by the more established NHL. [Wikipedia; Playing Hockey The World Over...what.htm; The Hockey News; billsportsmaps.com; whahockey. com; hockeyfights.com]

Even the Selects on this tour began to sense a black cloud of uncertainty that hung overhead some of the teams on the ice they faced. It showed in a bit of spillover in some of the opponent's play as well. Mekkar had not yet made a previous correlation of the behind-the-scenes activity of the league and on ice product beforehand. Mekkar felt this pressure might have contributed to a measure of success on the part of the visiting Selects squad versus these WHA teams. His opinion is that off-ice and outside work structured environment distractions normally affect any individual's job performance. Plus, hockey insiders knew about the instability surrounding the WHA.

What was the most disappointing to Mekkar about the 1979 consolidation and absorption by the NHL was not only the loss of major league hockey positions. Added to that, no WHA awards, records, or statistics compiled would be recognized by the NHL ever. Unlike the similar situation involving the recent NBA merger by taking on the ABA New York Nets, Denver Nuggets, Indiana Pacers, and San Antonio Spurs. To Mekkar, it was like the top circuit (NHL) was intentionally trying to blot out any memories of the rival league. With that attempting to wipe out it existence or any of its accomplishments including the players who were there during its seven year life span. A great example of this attitude was the rejection of any WHA stars from the Canadian side in the 1972 Summit Series against the USSR. [Wikipedia; chidlovski.com; hhof. com/htmlTimeCapsule/GamesSummaryWHA1974; angelfire.com/tv2/ rainbowcountry/1972] More punishment for the upheaval caused by the upstart's serious challenge to NHL supremacy, which by the way changed pro hockey forever.

As a result of this conviction on the part of Mekkar, he will never set foot into what he deems as the NHL dominated and controlled Hockey Hall of Fame in Toronto. He makes a different distinction regarding the IIHF. He feels that The Hall is not complete nor a legit hockey shrine. Since it will admit some inductees with questionable credentials to meet certain candidate quotas. Even individuals that never played in the National Hockey League such as a few Russians and females.

Yet, the Hockey Hall of Fame directors have the gall to neglect and punish WHA stars that helped build the game for the current crop of today's players. Mekkar attributes that attitude and misuse of judgment as unfair, corrupt, and frontier injustice. He refuses to accept it or their positions on personal grounds. Especially, when there are some more qualified applicants in the career pool that he feels would be much better choices for admission. These biases and what he speculates as a political double-standard and why Mekkar only adopts International Ice Hockey Hall of Fame (IIHF) honored members list. He regards that as the true register which includes and exhibits players, builders, and referees from all over the globe. Particular issues to Mekkar are unwavering and non-negotiable. The other arrogantly so called (NHL) Hockey Hall of Fame is nothing but a sham in Mekkar's eyes. A testament to the claim of focusing on the center of the hockey universe, Toronto. It is an outward display dissing most everywhere else in the world outside North America and regarding them as nothing in the realm of hockey. [Wikipedia; triposo.com/poi/W__62255416; iihf.com/iihf-home/history/the-iihf/iihf-hall-of-fame.html; whahof.com/hofmembers.html]

Anyway, the World Hockey Association was attempting to be a proper world league and had future plans in place to carry this out. Many WHA clubs faced-off in a variety of matches against travelling National squads, top teams, and all-star contingents from a host of nations. These international matchups occurred in both formal and informal situations and exhibitions. Some of the outcomes which were reflected in reason season win-loss columns. Games materialized in different locales in many places even Tokyo, Japan. [angelfire.com/space/u_line/wha7778.htm]

There were formal matches that counted for more than just national, league, team, or individual pride. Those outcomes could affect the playoff positioning fate of a club. Thus, the results were definitely taken seriously. Those tilts exuded a realm of playoff intensity in them. Fortunately for the Selects their matchups did not count in the regular WHA standings or the tension would have been higher. The pairings against the Selects were mainly about continental and hometown dignity. There was still the need to prove which school or style of hockey, in a team sense and on an individual basis, was superior. Was it the strictly European/International or North American system? No one came up with a definite answer to that question.

Mekkar felt that it was a moot point anyway comparing which type of player was better between the two styles. To him the dividing lines were becoming more obscured and there would soon be players that would became like a hybrid type of athlete having the best attributes of both systems. The Arctic Warrior already possessed the mindset that these future athletes could have their origins from anywhere in the world. It turned out to be the case, since there are now ice hockey clubs and leagues in more than one hundred countries. Even in places no one would expect to see it such as in Mexico, Mongolia, and many nations.

This era was a time that furthered a lot of social change, which also included sports. It started a trend to take the best players available based on their skills and talent regardless of nationality. The idea was that, if done properly, both styles could be blended together. Mekkar wanted to give a shout out to those who really pioneered this pattern like Borje Salming and others. The World Hockey Association was basically the first star chef in the hockey world to truly mix those individual player ingredients (talents) to form a great drink or meal (successful team). This would forever alter

the fastest game on ice as we know it. [billsportsmaps.com; whahockey.
com; The Hockey News; Playing Hockey The World Over ... wha.htm;
Wikipedia; hcokeyfights.com]

Back home, Mekkar was taught that the World Championships and
Olympics were the real testing grounds to resolve this debate. Thus, the
priority on those huge events. The results from this tour would answer a
number of questions in Mekkar's mind. Despite the fact the Selects were
much less experienced and younger than their professional counterparts.
Mekkar thought other matches against collegiate and major junior clubs
later on in the schedule would probably be a better indicator to test the
Selects players at a similar level. It turned out that the teenager was right
on the money with his analysis.

Not to discount another overlooked item by Mekkar and his teammates
regarding this jaunt through the North American continent. The small
expense and easy accessibility for the pro teams here to scout fresh, new,
and young talent. Potential draft selection by major league clubs all over
the map was already occurring but this is when the floodgates opened wide.
In some cases the farm team or one that trained and developed the player
up through the young ranks could be compensated. In other instances, the
sports federations back in that individual's home nation would be bribed
with a handsome sum of dough. Then, that individual hockey rights were
now owned by a particular franchise for a specific amount of time. Not
surprisingly every member of the Selects squad was chosen, acquired, or
put on some protected talent list in some form or another. A few of the
professional teams did this, even by some of the Selects opponents on this
tour that saw the future potential and were impressed by their poise.

All of the home pro teams on this journey versus the Selects were
stubborn and staunch in their way and all wanted to make a show of
defending their turf as comparable to gang warfare. This was true especially
for players that were on the bubble of claiming, keeping, and not losing the
last few roster spots on their own squads. Since training camp had past
and a few of these teams were in the middle of their long season no one
wanted to be shipped off to the minors. Think of a peacock strutting their
stuff to be the most noticeable, attractive, and ultimately selected to stay
with the big club, as Mekkar referred to it. Mekkar was amused by all the
posturing behavior and had encountered this before. This activity of what
is called talk, but talk is cheap. Only results matter to Mekkar, everything
else leading up to it is a crock.

Mekkar also saw a couple more main positives that the newer circuit brought to the realm of hockey. He was hoping to grow up fast enough and take advantage of this competitive, rapidly changing atmosphere for himself and his own personal benefit. The pay at home in the top league was a joke in comparison to what he could possibly earn over here in North America. On the other hand, some scouts had doubts about a positive transition for Mekkar. Comments such as could he take all of the punishment as an outsider trained in that other style of play? What about the adjustment to much longer length of schedule? How would he fare come playoff off time? Or would the youngster already be suffering from a number of injuries to limit his effectiveness on the ice?

As the team bus was coming nearer to the San Diego International Sports Arena, Mekkar looked out the window and saw a large advertising billboard high in the sky which caught his eye. He strained to read the hockey slogan on it. It said, "Mean. Mad, Menacing, Major League Mariners" on it with the picture of a player and their logo. First of all, Mekkar thinks the San Diego Mariners skating Sailor with a boat steering wheel in the background logo is fantastic and one of the best in hockey history. [WHA San Diego Mariners Historical Site – sdmariners.htm; whahockey.com; sportslogos.net; fanbase.com/San-Diego-Mariners; Wikipedia] Mekkar thought to himself Oh, No! I hope they are not that type of goon squad that we faced earlier. It was not supposed to be this type of rough and tumble affair, well according to his own preliminary report and analysis. Yet, you never know because this is the WHA. A nineteen seventies hockey version of the wild, wild west trying to be different and at the same time insert itself into the public sports consciousness. Mekkar needed a break from that type of physical abuse especially to his now badly damaged paw. Next he went deep into his memory bank and thought about home and how tough it was living there. He recalled how you don't get a second chance to make first impression with a polar bear. The bear is either scared and flees or is desperate, hungry, scared, surprised, or annoyed. In other words, the white beast could look at you as a threat, an object to tear apart, or maybe as a snack. Since they can usually sense, hear, and smell a human and depending on the great white bear's mood be violently aggressive and attack. After dwelling on this thought Mekkar felt better and became inspired for that evening's matchup.

Due to Mekkar's pre-tour research he discovered a few items about sports teams in San Diego. He heard and read about statements, on more than one occasion, that clubs from America's Finest City have a habit of choking when the pressure is on. That there is a supposed sports curse on teams as well as an inability to claim a modern North American major league professional sports championship. The last one was the American Football League Chargers in nineteen sixty-three. Of course, the exception is the San Diego Sockers and minor league San Diego Gulls who both won many titles, but both are not in the big three sports on the continent. [Wikipedia]

Nonetheless, when the Selects arrived to the arena, Mekkar first went out to survey the rink itself. It was his normal custom, and part of Mekkar's pre-game ritual, for the specific scheduled game for that day or evening. Mekkar noticed the uncluttered boards. In most rinks then used by professional franchises in North America there was little and sometimes no signage. Advertising logos did not surround the rink at the highest levels, unlike today. The reasoning was that it was considered so minor league and extremely unprofessional back then. Now, it is the opposite perspective where the goal is to maximize all possible revenue streams. Mekkar then saw there was something that resembled chicken-wire in some areas, as he referred to it. Instead of Plexiglas, there were wire-mesh gates in top of the dasher and boards surrounding the rink. It existed where there might be protective netting or higher glass today. Mekkar shook his head and did a double-take to focus and confirm what he thought he just observed. Maybe, he was mistaken or hallucinating from the pain medications he was taking like candy for the injuries. Added to that the extra alcohol mixed in to wash them down or the fatigued state he was in. The tiredness had come back in full force and was affecting his senses greatly along with the other factors. Mekkar wanted to stay away from fans who could throw things or pour drinks on him through the wire as it was common during this era. [The Rebel League: The Short and Unruly Life of the World Hockey Association by Ed Willes, 2005]

During Mekkar's heyday most, not all, arenas only had higher plexiglass above the dasher and boards normally at the far ends of the ice. That is where the majority of shots on net are taken and they appeared to be much heavier panes of glass unlike what is used in the current time. There was usually less, or none at all, glass extruding above the boards on both sides of the ice surface even with respect to the penalty boxes. As one might guess fans took advantage of this aspect in many places. They also took liberties by pouring beer and throw food, as well as, toss an assortment of items onto and at opposing players. Especially, enemy players who would be serving their infraction time in the sin bin in those days.

Mekkar experienced this phenomenon on a first-hand basis since he was a frequent visitor to the penalty box. Alf called it, "His home away from home!" Mekkar was on many occasions a target of fan wrath for that type of mistreatment. Being doused with items while doing his time in the box, waiting to get free, was a regular occurrence. Much of the time hometown security agents and police officers assigned to work that particular area during the match were reluctant to try to stop that type of unruly fan behavior. At times, they would willfully ignore the actions, laugh and snicker, or watch gleefully at the abuse against visiting players. Surprisingly, this also happened in his home rink also because of his style of play and unconcern of making people angry while the game was ongoing. Mekkar did not miss being the mark of repetitive drenching by foreign objects after his hockey career was over.

A person has to remember that hockey is a sport that has allowed fans to throw hats onto to ice. The hats are a symbol for a hat trick (three goal performance) in one game by a hometown player. Next, the hats are gathered by the arena crew and normally donated to charity. Other objects are deposited on the ice also such as an octopus for the first goal by the home club in a playoff game to signify an old standard. The tradition began in Detroit when it only took eight victories to win the Stanley Cup before the first NHL expansion in nineteen sixty-seven. These are practices and rituals that have been present in hockey for many years. [Wikipedia; The Hockey News]

Since, several arenas at that time had much shorter, and in a few cases no, glass rising from the top of the boards on the sides of the rink. Mekkar figured the excuse might have been used that shots on goal were not aimed there. Plus, it could be a quicker turn around process to convert to another scheduled activity in the venue. Younger fans, along with their families, that sat in those seats would often be seen with baseball gloves to catch deflected pucks. That is, if they could react fast enough. Mekkar thought it was mainly for their own personal protection because a wayward puck travelling at high speeds can maim a person. If that vulcanized rubber disc hits the right spot it can kill too, especially an individual who is unprepared, unaware, or not paying attention. Sadly, this instance has materialized on occasion with dire consequences for the victim.

Well, at the rink Mekkar ran into and started a brief chat with a couple of the home team equipment handling employees. He mentioned off-handedly about how his squad (the Selects) didn't have to bring so many of own toiletries, medications, drinking water, alcohol, daily use items, knickknacks, and more on this trip. Mainly because they could find and purchase those needed items here in the city. Mekkar brought up the subject related to stories he heard from other veteran players back home who performed for various travelling national and representative squads. More specifically, when those vets played in matches in other not so modern parts of the world. He commented about team members, players, officials, coaches, and other club employees were unable to find what they needed when they required it. The little band got a chuckle out of that one and reassured him that things were plentiful here in San Diego. [sportsillustrated.cnn.com; The Hockey News]

That was a relief to Mekkar and he did compliment those employees during their exchange. These little distractions were not large considerations occupying the mind or negative issues on this tour. Mekkar said that the trip organizers, outside of the game schedule, and even more so the host teams all took good care of the visiting Selects. The teen from the arctic understood this because he helped carry out and operate similar administrative functions for a previous squad; he also played for, prior to this journey.

Mekkar was well aware that home tilts against international squads could attract more fans than non-rivalry regular matches on the schedule. The employees told him how the Mariners drew a packed house, or close to it in comparison, in a previous match versus the USSR. It was brought up that the home side played one of their best games ever. However, San Diego received the shaft along with no power-plays due to the referee bias against them. The Soviet referee was accompanying with his own squad, so go figure! They mentioned that there were no homer calls for the Mariners that night!

The good draw of these visiting teams from overseas was the reasoning for continuing to book them on the schedule. These exhibition matches were a novelty for the fans and brought in extra cash and profits. This was especially key for some of the more financially strapped clubs struggling at the gate. It was pretty much expected to be a fairly even exchange of travelling and touring teams going over to the other's countries' overseas and vice versa. Play games in each other's backyard where these matches would bring in more fans and all involved would rake in the dough. Similar to dealing with tourists if you treat them well, they will probably come back.

Another option, they could pass the word onto their acquaintances that also might travel there. This was becoming a regular standard, led by the World Hockey Association, all over the hockey globe. The WHA never tried to hide the fact they were truly attempting to be a world league. Well as much as they could afford, since there wasn't the stability of the NHL. [Wikipedia; WHA San Diego Mariners Historical Site – sdmariners.htm; Playing Hockey The World Over … wha.htm; billsportsmaps.com; The Hockey News; whahockey.com; hockeyfights.com]

The arctic youngster was quite aware of this trend because he was present at a few of those events back home. That was before participating himself in a number of these special matches. Mekkar already knew about the accompanying extra local media hype before and during the attraction as he had been part of it on multiple levels. Thus, it resulted in increased swelled size crowds over the norm during the festivities and exhibition games. The North American visiting clubs did the smart thing by bring back local and national heroes and star athletes as part of the games exchanges. When they came over to Mekkar's part of the world wisdom and profits prevailed. Former players would be included that the hometown fans would recognize. Bring the stars and fans will come! That normally meant great gains for the paying gate and regular occurrence of sellouts too! Mekkar felt that these overseas tilts benefitted the hockey industry on a worldwide basis more than anyone could have predicted.

He had the impression that the trend further helped and molded the blending process of individual player's talents, teams, playing styles, preparation, and more, as Mekkar referred to it. Now, all of the big boys (NHL) play the game and follow suit in this ground breaking path along with other sports, like basketball, etc. that was began in great measure by the WHA. Perhaps Mekkar thought, unlike many other people, that he caught a glimpse of a future big picture way ahead of time in some respects. Well, it is important to note that the teenager was partially named after the shaman who helped deliver him at a precarious birth, after all. Could this be a factor? Did Mekkar have any special insight abilities that were not developed yet? Only time would tell. [Playing Hockey The World Over … wha.htm; whahockey.com]

Lasse's best friend, Mekkar, became more excited and antsy as game time approached. He usually got revved up prior to the start of a match similar to a boxer warming up in his dressing room before arriving at ringside in tow with their entourage. Despite the certainty that Mekkar's recent injuries would significantly cut down his playing time didn't matter in this regard. Added to the fact he would get to face off against one of favorite hockey players Andre "The Magician" Lacroix. Mekkar's eyes would be peeled on Lacroix's number seven jersey. The number seven is also worn by the icon in the team logo. Mekkar didn't believe this was a coincidence but intentional to honor the superstar of the home team. The youngster thought that Lacroix was so smooth, fluid, and made the game look so effortlessly on the ice. Mekkar also disagreed with one of Andre's previous team's coaches that knocked on Lacroix's lack of skating ability. The arctic warrior esteemed his Mariner rival's on ice movement as elusive and plus he could stickhandle in a phone booth to set up goals. [whahof.com]

Statistically Lacroix and Mekkar were fairly similar in size, yet they had different physical builds. Mekkar was stockier and one could hear the crunch of the razor sharp skate cutting into the surface as a result of a powerful stride that took a bit to get going to get to full speed. While The Magician or Magic Man as Andre was also referred to, seemed to float over the ice in comparison with a wick, wick sound of his skates in flight always looking to make a play. Lacroix, in Mekkar's mind, resembled as if he knew where everyone was on the ice at all times. It also appeared that Andre consistently found the open man with a tape-to-tape pass. Lacroix had many capabilities that Mekkar lacked in his own skill set and thus the reason why San Diego's number seven was one of his favorites. Mekkar admired strengths and talents in areas that were weaknesses in his game and used that to improve in those abilities. Alf commented that Andre had qualities that were totally different and even the complete opposite from his older sibling. This was very evident on the frozen pond too. Lacroix wasn't called The Magician when he had the puck on his stick for no reason!

The match began but Mekkar was not in the starting lineup as he hoped. The adrenaline was pumping in Mekkar's body as he was still dealing with his seriously injured right hand suffered in the match right before this one. The team trainers did an incredible job wrapping the hand extremely well and put Mekkar's glove over it. However, they were unable to tie it down and left it, as is, for the duration. They were able to hide the extensive tape job inside the glove and told Mekkar to not tie down the left gauntlet either. This way it would not stand out as odd and possibly keep it from the immediate view of opposing players. The idea was to not make the hand a target for further injury through slashes or other devious stickwork.

Fortunately, the Selects opposition on this evening was more of a skating team and not a flat out brawling; goon squad that Mekkar's team encountered earlier on this tour. The Mariners had some individuals who could play the rougher style if desired, but thankfully for Mekkar's sake they didn't.

Trouble was Mekkar's injury made him less effective in his on ice responsibilities than he normally was. The other physical aspects of meds, plus alcoholic drink, were used in combination to create a pain numbing effect. Added to that, his fatigue combined with that impairment made The Arctic Warrior more unpredictable and outright goofy in his behavior.

The first time Mekkar climbed over the boards for his shift in the game was during a stoppage in play. After a score by the hometown club and before the drop of the puck at the center ice dot, Mekkar looked at the Mariners' center ice logo. Part of the emblem resembled a wooden steering wheel of an old fashioned boat. The somewhat out of his mind youngster chanted in an audible voice, "Ho Ho Ho and a bottle of rum". The referee nearby told him to shut up as the puck was about to be dropped for the face-off. But. Mekkar, rebel that he is, defied authority and continued the same chant again. The ref responded with the same answer in a stronger tone to, "Zip it or you will get an unsportsmanlike penalty." Wouldn't you know it, Mekkar did it once again. Alf called his older brother a stupid moron from the bench. Lasse shouted his own response. Since, Lasse had been ready and waiting for the face off to take place. Before playing one official second of this match Mekkar had incurred a trip to the sin bin. It was for delay of game infraction against his team. Guess who scored approximately forty-five seconds later as a result of Mekkar's two minute minor penalty – Lacroix. The Selects coaching staff was not amused and after the goal against they made Mekkar skip a few regular shifts and get comfortable sitting on the bench. It was punishment for taking a foolish penalty and costing his team.

Later on in the game, during another stoppage in play, Mekkar had the gall to skate near Andre and offer him money to purchase the Mariners star's game sweater right after the match. The response back to Mekkar was not what he expected at all. The reply went something like the following, "One previous owner deserted us during the season. We, for a time had no owner and were playing for free. So, there is a possibility I might not be able to replace it or any of my gear with the way things are."

A local baseball team owner (Ray Kroc of McDonald's fame) had purchased the San Diego WHA franchise and assigned his management team to run it. The problem was they had no experience with hockey and the Mariners were not considered a priority endeavor like the Major League Baseball club. Thus, they neglected the squad. Ownership lacked patience to hold onto a good team which only needed a few more pieces to truly become a championship contender. The Mariners made the playoffs all of the three years during their run in San Diego. If the group would have kept the club a couple of years longer, this team probably would have been absorbed into the NHL due to having a big name owner. The Los Angeles Kings would have had a California rival instead of waiting for the expansion San Jose Sharks in 1991. Unfortunately, Kings owner Jack Kent Cooke's greedy desire to also have the San Diego market to himself helped doom the Mariners as well. Plus, Kroc's new administrators lacked vision and as a result sold the squad after one year and the Mariners folded into obscurity. [whahockey.com/mariners.html; Wikipedia]

It seemed to Mekkar that he could do no right in this game. Lacroix knotted two goals and two assists while Mekkar either failed to do an adequate job covering him or rode the pine in the sin bin. San Diego spanked the Selects by a score of seven to two. It could have been much worse. The home side drew well that evening versus the Selects, much higher than normal for that season. Mekkar didn't think the Selects were of the caliber like a national squad to pull in a lot of fans, so he assumed it some sort of promotional giveaway night.

Mekkar had read one of the local newspapers prior to the match regarding ownership unhappiness about the usual low fan attendance. There was a minimum level of paying patrons expected to be drawn on a nightly game basis and expectations were not being met. Mekkar summarized from the articles and other local sources he read that hardcore fans of the previous team that the Mariners replaced never accepted the WHA club. The Western Hockey League San Diego Gulls had been established for awhile and developed a rabid fan base but the team had to fold with the Mariners' arrival in town and was not happy regarding the demise of the minor league operation. Mekkar was aware from back home that when a fair amount of the most knowledgeable hockey attendees in a city stay away from the new squad's matches that negatively impacts the long term viability of any new franchise. [Wikipedia; WHA San Diego Mariner Historical Site – sdmariners.htm; WHL San Diego Gulls Historical Site – sdhulls.htm; whahockey.com;

Playing Hockey The World Over … wha.htm; billsportsmaps.com; The San Diego Union Tribune; Other Local Media Sources]

As Mekkar searched for perspective on his opponent during his pre-game ritual process, he remembered a statement that Sirga made that became ingrained into his and younger brother Alf's heads. A concept that reading makes a person smarter. The subject was brought up so often by their mama, they it became a habit for all of her children to just get her off their back.

Since the Selects players have a few days off until the next matchup they decided to do some sightseeing of the area. During the next day after the game it dawned on Mekkar that he wanted to eventually play for the Mariners club and live in San Diego too! However, it was not to be due to future events making that dream impossible. Unless, San Diego received another franchise …

The city was also an option for Mekkar and it was his choice of where he wanted to go for his high school exchange program location. The arctic boy chose San Diego because he liked it. Questions of how would he survive during the summers, which are much warmer than back home. That could be an issue, but he did not consider it as a factor at the time. His views like most teenagers, are very short-term and limited whether they admit it or not. Mekkar wasn't very enthused about his mama's preference for him to do his overseas studies in the United Kingdom. She wanted him to be closer to the family and not almost half way around the globe. Sirga wanted her oldest son to go to a place where he would improve his English speaking and language skills.

She had a vision into the future about the state of affairs in regard to their home nation's economic status and it was with dread when she mentioned it to Mekkar. Well, Mekkar thought that he could cover all the bases and fulfill her language requirements for him here in this location. It's not like he had not been to this city before. He journeyed with his papa when he was younger. Since Far North Native's choice and decision was against his mama's wishes, Mekkar tried to get his papa involved to help convince Sirga. The thought was to have Henrik arrange all of the details. Mainly, because he was so experienced at those aspects as shown on other previous occasions.

When Sirga heard about Mekkar's selection, she knew that this situation would be a showdown and it wouldn't be easy to turn the older son back to her way. Primarily, because Mekkar is just like her, stubborn as a mule.

The whole idea behind Sirga's determination in this matter was to help him grow up and adapt to the modern world lifestyle. So, he could make a successful transition like she did and expand his mind by relying on himself more. Added to that, was growing into full adulthood by weaning him off from the family safety net support system, if necessary. This planning was all predicated on her premonition based on future events. Calamities such as a down-swing or eventual collapse of the national economy were taken into account. Lack of opportunities for her son's skill set in relation to the region employment market was another foreseen factor. This prediction came to pass by nineteen eighty eight. However, by that time, Mekkar was already gone due to other catastrophic circumstances that affected him.

Mekkar saw a brochure in a rack located in the hotel lobby that interested him. He doesn't remember the title exactly, so he called it Beach On The Border. After some cajoling Alf, Lasse, Johan, and Stig decided to accompany him on this trip.

Their group bribed one of the hotel employees who also drove the transport vans for picking up and dropping guest staying there. The band of five also paid him for his time and asked him if he was familiar with the area they wanted to travel to. The employee said he used to live in the area and still has friends living nearby.

They first stopped off, at a hardware store, to pickup some supplies for their little project. The crew searched and purchased tools such as a couple of shovels, buckets, trash cans, and some pieces of lumber. Also, they stopped somewhere else and got some alcohol. Mekkar told the hotel staff member that this equipment they had purchased would be donated to the hotel landscaping staff after this journey.

Then, the small group set off down the highway until they reached one of the last exits before reaching the border and headed west to the water. The driver warned them that the water might be polluted so be careful.

He also told them a small amount about the Tijuana Bullring by the Sea nearby. When the guys got out and removed the tools, they asked him to pick them up in about three hours. The van took off and the crew went down to the deserted beach with the overcast skies above them.

The group got to work building a sand castle. While at the same time, hoping no one would notice them. Since Mekkar's one hand was damaged his job was to pat down the dirt in place with his good paw. The task happened quickly with all five putting forth some effort.

They build one tiny room with dirt support that even a six foot tall individual could stand straight up in with touching the ceiling or the inside walls. It was a tight squeeze with little clearance room inside for Alf or Mekkar, as Lasse was much too large or tall.

Since there were not the problems with the border in those days, Mekkar went around the poles on the beach and just took a couple steps onto the Mexico side. The fence was not as large, extensive, restricted, or fortified as it is today.

Mekkar twirled around in a circle a couple of times and yelled out to others, "I am in Mexico!" It sort of looked like a shortened version of the hokey-pokey. A couple of strides later and he was back on the United States side. They all noticed the bullring since it stands out from anything else there. Their reward for building the sand structure was they all got drunk together on the peaceful beach. By the time the van came back they were tired from their physical exertion and well lubricated as well.

Later on unaware, the gang of five found out that it was illegal to dig on the beach, cross the border, and consume alcohol in a state park without permission. Fortunately for them no authorities showed up to reprimand them or give them a fine to pay. From there, Mekkar and his buddies embarked on other adventures throughout the area until their next match.

World Wide Hockey Tour - Los Angeles

After the portion of the schedule with the matches against the World Hockey Association (WHA) clubs was completed the attention turned forward. Now it was onto to the games against the mighty National Hockey League (NHL) squads. The first trip of this leg led the Selects to the Los Angeles Forum. It was an auspicious beginning too! Mekkar thought it could be a sign of things to come. However, The Native from the North still had this image in his mind about West Coast fans. It was formed from listening to Beach Boys, Jan & Dean, The Ventures, etc. songs. Those tunes, in reality, only referred to one segment of the local population – that is, Beachgoers & Surfers.

The Kings had those regal purple and gold clad jerseys and a flair for offense. It was not a coincidence the team shared the same color scheme with the Los Angeles Lakers since the same owner possessed both clubs along with their home arena.

Los Angeles was not considered by pundits to be strong on defense but it was balanced out by having the great Rogie Vachon in net behind them. The Kings also had a couple of tough guys also. The notorious and once former Broad Street Bully Dave "The Hammer" Schultz had been acquired for his muscle from Philadelphia. Schultz would make his mark on Mekkar in the matchup.

There was not a large concern of the Selects by the home team because they felt they could handle this travelling barn-storming squad quite easily. That turned out to be the case in the matchup that night too!

However, everything changed during an incident in the final period in which unidentified fans began throwing items at the visitors on the ice as well as at their Selects' bench area. The Arctic Warrior commented, "I guess the normally laid back fans here resemble the East Coast fans that I saw on film." When Mekkar received a thump on the noggin by an unidentified flying object, he led the charge over the shorter glass seeking revenge against the perpetrator.

As he was dishing out his own brand of vigilante retaliation in the stands, Mekkar planted the middle of a guy's forehand with a forceful move. He had taken one of his fighting sticks with him and was using it like a medieval lance. He proceeded to knock out cold a person charging at him.

Then, a group of patrons responded with a rush and pushed him back down the stairs. Mekkar rolled the short distance all the way back to the front row and landed next to the boards. Since Mekkar was advancing up the stairs in his skates in the first place, his balance was tenuous at best.

At the very least, Mekkar was glad that he wasn't a teammate who wanted to go into the stands after him to retaliate against the oncoming mob. That Selects' player never got to join the melee before being smashed over the head with a mysterious item that was never located. That hockey player was pretty much incapacitated after that with a serious head wound.

There were supporters that had battled opposing visiting team players on occasion in the past. This behavior was not an uncommon theme for the era unlike the present time. Still Mekkar was rewarded by receiving a game misconduct penalty and was tossed from the match at that point.

That was just one incident among many in a penalty filled affair in which the Kings prevailed six to three. Mekkar was beginning to believe that this was going to be a regular trend on the tour schedule. What influenced his opinion in this regard was the Selects were previously exposed to these on ice antics in Birmingham and Saint Paul. Now it was bleeding out into the stands now.

World Wide Hockey Tour – Chicago

The previous match versus Los Angeles was much different than Mekkar anticipated beforehand. The Selects also didn't expect to encounter a rough and tumble style strategy game by the Kings and their fans especially in regard to exhibition matchups. Mekkar was caught unaware also because his pre-tour research indicated a different performance and alternative match. One that would be focused on skill and scoring prowess similar to the earlier game on this jaunt against the Houston Aeros. The attitude that was put out there was contrary however with an aire of welcome to the National Hockey League brand of hockey. Not only that, it seemed to Mekkar that the Kings wanted to send a message to the Selects squad and teach them a lesson at the same time. The vibe given off by the established franchised was we have the very best hockey players in the world here and we will display it to you. The smugness and arrogance continued throughout that match.

Mekkar was perceptive enough to see through the smokescreen. He knew that other locations and hockey circuits around the globe also had top notch athletes. This was evidenced by the results of the well known 1972 Summit Series between Canada and the USSR. Not to forget the matchups between the Canadian representatives and other European national squads during that period. Added to the fact the increase and incorporation of non-Canadian draft selections in the past few years. One who could see the effects and dotting of team rosters with players from many nations currently in professional leagues of North America.

Since Mekkar and the Selects were wrong about the first game in this leg of the journey they were not sure what to expect now. Yet, Mekkar was now prepared and ready for almost anything to occur. His demeanor was if you to mix it up then let's tango knucklehead or a more slick match if it were to manifest itself. He didn't avoid the rough stuff but actually embraced the violence as just part of the game.

He even stated to a couple of his teammates on the bus to the arena for this portion of the journey, "If they want to goon it up, I will be rearing to go." Mekkar was not concerned about further damage to his already injured body parts.

The Arctic Native saw it as a tale of the biggest bear in the forest. You should let that bear hibernate and not provoke or disturb him. But, if you want to intentionally make the mistake and wake the bear to tick him off, then you get to experience the consequences of your actions. Mekkar thought of himself as the big bear. Of course, it would be a joke if he was referring to only to his physically statue. However, Mekkar also includes other factors of his being in the equation such as his drive, determination, and heart. In some aspects he was nuts on ice, but he believed this state of mind helped to protect him. Mekkar is of the presumption that he is like no one else and one of a kind. Plus, he is always willing to hammer home that point to somebody's dome if necessary, if only to get their attention.

As per his custom when Mekkar's team entered the arena he went straight away to survey it. He had read previous stories about this place. Remember, Mekkar was still a curious youngster like many kids. He searched around for the location of where the famous arena organ was. Mekkar eventually found it and met the organist there in this area. They conversed about subjects about the history of the building and how the Chicago Stadium organ was built into the facility. {Wikipedia]

Mekkar asked the guy there if he could teach the teenager any easy songs to play on the organ. The maestro did oblige and let Mekkar try to play them back on his own. Was startled when he held one of the bass keys down longer than normal. It seemed that the whole building shook. "Wow, what a feeling!" Mekkar exclaimed later. He learned two short ditties during that brief time, even though he was unfamiliar with piano or organ keys. Now Mekkar can play a version of Charge and another short hockey tune to get the crowd going and finishes with a deep bass sound at the end.

Sirga's oldest offspring stated back to the organist there, "What a home advantage you have. Especially when the opposing team has to carry and control the puck during the game." The virtuoso only responded with a sly grin, but no words. With that Mekkar had to rejoin his team in the visitor's lockerroom.

Later on, he pondered about having to stickhandle and corral the rubber disc when skating up ice with it. He asked himself if the monster organ would be going full tilt or not. Potential issues were raised by Mekkar in his consciousness. He recognized that he might have to look down to make sure the frozen biscuit stayed on his stick due to the vibrational effects. Mekkar found out in the pre-game warm-ups for real that he was indeed correct in his analysis.

All hockey players are taught ever since they are young and just starting out in the sport to always keep your head up. This is especially the case while skating through the neutral zone. Otherwise, you could risk getting walloped hard and also knocked out. Even pro players make this grave error occasionally and pay dearly for it. Being on the receiving end of open ice hits have resulted in quite a few career ending injuries.

This match against the Chicago Blackhawks was a pretty clean affair unlike the last one. It was surprising because the home side didn't feel they needed to take advantage of the smaller than the normal ice size standard for the North American continent. {Wikipedia] Unfortunately for Mekkar and the Selects the result was the same, a defeat by a 5-2 margin.

The one thing that stood out for Mekkar was being the ice and playing at the same time as the great Bobby Orr. Although, it wasn't the same Orr as Mekkar remembered from watching the films and tapes back home. Due to the many knee injuries and other maladies Orr was almost at the completion of his hockey career. Mekkar noticed that Bobby's skating ability was clearly not the same as before and that Orr's playing days would soon be coming to an end. This, in fact, transpired. However, a fifty percent Bobby Orr is still better than eighty percent of the players that have ever suited up, even if not up to his own lofty standards. [Wikipedia; The Hockey News; and various other media sources]

World Wide Hockey Tour – Toronto

When Mekkar and his team arrived at Maple Leaf Gardens in Toronto, Ontario, Canada they were initially directed down a pathway to the visitor's dressing room. He noticed along this corridor were pictures of past star players of the homeside. There were also quite a few plaques and lists showing the different accomplishments and awards involving various Maple Leaf players throughout the years.

The skeptical youngster that he is saw this as a type of tactic to try to throw the Selects squad off of their game. Furthermore, it was just basically to get inside their heads prior to gametime. Mekkar concluded that this was just another intimidation endeavor but carried out in a psychological way. He was not affected by it because he could see through the tactic, but figured that some of the other Selects' might be.

Anyway, Mekkar was excited to play against one of his heroes, Borje "The King" Salming. Despite realizing that due to both of their positions as defensemen and the natural flow of the match, they would come into direct contact with each other very little, if at all. Plus, Mekkar's on ice minutes were sharply reduced due to injury.

Many of the Selects' members observed the rabid parts of the crowd as they came onto the ice for the normal pre-game warmup ritual. It was a larger crowd than almost anywhere back home, but still overall less rowdy. Mekkar didn't hear songs directed toward individual players like his home rink nor see large flags and banners waving in the stands. Here was tame in comparison but the sheer mass of people in the arena energized the home team with their pockets of exuberance.

Mekkar had trained himself long ago to accept any cheering or positive reinforcement and incorporate it as his own, no matter whom it was directed at, the source or location. This would always increase the confidence in Mekkar. Lasse and Alf deemed it as more like cockiness which Mekkar was not undersupplied. This mindset was beneficial for Mekkar's on ice performances during the actual games. He said this attitude made him more successful.

The Leafs sported a starting lineup that could rival that very best clubs in the world. However, their troubles stemmed from bad management and in the lack of quality depth on the roster departments. Who Toronto sent over the boards to start the match was impressive. Lanny McDonald up front with Darryl Sittler centering the first line and Left Wing Dave "Tiger" Williams protecting everyone's back. On the back line were Salming and Ian Turnbull with Mike Palmateer in goal. [Wikipedia] Formidable indeed thought Mekkar and his teammates. When the top Toronto unit was on the ice they totally controlled the pay and dictated the pace, which the Selects were unable to counteract.

As the Selects' coaching staff behind the bench accepted this and desired their team to push the tempo when the other Leaf lines were on the ice to balance it all out. The game did not accurately reflect the dominance in the box score in a 4-2 Maple Leaf win. Mekkar felt fortunate to avoid a blowout. The Selects only took one minor penalty and negated that opportunity by keeping Toronto from converting their powerplay. Guess who took the penalty? Yes, it was Mekkar! The netminding for the visitors on this night was excellent and helped to keep the match from being a runaway for the hosts. As a result, the Far North Native stated, "A hot goalie can make up for the rest of the team's mistakes." Nevertheless, the cynical Mekkar thought that the Leafs were sort of toying with his travelling team.

The best part of the night for Mekkar was the post game brief chat with Salming, who is one of his hockey role models. He did try to pick to pick the classy Borje's mind a bit. However, there was just so much information and experience there. Salming's vast resource knowledge was overwhelming to the young arctic teen and it was hard to grasp, even a small bit of it.

World Wide Hockey Tour – Buffalo

This was a game for Mekkar to test how much he had developed his hockey acumen and skill set. It was hard to judge without considering his injury against him. It was also a barometer of the work that still needed to be done for him to reach a reasonable professional level. The gap between the two degrees was still evident and obvious, even to Mekkar himself.

He had to show his stuff even though by this matchup in Buffalo the teenager had his playing minutes greatly reduced to hopefully further the healing of his badly broken hand. It had not gotten any better by this point due to the fact of his not taking time off from missing matches on this tour. Mekkar was too stubborn for that and only watching the matches as a scratched Black Ace would drastically increase his growing frustration levels. The damage incurred to his right paw and wrist also affected the roll over and snap of the wrist required for different and effective passes to teammates or shots on net. Since, Mekkar did not possess a howitzer slap shot from the point anyway.

The lower extended extremity meant the loss of power and control in all things related to handling of the hard rubber flying disc. This placed an adaptation of more emphasis on the top hand on his stick that can guide direction of passes to open fellow members of his team. Mekkar distinguished that due to the upper body issue it was still more important to put the biscuit in the basket or at least directly on net. That way to also create any rebound opportunities for his club to score more scrappy goals.

Not counting the matter regarding a few assumptions on behalf of the Selects coaching staff about their opponent this evening, the Buffalo Sabres. The viewpoint was despite the slightly small non-regular sized rink dimensions the Sabres wouldn't play a goon it up style. The fear was that Buffalo might light-up the Selects on the scoreboard instead. The Sabres first forward line made them an offensive juggernaut led by the dynamic French Connection Line of Gilbert Perreault, Rene Robert, and Rick Martin. In addition, they had good goaltending behind them.

The matchup was expected to be similar to the Kings who the Selects already faced off against. However, it was predicted there would not be a repeat of the pugilistic affair like the one in Los Angeles. This would be highly beneficial for Mekkar in that he could take a break and hold back from having to punch any rival combatants in the noggin during on-ice tangos. Then, he recalled that is also what the Selects' team staff said prior to the match in Southern California and look how that episode turned out.

Some of Mekkar's buddies on the squad agreed with him on his cautious assessment regarding this match against the Sabres. Mekkar asked the question, "Could we fall for the club management intelligence again and trust in their judgment one more time regarding this?" Nevertheless, cultural factors and influences took precedence over their emotions and were applied to not challenge or ruffle the feathers of the Selects coaches. Mekkar was at the forefront of non-acceptance of the authoritative opinion regarding them team's next opponent. It is because those in coaching positions have the power to ultimately mete out individual playing time and discipline toward each athlete.

There is always a fear of being known as a person with a reputation of rocking the (team) boat. This is seen as very detrimental in hockey, sports, and business circles and can affect one's career especially at the higher levels. In many cases, the temperament does not match the individual athlete's talent level and might not be deserved but just perceived. There is also the tendency, where Mekkar is originally from, to avoid most confrontational situations especially involving authority figures. Staying away from all the drama that usually goes with a prickly personality is the road taken by most people as a matter of self preservation.

Yet, Mekkar was pretty much unlike anyone else and didn't care what others thought of him. Definitely those creatures in authoritative positions, even ones placed above him. His typical attitude did not follow the accepted norms of most civilized societies nor in his own native environment for that matter. This part of Mekkar's psyche steadily grew stronger as he reached maturity as a fully developed adult.

Anyway, in spite of Mekkar's insolence and a position of relative non-conformance he seemed to commonly make it through with minimal setbacks. That was not the reality for the Selects on this night as Buffalo's French Connection top line ripped Mekkar's team apart in an 8-3 Sabre victory.

World Wide Hockey Tour – Boston

After matches against a few of the other league teams, the Selects were to face off against the big bad powerful Boston Bruins. The Bruins' had a lineup that was specifically built and tailored to more effective in the friendly confines of the Boston Garden. Once again, another shorter dimensions ice rink. That way they could be on a player much quicker and close any distances more rapidly. This was especially true when Mekkar or his teammates had the puck on their stick. Their youthfulness and relative inexperience could be very much exposed in panic situations like that.

The Bruins were also a very scrappy squad through the decade and maximized the use of their smaller rink to physically intimidate most of the visiting reams. They had tough players such as Stan Jonathan, Mike Milbury, Terry O'Reilly, Brad Park, & others. However, it was not on the scale of The Broad Street Bully teams that were in their championship glory period down south. The pundits were quick to note there was a balance of toughness and talent in Boston which the Bruins had in abundance too!

Also, the Garden was constructed so long ago before modern building techniques were instituted. Humidity and arena temperatures could fluctuate greatly and affect the playing surface and game conditions in the facility. Mekkar was aware of this through his earlier research that issues more often arise during the warmer parts of the year. It should not be a factor now for this matchup, Mekkar thought. It turned out it wasn't a problem involving the Selects during this game. The travelling squad had more pressing matters to deal with.

For the fans of the current day, the closest one can experience the old time styled buildings would be in a few minor pro leagues or top tier junior circuits. That is, if the old barns are still in existence before being torn down and replaced by more sterile places. Some of those aged rinks are tiny in comparison to the smaller than the normal sized Garden. Mekkar has seen some rinks where shots toward the opposition net from the offensive blue line were equivalent to being far inside the offensive zone. That is, more than anywhere else with standard hockey dimensions.

Mekkar had one source of reference as to the style of the Bruins. He remembered there is only one league in Europe, when facing clubs there, which was more like the North American linear and rougher style of hockey. This mode was contrary to other comparable elite ice hockey circuits around the world.

Thankfully for Mekkar, there were no line brawls in the Bruins – Selects match like Mekkar had previously watched on tape versus some of Boston's main rivals. It was more common theme in the nineteen seventies games and every so often included fans also. Still, it was a physical, if non-descript affair. Mekkar was of the opinion that the Bruins didn't have the desire nor motivation to really put the hurt on the visitor's on this evening.

On the other hand, Boston has a bruising manner of hockey instilled in their fabric as a team and it would be hard for them to adopt any other way. Mekkar said, "The Bruins were compelled to take advantage of their home's idiosyncrasies and they did so during this game." Boston pushed the young Selects around most of the night and banged the road weary Selects 6-2. Only Mekkar, Lasse, and a couple of others on their squad were not affected by the Bruins system of breaking teams down.

World Wide Hockey Tour – Philadelphia

Mekkar was still young but he was growing up pretty fast on this tour. He felt that he was learning lessons that could not be acquired anywhere else and that he could draw upon in the future. Nevertheless, being an immature teen has its drawbacks. Mekkar still had a bad problem or Alf would refer to it as a flaw in his character. Alf mentioned that his older sibling was often bravely dumb or just flat out crazy and stupid. Alf could not decide which was the case. It is a fine line between acting brave and being stupid. This description fit Mekkar to a tee. This defect was shown when Mekkar would refuse to back down from a battle or a fight, even when it might be more prudent to do so. The hand injury just compounded the situation.

The arctic native needed to be wary of combining his problems as a result of the increasing issues of bodily damage including the head area. The blunt force trauma endured by Mekkar was a consequence of short term thinking and the amount of brawls he participated in. Not realizing it then, many of Mekkar's future activities in life would be drastically affected.

It is well known that other collision sports athletes from other sports appreciate the skills needed to play ice hockey. Many would be surprised how many NFL football players go to watch pro hockey games today. Like other fans, a few go to watch the fights. Similar to the small number of car racing fans watching only to observe the accidents.

People forget how loaded with talent and toughness the Flyers were with Andre "Moose" Dupont, Bobby Clarke, Rick MacLeish, Bill Barber, Bernie Parent, and more. In one instance, one of the members of the Flyers was engaged in a round a fista-a-cuffs with Mekkar. Rapid Fire as Mekkar referred to his fellow combatant in contrast to the well known Hound Dog nickname by others. [Wikipedia] Two reasons why Mekkar called Bob Kelly by this term. One reason was the rapid firing punching hand at Mekkar's noggin and the other was a slight reference to gangster Machine Gun Kelly. Mekkar's normal tactic of using the boards as a brace behind him from falling backwards and hitting his head on the ice on this occasion backfired. Once they were squared off halfway from the face-off dot near the corner of the rink; Rapid Fire alternatively grabbed Mekkar's head by its sides and repeatedly kept slamming it against the glass.

He was now in sort of a fog and Mekkar's mind began to wander. As he was taking this throttling he strained to look up in The Spectrum and noticed different items up there on high. Mekkar also observed other aspects upward that many arena patrons might never notice. Then, the reality of Mekkar's setting knocked him back into focus enough to gain his bearings. The Arctic Warrior realized that he must turn the tide against his aggressor somehow. He lifted his knee upward, while still balanced against those side boards, and thrusted it into the groin of his adversary. His opponent's cup moved slightly to one side enough to inflict enough pain. Finally, the action of the head-to-glass pounding against Mekkar ceased. He was just thankful that he didn't slump backwards during that maneuver and hit his skull directly on the ice. As Mekkar often quips, "Because ice always wins!"

During another part of the same exhibition matchup, one of the Philadelphia players' took a nasty cheap shot against a Selects' member. That same Flyer player had taken these actions before because that strategy had been employed beforehand against other visiting squads. It was used to create an environment of intimidation, even though the Flyers had plenty of skill and great goaltending to be successful with any style they wished. Mekkar was having none of this and chased after the infractor and sought revenge - ready to beat his butt.

That individual hurriedly fled behind tougher Philadelphia teammates instead of defending those actions. In true smack and run pest mode did not have to face the music in retaliation for their own despicable behavior on the ice. So, Mekkar went right back to taking up arms against one of the other Flyer goons. Mekkar despises that Flyer alum right up to the current day because they didn't have the guts to physically defend their dirty actions on the ice that day.

Due to the nature of this match and the multiple concussions he suffered as a result, Mekkar remembered almost no details afterward. Fortunately, his younger brother Alf, his best friend Lasse, and other teammates filled him in later. They had to wait to plug in the details after his mind had cleared a bit from the head trauma. Mekkar essentially lost a week of his memory at the time. As was a common practice among his squad, the others' around him filled in and completed the information of the time he was there in person, but absent otherwise. For example, that the Selects were beaten up and defeated 6-1. That is, until the young Mekkar gained his faculties back from all the whacks to his crown, ready to do it some more later on.

World Wide Hockey Tour – Pittsburgh

Unknown to the young Mekkar and by the time of this matchup versus the Penguins, they were already interested parties in acquiring his future services. Clubs from both the WHA & NHL observed his play and loved his toughness. They appreciated the fact he soldiered on and was still effective in a limited role despite the serious hand injury. Plus, the fact that he missed no games on the Selects barn-storming tour. The scouts had their ways of founding out hard to discover inside information from their sources about hockey personnel.

It was a good thing that Mekkar was not cognizant of the interest in him because that might have put too much pressure on him. He might have tried too hard to impress the pro hockey brass with the result of more on ice frequent mistakes and errors. It was already tough enough to draw from the well of his full capacity of skills being exhibited because of the upper body injury. The physical diminishment was considerable, but the determination and heart was extremely visible.

Mekkar learned some new inside lessons during this matchup. He learned the art of sending a message to on ice officials for disparate rulings. Rulings that greatly favored one team over another and ultimately impacted the outcome of the game. He saw examples of individuals trying to line up body checks, usually near the boards, of opponents that would include hopefully clip the refs in the process also. He also overheard statements such as "Be more consistent in your calls for both sides!" The reasoning was to get the attention of the on ice decision makers and send a message to them. That is, if they are going to be awful, at least be consistently bad for both teams as much as possible. Show no favoritism because players and fans eventually learn the referees' tendencies and recognize these erratic stances. He wanted to incorporate these elements into his game as well.

Other previously unknown perspectives to Mekkar were introduced to him during this part of the trip as well. Whether he want to be or not, Mekkar would be introduced to more insight about the game he loved. For instance, this was an era where dubious activities were always taking place. Members of one squad would place bounties as a reward of carrying out aggressive moves. Violence against individual opposition players, coaches, referees, whole teams, what have you, were common. Mekkar found out that these spirited undertakings have been present for a long time. It could be found in a myriad of athletics such as hockey, football, and many others. At many levels of sports too! Such an environment exists in other realms like the cutthroat business world also. If one needs proof do a research on the mafia and hidden government operations. So, it was not a new phenomenon.

Whoever says they do not know about it is either lying, involved somehow, or willfully ignorant. This includes coaches, managers, executives, etc. Thus, the reason why these deeds of intent are still conducted regularly today.

Management and executives usually turn a blind eye to this type of behavior, but they are acutely aware that it happens as most were athletes at one time or another. However, the suits who are just politician lawyers do target their specific punishment decrees and mete out retribution based on a host of reasons. Some reactions are in reaction to public outcry and perception. Others are due to hidden jealousy, choosing sides in a rivalry, or flat out hatred.

Many excuses are made to conceal the dictatorial mandates and exercise of authoritative power which in turn has an extremely high potential for abuse. There is truth in the saying that: Power corrupts and absolute power corrupts absolutely. [Lord Acton, 1887; William Pitt the Younger, The Earl of Chatham, 1770]

Overbearing answers are given in regard to legality issues as to avoid lawsuits in sue-happy North America to cover the speaker's tracks. However, it is evident for all to see through the smokescreen, if a person is truly alert to conditions that surround them. Aslak's discussions with Mekkar back home made him very enlightened. That is of the premise that everyone has some sort of agenda and will take actions to promote it, if they are able.

The match itself was fairly non-descript in that the young Selects squad were vanquished by the Penguins club by a seven to four margin. Jean Pronovost and Rick Kehoe contributed to the scoring. Another player on the Pittsburgh side - Bob "Battleship" Kelly was given way too much room on the ice as a result of his pugilistic prowess. He wasn't just a goon, but also had a good slap shot and knotted two goals in this match sending the Selects off with another loss. [Wikipedia; penguinslegends.blogspot.com; penguinpoop.com]

World Wide Hockey Tour -
Bombed in the Box

The Selects as a team were on a high note because they won six straight games versus collegiate teams. Next up was a matchup against two junior hockey squads. This story refers to the first game of the two.

Mekkar was in a bad mood on this evening and that attitude resulted in more than his usual aggressive nastiness on the ice. About midway through the first period of the match The Arctic Warrior was whistled for roughing. Then, he was sent to his hockey home away from home, the penalty box. At first, he was aware by the booing that he was a target of crowd displeasure. Then, hometown fans began to give him some more grief. Mekkar responded by squirting some water, from the water bottle, at fans over the short glass. However, the home fans got their revenge. The Native from the North proceeded to get bombed during this particular visit to the sin bin.

However, he didn't recognize the onslaught of objects being thrown at him while doing his time in the box. That was, until he caught one with his hand and exclaimed, "What! It looks like cherries!" He flicked a few right back into the crowd which incited them even more to continue the rain upon him.

Well, he was playing a club that resided in a region for its bountiful assortment of fruits. Mekkar thought to himself out loud as usual, but normally unaware of it, and asked "Where did the fans get all of those cherries?" Cherries, like marshmallows, are a symbol used by the fans to show who they think is not tough and to get under a player's skin. All who know Mekkar definitely wouldn't place him in the soft category.

Before this trip to the penalty box, Mekkar was involved in this game against a well known junior squad on the continent. He was playing with extra roughness due to his mood. Since Mekkar doesn't care what people in general and especially enemy fans think of him, he was unrepentant. He clearly was not planning on modifying his behavior.

This attitude was straddling a fine line because he was still performing for a team that was representing his country. The Selects team executives had minimum standards and codes of conduct for players to follow. It was even applied in the face of taunts and worse actions taken against him and his teammates. This conflicted with Mekkar's disposition and style of play which to him elevated his effectiveness on the ice.

The young man from the Arctic fought his inner being with its urge to taunt the unfriendly and downright hostile crowd there. He did respond as his normal self to opposing players who gave him grief with comments such as, "I have encountered bears, so fear of humans Ha! You have to be kidding me!"

Alf's sibling felt that the ice surface was not in prime shape and intentionally prepped in that manner to slow down the speed advantage of his team. Any way to help the plodding and slower home side, huh! Mekkar suspected this treachery because he knew it was odd for a rink in this area to have such a poorly maintained ice surface. One could tell there was a pride about that. Mekkar also felt that the building was warmer than it should be because he acutely familiar with arena operations in general.

Mekkar wasn't sure if the cherries and possibly other fruits were given out in bunches, bags, or gift baskets as a promotional giveaway items to induce greater attendance to the game. He thought the idea was one that was outside of the box. He was of the opinion maybe the local community was having a fruit festival and might have had a different incentive item given to the fans each night. He also asked the question of why let the fans bring these outside things into the arena in the first place? Would it hurt the concession sales there which all or at least a portion of food sales and parking fees from an event go directly to the home team.

These are things Mekkar had running through his mind while serving his sentence in the penalty box. It was quite a regular spot for him and a very well known part to Mekkar, especially back home. Well, since he had such a penchant for taking aggressive penalties.

On this evening, Mr. Bad Attitude, Mekkar had heard of rowdy fans at junior rinks in other locations around North America doing crazy stunts like this. Like tossing batteries, red dyed and colored rice, or spraying various substances at visiting team benches and on individual players themselves. In a few locations heavy tarps and temporary roofs would be used to cover non-homeside benches and tunnels to and from the dressing room to combat these unruly fan behaviors. Since Mekkar had heard about stories such as these before he could not just discount the notion or possibilities. He understood that these fan responses could erupt and arise at any moment. Thus, Mekkar needed to always be ready and prepared like as if he was on a reindeer trek watching out for predators.

Back when he, at home earlier in the decade, first observed in person the nasty tempered clubs coming from North American hooligan hockey breeding grounds. Those visitors acted in the same manner and brought some of their drunken supporters with them. Mekkar figured the squads where imitating the behaviors of belligerent, rowdy, and downright rude to almost everyone around them fans. Monkey see, Monkey do!

Then, the effects of the cherry and possibly other fruits as well bombing raid set in. Mekkar's uniform and some items underneath were now soaked with juice mixed with his own sweat and it began to run down into all parts of his gear and undergarments. Mekkar felt like people in the seats nearby had also poured more cups of juice or a liquid that smelled like beer all over him. It was starting to feel sticky to the touch.

When Mekkar had served his crime time in the hockey jail there was a break in the action during the game. He made a bee-line from the sin bin straight to the lockerroom across the ice. Mekkar also left his own unintentional small streak from the assault to mark his journey off to the bowels of the arena. The game officials called for time to repair the ice surface and try to lessen the visibility of the new line created by the Mekkar mess.

Selects' players thought the whole situation was pretty funny and saw that Mekkar was steamed. They knew he would be back for more extraction and retaliation for this act against him. Mekkar hurried to get out of the drenched juice soaked gear and clothing he was wearing and took a quick shower. He had insufficient backup equipment of his own and so had to scramble up some other items to be fully outfitted to participate in the third and final period of the game.

Mekkar subsequently stated out loud and directed his comments to anyone nearby who would listen regarding his theory of why the home team was wearing their dark colored sweaters at home for this matchup. Since the home club gets to choose this meant the visitors had to don their light background jerseys. Now this is a common theme with the advent of third or alternate jerseys for the teams playing in their own backyard.

However, the normal trend during this era was the home teams wore the whites or in the case of the NBA Los Angeles Lakers donned their yellow jerseys at home with the darken shades being worn on the road. Special occasions were a whole different environment entirely and excluded from these tendencies. Mekkar was now extra suspicious as he changed and cleaned himself up for more activity in the last period.

He just wanted revenge and was about to take it out on any opposing player foolish enough to venture in his space on the ice. A cruising for a bruising in a brutal physical manner was to be unleashed as a result of the fans display against him. Until, he was kicked out of the game altogether.

In the course of his first shift of the third stanza, one of the home players made a smart remark to Mekkar. This set him off and Mekkar went on the attack. After knocking out that player with a good right hook to the chin, he let gravity take over and the victim fell to the ice in a heap. The enraged teen was happy to see his favorite color of red blood flowing from his victim. Right then Mekkar received his fighting major infraction along with a game misconduct penalty and was ejected from the match.

This led to the crowd serenading him while the chorus of the song Na Na Na Na Hey Hey Hey Good Bye by Steam played in the background. In addition, The Arctic Warrior received a personal escort to the lockeroom where he got to listen to the rest of the game on a local radio station. Mekkar is completely different from most people in that he believes in getting mad and getting even with his target. He was still ticked off because Mekkar felt that he didn't really accomplish his due amount of retaliation. Nonetheless, it is wise to not to mess with Mekkar and pick another mark to heap abuse upon. Oh! Yeah, the Selects won the game 5-1 and totally turned the tables after Mekkar's forced departure from the match.

World Wide Hockey Tour – Southern Europe

The Selects had a record of two wins and five losses against the WHA squads and no victories in the seven matches they faced off against NHL teams. Actually, they did better than expected by winning a couple of the earlier games against the pro teams. It was expected that they would lose them all, even get crushed in most of them. The Selects' club did meet the forecast by prevailing in the next eight games without a loss versus the collegiate plus a couple of Canadian major junior clubs. Mekkar and teammates showed dominance in those matches except the last one due to the fatigue factor. This despite having a roster that was younger overall than all of the squads so far on this portion of the hockey tour.

Mekkar recalled that the coaches and team officials still always expected more from the team. At the same time, the Selects' players were being constantly reminded to be on their best behavior and frequently told, "You are goodwill ambassadors representing your country". Mekkar joked to some of his teammates, "If that were true, those in charge would have sent the real top tier national team instead of us. The one that plays in the annual World Championships, the Olympics, and big tournaments like that! Our squad was sent to fulfill previously made exchange agreements." All of his teammates that heard the rebellious native's comments laughed as they knew he was absolutely correct in his assessment.

This travelling circus as Mekkar referred to it still had other stops to play more matches after the stint in North America. The schedule was supposed to be very packed and have the team arrive in quite a few cities all over. Yet, the reality of the daily news passed onto to the players became a running comedy of errors in their minds. The whole farce seemed to Mekkar that whoever was arranging the different matches to be played was ill-prepared. The lack of organization of the tour was turning out to be more like a continuing gag. The team members didn't know from one to the next if the schedule match would take place that day or not. Cancellations and changes in the calendar would at times be discovered the very morning of that particular game day. It was frustrating to say the least for Mekkar and many of the others.

Maybe, Mekkar figured it was just an absence of finding quality opponents for the Selects to face off against. Of course, neither he nor any of them really knew for sure. Sometimes the players were informed with excuses of arena scheduling changes along with a host of other justifications. Mekkar thought many of those admissions were untrue. He knew better through what he learned about prearranging playing time and space availability planned far in advance. He did just recently help manage, along with teammates, a team and home facility while performing on the ice at the same time. There were matches already cancelled on this tour that would have taken the Selects to Brazil, Australia, Japan, Thailand, France, Germany, England, and South Africa. At least there still a few games left thought Mekkar. Anyway, the Selects next game on the docket was in Switzerland and they now had no idea what to expect.

Well, Mekkar was notified that he is now not welcome from participating in some engagements and cities in Canada. This was due to some altercations with opposing fans, coaches, and players. From what even a few of Mekkar's own team members considered as over-the-top taunting, swearing, and object throwing in retaliation to having items poured on him in the sin bin. Mekkar didn't care what they said about or how they labeled him. As a pest, Mekkar was not about to let up with respect to his behavior either. His attitude was if management wants to send me back home then do it otherwise shut up and move on. As for the objects thrown back at the crowd Mekkar now admitted he might have went too far in his reaction because it incited the fans even more against him.

On one occasion, Mekkar went to his bench to retrieve one of the two of his heavier twigs encased with a thicker layer of fiberglass. He called them his special fighting sticks and proceeded to engage another combatant in a stick fight by the home bench. Mekkar thought of these fights while wielding the lumber as like a dual between medieval knights aiming their lances. In this case he was on sharp blades on frozen water instead of on horseback. Mekkar had practiced this type of one-on-one battle back home. He became extremely adept at it. This time he knocked the other guy's wood club from his grasp.

In Mekkar's fury he swung his stick at the fellow willing belligerent's head in a downward chopping motion. The adversary ducked out of the way and one of the homeside coaches received a vicious slash across the face instead. It goes without saying that Mekkar was kicked out of the game and then later reprimanded by his squad's officials for his violent conduct. Mekkar later felt that someone in the Selects management must have appeased another important individual in that city. He was lucky that no assault charges were filed against him in a court of law. It was a different time and place, but he would not be able to escape in the same manner today. Mekkar got to continue on the rest of the tour and was not sent back home at this point. Still, Mekkar was on a very short leash.

The panorama in Switzerland to Mekkar was so beautiful in some areas of the country he thought they should put them on touristy postcards or for sale paintings. Since the Selects came into town early the day before Mekkar got to check out some of the surrounding sights. Yet, he was really tired and the rapid travel time zone changes affected his body today. He learned from working at the airline with his mama, well dragged along by her, that a good rule to follow was one day of rest for crossing every three time zones travelled. Utterly the recovery time was going to be shortened in preparation for this matchup and its 2pm local start time.

Arctic warrior that he is, Mekkar thought that it was a weird time to begin a hockey game. He attributed it to some type of local media broadcast reasoning or cause. Mekkar would soon learn why this oddity was in effect. When his squad arrived at the rink about an hour prior to game time, Mekkar went to check it out. Wow, he quickly noticed the differences and then went directly to the visitor's lockerroom area to change and get ready. Mekkar described what he saw to a few of other teammates. Most of the Selects' players were already into their pre-game rituals and ignored him. A few others on the team didn't believe his story at all.

Mekkar didn't even bother to converse with any of the netminders, just because to him they are aliens or from space. He felt that goalies are the only individuals crazy, weird, or stupid enough to accept a position where they received rapidly firing discs at themselves. Plus, other players coming at them too! Mekkar has performed netminding duties in the past but only in practices. Additionally, the assignments were by his coaches under duress and desperate to fill a need. The net duties taken by him were always against his better judgment and wishes. Even though it was to help the team, he thought who in their right mind would be crazy enough to play this position as a regular job.

No wonder the goalies are all nuts to accept hard solid rubber pucks flying at them at dangerous speeds. Only recently the last of the maskless guardians of the net had retired. At least by carrying this function outside of formal games Mekkar gained an appreciation of what he personally knew what the netminders go through. However, Mekkar was not about to change his game because he believed it would render him less effective on the ice.

As the team came out onto the ice Lasse discerned that yes there was a roof, but no building walls around the outside the stands and the arena. The overhead lighting was not the brightest either. Fortunately there was some day light that contributed to the atmosphere there. Mekkar had earlier tried to warn his teammates but they did not listen or rebuffed him altogether. So, he didn't speak anymore about the conditions and would let them find out for themselves.

He figured this environment would not have been so if the Selects were facing off against a team in one of the larger cities, would it? But, in Mekkar's intellect and reasoning, once again thanks to the idiotic organizers of this tour the squad was stuck in a small town. As well as performing in this partially constructed building as he pointed out. Mekkar was about to change his perspective to further prepare himself for the upcoming matchup.

In the first period when the winter wind blew through the arena Mekkar could have swore he heard the crowd make a shivering noise in unison. The Native from the North decided to treat this match as if they were outdoors. Similar to, when he was younger, playing on the frozen lake back home in the arctic. That way he could play his normal style with boldness despite the elemental effects on his team as a whole.

Lasse, Mekkar, and Alf all had a huge advantage over most of their spoiled squad members who were used to more modern game conditions. The arctic three had played hockey in much colder weather outdoors and had better adapted to chilly breezes back in the village. Mekkar spoke up and said that, "This was nothing you babies!" Still some of traveler teammates were quite miserable throughout this game. The coaching staff gave more playing minutes to some of the Selects' team members that were less used to the colder climates. So that to keep their body temperatures warmer and not let it drop too far.

Alf, Lasse, and Mekkar always came prepared and had packed, in their minimal hand carry luggage, beanie caps or toques to put on under their helmets. Growing up in the colder regions teaches one that the top of the head is where the most body heat escapes. They all had extra mittens to put fit under the gloves also. Mekkar's hand was heavily taped so he was unable to use the gloves or had no need for them. He loaned them to a team member who needed them badly, but charged him to wash them thoroughly before return them back to him. Otherwise, a butt kicking would be in store.

Mekkar also saw during his own quick rink inspection and observation that the glass at the far ends of that rink was shorter than normal. He realized that the home club must prefer puck possession, thus it was a priority in this game. During this match Mekkar also noticed that children would stand right up against the glass to watch the game. Furthermore they would be protected from the crisp wind gusts that whipped through the rink every so often. There was a set of stands on each side of the rink. Even though there wasn't a large crowd to view the festivities, the sound from the voices would carry. It was much louder than it should have been for the small number of fans in attendance. Most of the Selects were motivated through efforts to retain their body heat and desire to feel warmth on the day. Subsequently, the visitors completely dominated their competition that afternoon by a score of fourteen to one. Mekkar quipped, "This time the shoe is on the other foot and we get to enjoy a blowout for a change."

If Mekkar thought the last place was an odd environment to have a hockey game, the next match in Italy topped it. After the last tilt, the Selects left by way of a charter airplane along with other modes of transportation. The squad arrived at their destination the next evening.

After checking into their meager accommodations and getting settled Mekkar, Lasse, Alf and Johan headed out on the hunt to find any nightlife. Well, at the very least round up some of the local talent. They all had drinks in their hands during the search. The club they wandered into was not the greatest but Mekkar replied, "The chicks are just okay here but they will look a lot better when we are drunk."

Those four opportunistic guys all were hooked for the rest of the crisp night. It was tough to get going the next morning when the whole team met together at the hotel a couple of hours before the one o'clock afternoon match. Mekkar felt in the course of the pre-game preparation session that these early game starting times were beginning to cut into his regular party time. He was hoping and embarked on lobbying team management for evening matchups. Favorably for Mekkar, he still had some strong medications for his injuries to help him cope with the unexpected changes.

The native from the north had a sense that something was going to be peculiar for this match. Ever since he became aware that it was going to start earlier than the previous one. When the team arrived at the rink, if one wanted to call it that, Mekkar's nagging intuition was right on the money.

In Mekkar's view this match was about to take the form similar to an outdoor pond hockey game. There were boards with very short glass around the ice surface. However, the boards did not completely surround the rink as they were supplemented by a few huge boulders without any plexiglass on top of them in some spots. The big stones appeared to have been there previously or specifically laid in place by large machinery, thought Mekkar.

Promptly at 1pm the match began. It took full advantage of the daylight since there was no roof, building walls of any kind ringing the area, and only a few light poles existent. Sort of like one would find at your local tennis courts. There were older fans sitting in the portable metal stands on one side of the rink. The rest were standing all around and singing songs, chanting, and making noise in support of their local club.

The Selects skated their rear-ends off as prodded by the coaches and turned in a masterful performance. They had possession of the puck more than eighty percent of the game. It was even more of a dominant performance than the last time out. The drawback was that the home team began to play the body more than the puck. A couple of the Selects were hammered into the big rocks that were part of the rink. Mekkar was involved in one of those incidents too and paid the price. He stated as he was coming to the bench after the hit, "At least the boards have some give, but those rocks are sturdy with no leeway." Mekkar, unlike a couple of his other fallen and injured teammates, finished the match. Although, not without some discomfort on his part.

World Wide Hockey Tour - Down the Nile

The next tilt for the Selects was in the most unlikely of places, Cairo Egypt. It wasn't explained to the players as to who their actual opponent was. Just that an ice rink had been set up for this exhibition match. The coaching staff passes the word from the tour organizers that this game was for the benefit of international relations. Mekkar mocked them after delivering the news to the team. He joked, "It is just some politician speak phrases to cover for the freshly arranged match against probably some scrub club. After that, who knows what is next!"

Since the beginning of the worldwide hockey journey the team members had been informed of current and possible developments only on a need to know basis. At least it seemed that way when Mekkar, Lasse, and other players were discussing this subject together. Mekkar snapped, "Those individuals at the top are just toying with us and think it is hilarious." He also audibly expressed himself, in his original bold manner, regarding the player's frustration of the fact that anything was subject to change at any moment. Unfortunately, for them it usually did without warning. Mekkar had the inkling to find and beat a few answers out of one or more of those pencil pushers as he referred to the Selects management.

Nevertheless, there was a perception that the coaching staff was much better informed than were the players. It gave off an impression that the coaches didn't always tell all of what they knew regarding the behind the scenes activities and shenanigans related to the tour. A few of the other athletes tried to wring more details from members of the Selects staff but it was unsuccessful. Mekkar scoffed out loud in the dressing room prior to this matchup, "To somebody else's whim we go!"

Mekkar pondered several thoughts before this game. It was due to his belief that when you are not familiar with your opponent it is hard to judge their skill quality and abilities. He never underestimated anyone. Thus, the reason why the Native from the North always gave his full out, maximum effort every game. Part of it was the abhorrence of being part of a team that might suffer indignity and become a footnote in history. He didn't want to be on the wrong side in the list of great sports upsets, ever. He figured no one wants that shame, especially him. Otherwise, Mekkar would dish out an extensive physical whipping among his own teammates to go along with the embarrassment on the scoreboard. His distaste of losing was quite clear to everyone who knew him.

Sirga and Henrik had advised Mekkar on a few occasions that it is okay to do a psychological job on your enemy for whatever reasons. For him to look at it like marketing similar to hyping a boxing match or any type of event. They also strongly infused their son to never disregard or underestimate any opponent or combatant. It is foolish to do so they would expound. Just when you think you know your foe, they can surprise you with something new they learned recently was maintained to the teenager.

Due to the last match and the Selects injury situation there was only six defensemen for this game, less than normal. So, Mekkar would be suited up even though the staff wanted to scratch him from the lineup. The wanted to hold him out for this match to let his hand heal more, so he could be more effective later on. The Selects felt they didn't really need him for this matchup. Healthy game time scratches are usually known in hockey as Black Aces. [blackaceshockey.com/origin.htm] The problem was there were no more forward or defensive reserves left to insert into the lineup for tonight. The travel time ensured that none could arrive on the horizon in time for the game either. There was an exception, a non-dressed third string goalie. Trouble is, netminders have their own unique standards and rules that most other players don't fully understand, including Mekkar.

After realizing how bad the opposing squad was skill-wise the Selects would face on this night in comparison, the travelling team offered the use of one of the Selects' goalies for this clash. Since the netminders were of a much lower quality than any of them on Mekkar's squad. The rivals on this evening were even given a choice of goalie selections to choose from, but the Selects' generous offer was refused. They figured that this way even the backups could gain some more playing time and help provide a competitive tilt. The Selects starting number one goalie was already scheduled to sit this match out, so the other two on the roster could split the duties.

Mekkar himself was not expected to be available, but he was needed so he was given minimal playing minutes. The members of the team, on the non-top lines, who normally received less in-game shifts & time substantially had theirs increased. The situation was similar to when a club has already clinched a playoff spot near the end of the regular season. With the second or post season seedings already set, top players get a break with reduced minutes or complete rest to nurse injuries. That is, before the ramp up of more grueling playoff action soon after.

No matter, the Selects non-top athletes clearly outclassed the other team and were far superior on this night. To avoid humiliation upon the home side and in the context of positive international relations the coaches were instructed to have Mekkar & his teammates change strategy. The Selects were commanded to work on puck passing skills and shoot less frequently on the enemy net. The reality was the Selects would have had a more competitive atmosphere between themselves in one of their own practices. The match itself was still a total rout of great proportions.

During a stoppage in play toward the end of the game due to an icing call, Mekkar perceived that the fans in the building must have realized that their team was being thoroughly crushed. The players on the ice understood that the homeside had no chance of catching up on the scoreboard to make it a competitive game again. Mekkar wondered while sitting on the Selects bench if anyone in this crowd actually grasped the game of ice hockey. Much less how many of them had ever seen a hockey match live before. He questioned whether this adversary was a local one or a team brought in to face the Selects on short notice. Mekkar also inquired just how much of each of the individuals in the restless crowd's wages had been used to purchase tickets to this sham of an exhibition.

Then the mob in the stands took a hostile tone and was shouting out statements. None of the members on the Selects team could decipher except for Alf and another on the team. Only because they could speak any Arabic at all. Yet, Alf kept silent and reserved. He went into his own shell, his own cone of silence as was his personality. [Get Smart TV Show, 1965-70] Some people in the crowd began to throw various food items at the players on both teams whether they were on the ice or not. The now unruly mass of humanity did not discriminate with regard to the targets of their wrath. Mekkar thought he was lucky enough to catch a homemade loaf of bread right after he had rotated his spot on the Selects bench.

The arctic boy even exclaimed to some of his teammates, "Hey, bread! I am going to eat it because it looks good and I am kind of hungry." Mekkar loved heavy, fresh homemade bread which then reminded him of home. Unhappily for Mekkar and the rest of his squad the coaches were tapping them all on the shoulder. It was not for a line change this time, but to gain their attention and to tell each one of them not to consume the food. No matter how delicious the food might appear. The staff explained that it could be contaminated and could have bacteria, plus who knows what else. They were concerned about potential illness because it seems that someone on the team is always sick. On top of that, colds and other illnesses are spread through the whole squad around and around throughout the season.

Behind the Selects bench players were being implored with comments and questions about the possible lack of hygiene habits of the individuals tossing the edibles at them. Mekkar snickered to Alf and Lasse nearby, "So much for good relations, what a crock!" The ice surface then took quite awhile to be cleared of all the items that littered it. Due to that the rest of the game was cancelled and called completed as a result, even though it there was a few minutes left to go. The lopsided score was a foregone conclusion anyway.

Lasse led the team to escape the madness back to the lockerroom because there was no telling how the rowdy multitude might respond next. Plus, the Selects still had to reach the parking lot. A few of the team members now felt that factions of the hostile mob might want to attempt to physically attack them or possibly shoot at them. Once the Selects all reached the bus safely, there was a sense of relief. Nevertheless, they were not out of the woods. There was another announcement for all the passengers to hear. There would be a change in the itinerary again. This time it would include a break with no matches coming up soon and a sightseeing trip too! The staff person didn't really give more details about the detour so there were some doubts. Still, Mekkar and some of the injured Selects players welcomed the interlude to heal. Mekkar joked with Lasse and uttered, "Well, at least the incompetent organizers of this tour did something right for a change. They needed to make up for the scheduling screw ups during this whole trip around the globe."

Relayed by the coaching crew as the current word to the players was that this break would last anywhere from a week to twenty one days. Mekkar knew that this could always be changed at any juncture, so he just considered the info fed to them with skepticism. It frankly became like a joke among the team members. Mekkar expressed himself, "I will believe they (the team management) will keep their word, when I see it. Otherwise, they are all full of lies and more lies!"

Mekkar was the lone exception among the individuals that had suffered afflictions on the tour. The rest were sent back home already due to the declaration of those players being unfit to continue in any more matches on this journey. Whew! Mekkar was relieved that the contentious environment at the arena had been swept away when the Selects checked out of the hotel the next day. At least, they got to see a few sites around Cairo. Afterward they gathered together all of the remaining members of the Selects at a specific rendezvous point in the south part of the city center. Fortunately there were no confrontations or conflicts as a result of the match the night before.

A lineup of well maintained in appearance off-road Range Rover vehicles were there to whisk them to destinations unknown. None of the players, including Mekkar, had an inkling as to the direction that was to be travelled or locations they were steered towards. Like most athletes they, most of the time anyways, do as they are told and follow the directives of those in charge. The life of high level athletes is in many ways as structured as the military including the family schedules at home also. Mekkar thought it must a surprise for the reason we are not being informed as to where we are going. He snapped, "In the dark much like the rest of this debacle of a journey."

Even in unfamiliar surroundings Mekkar aligned himself with those on the team he knew best. So Mekkar, Lasse, Alf, and Johan were all together in the same vehicle. Similar personalities hanging out together. Well, at least the gang of four rebels on the squad still had undiscovered alcohol in their bags to make the trip more enjoyable. They were unable to acquire more booze in the city so it had to last - but still must be consumed. Even though it was fully past the darkest part of winter back home, Mekkar deemed it crazy that some locals in this area would be wearing outer garments or jackets when it was ninety degrees Fahrenheit (32.22° Celsius) outside. He was still an arctic boy at heart. Mekkar inquired of the driver regarding what he saw and was told that temperature was downright chilly here in the Northern Africa desert region. Think of Phoenix, Arizona during the middle of the summer heat and one would get the idea of the norm.

The group of motorized transport machines headed out toward the great river Nile and then turned south. It was an awfully quick trip thought Mekkar as they first arrived at the Gaza area where the mighty pyramids, built long ago, towered nearby. Right at the entrance to their destination, the line of trucks stopped and everyone got out. The Great Sphinx was there as if to greet the visitors to its domain. Mekkar figured that this was part of the intentional design of the area back in ancient times to invoke an automatic response of respect. He guessed that the Sphinx was there as a symbol to protect this place and display the glory of the kingdom. After moving around the various blocks of carved stone, Mekkar stood near the head of the statue looking up at it in awe. He wondered why it had crumbled somewhat especially in the facial region. He also, at the same time, wondered why am I basically standing near the face and underneath this monument? Some of this deteriorating figure might fall directly upon me while I am here in this position. That realization forced him to quickly move away abit.

Mekkar must have stated his concerns in his mind and also out loud because another person there told him that the nose had been shot off by way of a cannon ball. A misfire that was done by one of Napoleon's soldiers long ago and that he was not in any danger of falling debris. [Wikipedia] The young man was hoping to see the rest of this vast pyramid complex on this day and he accomplished this. As dusk approached they loaded back up into the same vehicles and continued on. Happily the vehicles were supplied with snacks, drinks, and whatnot as they caravan travelled south through the desert with the great river nearby flowing in the opposite direction northward.

As he was leaving the pyramids in the distance of the rear view window, Mekkar felt sad for the long lost people who built those magnificent symbols. Masterpieces that are still around thousands of years later to be treasured by the earth's inhabitants today. He also reflected about the culture and the people who lived during that time period. Would they be pretty much forgotten today if these manmade structures no longer existed? Would their past accomplishments be basically erased today and banished to the annals of history? Mekkar pondered on these questions.

The native from the north was still a product of his upbringing and environment. He thought that hopefully some in the future will still remember us as a people. That our good deeds might be recognized long after our own native culture is no longer present in the world. That maybe we failed to leave any massive makers of a culture long passed like these the Egyptians did under the Pharaohs. He realized right then the future fate of his own indigenous civilization. Mekkar felt somber because many ancient peoples along with native societies have come and gone.

They disappeared and those stepping stones for progress, as well as, the lessons that could have been gained now are perished forever. The usefulness can't help us in the current age, even though there are some areas where mankind has gained ground. The basic truth is people have changed little in their nature throughout the sands of time. Mekkar is of the opinion that ancient peoples lived in the same vein as today's native environments. They both face similar dilemmas in that many of their contributions are rarely recognized by the dominating and overwhelming surrounding modern lifestyles. Mekkar knows one thing for sure, that concrete jungle dwellers are fairly inflexible and unadaptable in comparison to his tribe and society.

Whereas a passenger in the moving transport during that first night Mekkar had plenty of time to think about things, that is, when he was awake. He deliberated that everyone has their own agenda, no matter whom they are or when they lived. The team's visit to the pyramid valley reinforced this belief in his head. Mekkar kept speculating ways to show others those native manners of living also have their benefits. He affirms those are, on a smaller scale, excellent examples that resemble provision of a more equal distribution of resources. Which in turn raises the overall prosperity to the group as a whole due to sharing concept among its inhabitants. As long as everyone works and contributes their fare share of the load, and not sit on their rear end expecting others to take care of them. It is not a welfare system but a matter of survival just like, in a sense, a pack mentality of sorts.

Emerging from Mekkar's concept is that he feels modern societies have a very different screwed up viewpoint. For the most part those in charge do not care about their overall populations, except perhaps as slave classes to provide for the state and the benefit of the elites. This is a result of the dog eat dog greed mentality that is embedded into the consciousness of each modern society. Mekkar says it has also been imparted into the subconscious of the people by way of design as designated by the elites. It's all one facet of a greater overall plan to brainwash the people. This has not changed since the beginning of time.

The Wanderer from the Arctic considers it is ironic that the more technological civilizations are in many ways more backward and regressive. It is due to the impersonal, detached, and narcissistic attitude that infects and permeates the various societies. While at the same time delude them also. It is quite a quandary that he hasn't yet internally solved. Mekkar let these type of thoughts swirl through his noggin while he took in the majesty and expanse of this area. He appreciated how long these natural and interspersed manmade objects have stood the test of time. Mekkar answered some of his own questions regarding how these lasting wonders of the ancient world were built and still remain today.

Mekkar realized that even back then the same issues plagued mankind and the powers that be. That those in charge still will do or say anything to retain their status, positions of power, and influence just like today.

Unfortunately, the human species never appears in Mekkar's mind to learn from their own past history with its flaws and errors. If they did, he questioned whether the supposedly civilized human race would continue the same courses of action to their own folly. Mekkar would respond with a definite - I think not! He saw these physical symbols as just a part of another empire and culture. One that has come and gone in a long line of successive great powers who existed for at least awhile, but fell due to internal decay and inefficiency. His inquiry of when will it ever end never was resolved during this consideration process.

These crazy ideas kept popping into Mekkar's head to fight the absolute boredom during the transportation travel period along the stout Nile River. He could only be fascinated by sand for so long. Still, much to his chagrin, was the long journey to the next destination wherever that may be. It was an unknown factor as Mekkar was kept in the dark about this just like the rest of the players. He was not amused, as it was Mekkar's nature and preference to be in the know of upcoming developments.

This line of vehicles on the desert frontier kept moving at quite a rapid clip and distance. Basically stopping only for short pit-stops to refuel, reload with supplies, or have all empty their bladders, etc. When they reached the temple ruins of Luxor everyone checked it out. However, the group didn't spend near the amount of time in comparison when they previously visited the pyramids. Mekkar was definitely feeling groggy and listless at this point on the journey. He figured that he saw the pinnacle earlier on at the pyramids. Thus, Mekkar was sort of indifferent to the Luxor site. It was different from the manmade similarly named hotel near the Las Vegas strip. The contrast between the beautiful oases here along the Nile amidst the desert was most striking. The column of trucks, well more like sport utility vehicles, journeyed on. It was estimated the group covered a stretch further than the equivalent from San Diego to San Francisco everyday so far and this travel trend would continue as is.

Other sites passed by and viewed by Mekkar, when he was awake, was the large Aswan Dam & Lake Nasser. They were going to exit Egypt soon. Yet the voyage continued as they advanced through the desert like so many before them had. Mekkar reflected to his studies in an instant and thought just like Erwin "The Desert Fox" Rommel's tanks would have if they had reached this far south. Of course, Mekkar was quite aware that travelling companions were a very different type of warrior, on ice. The only true uniformed and active soldiers accompanying them were in service to the Egyptian military. Their tasks on this trip were not military in nature, just as drivers. Mekkar felt it was not wise for their guides and chauffeurs to wear any uniforms since it would just cause trouble down the road. Especially since they would be crossing into another country real soon and later on during this trip.

Ever a student of history and from research, Mekkar was only slightly perceptive of the deep animosity of various tribes and nations in this region of the planet. But, not the full extent. The Native from the North discerned and decided that former colonization and imperialism of these parts of the world created a sphere of issues still existent today as a result. Elites drawing up national borders while at the same disregarding the local populations and dividing homogeneous tribes. Of course, he reasoned there would be future complications and it happened.

It was another day or so until the Selects reached another large metropolis but they were all dwarfed by Cairo in comparison and where this excursion began. After passing a generous bend in the river and near the Sudanese capital Khartoum the Nile joins together from multiple branches. Despite many efforts by the surrounding people to harness resources from the longest watercourse on the planet to meet ever expanding power requirements, the ancient river still flows on. It has not been brought to a halt at all. Now Mekkar and his caravan crew can enjoy the fruits provided by the waterway as a result. Assorted construction of bridges and other crossings assure that locals have access to all the benefits the Nils provides on both sides of the river.

Mekkar recalled this was one of the places where the ancients were able to build whole civilizations without the modern tools of today. He guessed that the area was probably more despite deforestation. The desert has claimed much of the land in our times in his opinion. Even historians that Mekkar has read about have admitted to this trend. However, the Great River has not been completely conquered, like his own dwindling people, and the water still flows.

Some of the days still seemed warmer to Mekkar and he would request that the driver turn up the air conditioning in the truck. The boys from the coldest regions of their nation were here, so there were no outward complaints from the other passengers. Yet, none of the others including Alf or Lasse preferred it as chilly as Mekkar. They were always teasing him about having ice in his veins. Mekkar had too much time on his hands and was examining the potential change of seasons and possible effects upon him as they reached closer to the equator. He has enough trouble with hot weather because his regular body temperature is much lower than the normal 98.6° F (37° C). The funny thing is that his friends notice that heat radiates and emanates from Mekkar more than anyone they know. Alf mentions that his older sibling is unable to keep his heat within but at the same time prefers it colder, when healthy. Not surprisingly, no one who knows Mekkar is astounded that he is contrary to accepted scientific norms and conventional wisdom, but accepts him as an oddball in many ways. The poor driver ended up wearing a heavy coat while doing his duty. He didn't even mentioned anything about it nor bring up the subject at all. The guide kept speaking about details of the sites the crew arrived at or passed on by without a beat. Alf had a theory that the coachman was talking so much to keep warm, who knows!

Khartoum was almost the half way point to Lake Victoria, but the White Nile runs past that onto Burundi. However, even scientists were unaware of this continuation at the time and the true source in Burundi was discovered in the early twenty-first century. [Wikipedia] The group didn't stay long, but solely needed to replenish and resupply and be on their way.

As the chain passed past various regions they finally approached and journeyed through Uganda, the locals there cast their gaze at them with a lot of suspicion. Mekkar had the concept that the possible reason for the distrust could have been because their group was viewed as guests of Idi Amin. An off-handed comment regarding how the visitors were travelling by land instead of by boat on the water was the basis of this misjudgment. The regular custom was that normal tourists followed the locals and moved between different stopping points on the water.

When the Selects and their small entourage arrived in the Ugandan capital Mekkar contacted a person he was acquainted with, Tazil. Tazil's mother worked with Sirga in some capacity for a short time up north. Mekkar was unclear on the actual connections and details between the two women and didn't really care too much. However, he befriended Tazil during that time. Mekkar had previously contacted the Ugandan and his family when they got closer and told them that he might make it there, if it all works out right. He said it would depend on the time frame and possible schedule to the area excluding any unforeseen changes that were very common on this trip. Thus, Mekkar was not definite in the planned visit, just estimating a potential occurrence.

Nilla, Tazil's mother, had a hearty laugh and an outgoing disposition. She said to Mekkar, "When you get here give us a ring and we will come to see you." Her education was relayed into work as a civil servant in a national government building there. The brutal dictator killed her husband for some unknown reason and no one has ever given any explanation. She seemed to have a joyful disposition despite the outward circumstances that easily could have left her extremely bitter.

The Selects players, staff, and their transportation crew were booked into the swankiest hotel in Kampala. However, on the second night Mekkar, Alf, and Lasse went and stayed overnight at Tazil's more humble residence instead. The youngsters played diverse games while they were there with the family. Others in the neighborhood dropped by to take part in the activities. Mekkar even teased Tazil about wearing a coat when it was so warm (about 90 degrees Fahrenheit). Next, the three arctic boys retrieved their hockey sticks and pucks among the gear and taught the kids there about the game in a number of aspects like how to properly hold a stick and shoot. Some of the children had never seen anything that resembled ice hockey in any form. Mekkar wished they had more time to spend there and additional items to give away there. The three Selects players even autographed a few of the goodies also. Mekkar figured that they could acquire a few extra sticks and related items from equipment managers to replace what he gave to the kids there. He knew it was up to them to customize the fresh gear to their liking for future contests.

What the Native from the North remembers best is the animal chasing contest during the festivities. Tazil was very quick and extremely proficient at this enterprise. He told Mekkar why and how he became so exceptional at it, "The reason is you become good at this to prevent from going hungry." Tazil also mentioned that this was the case before his mother got that good government job to feed the family especially after his father had died. Tazil went on to say, "Now catching the food is just a hobby to keep his skills sharp and improved my futbol (soccer) goalie reactions."

Team staff and their vehicles then arrived to entreat Mekkar, Alf, and Lasse to get ready quickly so they could depart the city. The powers that be wanted them to join the rest of the team to forge ahead on the journey. Both sides waved their goodbyes and the Selects headed off to explore around one of the largest freshwater lakes on the global map. The assembly took them through the Masai Mara wildlife area in Kenya to reach the well-known Serengeti National Park in Tanzania. Mekkar wished Tazil could have been with him on this part of the trip because he knew the region so well. Yet, Mekkar thought it was probably no big deal to the Ugandan since he lived so close by and has seen these different animals in person many times over.

As the vehicles were in the northern part of the park and not far from the border and the lake they stopped to take a break. The idea was let all of them just enjoy the scenery. Soon afterward a herd of elephants went strolling by. Mekkar was glad it wasn't too close because he didn't know the temperament of pachyderms in relation to people. "Hopefully, those big beasts don't see us," stated Mekkar. It was still close enough to make the ground tremble as they rolled past. Mekkar commented that it felt like an earthquake on the Richter scale. The vehicle was rocking and swaying from side to side while also stirring up everyone's meal from earlier. The tusked creatures were not quite stampeding, but at the same time they were not walking slowly either.

Mekkar came prepared, as always, with a few sets of binoculars for those in the transport to use. Some of the others had their own as well. After the distance widened between them and the animals, the vehicle Mekkar was in headed off in pursuit. He had an overwhelming feeling to pursue the adventure even while doubting the wisdom of tracking the beasts. They followed the chase due to the strong urging and pestering of the driver by the majority of the passengers. Still the truck kept a wide gap between them and the moving herd. Mekkar and his buddies next saw something that he didn't believe at first. A male lion had gotten way too close for comfort. Mekkar felt it might have been hungry and possibly desperate but also asked the question, "Don't the female lions usually conduct the chase and hunt the prey instead?" The rest told Mekkar to keep quiet as to not attract any attention to them.

Well, one of larger pachyderms, Mekkar was unsure if it was a male or female elephant, kicked that displaced lion in the air like a field goal in American football. It seemed as though the big cat was dead before landing back to earth with a distinctive thud. Yet, they were too far away to feel the lion's punishment but could see it with a sense of empathy on behalf of the clawed cat. Mekkar right then stated out loud, "Whoever said that the lion is the King of the Jungle doesn't know what he is talking about! Oh, man!" He continued on to anyone there that was listening, "Did you see that lion get kicked like a field goal or a soccer ball? That was so cool!" They were all cracking up at that statement, but also told him to keep his voice down since Mekkar gets louder when he gets excited.

Soon after this they left to be out of range of the mammoth animals. A notification came over the sound box in the truck. When they came upon another location instructions were passed along that it was now time to go and resume the tour. The backtrack via a different route began. Mekkar pointed out a sight to the east. It was the highest mountain on the continent, Kilimanjaro. Mekkar was not a mountain climber and had no desire to he would only observe the peak's majesty from a reasonable distance. He would let the handheld field glasses amplify and focus the view of the famous mountain.

They were moving at a rapid pace to their next destination. Mekkar felt it was pretty amazing to view animals such as giraffes, etc. in the wildlife preserve with the Kenyan capital skyline silhouetted against the setting sun. It was then only quick jaunt to Nairobi nearby to fly out to unnamed locations northward.

World Wide Hockey Tour – Russia

Before the Selects embarked on their worldwide barnstorming hockey tour Mekkar, Alf, Lasse and some others watched tapes of the 1972 Summit Series. It pitted the Canadian NHL All-Stars against the Soviet Union's national team The boys also watched all the matches from the 1974 Summit Series featuring the WHA All-Stars versus the USSR. The others watched, but Mekkar studied.

Mekkar had seen other games involving Russian squads because of the large satellite his papa constructed back home. It was the only one of its kind in the area and stood out like a sore thumb. He even paid attention to a practice session of the Soviet national squad carrying out their precise drills to perfection on the ice. All the while they were blindfolded. Mekkar thought that was incredible!

He attributed it to the environment those players' trained in and it appeared to him as intense. That is how they became the well-oiled Red Machine as he described it. Mekkar had the feeling that sometimes the Soviet players were so extremely well drilled, like the soldiers they were, they gave him the perception they were more machine than human. Mekkar also saw the other side of the coin and that might be a possible flaw in the system to be exploited.

Most of the Soviets did not seem to him to exhibit that internal drive in an outward way much of the time. Although there were a few exceptions that displayed their emotions on an individual basis, it was very rare. Maybe it was a tactic used to show that the Eastern European powerhouse was not at all intimidated by extroverted Canucks, examined Mekkar. This was contrary and very unlike the players from Canada and to a lesser extent, America. There was no quit in the North Americans and a continual non-stop striving for victory until the gametime clock had expired. [1972summitseries.com; Wikipedia]

The Native from the North noticed this lack of excess outward emotion as a visible behavioral trend in the great majority of Russian athletes of the time. Yet, there were still pointed exceptions. Mekkar applied those expressed unmanifested characteristics and demeanor to individuals in all sports behind The Iron Curtain, not just hockey players. He was of the opinion that this psychological profile trend was a by-product of the Soviet sports system itself and could be possibly attributed to the Russian culture as a whole. Out of a historical subjection to dictatorial national leaders and the expectations for complete obedience of the population. Mekkar labeled many of the European players in this manner also. Outward displays of emotion on the ice were frowned upon by high ranking officials and subordinates. It seemed to Mekkar as if there was a waiting for a specific reaction from a superior before a display of their own. Many things resembled being contrived and much too calculated for Mekkar's taste.

The Arctic Warrior did not want to live his life that way, where he would be always on pins and needles. He couldn't do it because he was too bold and brash for that. Mekkar acknowledges he never could be successful in any venture with such extreme structure and protocol. Mekkar many times acts before he thinks without the extensive thought process of possible scenarios and actions beforehand. He would have done his own thing anyway and somewhere along the line eventually snap. The reaction would be something totally stupid while at the same times ticking off the authorities, thus, sabotaging future opportunities. Especially people who have the power to make decisions with regard to Mekkar's now growing hockey career aspirations.

He recalled prior to this hockey barnstorming tour some veterans were brought in to give advice, tips, and answer any questions of the Selects players regarding this trip. The guest speakers had been involved in numerous hockey games in many places around the globe. They gave Mekkar and his teammates some good hints and insights especially relating to issues they probably would encounter behind the Iron Curtain of Eastern Europe and Russia.

Some of the topic points were: First, don't expect to like the food and find alternatives to fit your taste. Second, put all of your hockey gear in other bags that are not on your person because those will get searched. It will almost definitely be the case when you are not near them and more specifically at the airport for your inbound flight. Third, bring any normally used personal accessories and utility items. Plus, carry any goods that are hard to find at your destination in your one carry-on bag and never let it leave your sight. Keep that tote with you at all times. So you can jettison the contents as quickly as possible to make some extra cash.

Fourth, assume that you and your entourage will always be watched and followed by the KGB, secret police, or some type of security agent at all times. Travel everywhere in groups so that individuals can split up at any time to hopefully lose them. Unload through selling your snuck in contraband items to black market sources as quickly as possible. Don't forget about the back end of the official political party stores which are not ordinarily noticed by much of the general public. Those goods will bring a nice profit for you. Bring scarce things like Levi's and other items from outside the area, but in all instances be careful.

We can give you guys more detailed information of where to go and who to speak to. Be sure to make friends with the hotel concierges by bribing them with products and money. They are resourceful and a wealth of good information of the best deals to be had for you. Each one of them is usually hooked up with particular black market connections that will purchase the goods. Remember to set aside and keep a few hockey related items in the bag as a cover to hide the other products from peering eyes. You might also have to give gifts to local police and agents to stay out of trouble if you get caught. Bribery will get you everywhere there.

Fifth, expect bad service and poor treatment towards you for everything because they want to get into your head beforehand. They believe the mind games always help the home teams to achieve victory. It is their way. You are not special; they have done this to all other visiting teams in the past. [whahof.com] This includes one sided refereeing in favor of the home sides on the ice too. [whahof.com/Europe-feature.html; chidlovski.com]

Sixth, expect your hotel rooms, cars, busses, etc. to be bugged so be careful as to what you say all times. Their goal is to make you paranoid and distracted in a manner as to negatively affect your performance during a match. Seventh, bring multiple sets of top notch ear plugs to help block out all noise and interruptions. The phone will certainly ring during your afternoon nap; late night phones calls to wake you up, and flicking hotel room lights. Plus, fire alarms will go off in the middle of the night to also disturb your sleep. Not to forget, bugging the phones of all of the visiting player's quarters. Many other out of the ordinary events will occur to throw you off of your routine.

Use these occasions as a trigger to foster more team building among yourselves. Increase the cohesiveness of this squad in a manner with a focus of it is us against the whole world and use it as motivation. Eighth, bring your own preferred alcohol and possess it on you. Otherwise it is assured to be stolen and you will be stuck having to borrow some from one of your teammates. Barring that, reduced to drinking nasty tasting homemade vodka most likely made from your own hand. There was a lot of additional advice and tips stressed to the players.

Anyway, Mekkar was still upset at the ever changing schedule and itinerary of this tour. He, along with his team, was informed in the air to be prepared to play three different clubs located in the Moscow area. This had been expanded from just one as originally planned. The Selects players were told that it was to make up for previously cancelled games and also for the long break they had in Africa.

When the Selects had touched down in Moscow and got off of the aircraft events happened almost exactly as they were described beforehand and warned about. It was fortunate that Mekkar heeded the pre-trip advice and purchased some less expensive goods during the North American part of the journey. Those items were originally intended to be taken back home. He now decided to sell those items behind the Iron Curtain for a tidy sum profit. Mekkar was not the only team member to do this, even a couple of the coaches got into the act by bringing alcohol that couldn't be found here. The players just expected those coaches to drink it in style instead. Boy, they were wrong!

The KGB agents and a few of the military personnel they encountered since disembarking their flight and on the way to the hotel appeared to Mekkar to be very smug toward them. It seemed that way throughout their whole stay there. Mekkar distinguished the steely eyed looks and cold stares as a type of borderline arrogance. Takes one to recognize another haughty person. Unknown to the hosts, Alf was a secret weapon in the Selects arsenal since he was fluent in the Russian language. Mekkar and other teammates were always pestering Alf to translate for them. They were continually asking Alf, "What did they say?" over and over again. Alf knew his older sibling was a pain in the butt and now he felt the rest of the squad was acquiring this defective trait from Mekkar. Well, Sirga's expansive language plan was at least being put to good use after all and outside the scope of the family business.

After checking in at their temporary quarters them boys ventured out around the capital city. They soon broke off into smaller groups and pairs to track down the locations to unload their goods. Mekkar was eager to make some exchangeable cash and wanted to get rid of the smuggled articles on his person. He had a sense that the government security people were following him, Lasse, Alf, & others were sort of letting them slide. Mekkar felt those authorities were overlooking minor breeches of the law and protocol with regard to bringing items from outside the country. He thought that they might pounce on the recipients after they leave. Mekkar was of the opinion that the agents were looking for a handout or a bribe to look the other way. He knew this is a normal practice with police and state figures all over the world. Yet, Mekkar did not dare to do this because he did not know who he could trust there.

It dawned on Mekkar when he looked around the place as to why the locals consumed a lot of alcohol, just like back home. He determined that many people there drank like a fish. He described the scene as kind of depressing and thus maybe the reason for these societal habits. To him people were not upbeat and didn't appear to be happy as a whole, at least not in public or in front of the visitors and most didn't try to hide it either. Most of the individual dour citizens also seemed to Mekkar as being cut from the same cloth with little variety in dress or mannerisms. Mekkar attributed it to being under the thumb of powerful communist rulers for so long in the vein of Joseph Stalin, etc. It was as though Mekkar had stepped back in time into the 1950's similar to an old black and white movie on television. Mekkar has never been a fan of tv shows and films that are from the pre-color period.

Could it be the host city residents and government employees knew something that he didn't? Thus the reason for displaying their overconfident attitude thought Mekkar. He let out a sigh of relief when the small contingent had gotten back to their hotel for the evening. Especially after trading their goods for money that could be switched for a real internationally valued currency before leaving the country. Mekkar definitely didn't want to get stuck with rubles afterward since they weren't accepted as payment back home.

In the Arctic Warrior's opinion, the Soviet players appeared to already believe they had victory over their opponents. Especially of opposition squads as inexperienced as Mekkar's team. Like a boxing match, a team can be scared and defeated before the game itself. The Selects players were already warned about these dubious tactics would increase when the home squad's own confidence waivered. Even more so, if there was a thought of potential defeat. Mekkar & his brother Alf both suspected the KGB's role behind various actions that might be taken against them. The intensity of the nefarious activities almost always increased the day before a game itself. The fatigue factor was the goal through paranoia and suspicion. That is, to have you wiped out by game time and to force mistakes on the ice.

Preparations during the next day for the Selects' focused on the matchup against the mighty Russian Red Army team, otherwise known as CSKA Moscow. The Red Army squad usually supplied most of the personnel to the powerhouse Soviet National team. Yes, Mekkar knew some the history and it was well known the USSR team had dominated the international hockey landscape since the nineteen sixties. The Selects' opponents also regularly defeated top-level pro clubs from North America and National teams on both sides of the Atlantic Ocean. The Red Army club (CSKA) was able to attract the best players because of the required military commitments of most males in the USSR. {Wikipedia}

The CSKA roster was filled with names acknowledged throughout the hockey world. Players such as Valeri Kharlamov who was as talented as Gretzky or Lemieux, one of the best goalies ever Vladislav Tretiak, Vladimir Petrov, the tenacious Boris Mikhailov, Alexander Gusev, Vladimir Lutchenko, Yuri Liapkin, a young budding superstar defenseman Vyacheslav Fetisov, and more. Many of those players had gained experience on the international stage and now were squaring off against kids. [Wikipedia; hockeydb.com; 1972summitseries.com; chidlovski.com; russkiyhockey.wordpress.com]

There was a barrage of constant interruptions throughout the night and on the day of the game as cautioned earlier. Mekkar was mindful of the intentional nature of these actions due to the forewarning before ever leaving home on this whirlwind tour. Despite this being aware of this environment Mekkar still became irritated. Mekkar considered this as a problem and was cherishing the chance to exercise his wrath. He would get his opportunity to dole out payback that night as a result. Mekkar's disposition is to get ticked off and get even by reacting in a specific manner while knocking some heads in.

Mekkar started the game and got his revenge in a physical manner and hit everything in sight on the ice. He judged most of the Selects squad and said they had too much respect for the Soviet champions. The Arctic Warrior was like a man possessed and showed no fear while carrying out his own sense of ice frontier justice of punishment. It got to a point where even the opposition players did not want to provoke him anymore with nasty stickwork. Mekkar spent a lot of time to think and ponder the ongoing match from the penalty box. Alf's older brother had seen quite a few tapes, etc. and knew what to expect in the game itself from the Red Army club.

The young man from the arctic had the best statistical night of all the Selects defensemen despite spending so much time in the sin bin. He was only a minus one which means that the other squad only scored one more goal than his team while he was on the ice. Lasse said the stats were misleading because it might have looked better if Mekkar had not made his team short-handed so often by taking frequent aggressive penalties. Still, the Russian club possessed quite a bit of speed and talent. Kharlamov himself undressed Mekkar on the ice with an incredible move and then immediately scored a goal.

Right before the match Mekkar had implored his Selects teammates to adopt a successful strategy that worked against the Soviets in Quebec City. He had Alf translate a newspaper article for him that revealed a tactic to interrupt the commonly used flow and weave game. Mekkar was willing to combat and overcome the well schooled style of smart, elegant, and officially clean hockey. A method with a penchant for connecting on longer breakout passes to create odd-man breakaways to rack up the goals. [1972summitseries.com; chidlovski.com]

However, Mekkar's teammates did not heed his advice and it was to their demise. Also, later on in the game several members of the Selects just ignored anything the Native from the North said and counted him responsible for the Selects handicapped situation. The Selects were effectively crushed eleven to two. They failed all over the ice that night even while Mekkar dished out some devastating hits. One of the few positives was that none of their players were seriously injured in this debacle. None of them wanted to visit any hospital facility there as a patient. The players had been previously told stories about the doctors performing operations without anesthesia while the subject is fully awake during the procedure. Mekkar's response was, "No way! I will wait until I get back home for anything like that. No surgery here for me."

After the drubbing and post-game formalities such as both squads exchanging of gifts, the fun part was about to begin thought Mekkar. Some of the Soviet players had invited a few of the Selects athletes over for a get together, that is - a party. The Russians had heard that their young opponents could consume considerable quantities of drink. So, they had to test Mekkar and a number of his teammates to see if the alcohol intake rumors were correct.

Mekkar got into one of the host's vehicles along with Alf, Lasse, Johan, and another to journey to unknown location. He didn't know where he was being taken to but felt, for some unexplained reason, secure in the fact he had some quality booze with him. As the crew started to roll along the streets further away from the city center some nagging thoughts crept into Mekkar's mind. Were the agents still watching them? He supposed, that finally, officers and the like would leave him alone and not hassle him or any of the other visiting hockey players. Mekkar's reasoning was where would they go when they didn't quite know where they were. Plus, they were with some of the most famous athletes in the country and were visible in that sense.

They finally reached the outskirts of the capital and arrived at one of the home side player's little home. Right then a numbers of cars rolled up onto the scene and Mekkar quipped, "Now! We have a party." Many of the cluster went inside and participated in activities like card games while ingesting copious amounts of drink. While the music was in the blaring in the background, Mekkar noticed that the host individual's family was absent from the premises. He then downed more booze and didn't concern himself with anymore trivial matters like that.

Both Mekkar and Lasse esteemed themselves lucky that Alf was there because he was the go between to break any language barriers. The young Alf was a valuable asset as to the interaction between the two team's players at the party. There were not a whole lot of people there including a lack of females. The goal was to get totally blasted and Mekkar was fine with that. In time, most of the group were so wasted that many had landed on the floor, sprawled across coaches, and a couple ended up under a table passed out drunk. There were only a small number that were even remotely conscious, as most were in a stupor.

When the phone rang there was a collective groan in the room and everyone just neglected to answer it including the property owner. He was sort of hanging halfway out one of the windows basically toasted. One person asked if anyone was going to pickup the phone. Another responded, "Who cares, leave it alone. Anyway, I am too drunk to get up off of the floor." Mekkar wouldn't answer it because he didn't speak the local language. Plus, it wasn't his residence. Plus, he was still in a semi-aware catatonic hammered state and fairly unmoved, along with others, on the floor also.

Alf was known as the go-between on both sides since he was the only one there who had a full command of both spoken tongues at the fiesta and inebriation session. Alf translated for Mekkar a comment made about him by one of the Russians as, "At least Mekkar is too drunk off to dish out anymore punishment right now like he did at the rink. That crazy dude! He (Mekkar) got worse when the score became lopsided and had gotten out of hand. He didn't care and played tonight like one of the vicious Canadian squads of past tournaments." However, Alf's translation abilities were hit and miss at this point because the youngster was also greatly affected by the spirits he had consumed. Alf was at the same time laying on the floor right next to his brother. One could hear Mekkar only sometimes acknowledge his sibling with a murmur or an undecipherable sound. The older one, Mekkar, was in his own dream-like state and was fortunate to drink the good vodka this night and thus avoiding the homemade alcohol. Despite that, even in this frame of mind Mekkar would have gulped down that booze too, if that is all there was available.

After the blowout of the last match and the drinking episode at the dacha, Mekkar thought the poor treatment and mind games on the part of the host authorities actually improved somewhat. Even so, it would have been better if they had not confiscated the last shipment of alcohol from home some of the Selects' players had arranged to tide them over. It was about then, Mekkar and those in his little clique among the squad began to overhear biting comments regarding his team. Government officials, police, and others on the street would make statements like, "We don't have to worry about them too much since they are young and not good competition for our players and teams. This showed when the Red Army kicked their butts so bad the other night." Of course, this is how Alf interpreted it for the guys. "At least, they gave us a break and less hassles since the drubbing," positively quipped Mekkar. Still, the Arctic Warrior was still not amused.

The Native from the North had an inkling that the result could have been much more lopsided regarding the score. Mekkar was of the opinion the host Russian club let up a bit in the latter part of the game. He thought they started to eventually use the match as an opportunity to get some work in against live competition. In other words, shore up and focus on some weaker aspects of their game strategy and tactics for future tougher opponents.

Lasse and Mekkar had a discussion at the beginning of this world wide tour about the perception regarding the Selects as a squad. The Selects were aptly described as a collection of misfits, trouble makers, rebel rousers, and cast offs which in a way fit Mekkar. There was also a sense on Mekkar's part that their skilled opponents could see those aspects as well. In his mind the Russians saw that Mekkar's squad was hastily put together and they took advantage. The Soviets always used the opportunity to show that their sports system and clubs were superior in every respect as compared to the rest of the world. Mekkar distinguished this same haughty attitude as being displayed in major international tournaments, as well as, the annual World Championships and The Olympics.

Alf's older brother, Mekkar was not the only one on the team who felt that the leadership of his nation's hockey federation sought to find out if this group could jell as a team. However, it was a hard thing to ask for a lot of successful cohesion in such a rapid manner. The Selects executives and their bosses wanted to observe any individual examples of responsiveness and the ability to thrive under pressure. It was determined that those factors would go a long way to decide who does and doesn't participate in other pursuits with various hockey possibilities at higher echelons. Mekkar thought that it was just another exhibition of position where head honchos always want to assert their power and influence on any given situation.

The Selects next opponent was no slouch either. Dynamo Moscow was usually looked at as the second best hockey club in the whole of the Soviet Union. They had talented athletes who also performed admirably against the professionals and squads from Canada and the United States. Since the Red Army first string team only had a limited number of slots available some of the other similarly talented Russian hockey players would land here. Other squads that called the capital their home would absorb talented individuals also. Alexander Maltsev and Valeri Vasiliev were two of the better known players that dotted this Dynamo roster. They were well known for their participation in the 1972 Summit Series versus Canada [hockeydb.com; eurohockey.net; chidlovski.com; Wikipedia]

Due to his Russian language skills, Alf warned his Selects teammates and especially his maniacal brother Mekkar about this matchup. Alf mentioned that this club was related in some manner to a security apparatus or organization like the police or the infamous and dreaded KGB. The young Alf said that most, if not all, Dynamo squads are set up in this way. Alf flatly said to his older sibling, "Don't get too outrageous or do something really stupid in this game against this team or they might throw you in jail here in Russia. I would feel sorry for you. They could also still later on banish you to a gulag in the eastern part of the country. Good luck ever getting back home, if that happens. Many World War II prisoners from the German military never made it back home following the war, if you are familiar with past history."

Not that Alf realized it or not but his comments unintentionally screwed up the Selects in their game preparation for this match. Due to their lack of aggressiveness as a team the game plan execution was lacking also. Mekkar was even less effective as well because his game relies so much on his drive and aggressiveness factors for success. The result ended up with the Selects being stomped nine to one and it could have been much worse.

Even though the Selects were not scheduled to face off versus a more talented Moscow Spartak club, they did have to have to square off against a younger and hungrier team. The Soviet Wings squad was not short on skills or ability either. The Wings would achieve an overall winning record when matched against pro franchises in North America during this era. Despite not being as well known as some other Soviet star players, the Wings' roster still was represented by players who donned the USSR jersey in international play. Alexander Bodunov, Yuri Shatalov, Yuri Lebedev, Yevgeny Zimin, Alexander Sidelnikov and more filled in at times, on those powerhouse squads, versus the world.

Mekkar remembered the ice surface that day as being more conducive for speed. The Wings took a decided advantage of their speed and experience over the Selects by running away with a ten to three victory. Mekkar didn't feel that the Soviet Wings club were very physical but he exclaimed, "Boy they could skate and were fast too!" Mekkar thought that weariness of his team contributed to the shellacking they received. Since Mekkar hated to lose the only positive he could see was the barometer of what he needed to do and continue to develop. There were many more lessons for him to learn to elevate him to higher levels in the hockey world. Now the trip home would give him some time to heal up the bumps, bruises, and that shattered hand to prepare him for future battles on the ice. Unfortunately, Mekkar wouldn't get as much time as he hoped.

Zooming By

After Mekkar had got back from his first long worldwide hockey tour around the globe, he acted like a typical teenager and hung out with his closest buddies. Their little posse had their usual drinking session and then took off. The idea was to look for some fun of any kind. In this area, a person's options to fight against boredom are limited and creativity is needed. The small group were joking and laughing together. They were just glad to be out of the house with no adults around. The gang strolled alongside the road with the intent to make their way over to another friend's place. In short order the four of them would witness something they had not seen before and probably never will again.

Their small clique saw this shiny candy apple red Ferrari, none of them could ascertain the exact model but they knew it was a Ferrari by the car's body type. Mekkar recognized the vehicle as similar in type to the one that his relative Gunna had. He wanted so badly to take Gunna's car for a fast spin. Mekkar next began to convince the rest of the pack that he was right. Mekkar always wanted to be right about everything, even when he is wrong. Henrik's oldest boy was of the opinion that cars were more distinctive in those days and had more character, both on the inside and out. Most vehicles today appear to him to be very similar at first glance and harder to distinguish.

They were close enough to admire the cool chick magnet red Ferrari. Yet, as they did it seemed to pull out a little too much into the regional highway, with one lane going each way. Suddenly all four of them felt a swoosh. A great rush of wind blew past them as a screaming fast car went racing by. It appeared to be another fancy expensive sports car. Mekkar stated to the others that it looked like a yellow Lamborghini. It was an estimated guess on his part based on the shape and other factors. None of them could really identify the swift auto due to it was going by so fast. It was like a blur.

It was moving so rapidly, it sliced the front part of the red Ferrari off all the way to firewall in front of the driver. Just like cutting through butter. Mekkar and his buddies continued to approach the red sports car now dead in its tracks. They heard the driver in the red vehicle yell with a loud voice, "What the hell?" There was also a look of disbelief as that individual sat there in his formerly pricy car now without a front end. At the same time the yellow sport machine just kept going and it was instantly out of sight.

The guys knew that the yellow car that zoomed by had to have sustained severe damage. They were sure that it got messed up, but no one there saw the debasement of that expensive car because it was soon gone. Mekkar frowned and quipped, "What a waste of a prime piece of machinery." He wished he could afford one. Only small pieces of breakage remained and most of them were from the red ride. Lasse asked the other boys in their group with a surprised look, "Did you see that?" None of them could answer back eight then because they were paralyzed with a myriad of emotions at that point. They just stood there with their mouths open. Shock, awe, amazement, along with speechlessness was the response. No one said a word again until they reached the other friend's place. Then, they couldn't stop talking about they had witnessed. That episode continued to be the topic of conversation for quite awhile between them. Well, until something else comes along.

Lunch at the River

When Mekkar was younger he inquired to his mama concerning the noon meal time. Sirga replied sharply, "You know where the river is. If you want your lunch, get yourself down to the river and catch it or you don't eat. You know that the food made in the restaurant is for the tourists, not for you. Unless, you are working serving the visitors. The main reason is because you boys would eat all the profits!"

So early on, Mekkar and Lasse would walk down to the riverbank, near the old stone bridge. Here the river was not as wide or the water as deep. The boys had to first prepare and setup the spot to be able to catch fish. This is key, if they wanted to incur success. It began with the boys wading out in the water away from the riverbank where the flow was slightly calmer. Rocks and stones that lay along the bottom of the river would be arranged by them to force the fish to travel closer near the edge. That is, if the fish planned on continuing downstream to the sea. The goal was to make it easier for the youngsters to snag a meal to quench their hunger.

Many rivers in the far north area flow northward to the ocean, if there is an outlet in that direction. Those rivers are mainly fed and supplied by water sources that come from runoff of the nearby hills and low lying mountains. Thus, the water quality in these waters' is normally very good. Mekkar says that is fairly clean water. He is picky about that and expresses this often if his standard is not met. To him it was good enough to cup his hands together and scoop up the water to drink it right there.

On the first trip the boys constructed a permanent riverbank fire pit base with stones, rocks, and other items they had gathered from the surrounding area. Lasse's papa had forged a metal grill rack that fit perfectly to cook on, so that became part of their pit also. Thus, taking a couple of fishing spears, matches, small branches and twigs plus other easily retrievable supplies with them was all they would need each time they arrived.

Mekkar and Lasse would alternate, at different times, their turn to catch the fish in the shallow part of the river's edge they previously setup.

On some occasions, some of their buddies and young relatives around their same age range would join them for these escapades. The knee high waterproof boots of the fish retriever would make a sloshing sound with each step after journeying into the water. Whoever was doing the fishing would have a spear with a pointed tip at the ready to bring the hammer down and impale the fish.

Mekkar liked to raise the fish out of the water, in triumph, while the impaled prey was still wiggling on the hook. There was no use of fishing poles for this task. If the fish was too small, they would get upset that they had wasted their time. The reaction was a yank of the fish from the hook and a toss back into the flowing water as a sign of disgust. Mekkar responded frequently, "Let's get a real sized fish!" Mekkar was the worst in his outward dislike in this regard as he expected to get what he wanted on the first attempt, every time.

When the boys would collect one to their satisfaction, the next step was a release from the sharp point and clasp. After that was a smack of the fish's head against one of the rocks and cutting off the head and tail. They didn't bother eating the ends. Next, would be to fillet it with a slice down the middle and opening the fish to remove the spine and larger bones. Mekkar, Lasse, and the others that came down to the river didn't worry about eating the smaller fish bones. The fire cooking process would soften those to keep from becoming an issue. Later on the boys, along with Alf when he grew older, would bring an assortment of condiments and toppings with them. Other selections were also added such as a few side dishes, accessories, and other items to enjoy the crooked fish.

This routine became a regular mid day activity for a long time. Even when Mekkar and his buddies would come back to visit after moving away from the village. There was one instance in particular when Lasse was older that stood out. It was after the boys had started off by drinking some alcohol. As he went to go catch a fish in the water, Lasse stepped forward with the wrong foot in front of him. Mekkar's best friend then thrust the spear in his hand in a downward motion to get the fish. However, he impaled something else, his own foot, from the top piercing through the middle of his limb. Lasse had to jerk hard to dislodge the spear's point from the dirt of the riverbank underneath. The problem was the spear went through his foot and the boot straight into the ground when he thrust it.

His brow was furled as Lasse ripped the end of the spear from his foot and limped away from the river. Not to forget, he was a hockey player and as a result he was tough. Mekkar, Alf, and a couple others there were howling with laughter over this situation and even had the nerve to tease Lasse about it. They spewed out comments such as "Look at big, tough, mighty Lasse now. He speared himself to the riverbank!" Mekkar led the gang by giving Lasse the business regarding the incident. Even though Lasse was now bleeding from the hole in his foot, he didn't seem too hurt about it. Perhaps, he just didn't want to show his suffering in front of his friends. Lasse was more bothered by the teasing of his peers and increasingly became more ticked off at them. Lasse's wrath grew at this treatment and subsequently he wanted to rumble. Mekkar would be first up.

Tourist Business & Family Restaurant

After working on the fishing boat, his mama demanded that he learn the English language for the family business because there was a need and she thought that he would be a good candidate. There was also pressure on her due to the increasing number of tourists: Yanks (Americans), Canucks (Canadians), Roos (Aussies), Kiwis (New Zealanders), Springboks (South Africans), and most of all Brits (those from the United Kingdom, specifically Great Britain) that had English as their primary spoken tongue.

Thus, her impatience in this regard was understandable. Mekkar was his mama's choice and she was determined to make him fulfill this role she set out for him even if it killed her. His mama set up home schooling with tutors along with his special foreign language studies. Sirga also felt that this was a good reflection, in one aspect, of her parenting abilities.

When Mekkar's papa Henrik would go to the United States, Britain, or another nation with English as a mother tongue for business, Mekkar's mama made requests of him. In her mind, the requests were mainly for Mekkar's benefit. Sirga would tell Henrik to purchase and bring back English speaking only sports tapes, films, and videos for Mekkar. Mekkar's mama would gather related items for him during her own modeling junkets as well.

She knew that would the best and quickest way for Mekkar to grasp the correct interaction phraseology was through his passion of sports. Sirga never failed to remind Henrik to tell his translators these things also. She would do this herself on the rare occasions when she met the go betweens directly that would travel with her husband on those business trips. It was important due to the fact that Henrik never learned nor spoke English himself. He admitted being taught a few of the swear words as part of the Allied air group during the Korean conflict, but long since forgotten them. Henrik was able to converse fluently in ten other languages, with business vocabulary in German being most important for his employer at that time.

Henrik would buy in North America, at the behest of Sirga; National Football League (NFL), National Basketball Association (NBA), Major

League Baseball (MLB), World Hockey Association (WHA), National Hockey League (NHL), & English Futbol (Soccer) items for Mekkar. Henrik would bring back whole boxes of items. This was done to encourage Mekkar to continue on and to help him develop the skills needed as soon as possible. She designed it as an incentive program for the boy.

Sirga had confidence that Mekkar would succeed in the immediate and difficult task she had given him. Still she had a plan; otherwise consequences would be carried out. Yet, Sirga was not averse to taking that route and could use harsh measures as a last resort to motivate him. Frequently for her oldest son, Sirga held back whipping his rear end on a regular basis and other forms of punishment until the job was done. That is, in a satisfactory manner up to her standard. These factors caused Mekkar to accelerate his learning curve until his mama felt confident that he was ready enough for continuous customer interaction. Then, she placed him "into the fire" by pressing Mekkar into service for business reasons.

On one of the first days of dealing with the tourists in the family restaurant Mekkar was busing tables and took a couple of orders. One early example was a group of tourists that had arrived into their small 15 table specialty diner. The visitors from the United Kingdom appeared to be astonished when a boy came over to their order. One of the customers commented out load about their order taker's fairly broken English skills.

Even so, it seemed as though both parties understood each other well enough to converse and get the point across after his first order was received in the foreign language, Mekkar approached the kitchen. Mekkar beamed with confidence, well as much as a little boy could muster. In his eagerness, he sought out more opportunities to exercise his foreign language skills that day.

Later on, another kid from another tourist family taught Mekkar a few new phrases in English. However, Mekkar was given inaccurate information as to the true meanings of some of those expressions. The visitor told Mekkar that one of the words was referred to as a type of greeting instead. Why Mekkar took it at face value, without question, from the slightly older visitor we will never know. Not long afterward, Mekkar thought that he was being cool and uttered that greeting to other travelers. He became confused when he received an appalled reaction which caused them to flee out of the restaurant. When Sirga got wind of it, she was angry at Mekkar and smacked him upside the head. The Arctic boy was puzzled and bewildered by his mama's response. Mekkar thought that he was being friendly. The young boy was unaware that his specific choice of terminology were used as swear words instead of friendly introductions. Unknown to Mekkar, his mama had been warned by one of her friends who happened to be nearby and spoke English fairly well. She revealed what he was really saying. After some embarrassment and attempts to pass the blame, the lesson was learned. Of course, this was all before Sirga began her own process of absorbing English. She felt it was best for her to be relatable to different tourist groups that might arrive in the future.

This was one of the few slip ups by Mekkar. Overall, he was given praise for a job well done. After closing hours, Mekkar was rewarded with the washing of pots, pans, dishes, & other general cleaning duties. He felt that maybe that this was punishment due to his swearing at the tourists earlier in the day. Mekkar began to come up with alternate justifications and possibilities. He told himself the reason for doing these tasks was that his little brother needed to have an example to follow. For Alf to be groomed to carry out the same tasks, when he got older. The problem was there was a lack of available bodies to fill all the positions at the time to complete the work.

Eventually, the family business expanded into other areas and branched out. Sirga also forced Mekkar along with his siblings and friends to expand their foreign speaking skills by hook or by crook. Employment requirements needed to be filled. Mekkar didn't go to the formal school anyway and instead had tutors, training aids, plus other methods to help him learn. This way he could spend more time working. Any additional time was spent playing sports and being a kid as much as he could. In this culture, it was expected that children had to grow up more quickly and contribute to the family's welfare. When he got older formal classroom schooling was also sacrificed on the altar of sports and job assignments.

When he was younger, Mekkar was also in the process of learning not only his native tongue, but another nearby dialect of it, the national language of the country he lived in, a regional speech, a couple of continental languages, along with communication in English as his mama required. His plate was quite full at this time. This was all reinforced by the force of his mama's personality backed by statements of "Do it my way or I'll beat your butt!" There was no double standard or dual meaning to interpret regarding Sirga's words or intentions. She did not speak in double meanings or with a lying tongue unlike today's politicians. The goals were made very clear and defined. She always meant what she said and their native language was constructed in that manner.

Sirga also made his brothers, when they reached a certain age as he did, learn other foreign tongues to fulfill various other needs according to her perceptions. Alf would eventually become fluent in easily over twenty languages including Hungarian, which is considered by many to be the hardest language on earth. In the course of time, Alf could converse in Cantonese Chinese, Japanese, Arabic, Greek, as well as prominent Finno-Ugric, Germanic, Slavic, and Romance languages. Mekkar, on the other hand, was considered a slacker in his family for speaking less than ten languages himself. However, he spoke English which others in his family did not speak at the time. Due to lack of use and practice, in time Mekkar would forget a couple of the tongues he learned when he was a kid. He still remembers odd words however. English was here to stay and would be of more use in the future unbeknownst to Mekkar. This was the case almost exclusively in the future, when he had to flee his home forever due to extenuating circumstances.

Another time when Mekkar was a teenager outside tending watching over some of his reindeer, to keep them healthy for the tourist business, other visitors drove by slowly. The vehicle stopped suddenly where he was and a man, his wife along with two children got out. Mekkar instantly recognized them as non locals because of their clothes. His judgment was based on previous interaction with them in their own language earlier. This time, The Arctic herder kept his back turned toward their group and continued his duties while pretending to ignore the family. The man approached Mekkar within speaking distance. The tourist called out disparagingly, "Hey reindeer boy, turn around and look at us, so we can get a picture of you with the animals." Mekkar heard him and thought that maybe the out-of-towner had not recognized him from earlier. The young man from the far north surmised that the visitor thought he was speaking to someone else. Despite, the fact there was no other native person with Mekkar at that moment.

Mekkar became perturbed at the condescending comment and responded by turning slowly to his right. He responded, what he referred to as those arrogant bastards, with the native version of flipping the bird at them. It occurred to Mekkar that the visitors might not have understood the meaning behind his reaction. Just to make sure they received his response properly so they would get a clearer picture, he then proceeded to drop his pants to his ankles and moon the tourists there. He even patted his bare bottom in their direction for added emphasis. Mekkar intentionally had reacted with a flippant attitude in this manner. He did what he thought was an appropriate comeback to combat the snobbish attitude and comments on the part of the sightseers.

Against the Tide

Mekkar, Eppu, and the guys were in the mood to get something different for themselves. Kallio mentioned that, but didn't remember where; he saw an ad about these special colored shorts in the city. These were the 1970's type not the baggy down to the knees ones of today. Juha heard that they were the rage at the time and thought everyone in their little group should get them. Mekkar's sibling, Alf was not with them this time. When they finally arrived at the shop for each of them to purchase the item Juha referred to, Mekkar resisted. Mekkar implored the guys not to waste their money on a fad that would phase out quickly.

He was alone in his opinion among the group. In fact, he hated the item and disregarded the shorts as totally foolish. To him, they looked outrageous and just awful: A pink colored garment with a small yellow panther image on the lower left front side. Mekkar wouldn't be caught dead wearing anything in the color of pink as he extremely disliked the hue itself. He would rather wear his favorite of red instead without the panther icon.

Mekkar was not hesitant to say so either, "I can't believe any of you are buying these ridiculous shorts for this much money. Are you all crazy, drunk, stupid, or just lost your minds? Maybe it is a combination of all of it!"

The fact was that Mekkar had been previously exposed to the Pink Panther cartoon book character. Alf had some of those comic books in his room back home. The older sibling also knew that Alf was a big fan. Mekkar's younger brother had watched a show on television and tapes of Pink Panther cartoon episodes in a host of languages. The mystery was that only a couple of people were actually aware of the source where these materials came from. Mekkar wanted no part of that and definitely not at those outrageous prices. All those in their circle, except Mekkar, bought the garb anyway over Mekkar's objections. He concluded if Alf really wanted to buy this unauthentic apparel he would have to do it himself the next time he was in the area. Mekkar spouted off, "My brother should know better than my insane, drunk friends who waste their hard earned money on almost anything."

Machines are Taking Over

Long before the widespread public accessible World Wide Web, Mekkar's best friend Lasse had completed his custom made computer system for use at his house. Lasse had taught himself to become up to date in his knowledge of hardware and other related issues. The two boys had used other means to hack into satellites and information databases around the world. The technology and capabilities were expanding very quickly during this time.

Many times in the past, Mekkar and Lasse had both picked Henrik's brain often since Mekkar's papa was considered an electronics guru. Henrik was enlisted by the national government and military departments due to his expertise in those fields. Of course, Henrik would share some helpful information and demonstrate their applications to his oldest son and his friends. Mekkar figured it would be an honor for any papa to be able to pass on something to his offspring.

The system was extensive and too up the whole side of Lasse's bedroom wall with an assortment of tables and various separating constructs. Wires and cables seemed to be everywhere. They were marked with different color tape with written indicators as to function and where to be connected. The servers and makeshift other equipment had symbols on the back as well to identify how all of it must be set up. Lasse had other written his own software to make the whole thing operate as intended. The complete system itself was not cheap and the cost was in excess of sixty thousand dollars. Lasse had worked hard to gather the funds to pay for it.

That same day when a couple of the last parts, that Lasse ordered, had arrived he was excited. He couldn't resist and had to share the news with Mekkar. After reaching Mekkar's house, he waited about an hour for his best friend to finish his work in one of the family businesses. Mekkar licked his lips in anticipation upon his hearing his buddy's news. They went back a few roads over to Lasse's house to test out the newest prize. However, when these two get together there is mischief to be carried out.

It took awhile for Lasse to sort out the parts to set up the last pieces of equipment and integrate them into his system. Mekkar always hated that part because he expects most mechanical items to be already preassembled and ready function properly upon startup. Mainly, because Mekkar has no tolerance or patience for any nonsense. Plus, Mekkar does not sense how fortunate he was by being surrounded by individuals that are very mechanical. People that can fix or put together most things like Lasse, Alf, and Henrik are able to. Individuals that are closest to him. As Mekkar lacks those mechanical construction and repair abilities. Mekkar has other special talents. Unfortunately, contrary to Mekkar's wants, this was the not the plug and play era of the twenty-first century. Mach of the required know-how was not common and had to be diligently researched and put into practice to understand its inner workings. Lasse was blessed with an attention to details in his character makeup. Thus, he went through every step of the instructions a few times previously before actually setting up the additional machines. Lasse didn't want to damage what he already had.

Mekkar's attitude is let's play and see what we can do with it. A more haphazard and risky approach in many respects. Mekkar learns by doing it himself; not by merely reading, hearing about, or watching another person doing something. Unknown to Mekkar, his buddy had prearranged for a visitor from somewhere else to show up around that time and show them how to increase and maximize the configuration's abilities.

Eventually after the helper left, the two boys were able to connect with other aquaintenances. Also, people they knew from hockey in other regions outside of their own. Mekkar and Lasse contacted some going to school or living, with their relatives, in Switzerland, India, Hong Kong, and other locales. There was basic interaction, new jokes received back and forth, and updated news. It was painfully slow, in its infancy, with frustrating delays compared to later online chats like the Telnet Relay, ICQ, Windows Messenger, and later more advanced programs. Another future world was opening up to the Arctic boys, Mekkar thought.

With rapid technological improvements over time, in the computer and communications industries, Mekkar and Lasse further tested the boundaries. They began to access University and United States Department of Defense mainframes, and other places via the ARPANET. They wanted freedom and this was one way for them to get it. The system was restricted for only their use, as no one else in the village knew how to operate it and left it alone. Later on, WordStar was used for creating their own documents and other tasks. There were color limits such as the word processing, messaging, and transmission programs usually had the option of orange or green letters on a black background or the reverse. The black color in actuality appeared to be a dark brownish color instead of black on some screens. Some time later, Lasse did add video game consoles to the mix. Games were not Mekkar's focus. He observed Alf spend a lot of time playing Zaxxon and Super Zaxxon arcade game at the nearby store. Niillas was consumed by the other video game unit at the store, Donkey Kong and subsequent versions. Mekkar said that, "Those two put enough coins into those machines and played them so often, they could have bought the machines many times over."

Mekkar did maneuver his way into a couple of early game company sites. He had done this to help gain an advantage of a few games. Maybe, they could make some extra cash by selling secrets to the unknowing. Both of them were entrepreneurial in many respects. On one occasion, Mekkar thought that he had an answer to shrink the player spacecraft and create a surrounding force field to make the user harder to hit against the oncoming enemies. Instead, Mekkar ruined Lasse's game after applied the new hack. On top of that, this action by Mekkar, also did minor damage to Lasse's system. Less costly for Mekkar, his best friend was able to repair his system and get a brand new copy of that particular video game. Still, they would not be deterred.

The next day after watching a western movie from television, Lasse and Mekkar felt that they were in the computer Wild West just like the movie. Mekkar even accidently accessed into a program that was originally used for functions related to nuclear weapons. This online program could track their trajectories, if fired from a certain place to another. There were displays that showed the calculated distances, time of flight, etc. Lasse and Mekkar did play the simulated games a few times. They wanted to see how long it would take to fire a large nuke from various underground silos and reach the intended targets they chose, anywhere in the world. It lost its fascination quickly and they never accessed it again. The original program name has been changed and the former title now is a very different application that is familiar in today's society.

This is how Mekkar and his best friend gained insights on not so well known underground sites, military installations, and information that governments hide from their citizens. The boys discovered began to learn who had what capabilities and now knew where to find them. They grasped the pervasiveness of the industry and were exposed to plans regarding future, more advanced weapons and systems. Mekkar and Lasse tried to comprehend how much more extensive the internet was by reading and examining its history, but only touched the surface. Thus, little surprised the two when they were required to conduct their own national conscription military service, later on.

The Arctic reindeer herder comments that he is spoiled now regarding the development of The Web. He decided to rid himself, quite awhile ago, of his old hacking ways along with his code and cheat books that Mekkar had developed for himself. Making it easier and shortening the time processes to access anything was important to him. Mekkar stopped hacking because it became to too tempting to steal large amounts of money online. It would have so easy to make him a very rich man. However, he did have to perform a final act before giving up his freewheeling approach in this area. Getting even with some adversaries through satellite services had to be carried out first. It was paramount that Mekkar go out with a literal bang and he did.

Happiness on the Ferry

On a few occasions Mekkar and an assortment of his buddies would board a round trip excursion ferry from one of the larger cities to another and back. There were a host of different routes to choose from that left from that spot to a variety of intended destinations. They all said the main reason for this jaunt was they wanted to visit other people they knew across the water. Mekkar himself did not believe it and mentioned that was not the main intention at all. Since the trip itself was an overnight journey the collection of rebels figured why not party and have some outrageous fun.

At the time underagers could have a run of the boat minus a lot of restrictions they encountered on land. It did help that everyone in their bunch appeared to look older than they really were. First of all they could drink duty-free and was much cheaper in cost. Sometimes, that meant also getting hammered with a small number of crew members. The gang had done this sporadically, so they were on a first name basis with a portion of boat employees. Mekkar and his pals were seen by the crew as relatively harmless. The chums all thought the junket and the coastal stop in between was a good place to meet different women too.

As soon as the transport pushed away from the dock Mekkar, Eppu, Kallio, Vanha, Mikko, and a revolving cast of characters would start up the flurry of inebriation. Engaging in revelry was part of the action as well. In other words, party throughout the night. A wide selection of booze was available for consumption: Beer, vodka, other grain spirits, rum, bourbon, tequila, and more. Mekkar endeavored to try and experience as much of the different flavors at his disposal each time. Well, as much as his body could tolerate. Not forgetting the basic staples of alcoholic beverages the Arctic warrior already enjoyed.

Mekkar problem occurred when he would mix the hard stuff with beer. His system, especially his stomach, did not like this too much. As it would happen, he would feel the effects quickly. Then, proceed to get sick due to the mixing of the two different types of drink. Otherwise, when Mekkar stuck to one or the other he would arrive in a good festive state without the sickness and nausea.

The lack of extra taxes on the spirits on the boat made the liquor prices less expensive. Thus, the gang ingested more. Mekkar and his friends also saved a bundle of cash by usually renting one room or two at most. Not a cabin for each individual which would have cut into the amount of money on hand for partying. The troop rarely stayed in any of the rooms they did hire unless it was to place to pass out or bring female companions back to. Much of the time was spent run around the decks in a crazed state of drunken madness or playing pranks on others. To many outsiders it would be hilarious to watch them in action.

This type of activity on their part would be in full swing early in the journey. That is, way before reaching any halfway point of the shortest trip between two distinct locales. A few other forays might involve short stops at islands and coastal entrances along the way.

The pack would party all night long. On this particular trip there was a band onboard. So, Mekkar and the group definitely took advantage of that! On some trips they would reach the main destination city and stay on the boat not bothering to go ashore. Then, depart on the same course back to where they originated, to do it all over again. On the sojourn back, the fellows could be quite loaded.

In one instance, Mekkar and his buddies were going down in one of the elevators and Mekkar got sick by mixing the consumed booze. He became queasy from the combination and assimilation of the different beverages. As a result, Mekkar threw up in a big way on the floor of that lift. His barfing session was followed by others who saw it, were affected, and did the same. It became a considerable mess. Mekkar and the gang reached their floor and got out rapidly. They didn't want anyone else to notice who had made the nasty mess.

As they walked away laughing, carousing, and carrying on, most of them noticed an older couple about to get into the same elevator they had just left. There was a thud. The old woman had slipped and fell on her bottom in their vomit. Mekkar thought those people should have noticed the puke on the floor. At the very least, the nasty smell of it before getting into the lift. He concluded the reason why the older ones were not aware beforehand because they might have been drunk too! Mekkar still muttered to himself, "They are so stupid". The little old maid started blurting out derogatory statements and swear words in a loud manner not caring who heard. She said, "Those spoiled brats. Uncontrolled heathen!" and she went on and on cursing for a bit.

The elderly couple probably assumed that Mekkar and his friends didn't understand what they were saying. The boys had been steady conversing in a totally different tongue on the boat and in the vicinity of the other guests. However, Mekkar and the gang understood every word that came from those seniors' mouths. They just pretended not to understand. Mekkar along with the rest of his posse just thought it was funny and continued to laugh and joke about it. Still, there was plenty of time to carry on their merry way to consume more booze and create more commotion.

Punk Band

Mekkar had already seen quite a few concerts of many varieties in his young life. Plus, he was a lover of music also. He had visited a large number of venues, both big and small, in many different countries. Some of these occurred when he would accompany with his mama to her modeling assignments or with travelling hockey teams.

Sirga would appear to work for modeling photo sessions, runway fashion shows, and what have you. When Mekkar was younger, being around that type of environment was exciting. On a few occasions, Sirga even got criticism from others related to the set and it almost result in a fistfight. Everyone there Sirga would have won those encounters easily since she was six foot two inches tall and adept at brawling. Sirga quipped at times that she could some things really well – drink, fight, _____, and do a little modeling. Yet, there were many times other models would go out of the way to be nice to the young boy as it was not a common thing in those days. Some of the well known models even brought Mekkar treats. The youngster didn't know who they were or anything regarding if the ladies were famous or not. Mekkar was focused on the goodies that he was receiving. As the developing Mekkar got older, the photo and stage sets were not interesting anymore. He became more independent and would leave his mama's side to journey and explore whatever place they had arrived in. Mekkar, at this time, often would go to watch live music to get away from what he considered as the madhouse fashion industry his mama was part of.

The native from the north had joined the legions of teens with the advent of punk rock in the 1970's by attending counter culture alternative punk rock band shows. Outfits like the Clash, The Damned, Dead Kennedy's, Iggy Pop & the Stooges, The Ramones, The Saints, Sex Pistols, The Stranglers, Stiff Little Fingers, The Voidoids, The Vibrators, the Buzzcocks, U.K. Subs, Generation X, Dead Kennedys, Ebba Grön, the Rude Kids, Eppu Normaali, and many more countless diverse punk groups. Even a couple of bands from Hungary that he doesn't remember the names of anymore. Mekkar was able view some of the bands live when they were still obscure. The Arctic Warrior even colored a part of his hair with a canary yellow streak on the left side of his head over the ear. It happened after going to a Sham 69 large outdoor gig near London and identifying himself as part of the Sham Army fan base.

This was a time where the teenage Mekkar began to develop an attitude that distrusted the overwhelming, all inclusive establishment as many his age do. He partially broke away and became a punk rebel in many ways. This posture was displayed in many areas especially in his expansion of chosen music genres listened to. Alf, his younger brother, and older best friend Lasse also followed Mekkar's nonconformist path. The advantage was Mekkar had been exposed to the type first; otherwise, he would have followed one of them. The adolescent also checked out other groups during this period such as ACDC, Aerosmith, The Angels (Angel City), Black Sabbath, Blondie, the Commodores, David Bowie, Jefferson Starship, Kansas, The Kinks, Led Zeppelin, Pink Floyd, Queen, Rod Stewart, Rolling Stones, The Who, Hanoi Rocks, Raga Rockers, and hundreds of others at home and overseas. He was exposed to a host of styles and languages as well. The sound to Mekkar was always more important than the lyrics.

Hey, Mekkar's mama is the one that helped him obtain a top quality fake identification card. That ID would give him entry into music locations as some clubs had minimum age requirements. The limits applied even to non alcohol consuming patrons. He didn't need the high price drinks from the clubs anyway. He would be already buzzed by the time he arrived after slamming booze his mama got him earlier. It was normal in their regional traditions for young teens to drink with the parents. At least, she could observe and somewhat control the amounts being consumed by Mekkar. Sirga would tell her son before they would separate and go their own way, "Go and enjoy yourself at the shows and stay out of trouble. I don't want to have to bail you out of jail." He knew that he could take a cab afterward back to the hotel where they were registered to rejoin his mama. On some occasions Mekkar and Sirga would set up a plan beforehand to meet at a specific location by a certain time. The place was usually close enough for Mekkar to reach by foot. Then, it was time to travel back home and do it all over again later on.

Sirga grew up and admired the tunes of Elvis Presley, The Beatles, The Kinks, and a part of the first British wave of rock n' roll in the 1960's that soon afterward invaded North America. Her sons liked those groups but also had a disposition for heavier music such as later classic rock and so on. When Mekkar was younger his mama took him to concerts of the Beatles & Elvis (her two favorites). She wanted to take her best friend - but the person who usually watches Mekkar was also at those two same concerts. So, Mekkar's mama was not amused and dragged him along against her will. Sirga continued to give him grief about it as Mekkar grew up. The youngster now only remembers the introductions and sticking of his fingers in his ears due to all of the screaming, yelling, crying young girls during those concerts.

Both Alf & Mekkar still to this day recall words to obscure songs from records, tapes, compact discs, radio, etc. sources. The reason was their mama would have the record player operating repeatedly while she was home. Sirga would play Kinks records until they wore out and then replace them. It was part of her own process to accelerate her learning of the English language. The young Mekkar was unhappy when he had to accompany his mama on a side trip to visit Elvis' home, Graceland. In those days, when they still conducted on-site tours. The boy was bored stiff throughout the experience and appreciates it more now for nostalgic reasons, even though many details have been forgotten.

It made perfect sense for Mekkar to start a band since all the potential members lived in the same big city together. It didn't matter that some of the pack were not originally from the area. Besides that, Mekkar was inspired to form the group after attending over hundreds of distinct gigs during the decade alone. All the members were influenced by a fair amount of other bands from the international outlaw scene and colorful spectacles of the time. He just fell in love with the rawness of the punk sound. Alf, Lasse, and Mekkar had practiced together a bit with their instruments in the barn on the property back home. They all moved down south at various points for sports and now were back with each other again. This was not the arctic anymore, but it was like old times. They were adventures and it was time to spread their wings. Mekkar thought there were more available options and opportunity in the large metropolis. The crew had chosen a name for their ensemble. Yet, there was a need for a lead guitarist as none of them were close to being qualified. Fortunately, Mekkar was aware of a local hockey player that he played with and against in the ranks. Timo was not only an aspiring athlete but was also an up and coming studio axe man around the city. He was good enough to be asked to perform in a slew of recording sessions with quite a few other musicians.

Mekkar had heard him jam out previously and was of the opinion that he kicked it good. Not long afterward, he ran into Timo as part of a crowd at a local concert. He invited Timo to join the fledgling crew. Timo agreed and had access to a warehouse nearby the sports house. The building was prefect for practicing their raw noise with no one around to complain and at no cost to them also. It was exciting because the newest member also had contacts related to booking gigs. The tribe of four youngsters had to manage all things related to the band, themselves. All of them understood the basic reason for forming a group was not for money. Of course, that would have been nice. The real purpose was to get more women, have fun, and have another excuse to party. It was something different from sports for a change. The Arctic Warrior was convinced that chicks love people affiliated with music and especially members of a band. Mekkar figured it must be an aspect related to sound waves or vibes. They only had a couple of their own songs that they created and performed mostly covers. Even some popular songs in their own unique style. It was similar to punk rebel rock at its phoenix and during peak period of the overall world wide movement. There was plenty of material to choose from and inspiration to be garnered by or they could make it up as they go.

Sirga hated that music genre. She thought it was too fast, had no substance, obnoxious, and just plainly sounded like garbage. Both of her son's musical tastes definitely did not completely match hers. Mekkar's mama didn't hesitate in telling them either. Especially when they were back home practicing in the barn. On those occasions, the audience consisted of animals. Maybe it was a good thing that Mekkar was unable to gauge their reaction. It didn't seem to irritate the beasts too much in his opinion. Of course, Mekkar's cocky reasoning claimed, at the very least, the sound didn't put the animals to sleep.

The foursome had Mekkar's younger brother Alf as the drummer. Alf basically got stuck there in the beginning back home because he was the youngest and the age trend determined his placement. The fact is, nobody else wanted to bang the drums. Plus, he showed a knack for it, which helped. The positive was his six foot one inch height despite being about three and a half years more youthful than the rest of the band. Alf's height at such a young age benefited him and he appeared to most outsiders as rivaling Mekkar in age. Lasse was the lead vocalist while playing the bass guitar at the same time. He was the best of the group by far to audibly carry a note. An added benefit was that Lasse at this time was physically fit and not an individual to mess with. He stood at around six foot four inches tall and a weighed a muscular two hundred and forty pounds. He always wished to take his shirt off during their gigs unlike the rest of them. Mekkar thought it was to show off his physique to impress women in the crowd. At the beginning of their set Lasse would usually fling his t-shirt toward a hot girl in the crowd. It was an intentional directional and targeted toss. Lasse hoped he could score with her later in the night.

It was characteristic during gigs of the time for foolish drunk people in the rowdy crowds, to take swings at various front men in punk bands. Adolescent fury and aggression was the order of the day. So, it was a positive to have a singer who could kick some butt, if necessary, to protect them on stage. Truth was the whole group was made up of hockey players who are known for their toughness. All of the four could brawl pretty well. Even Alf could, but didn't prefer to scrap like the others, if he could avoid it. This happened on occasion when a few rambunctious individuals in the audience would start a commotion in their direction. If someone desired to start trouble directly with the group, they were always ready to end it right then and there. No prisoners would be taken, only a beat down. Beforehand, Mekkar like to spew out his venom as a warning, "Don't mess with us or we whip your rear ends hard! We don't care who you think you are." When that sort of rabid activity materialized, usually their set commenced for the night. Mekkar's band was normally just a warm up band that attempted to get the crowd riled up and into the mood. The whole idea was to blend into the scene and match the flowing booze with fast, sharp, high tempo minimal punk riffs.

The one who originally came up with the idea to form this group was the rhythm guitarist, Mekkar. He was self taught and at the beginning knew only the basics. He could easily handle three cord punk scores. When stayed at a friend's home, for a short time, he improved his guitar skills from just being a hack and thrashing out like a buzz saw. Mekkar filled in during practice sessions in the basement, to keep them on beat, because the drummer was frequently late. Both Alf and Lasse always teased Mekkar and said, "Don't ever give him a microphone on stage because he can't sing on key for anything. He doesn't even hit the right notes in his native music ditties or when listening to his favorite bands." They cringed every time after often overhearing Mekkar sing along to various songs. It was all due to Mekkar's habit of singing out loud in the shower or in his car. The Arctic native was bold enough not to care if anyone else heard him or not.

Lasse and Alf were the better singers in the bunch in Mekkar's opinion and the other member was good enough to sing in a backup role only. If he knew most of the words to a particular song Mekkar would sometimes mouth it silently. He would do this while hammering his strings because he was aware that his audible music voice sucked. Mekkar never sang out loud during performances as he didn't want to throw everyone else off their rhythm and ruin it for all of them. This off key and lack of tone phenomenon was blamed on an earlier sports injury where Mekkar broke his jaw. The worse part was that a portion of the bone went upward and also damaged his left eardrum. Mekkar's hearing has never been the same as before the trauma occurred. Constant drainage and fluid buildup issues have affected that left ear ever since. A number of early concussions didn't help matters either.

What was weird to acquaintances of Mekkar is that he seems to grasp music sounds better than human voices. Those who are close to him know that he even catches slight changes and musical nuances in a heightened way. It is no surprise to the other band members when Mekkar removed his shoes and socks for band practice. He would usually also be barefoot on the cleaner stages for gigs. Mekkar explained it as being better able to feel the music in his feet and body. Similar to a deaf Beethoven, who still used his hands and fingers to master the piano. Mekkar needed to be in the spirit of the resonance because he is a rhythmatic person by nature anyway. Not to forget, Mekkar is related to and partially named after a shaman. He has trouble describing this sensation that he experienced and found almost no one who could relate to the particular phenomenon he described. Mekkar said that he was sensitive to vibrations, rhythms, and other things like moving vehicles under his feet. He went onto to say it was much less when he wore his footwear. Mekkar thought this anomaly became more intense after he had suffered the hearing loss. Comparable to a blind person having increased other senses, which become better over time.

The teen claimed that he had always had a little of this ability throughout his life. Thus, the reason why Mekkar could play strands of tunes through hearing and feeling despite a limited knowledge of cords and score comprehension. Mekkar also did realize that he would need to expand his horizons in those weak areas for the band's sake. A much later demonstration revealed this ability when he jammed a bit with another teenage group. The only axe available there was a bass guitar with a couple of broken strings. They asked Mekkar to join them for their rehearsal until that regular band member showed up. Later on, they all complimented Mekkar on his savvy saying he did a good job filling in with such a messed up guitar. Alf, on the other hand, has responded to his older brothers' explanations and told him to his face repeatedly with, "That interpretation is so untrue!" That is, regarding Mekkar and his sensing of music through his feet and up. It would make Mekkar hot tempered and he wanted to brawl with Alf when he said stuff like that. For the good of their band the scuffle between the two brothers never came to fruition.

Now, Timo was a most interesting character. According to Mekkar, Timo was the most fanatical person in the group. Especially, when related to make believe icons and comic book character themes. Timo was extremely into Batman and many things which had a Caped Crusader flavor to it. His guitar, the Axe, was in the shape of a gadget that Batman would have used. Everything, it seemed, in Timo's existence revolved around Superheroes and the 1960's American television series Batman mystique in particular. Mekkar thought the whole theme was truly ridiculous. Timo even modified his classic vehicle to resemble like the Batmobile pictured in the comic books he collected. There was even had a mostly black colored with yellow trim refrigerator. Mekkar's bandmate referred to it as the Batfrig and it was always stocked full of alcohol. It was a good thing the Batfrig had a small amount of yellow coloring. Sometimes, it was hard to find, when the lights were off and one is so hammered. That is, when Timo and the guys would have a case of the beer goggles and feeling like booze hounds. In that condition they still were able to locate the chilled alcohol box. There were a great number of items collected that decorated Timo's apartment which matched the superhero motif. Timo also followed Wonder Woman only because he was attracted to her in real life. At least, the actresses who embodied the super heroine in full costume.

Axeman, as Mekkar like to call him, Timo would go off every so often on his guitar solos in the middle of a gig. This was customary in songs of that decade, but not punk music. The rub was Timo would run outside in front of the joint while still continuing to jam on his axe. The rest of the band continued on, in tune, with the music as well. During those escapades, the Axeman would approach people outside the venue. It was especially certain if there any hot women that might be passing by or about to enter in. Mekkar quipped that Timo did this just to show off and impress the females. Trouble was, it seemed to work well and the business owner's usually approved because of its success as a marketing ploy to bring in more people. Similar to an on-site media promotion. It was easy for their group to book shows, but the main reason wasn't because of great overall musical skill. However, they knew a lot of people who showed up, on a regular basis, to see them play at a club. Teammates and fans of their two different local teams frequently arrived on the scene. A few opposing players would drop by, if the club was right and close enough. Other friends in the music scene might turn up. The small venue owners loved the band for their attraction ability. It was almost a guaranteed packed house to increase profits for the proprietor, on those nights the band performed.

The really cool thing about the Axeman's guitar was its rarity and technology wise slightly ahead of its time. A relative of Timo's personally fashioned all of his stringed instruments to be wireless up to a specific distance away from the source. His devices could be used without the need to be connected to an amplifier via a cord or cable. The amps were adapted as well, with little distortion, to handle this special capability. Mekkar never could recall an instance where the sounds, played by Timo, cut out. What was special is that these alterations wouldn't become more commonplace for awhile. The problem was there were only a limited number of doctored equipment pieces at his disposal. So, he was extremely careful and gentle with his gear and avoided even scratching them. Any thought of damaging the equipment was totally out of the question. There was no imitation of famous rock n' roll musicians like Pete Townshend smashing his guitar into pieces on stage. Also, there never would be any lighting of the axe on fire like Jimi Hendrix either. None of them could afford the continual replacement of instruments, along with the many accessories, as a result of those displays of raw emotion.

Timo was so protective and guarded regarding all of his musical items too. He didn't want anyone else near it or touch it. Also, it was forbidden, for anyone besides Timo, to move his instruments in any way. That also applied to the setup process before and the subsequent takedown after gigs. Timo took care of his stuff himself and preferred it in that manner. He was like a hockey netminder in that sense. Mekkar thought it based on Timo's athlete and musician superstitions. No one else understood the reasoning, thus no one else ever brought up the subject. The rest of the group and everyone that hung around them, in time, got used to it and accepted this as normal behavior. In the vein as the sports world, many athletes have their own irrational behavior and rituals that they believe help them perform better. Mekkar wanted his papa to do the same for his instruments too. Henrik was an electronics master and could have easily completed the conversions. However, his papa didn't have the time and this request made by Mekkar was low on Henrik's project priority list.

The group never recorded any original songs or covered anyone else's songs in the studio. No pressings or vinyl records were produced by the band. Mekkar also doubts that anyone made any bootleg records from their gigs, however it is possible. They weren't originally in this band to develop and grow into a future monstrosity to go on tours or make big cash with this project. This was just for fun, not another job, as they already had employment outside of sports. Frankly, only Timo was the only one of the four who excelled with enough musical talent to eventually make money in the scene after his hockey playing days ended.

Their contracted pay was based on the number of paying patrons brought into the venue. A bonus was given when the crowd exceeded the expected certain minimum level. Well, the group was at least simply good enough to get gigs and run an alcohol tab at the clubs and dives they performed at. Mekkar remembered the funny thing was this usually was in exchange for actual cash. To explain it further the compensation was arranged in a certain way and rarely, if ever, covered them and their closest buddies' drink tab. If the four local team hockey players in the band didn't bring a lot of people, the band would have owed much more out of pocket. Fortunately, it takes only a few friends who then bring along their buddies that can rapidly add to the numbers and the tab is surpassed easily. Even acquaintances of the crew were encouraged to bring a high ratio of females along with them. Combine the massive consumption of booze, the motley crew of the band members' buddies, and the added amount of women along for the ride. The result usually surpassed the prearranged reimbursement for services rendered. In other words, the band and their entourage always seemed to far exceed the tab limits and then some. They were required to make up the difference at the end of the night with cash. So, it was good they all had jobs to pay for the difference.

The whole experience was viewed by all of them in the group as just a fun hobby for a limited amount of time. Mekkar felt it was just a needed break and distraction from the rigors of sports. Well, just until they had to cease the crew to continue each one of their potential sporting careers going forward. Mekkar said it best, "It was fun the short time it lasted. Now, it is time to move up to higher levels because we know others are watching."

Home Game

There was a home game in front of the same fans that support the local team Mekkar was a defenseman of. The opponent that night was the mighty and experienced USSR National hockey squad. Yes, that one that had been victorious against international teams from all around the globe. It was also the same group that had a high winning percentage versus professional teams from top leagues everywhere. The Soviets delivering the goods on a consistent basis in international tournaments too! Many considered Mekkar's opponents on this night as the best squad in the world, including the National Hockey League.

At first, Mekkar thought it was a prank setup by some of his teammates and didn't believe it. Soon enough, he found out the game was on and the true foe was confirmed. The teen from the Arctic made a crack to a media acquaintance of his, "Maybe we are just a warm up until their next match versus a top notch adversary." The Stars team Mekkar was playing for during this time was young in comparison. A scant number of members on his squad had not even participated in any matches outside of the country yet. However, the home side was still a quality minor league equivalent professional team with a winning record.

Mekkar was still not awed by the Soviets as many in the building and most of his team were. He had encountered wild animals in their habitat, so to him no person could ever intimidate him. Even though Mekkar was quite aware that his team was greatly overmatched, he always strived for victory each time. Still, it would take a massive effort for his club to defeat their rival on this evening. Mekkar expected a monumental upset to occur.

When the game began the Russians jumped on the Stars early and often. It was quickly become a rout. At least, Mekkar salvaged a little local pride by scoring the only two goals for his team during the first two periods. One of the defenseman, on Mekkar's side, had previously faced off against powerful squads in the Soviet Union and had experienced this same result. Mekkar was not amused and by the third period, he turned physically vicious and continued to hit everyone on the other side. He crossed the line himself in regard to the rule book, but it didn't matter to him at this point. He told a friend afterward, "I was returning the favor for the nasty stickwork and uncalled cheap shots that were not penalized. You know me; I will not tolerate that under any circumstances."

The Stars coaching staff was not happy with the team's on-ice performance because the Soviets crushed them 10-2. They also told Mekkar flatly, "It is not your job to pot goals and be that deep into the offensive zone. That is, so close to the opposition net. Your main task is to prevent scoring by the other squad against us. Look at the scoreboard, they tallied ten." Mekkar snapped back, "Those guys did not score any goals versus our team while I was on the ice. I was a plus two in the plus/minus rating for the match. Exactly, what is the problem?" This response by the insolent youngster infuriated the team coaches and administrators that were present and embarrassed. They were indignant with Mekkar's remarks considering the fact the Stars simply got their rear ends whipped.

Team management responded forcefully before Mekkar left the bench area by telling him that he was suspended a game for each goal he had scored that evening. Thus, the suspension was for the duration of two matches that he would miss as a result. Mekkar was ticked off after hearing these words and shouted at the club officials. Anyone who was close enough could hear his response of, "Screw You!" He proceeded to the dressing room and rapidly changed out of his gear. Next, the young hothead avoided everyone, including any reporters, and left the arena in a foul mood.

Mekkar interpreted the situation and overreaction by the club as being extremely unreasonable. The Arctic Warrior felt that he had performed very well against a high quality opponent for the first part of the match. He also saw his ferocity in the last portion as a type of exhibition in civic pride. Mekkar refused to return to represent that Stars team in any more games remaining on their schedule for that particular campaign. He stated that he might consider coming back, in the future, if those in charge and the coaching staff were replaced. Therefore, Mekkar went back to play for his regular regional squad. He felt they better appreciated for his all around contributions while continuing to pile up victories because Mekkar loved winning more than anything else.

Visiting Alf

After arriving back & visiting his home village for a short time Mekkar was restless. As a result he decided to journey down south to visit his younger brother, Alf. The travel distance was over 400 miles (643.74 kilometers) away. Mekkar, Karku, Lasse, & Niillas took the train to get there and hang with him like they used to back home. Alf was currently going to school in an actual city where everything was much larger. The differences were vast as compared to the village they originated from. The middle child in Mekkar's family was also now involved in the town's local hockey system. Alf was progressing quickly and currently playing for a top level team for his age group. They all wanted to witness him in action before surprising Alf in person.

The oldest three of this crew got pretty rowdy during their drinking session while travelling. It was fortunate for them they didn't have their items confiscated. The gang almost got thrown off of the train for their obnoxious behavior. So, it was a good thing each of them brought extra pocket money for the trip, just in case. Like at home, they made wagers on anything and everything they could think of. Some of it was on stupid ridiculous things too as kids bet on all kinds of stuff. They had their own small version of Las Vegas. The betting that went on was limited to their clique, and always excluded any outsiders, due to lack of trust of strangers. This type of activity was considered normal and routine among their age group back home in the village. Many others observed their actions as strange behavior that should be reserved for fully grown adults. It was normal conduct in their view and they didn't care what other people thought.

Finally the band of four reached their destination and went to see Alf play some hockey. Mekkar's brother stood out as the star of his squad. Alf conversed with them near the bench after the game was over. He told Mekkar that he would them back there after he showered and changed. For anyone familiar with a hockey locker room, the foul odor can be overwhelming at first. You know who the new reporters are by their offense at the smell in the air. Most get used to it very soon and they are gone. The boys all played sports, so that wasn't an issue. Arrangements for lodging had previously been made. The crew set up a time and place to meet Alf after he got out of school the next day. Mekkar thought to himself, and then the real mischief could begin. Would the town be ready was the question.

On one occasion Karku, Lasse, & the ringleader Mekkar put out a dare to the youngest in the group, Mekkar's youngest brother, Niillas. Part of the conditions was that Niillas had to run out quickly into the middle of a four way stop light intersection. There must be a predetermined minimum amount of traffic present. Another part of the challenge was that Niillas had to pull down his pants and take a dump right in the middle of the junction. After he would finish his business, Niillas would rejoin the group nearby and cleanup with items they had available.

The promised reward if Mekkar's youngest brother carried out this action in its entirety was that each person in the party would give him forty dollars apiece. The posse was extremely cocky in their proposition. None of them ever thought that Niillas would have the guts to actually carry it out. It was test among the adolescents. The youngest potential members that wanted to hang with them had to show their stuff. They every so often had to show a willingness to ignore their fear and accept a challenge when given. Mekkar thought to himself, this is not back in their country village where they knew most everyone. At the same time, any leading adults back home would chalk it up as a harmless teenage prank. Like anywhere else in the world, human nature takes over to satisfy a need to be a part of something and fulfill a goal to gain acceptance.

There was a risk involved. Mekkar remembered that this is a city where if the police show up they all could get arrested. Mekkar whished that he would have thought of this idea regarding Niillas first. However, Karku came up with it and took all the credit for it. Since, they all had been drinking for awhile the group lost most of their inhibitions. Despite all his concerns, the setting forced Mekkar to display his brave face. Plus, Niillas desperately wanted to prove that he was worthy of hanging out with the older ones.

The gang was drinking, joking, and laughing together, hopefully inconspicuously behind a small berm, on the side of the road. Alf arrived late and finally met them there near the scene of the alleged misconduct that was about to take place. Mekkar thought this was good timing and proceeded to fill Alf in regarding the situation. Alf was game and he wanted to get in on the action. He was in an adventurous mood and desired a piece of the gamble. The money pot increased with another contributor. The crew had basically been eating and consuming non-stop during their waking hours since arriving in town. Thus, they had come prepared and brought plenty of resources for this endeavor.

Niillas got ready and loosened his belt that held up his pants. He briefly waited for vehicles to appear in all directions. Then, he suddenly dashed out into the middle of the crossway. Next, Niillas pulled down his drawers to his ankles, squatted, and left a medium sized pile right there. Without thinking of wiping his bottom, the boy quickly yanked up his pants. The surrounding cars were honking their horns at him. Catcalls and shouts from a few of the drivers came from all quarters. Right afterward, Niillas ran back to the side of the road to the relative safety where the group was. It was hilarious and everyone in the bunch was cracking up. At the same time, all of them were amazed that the boy did complete the dare.

Mekkar spoke to the group and said, "Let's get out of here before the cops show up or worse. First of all, we need to find a bathroom so Niillas can finish wiping himself and fully clean up." Subsequently, they fled the scene to avoid any potential trouble and arrived at a nearby restaurant. After cleaning himself up in the restroom, Niillas was ready to collect his prize. Each individual paid the money owed to the young guy for accomplishing the dare. Niillas raked in a total of one hundred and sixty bucks.

Not one of the guys believed enough to wager between themselves whether Mekkar & Alf's youngest sibling would complete the task in the middle of the road with vehicles there. Thus, no odds on that aspect were set up beforehand. Mekkar commented in front of the group, "Let's face it, we all lost our rear ends on this one!" Mekkar was also slightly perturbed that he lost the bet that separated some cash from his pocket. He was always ticked off when he lost anything because he hated losing so much. Yet, he had to admit that this was a stunt for the ages and probably was worth it despite the cost. Oh! The things that occur in boys club.

It is Better to Give than Receive

When it came to dishing out the sports related physical punishment Mekkar didn't hold back. He didn't realize it at the time but he should have played smarter when he was younger. Mekkar surely does understand his folly now as his body is crippled and falling apart. Some days it is a chore just to get out of bed for the day. He knew the risks and accepted willingly blaming no one else but himself.

It is too bad he didn't listen to others who had told him through their own past experiences about the possible end physical results. Mekkar now wishes he could have perceived or viewed the consequences of this harsh lesson and learned them sooner. He now attributes it as being young and the thought process that it will not happen to you. As the paraphrased saying goes, "Those who do not learn from past history are doomed to repeat it (and its past mistakes)." [Edmund Burke, 1729-1797] or something to that effect, according to Mekkar.

Sirga told Mekkar flat to his face on more than one occasion, "No matter how much you give, you always receive more in return. That is because there is only one of you and so many more of them ready to return the favor." This statement, or some variation of it, had been passed down to Sirga by her mama and through her lineage. Sirga applied this piece of wisdom to her oldest son in regard to a physical state. Yet, of course the young Mekkar did not take it to heart nor apply the message into his play on the ice.

There is a similar adage used during the Christmas season – It is better to give than to receive. Mekkar preferred this application instead. It showed itself to be especially true when he would throw his body around on the ice and wipe opposing players out with hard body checks of all types.

Still Mekkar, like most other teenagers, are prone to do blow off much of the advice and sage wisdom given to him by the adults. Mainly because he thought it was so old school thinking and that times had changed. Similar to many individuals that are growing into eventual adulthood, Mekkar thought he knew better. Young people in this stage of life tend to think they know it all and more than anyone else. Plus, Mekkar felt that no parent or relative could relate to him during this time with regard to his own life and his own chosen direction for it. There is the tendency to forget that all adults have already gone through those things beforehand and made it through.

The result usually is that the youthful person has to stubbornly learn various lessons in life the painful hard way and Mekkar eventually did as well. Yes, Mekkar would find out that when he thinks he knows it all, that attitude will soon make him look foolish in reality. It does happen when life kicks him around a bit and humbles him through tough circumstances. These trials and tests would come about sooner than he ever imagined. Then, finally the boy would become a man by gaining the required life instruction to go on to the next set of tasks.

On the Pitch

Mekkar was in town to visit his youngest brother Niillas. The younger sibling asked Mekkar to come and watch him play, the next day, in a soccer (futbol) match for charity. The game would include other pro players like Niillas that supported a specific cause. Initially, was not interested and came up with excuses to avoid coming to observe the game. To Mekkar, it would be only a glorified scrimmage. He prefers to attend real matches where a victory would count for something in the standings.

So, Niillas threw out another bone by telling his older brother that there would be some former International and World Cup stars in the game. Names that he would be familiar with. Niillas also told Mekkar that one side had his favorite player Giorgio Chinaglia along with Pele, and a German goalie. The other side had one of the greatest players from Germany, as well as, others that Mekkar would recognize from all over the globe (Mexico, Brazil, Italy, England, and more). The sell job worked and convinced Mekkar to agree to go. "After all, it was for charity," Mekkar quipped in justifying tone as if he was trying to convince himself that he had made the right decision.

The man from the Arctic expected to see a tiny member of people in the stands for the matchup. Boy, he was in for a surprise when about a half hour before the scheduled start time the crowd began to file in. There was a lot more than Mekkar originally anticipated. He then received the news why the event was happening at all. The match was put on in a rather hastily manner to raise funds for a fellow old footballer to meet medical expenses for a recently diagnosed disease. Mekkar made the assumption that the individual was a well respected in the soccer (futbol) community and some of his friends wanted to help any way they could.

However, Niillas came over to the bench to get a drink of water with a worried look on his face. Mekkar noticed this and inquired, "What is the problem?" Niillas told his brother that he was just informed that one of the players for his team was unable to get a connecting flight and unable to make it in time for the match. The younger brother asked Mekkar to play instead and said to him, "We have no subs to fill in the hole (in the lineup)." Mekkar came appropriately dressed in a t-shirt and shorts since it was a sunny day and didn't need to change his attire. Since, the older brother was reluctant, Niillas now pleaded with Mekkar to be the replacement. He told Niillas, "I am a former hockey player, not a soccer (futbol) player!" The younger sibling responded back, "Don't you think that I know that, but the choices were either you or that fat sports reporter over there on the sidelines. Not only are you in much better shape, you have played the game a few times and watched hundreds of top flight soccer (futbol) games, a number with me in them." Niillas continued on, "You already know how to play this game and you don't want us, especially me, to look bad do you?" Mekkar began to be suspicious, as it is his nature, and thought that this was all a big set up of some type, by his sibling. Even though it was not the case, Mekkar was not convinced.

The other side lacked any additional players as well with only the minimum of ten and a goaltender. Niillas influenced Mekkar by making him aware to not disappoint the crowd that had already shown up. Trouble was, it was too late for emergency reasons to turn back and Mekkar finally agreed. He decided to not make any additional enemies in a foreign stadium. Mekkar was not in the mood, at this point, to have a hostile crowd predisposed toward him. Especially, if they found out he might be the one responsible for today's event being called off. You never know how fans might react to the news, thought Mekkar.

The Arctic Warrior pressed his relative as to what his position would be and what was expected of him on the pitch. Niillas advised Mekkar, "I know that you were a defenseman in your sport and know all kinds of tricks, especially below the waist with the hips and positioning." Surprisingly, Niillas had never played ice hockey before and lacked excellent skating skills for the sport his older sibling excelled at. Mekkar's brother went on to say to his older kin, "Use the tactics I mentioned to you and try not to foul too often above the waist. Do that and you will be fine. You will have to mark number six when he pushes forward into his offensive zone, otherwise you will be a regular defender. Your teammates back there on the field will guide you." And Niillas went on to say, "During the one-on-one marking, the player you will be covering will get frustrated and probably swear at you. You do remember enough choice words to respond back in his own language, right?" Mekkar sot back with disdain in his voice, "Yes! Great, I get to be embarrassed by one of the greatest players ever and have him hate me forever by the time the match is over. Be a pest, I can do that! I was very good at that in hockey and got under opponents skin."

Yet, Mekkar had to change his mindset because as a hockey player he could get physical by body checking, even punching opposing players. But, in the Beautiful Game (soccer / futbol) it is the complete opposite and you are unable to manhandle other players. Mekkar could not afford to get red carded and removed from the game, thus forcing his side into a shorthanded scenario for the rest of the time. Unlike hockey, down a man to spend two minutes in the sin bin would be a minimum penalty. Fortunately, it never came to that. Niillas squad, which included Mekkar, won the match with a late goal in the last couple of minutes in regulation time. Mekkar was glad there was no tie score as he hated results where there is no clear winner.

After the final whistle from the referee blew, Mekkar began to approach some of teammates on the field that day. He figured that this might be his only chance to ever interact with some them. He wanted to meet Pele right after the match was over and who was on his side, but never was able to because the superstar was immediately surrounded by a thick throng of people. Mekkar did get to chat with some of the other athletes there that he had previously watched for years. He thought it was pretty cool. Plus, Mekkar got to spend some time talking with his favorite soccer (futbol) player in the whole world, Chinaglia.

Refusal

Mekkar's younger sibling, Alf has stated more than a few a times, that he refuses to learn the English language and never will do so. Contrary to Alf's normally laid-back demeanor, he is extremely blunt and forward in regards to this matter. In no way is it an issue of Alf not being able to learn the language. Alf already speaks over twenty different languages fluently from diverse areas of the world. Mekkar quips about his brother, "He can pick up other languages like drinking water. The only issue is desire." Plus, since Mekkar and their mama also learned English beforehand, Alf could get hints and tips. Both of them would be good sources to practice the learned skills on also. He would not be relegated to honing his English on their godparent's dog as Mekkar was required to do.

One time long ago, another person spoke plainly to Alf during a conversation and made the off-hand remark that "English is taking over the world". This angered Alf. He responded in the following manner with arrogant tone. "It is not taking over me nor anyone in my house. I will learn all of the other languages before I will learn English. Do you hear me?" Mekkar's younger brother already is fluent in what is considered the most difficult tongue in the world, Hungarian. For business, Alf travels all over the globe along to frequent trips to Asia. When in Hong Kong, Alf is articulate in Cantonese Chinese. He regularly conducts affairs in German, Russian, Korean, Japanese, French, Italian, and many others. This is a skill he inherited from his mama, Sirga. Sirga, herself spoke easily more than twenty languages and forty plus dialects. For Mekkar, it is not so effortless. The oldest had a head start in regards to English, mainly the United Kingdom Commonwealth or British Queen's version. Mekkar began that task, just after his fourth birthday, for use in the family businesses. Sirga needed the boys to be able to converse with the increased influx of tourists to the area. Who doesn't want to see real live reindeer and experience the great outdoors?

To this day when the brothers are conversing together in a variety of ways, they continually switch languages when choosing words because one might prefer a certain one. The siblings have their favorite phrases and words in specific languages. This repetitive switching is not a common habit, even among relatives. Since they can understand some of the same tongues, this is usually not a problem, until they reach a point where the one is unfamiliar. Mainly because Alf can easily speak over twenty languages and Mekkar has the same ability in only five. Mekkar basically lost three others due to lack of mental exercise and usage. However, the older sibling can still read a little bit of those three and remember the odd word or phrase.

The Arctic Warrior, Mekkar, must try to remember not to use English when expressing himself with his kin. This is especially true with regard to usage of slang terminology that Mekkar has picked up through time spent living overseas in North America. The same is true if Alf spoke Chinese to him, even more so when using casual lingo. Alf has three boys now and the middle one has come home attempting to apply new English words learned at school. The boys are required, as part of the curriculum, to learn and be proficient in another tongue that is away from their home region and part of the world. Part of the same unchanged educational standard that Mekkar, Alf, the youngest, Sirga, Henrik the papa, and everyone else experienced, where they grew up. Alf commented that the system wanted to instill more well roundedness to help individuals better prepare for the constantly changing international environment. The concept was that each person would eventually encounter interaction with people from very different places and new skills are always needed. Yet, Alf understands when he overhears English and bellows out, "I do not want to ever hear that in my house or my presence because it will never conquer anything that I can influence, which means you too!" He is almost militant regarding this, but no one knows why. Still, the man with vast vocabularies is mum on the subject. Mekkar chalks it up to plain cultural significance and prideful stubbornness, which he has in abundance also.

Unwelcome Visitor

Mekkar was seeking a rare moment of solitude on the back porch. He only needed a short break to recharge his physical and mental "batteries". The mischievous Mekkar had taken one the protective weapons, along with ammunition, from a specific unlocked cabinet inside his house. The young man planned on sneaking it back into the wood container later on, while hoping no one else had noticed.

The cabinet was within sight distance from the front door. Its strategic location was chosen based on past negative experiences involving older family members from the last Great War. The idea was to keep small weapons at home to be made available to the household. All members of the family dwelling there were trained in various weapon usage and maintenance. The reasoning behind it was because the closest military base was too far away – even further away than the largest adversary. It would take too long for any aircraft to be scrambled and airborne to provide any defense that might be required.

In the local custom, only strangers came to the front door. People you knew, such as friends and acquaintances normally showed up at the back porch. Nearby the same back door Mekkar was currently enjoying brief relaxation. The Native from the North intended to go with a few friends some distance from the village and fire off some rounds. At least, far enough away to avoid detection and possible trouble from any adults. Of course, there would be drinking involved. While Mekkar sat and waited for a few of his buddies, the fully loaded weapon lay within arm's length on the table. The Arctic Warrior was looking forward to some carousing.

However, his space was about to be invaded by an unwelcoming guest. The interloper appeared irritated and seemed to looking for food to get his hands on and satisfy its hunger. The animal the growled during its approach toward the porch. As it got closer – the bear stood up and let out a bellowing sound. Mekkar had the feeling that the animal was trying to intimidate him to get what it wanted. Yet, the Native from the Far North was not afraid.

He already played a sport during this time that automatically contained intimidation as par of its makeup – that is, ice hockey.

Next, Mekkar stood up and waited for the black bear to make his move first. The beast then moved quickly on all fours and began to climb the stairs. Mekkar was ready and willing to give a welcome that the bear was not expecting. The natives already knew the weak points of a bear such as its nose. The young man slightly turned his body to his right side and with great momentum brought his arm up to shoulder level. His fist proceeded forward, as the bear reached the top step, and connected with the animal's snout. The animal let out a sound of pain as it tumbled down the stairs from the powerful punch.

Alf, Mekkar's younger brother, heard the noise and came outside to find out what all the commotion was all about. But, he did not see the punch. The Arctic Warrior firmly stated to the animal that if it were to come back up and attack him, he would retrieve the fully loaded grenade launcher and would blow him apart. Mekkar did not think about the great chance that by firing the weapon at such a short distance – he would probably be killed as well. The close proximity between him and the bear would make that outcome almost a certainty. Well, the young man figured that the animal must have understood his warning and didn't want to risk it. Since, the bear turned around and left the area unsatisfied and worse for wear.

Waiting in Line

As Mekkar listens to the AC/DC song – Down Payment Blues, it takes him back in time to when he first heard it in the background. The Arctic Warrior wanted to buy the album - Powerage right then and there because he thought it rocked in a fantastic way. However, his wish was not granted during that particular stop on another Hockey Tour away from home. Mekkar was kept from making that purchase in person, due to the team bus was departing for the arena as part of the game day morning skate. All players on the team were required to be on that particular bus as to not miss the trip. In reality, the morning skate always ended up as a light practice instead of a familiarity skate in the rink. The idea was to get the team acquainted with the facility before participating in the game later on that day.

Sometime in the future, Mekkar heard news that a limited number of copies of the same album were going to be made available locally for purchase. He knew exactly when and where to be, as well as, hoping that no unforeseen obstacles were placed in his way. Mekkar was a creature of habit like many of his fellow citizens. However, he was very stubborn in his way and would be unamused if his plan did not work out as planned.

Mekkar was already living, down south, in the capital city and being employed by a local hockey team in the area. On the appropriate date, The Arctic Warrior woke up early and walked a few blocks to be outside the Import Shop. He was the first person there and waited for the small business to open its front door. Soon afterward, other stragglers shuffled up and formed a line behind him. This had occurred before, remembered Mekkar, when he concluded previous purchases there before. So, he did not expect any surprises. Yet, on this cold morning he was first in line with cash ready to be spent. There would be little time to waste once the store opened. The native from the north wanted to take care of this transaction quickly and be out the door. Ironically, Mekkar needed to head back to the arena to prepare himself for another morning skate. He felt this might be his last chance.

Down South

One time while Mekkar was living in the big city, he and a couple of friends walked toward the downtown area. They wanted to visit the large weekly open air marketplace for two reasons. One was to pickup some fresh fruit and vegetables because of their nutritional value. To them, the taste is better than the store bought brands as well. After all, they were still growing young athletes. The other reason was to meet the hordes of women that appeared there.

After the small group spent some time doing their thing, they split up in pairs to make the walk back home with their produce and a few phone numbers. Mekkar and the buddy with him soon saw, on a side street, two huge guys begin to move a vehicle out of a parking spot near the curb. Mekkar and his friend could not stop observing the scene unfold in front of them. Each one stood at least six foot nine inches (2.10 meters) tall and appeared to weigh 300 pounds (136.077 kilograms) or more. Those guys had shirts on that revealed muscular frames. The men each took a corner of the front side of the medium sized vehicle and scooted it over a bit. Then, they went to the rear of the car and did the same thing. This occurred a few times until the pair of large individuals got back into their own vehicle and moved it into the parking spot along the curb. The one they just physically created with their own brawn and brute strength.

The two men began to leave the newly relocated car alongside theirs, in the road and in a double parked situation. At that moment, it dawned on Mekkar that only a few individuals, he was aware of, could and the guts to attempt and carry out such a stunt like what he had just witnessed. Back home in his village there were some people who were big and strong enough to do it including his papa, he thought. He knew his papa was overseas on a business trip, so Mekkar right then dismissed that speculation altogether.

There is a saying that "curiosity killed the cat" and in this instance Mekkar and his buddy became the panthers as they approached within hearing distance of the ensuing conversation. The Arctic Warrior instantly recognized the large men's voices as soon he heard them. It was affirmed now that Mekkar was close enough to see and identify who the huge individuals were. Fortunately, Mekkar and his chum were still at a safe distance away from the action, in case they had to flee to avoid any trouble. Now, both were close enough to the action to see and hear everything that was happening. Still, the presence of Mekkar and his compatriot were never noticed.

Suddenly, an officer of the law arrived on the scene and Mekkar thought he also looked familiar. However, neither Mekkar nor his pal wanted to deal with the cops in any manner. The authority figure spoke to the two large individuals as if he knew who they were and discerned what had happened. He sternly told the men, "To put the other car back in its rightful place and take themselves somewhere else. Before you go, I am giving you both a ticket with a fine to be paid in court for your creative action." Afterwards, the policeman went away laughing.

Twin-Fin

Mekkar traveled to Australia on a reciprocal visit to stay with few friends he met when they previously sojourned to his hometown and stayed at the local youth hostel there. They turned Mekkar onto surfing, during this time, by taking him to watch a live surfing competition involving Mark Richards. The now legendary Richards would soon afterward conquer the world of Pro Surfing. Mekkar stood among the crowd on that Australian beach and pondered how he needed a new activity to pursue. He thought there must be some other physical activity to get away from it all. At the same time, supplant the martial arts disciplines he participated in for years with his brother and best friend.

The tendency is for Mekkar to get bored easily and seek out new challenges. There was a churning for something different, stimulating inside of him. It did not matter if he wanted it or not, it was a part of his inner being. The expression had to get out somehow. Also, he wanted to distance himself from the reason why he left the Asian fighting arts in the first place. The Arctic Warrior decided to move on when his instructors restricted his advancement and told him that he could not test for a black belt in both styles. The sensei's agreed that Mekkar's temperament was too violent and a risk to others, if the situation presented itself. Due to his learned proficiency, fighting, and athletic ability, the mentors explained that they did not want to feel responsible for the Native from the North's possible future actions. They had seen Mekkar go into a seemingly uncontrolled, frenzied mode with a potential to use excessive force in a relative minor encounter. So, Mekkar moved on.

During the trip in the Land of Plenty, Mekkar started with his buddies by floating on the long rideable waves off the coast that could last as long as fifteen minutes or more. It was a good thing that the waves were not large for him to learn to balance himself properly on the board. The Aussie group was quite surprised that Mekkar was able to move along with the wave as quickly he did. Mekkar convinced himself that he could grasp this and run with it. Soon, the Young Man from the Arctic caught the fever and surf as much as he could, while he was in the Land Down Under.

Even though he was hooked on the sport, he wasn't very good at it and still wet behind the ears. Mekkar made a decision then that he would have to find a spot nearby back home to continue on and improve. There were enough rough areas, with rapids, in the river near his house to practice. Top notch kayakers use those places on a frequent basis, he reasoned. His friends told him that it was imperative for him to get his own surf boards before he left. Someone in the group brought up that the Aussie-born Richards also did board shaping and modification as a part of his many talents. Mekkar recognized the name from the contest at the beach and had items he sought. He figured, what was he waiting for? The nice weather made a great time for a road trip to go get what he wanted, as soon as possible, two unique boards that expressed his personality.

Unfortunately, the time spent in the Great Southern Continent went by much too quickly and the fun had to end. By the time Mekkar was ready to leave from this journey, he did possess two custom painted Mark Richards (MR) Twin-fin surfboards made especially for him. They were blue, yellow, and white colored emblazoned with the MR logo in black. Mekkar would take his new possessions on the long flight back home with him and it was a costly venture. Those items, later on, would receive a lot more travel time to other far away locales.

Eventually, the native of the north used those MR sticks extensively to improve his skills on the water during his days as a foreign exchange student in San Diego. Surfing became to Mekkar a type if release similar to other sports related activities which he had done before. He saw it as a relationship in regard to a person's connection of yourself, your board, and the ocean environment. Mekkar remembered his interactions with Aslak when he was younger and took on a spiritual significance in a way. Even though he was dissed by a few of the much more highly skilled surfers as being below par, Mekkar gained a greater appreciation for the sport. He realized how easy it could become a lifestyle. Especially, if he stuck with it for a great length of time. Mekkar was aware that the true surfers are a very different breed than all of the other souls that invade the beach. The key for the Arctic teenager was could he somewhat tap into that mindset.

School itself bored Mekkar to death. Mekkar had learned a great many things during the education process instituted by his various hockey programs. There were long bus rides with extensive reading, paper writing, and homework assignments to keep the players engaged. A couple of the team trainers were always tutors and seemed to be always present for any questions. Mekkar sometimes felt as though he could never get away from them. The result was high school seemed fairly easy to him He felt that he was being loaded with plain busywork to keep occupied. The classroom setting was tedious in his mind. Teachers noticed Mekkar was inclined to daydream often or at least have his mind somewhere else. It was obvious to many around him. The Arctic Adventurer was not used to this type of setting. He never was involved in a formal school environment previous to this program. The learning environment he grew up with was unconventional and adapted to his pursuit of a future professional athletic career.

There was still the incessant desire to learn and undertake new things. Mekkar was still a teen at this point and had not adopted the concept of Older People's Syndrome as he termed it, yet. His viewpoint was awakened by observing people throughout his life and interaction with wiser individuals back home in the native culture which shaped Mekkar's particular theory. The terminology reflected a conviction that Mekkar believed about people in general. His idea was that younger people are more open to new adventures and experiences. However, that begins to change at various rates when a person reaches about thirty-five to forty years old. Mekkar admits that his application does not apply to everyone as each person is different, but is a generally applied principle. Anyway, the older person becomes set in their own ways and habits. Thus, much more than a teenager, eventually develops into a state which is more resistant to great changes in any area of their life. Reasons are that one gets to a place of relative comfort, can predict certain circumstances and outcomes, increasing dislike of uncertainty, and flat-out stubbornness levels increase exponentially. Experiencing the syndrome was still a long way off for the restless Northerner.

Mekkar normally would take his usual route to get to his favorite spot to hit the waves. His modified silver beach cruiser bike had a contraption welded to it on the ride side by a friend. It was setup with metal bars extended with a basket in the bottom to carry a bag with his wetsuit and other needed supplies. Mekkar would place his surfboard flat on the top of the rack and fastened it with bungee cords. His stick was secure and was not going anywhere. Plus, the side carriage as he referred to it had wheels at the bottom that rolled along the ground with the bike. It took some time to put it altogether to make it handy, even though it was odd to look at. Once in awhile the native from the north would get struck with a fondness to mix things up once in a while. Just to break up the monotony and boredom.

On one occasion, he decided to ride along a very different path to another beach, after checking the weather report to make sure it was worth the trip. In the water at this new location he looked down and noticed alongside his surfboard little creatures. They moved too quickly to be seaweed. Mekkar called them sand or beach sharks and knew they were much too small to be any danger to the people in the water. Usually they swam away when he would get too close. Only the braver ones might bump into his board with a thump sound or his leg unintentionally. Mekkar never saw larger sharks during his time in the water like they have in recent years. He quipped, "I guess, I could never have been mistaken for a seal as people are typically seen by the larger predator sharks." He had a blast that day and started back home at dusk. As Mekkar was passing a school, he noticed a film crew was shooting a scene in the parking area near one of the buildings. There were a lot of props, cameras, and people in that crowded space. It reminded him of the environment he was exposed to when his mama would take him on her modeling shoots. Later, when he watched the well-known movie with his buddies at the theatre, he recognized what he had seen on the school grounds that day. However at the time, Mekkar was focused on riding back home. It was a two-pronged race for his safety against both the sun's descent below the horizon and heavier evening vehicle traffic. He asked himself the question that if drivers have trouble seeing other cars, then how much easier can it be for them to miss seeing him? He did not have any desire to become an accident statistic.

When the young man was not occupied with school, related sports activities, and work he would make time to enjoy some waves. He received more than his share of beach time because of his penchant of being bored in class. Many times the teacher would present material that he had already learned back home in the continuous study sessions when not playing sports. Sometimes, he would act out in a ridiculous manner with an intention to be sent directly to the front office. It was not an exhibition of negative behavior for attention's sake, there was an agenda on his part. The school administrator asked the Arctic Warrior why he couldn't behave in a manner identical to other foreign students. Mekkar always had a comeback statement to the authority figure. He had a disposition that seem to automatic challenge or oppose those in charge. The teenager was quite creative in his defense with comments such as, "I am the valedictorian.

So, give me a hassle when I receive a B grade from a class." The result was various suspensions for mouthing off to the school's Vice Principal. Yet, he would flatly reply with the challenge, "Do it and you will add to my surfing time." Mekkar's bluff was repeatedly called and was he happy about that since he was not fond of the boring academic classroom atmosphere. Mekkar preferred the extra curricular activities anyway.

Most likely due to his athletic and fighting background, Mekkar carried the same attitude everywhere he went. It was natural for him not to be afraid of others in the sports arena, football field, or the beach. The Arctic young man grew up in an area where there were large bears and other wild animals. To him, people in comparison are no contest and not more intimidating. Mekkar also had experience going toe-to-toe fisticuffs, on skates, with opponents much larger than him in hockey rinks all around the globe.

The brazen teen never got as proficient as he would have liked at the newly found water sport. His effort was always there to improve and ensure the fun and freedom aspect of the activity. Unfortunately, Mekkar lost one of his prized sticks when it was broken while dancing among the rocks after being swept by the strong current. It was a particularly bad day for him on that occasion and he should probably have stayed onshore until conditions were better. In the end, Mekkar's athletic competitive spirit got the best of him and he paid the price. The Northern Native should have remembered advice he received from Aslak on the trek long ago. Lessons, whether he wanted to accept it or not, that taught him regarding the different skills needed for different environments. Being tough and able on land and ice did not translate the same in water elements; other abilities are needed to adapt in a different setting. This should have been completely installed into him long ago that nature is no respecter of persons. Maybe, he had forgotten part of this concept due to always being away from the village and his native culture? Was the modern world outlook changing Mekkar's perspective and viewpoints? Even, the Arctic teen was unable to arrive at those answers.

His best day in the water was the one time when he was inside a barrel-roll as he called it and made it most of the way through before wiping out at the end. The inside of the tube could have looked like one of those surfing pictures he had previously seen in magazines. Of course, the photos rarely show the surfer getting overwhelmed by the wave at the end, which happened in Mekkar's case. He always sought to repeat that one feat but never was able to duplicate it. The arctic native did steadily continue to improve his surfing ability, but he was not as competent at it as he thought he was. It didn't help that Mekkar's young cockiness and ultra competitive nature contributed to the overestimation of his actual abilities in the surf.

A couple of years later Mekkar received a true test of his water capabilities when he visited some friends in Hawaii. Mekkar had heard about and read about surfing in the Islands. He did his diligent research and could identify on the map where the major sunbather beaches were located and wanted to avoid those. When Mekkar landed, he wanted to try his hand where some his friends hit the waves. Mekkar got the itch to take one ride at The Banzai Beach Pipeline on the Oahu North Shore [wikipedia.com]. He was aware of the Shore's past history regarding how the Pipeline had taken the lives of pro surfers much better than him. Yet, he felt as though he must attempt one wave, at least one time or the trip would be a disappointment for him. The waves that day were larger than normal and his friends that lived in the area were used to surfing there, but he was not. In Mekkar's mind, they were still a great deal more imposing than the California coast where he had been. His friends, and some others on the shore, warned him that he was not ready for this and attempted to keep him away from possible danger. They were also aware of the landscape which Mekkar was not. Nevertheless, Mekkar is very stubborn when he wants to be and was not to be denied. The Arctic Native began to psych himself out into what he called a Water Warrior mode, similar to a Lion Tamer before getting into the cage with the animals. He next took his board and ran off diving into the water with a lack of fear in his eyes. He rode his board out toward the waves. It was customary for local master surfers to discourage the inexperienced from injuring themselves in the water. Intentionally, it seemed Mekkar chose to ignore all signals from everyone else. He felt that his friends didn't pay attention to his true prowess and ability, even though they had done this here for quite awhile.

This turned out to be a big mistake on Mekkar's part. Mekkar had a false confidence in his abilities in the water and grossly miscalculated them in this instance. Plus, he only said that he had been surfing for two years now. A time experience indicator, like an aircraft pilot, is applicable in the number of hours spent in the actual activity. The two year period didn't point how frequently or not he had the chance to participate in surfing with all the other distractions in his life. When his turn in the lineup came, he attacked that wave and caught it. The whoosh sound of the water around him lulled him into a temporary and imaginary assurance.

He was mesmerized by the sound of rushing water. Yet, it was short-lived. Suddenly, Mekkar was crushed by the full force of the wave and received a good hammering by the sheer mass of the ocean that enveloped him. He thought to himself, I have to get to the surface as quickly as I can to get air. At the same time, the thoughts raced in his mind as he started to question whether his time had finally run out. Maybe, the last of his nine lives was about to be unexpectedly snuffed out. Too bad it wasn't on his own terms. The rapidly crashing wave seemed to continue on forever and was kicking his rear-end. Mekkar reflected on the previous lives extinguished and hoped that he wouldn't be next. The truth and danger was being delivered with full force right at that moment. He realized that he had no control over the situation and was at the mercy of the ocean. He felt like he was a rag doll and was in a blender to be shaken and stirred. Then, it was over and calm set in. Mekkar wasn't sure if he was alive or dead until he appeared in the shallow water coughing up remaining water from his lungs.

The battering Mekkar took cut him up on the reef below and the foot leash had snapped. His separated board broke up. Later on, a remaining few pieces washed ashore. Some of the other local surfers rushed to rescue him from his potential calamity. They pointed out to him, later on, that a large chunk including one of fins almost hit him in the head. That might have sliced through and killed him for sure. Other people there, as well as his buddies, warned him that he was wacked for paddling out that day in the first place. Mekkar nearly paid with his life. The ocean taught him a lesson and had treated him harshly. He was ticked off, but was too exhausted to come back for another round to due battle. If the Arctic Warrior wanted to try again no one was willing to give or even rent him another surfboard. With his last own remaining board destroyed and feeling humiliated that was the last time Mekkar took his chances to test out the waves.

Understanding

One day Mekkar was having lunch, with his younger brother Alf, at an outdoor restaurant. It was in a foreign city where their team was about to play an ice hockey game that evening. The waiter approached the table soon after the brothers had seated themselves. Alf didn't say a word but just pointed at his selection on the menu. When Mekkar spoke regarding the order in english, the server discovered that he did not speak nor understand the local language. Automatic assumptions about Mekkar were made and disparaging comments were discerned in the waiter's speech.

It seemed as though there was an expectation that the Arctic Warrior would never find out what was being said about him in the local tongue. Big mistake! The restaurant employee could not have been more wrong in his judgment. Alf spoke the language of the country fluently and understood every word that was spoken. He was even aware of the arrogant tone and proceeded to translate every sentence to his older brother. In his true feisty manner, Mekkar became furious and expressed this in an outward display.

The two brothers ended up not ordering their meal. Instead Mekkar arose from his seat with intent to do some harm. Mekkar got in the waiter's face and responded with a few choice words in the server's tongue. Alf had quickly taught him a few simple phrases to respond with during their brief interaction at the table. Mekkar was now sure the waiter grasped that the snide words he had used previously about the Arctic Warrior were exposed. The countenance of the staff member changed to fear and he probably realized that he was in an inevitable position. There was no escape.

Next, the teenager from the far north stopped talking and threw a rapid fist, connecting in the middle of the server's face. This stunned the taller waiter as Mekkar could unleash a powerful blow from his hands. One more punch to the stomach bent the employee over at the waist. Mekkar exhibited the strength to pickup his adversary enough to toss him into a nearby plate glass window. Flying shards of glass were all over. Mekkar didn't foresee that much damage, but was in no mood to care. The brothers immediately decided to get out of there as quickly as they could. They wanted to avoid the local police, who they were sure had been called by a bystander observing the activity at the restaurant.

Mekkar and his younger sibling chased down a taxi to take them both back to the team hotel. They figured there was no need for further incidents and they could get some food at the team hotel or maybe even room service. The game day routine followed as usual without interruption.

However, when the match began that night Mekkar was still in a vicious state of mind and he wanted to take it out on someone. He would get his wish. The Arctic Warrior announced to his coaches on the bench for them to be ready to alter their lines. He commented that he was going to play forward and would probably receive an early ejection from the game. Mekkar's target in this case would be anyone in an opposition national squad uniform, it didn't matter whom. The bigger, the better!

The side that included Mekkar, his best friend Lasse, and Alf was far superior talent-wise. Thus, the team would have no problem winning the matchup without Mekkar, even though they would be one defenseman short for the whole game. Right at the beginning of his first shift, Mekkar exploded like a heat seeking missile. He sought out the toughest opposing player on the ice. After charging in and forcing a one-on-one tie-up, Mekkar unleashed a beatdown. The other guy quickly prostrated himself into a turtle position, but Mekkar continued his barrage. Mekkar, on this occasion, was sent to the sin bin for five minutes. His team scored a couple of short handed goals in the meantime.

When he was set free from the box, Mekkar did not join the flow on the ice. Instead, he chased after another potential victim and released the beast within. The intent was clear to all people in attendance. Mekkar's own squad knew what his fate would be on this night. He threw many right hand blasts at the head of his opponent. Blood was streaming from the face of the other player. Since, Mekkar adrenaline was escalated, along with his boiling over anger; the young man was charged up and felt neither pain in his hands nor anywhere else. His teammates quipped that his smashes likely broke his opponent's protective headgear at the same time. Mekkar didn't notice and had no capacity for any mercy during the encounter. The Arctic Warrior's attitude was taking no prisoners and Mekkar obeyed his fury.

It was ironic that Mekkar was ejected from the game, in the initial period, not for the pummeling he dished out. The action of picking up someone's hockey stick lying nearby and subsequently swinging it like a club is what got him tossed. Even though Mekkar missed connecting with anyone, his baseball bat striking attempt sealed his fate this night. Alf afterward commented, "Beware of what comes out your mouth because you never know who is listening and there might be consequences, especially around Mekkar."

Together Forever

Mekkar was home visiting for a short time to attend a gathering due to a family member passing onto the afterlife. He was not planning to stay long as he needed to go back and finish his high school education. He also had to get ready for the upcoming fall sports season of football and beyond. Mekkar was a person that lived by habit of consistent routines and liked it that way. No unforeseen surprises were a good thing to him. Being a creature of habit was too inbred by his cultural upbringing whether he realized it or not, so he wouldn't have been able to change it much anyway.

Henrik suggested that him, Sirga, and their oldest child Mekkar brighten up the mood and celebrate the recent deceased person's life by taking a fun trip. Of course, there would be travel incurred but Mekkar's papa didn't tell the other two where they were going. Well at least not up front but he would reveal their destination later on in the journey.

After a few hours of flying with the resulting change of planes, the trio arrived in Hamburg, Germany and picked up the black shiny new model Mercedes rental car. Mekkar figured if they were going to drive might as well go in style. When they got on the highway Henrik revealed where they were going and said he wanted to enjoy a nice drive on the super speed highway of Germany. Both of Mekkar's parents had fancy sports cars at home and liked to drive fast. They were very proficient at quick motoring also. However, the not too warm summer and sunny clear sky outside would belie the dark events that were soon to come.

Not long into the car ride Sirga first gave a complement to her son for participating in a recent international hockey tournament. Then, true to her nature as she had high expectations for him. Mekkar's mama next started to critique Mekkar's team by saying that his team should have won the whole tournament. Henrik agreed with her and stated that Mekkar's squad did not play to their full ability. Henrik should know as he had played ice hockey before having to change careers due to injury.

Mekkar did accept the criticism but pointed out a few points of his own. First, he took a shot off of his left foot and fractured it on his very first shift in the first period. This affected and reduced his top form throughout the tourney. Plus, Mekkar mentioned that any of the top six national powers in international ice hockey could win any event at any time. The six were Canada, United States, Soviet Union, Czechoslovakia, Sweden, and Finland. For any other non hockey power entrant like Norway or West Germany to win it or even medal was unlikely.

The powerful USSR National Team was the rightful favorite as they had regularly beaten NHL, WHA, and squads from all over the hockey world during the past decade in International matchups. They even shutout the NHL All-Stars 6-0 to win the 1979 Challenge Cup at Madison Square Garden. Many of the other players were flat out intimidated by the Soviet dominance, but Mekkar was not. Mekkar's parents knew that their son always compared the biggest individuals to bears from back home and this eliminated any fear of people on his part.

However, Mekkar was tired and wanted to exit himself from this conversation and the subsequent critique of his play from his parents. He then decided to ignore them and his eyelids got heavy. Soon, he laid down across the back seat to rest. He attempted to still secure himself with a seat belt while lying down in a side position but was fairly unsuccessful in that regard. It was probably a good thing too that he released that restrictive device and was not upright.

The accident happened in a 49.7 Kilometer (30.88 miles) stretch between Göttingen, Germany & Kassel, Germany less than 3 hours from their driving starting point in Hamburg.

Mekkar, who was lying across the backseat asleep was definitely now awake by the force of impact. The collision had woken him up from his nap but there was the fact that he was trapped by the tangled metal around him and now could only slightly sit upright. There was one thing he for sure aware of was the pain in his legs. He knew his body fairly well and he was aware from his previous personal experiences with sports injuries that it was serious. In regard to everything else, Mekkar was still in a state of shock and disbelief. Mekkar noticed that Sirga was unable to turn her head in either direction to inspect that status of her husband's or son's condition.

"Don't take any crap from anybody, ever! No matter whom they are. Remember, you are no respecter of persons and always stay true to yourself." was Sirga's last statement and advice to her oldest son Mekkar. She stated this while dying in the front passenger seat of a vehicle from a head-on collision accident on the German Autobahn that was not any fault of their own doing. Then, Mekkar's mama expired, as she took her last breath, due to the result of her considerable injuries. Mekkar's papa's head in the driver's seat was already visibly crushed upon impact and had already died. However, his status was still unknown to the teenager. Henrik's large legs were driven backward because part of the engine's placement in the cabin. This gruesome scene had unfolded right in front of a horror stricken Mekkar. His mind was engrossed on the situation at hand and it was not restricted just to his own physical suffering.

He was also distracted with worry about the condition of his parents in front of him and concerned if their lives could be saved. Unfortunately, Mekkar was not a doctor and would not have been able to ascertain his mama or papa's condition. Plus, even if he was qualified to help, he was unable to extract himself first. All Mekkar could do was hope for the best. Yet, there was always the dreadful feeling deep within him of the worst possible scenario that was unfolding before him. Mekkar stubbornly refused to accept that his parents might have been gone away from this realm as to their health and well being. The continual thoughts racing through his mind was not only from fear but also used as a distraction from his own predicament.

The young man from the arctic also expected his parents to evoke some power or conjure up a spell to get them all out of this predicament and make it all whole again. That is how much faith Mekkar had in his parents' special natures. Unfortunately, it didn't happen and he began to consider that it was their time to go. That is to advance into their next plane of existence for further self development that stems from an old tribal belief system.

Anyway, qualified or not as a medical professional Mekkar was not stupid and could see some of the considerable damage done to the vehicle. He was quite aware that his folk's survival was precarious at best. He had seen other car accidents back home where people had been killed. Mekkar had already been in a few winter weather related minor fender benders himself as a passenger. However, no where near on the scale of this.

What seemed like forever, even though in reality it was only a brief time, Mekkar heard the sounds of sirens and saw the reflection of red and blue colored lights of the emergency vehicles. Next, he heard noises and voices from the rescue workers despite his hazy state of mind. The boy listened to the discussions of the individuals describing what they saw, from their perspective, while at the same time attempting to free him. Mekkar overheard some of them say that they would be surprised if anyone in the accident was still alive. It helped that the boy from the north was still familiar with some the language spoken by those on the outside of the hunk of crushed metal. This desperation made Mekkar call out that he was trapped and wanted out of there.

At this point he was also beginning to feel claustrophobic in his unenviable confined situation. Added to the fact that he was also fully unaware of the nature of what had happened. There was a wide range of different emotions and thoughts clouding Mekkar's normal thought processes.

Finally, they cut their way through the mangled metal to first reach Mekkar and remove him from the wreckage. Mekkar told his liberators that he had probably broken both of his legs since he knew his body well. He asked to be careful as to not make the problem worse than it already was. Mekkar was soon given drugs to put him in a state of semi-consciousness to provide a numbing sensation to sustain him and most likely to keep him calm under the circumstances. His hope was that he was able to block out much of what just occurred. Mekkar was confused and confounded by his true situation but didn't realize the full measure.

As Mekkar was on a low lying stretcher, unable to walk, he saw where the other vehicle had crossed over into their lane in the accident and hit theirs head on. The other vehicle landed on their side of the highway. Mekkar knew then who was responsible for the disaster and felt helpless to reverse the timeline. His fierce anger overcame him at this point and he flung himself off of the stretcher. The enraged teenager crawled over to a sheet covered body on the road that was next to the other vehicle. Mekkar assumed that this was the individual who caused the smashup so he pulled back part of the covering. He attempted to kick at and rain down blows with his fists upon the now lifeless corpse of the other driver in front of him. In reality, he was incapable of making that person feel some of the full measure pain that he was dishing out. Mekkar was not able to take the correct position and executive his wrath in this physical manner very effectively. Then, the teenager followed up with an extensive barrage of expletives at the deceased person as he was pulled off the prone lifeless body. He had determined in his mind whom was responsible for this tragedy and aimed his spit at the other vehicle and other dead driver. Fury and shock at the same time can normally be lethal combination. He just didn't care what anyone else thought about him at this juncture. Mekkar was in a mood for revenge and desired to extinguish the pain he was feeling inside. However, the full measure of psychological affects as a result of this incident wouldn't be evident for some time.

Someone in the ambulance, on the way to the hospital, pointed out to Mekkar that lying down across the back bench seat probably saved him from being another deceased statistic. But, this news was no consolation to him right now. Other details of the incident came out not long after evidence was gathered from witness statements and physical calculations of how it happened. However, there was nothing to be done to change the outcome which was already obvious. After the shock effect and medical remedies wore off, the nagging reality of his situation of losing both parents as a teenager hit him harder than any punch to his gut or noggin on the ice. He wondered why he was the only one to survive the accident? Why didn't he join his parents into the next life?

Many questions ran through Mekkar's mind such as, "Why did my mama and papa leave me?" and "Why where they now taken away from me?" Mekkar was clueless as to their new location and realm or what form his parents now possessed. The teen had little adult understanding of what that all entailed and hoped the wise elder Aslak back home might fill him in. He became overwhelmed by these types of feelings for some time. He realized that he was also helpless to change the sequence or effects of this series of events.

Mekkar's temperament became much shorter and fiery when remembering back and the thoughts about the crash continued to creep into his mind. He did his best to try to forget the whole incident to speed up the healing and recovery process. Unfortunately, the now missing gap in his life was too much for him to not notice. The constant physical reminder from his injured legs made him aware as well.

No matter what Mekkar still had to resume his life without two gigantic influences upon him and he wasn't even out of high school yet. The realization at times hit him like a brick wall. His parents were now gone together forever. It was a permanent journey into the great beyond, an extended unknown realm of the dead. The young man attempted to perceive what his parents would have wanted him to do, that is, continue on with his life.

Putting the tragedy out of his mind was a much more difficult task. What helped him was statements from both of his parents such as, "You can only change and control what is within your capability and desire to do so." Another related comment was "There are some other things that are beyond you." Of course, it was not so easy for a traumatized teenager to just forget what he witnessed. Plus, the physical injuries he sustained would force him to relive much of the details, in his mind, for quite some time.

Mekkar was still a young developing man trying to find his way in life, but he was still far from being fully grown up yet. This is despite the fact that teenagers think they know everything with little life experience to back up their perceptions. Another factor was his own native culture considered Mekkar, for all intensive purposes, as an adult already for a year when he was only seventeen. After the shock of the accident had truly worn off the reality of the situation was extremely painful. Later, other deeply hidden effects would manifest themselves later on. For awhile, it got much worse before it got better. Outward fits of rage, anger, loneliness, and disbelief exhibited themselves far worse than he ever anticipated. Disastrously, Henrik and Sirga's untimely deaths affected the youngest and least mature of the three sons, Niillas, most of all.

The incident adversely drove Niillas to exhibit deep character flaws such as he started to steal when away from the area. This was due to punishment of body part removal, such as loss of a hand, if he was ever caught stealing at home. The rules in place had been in place for a very long time. Everyone drank alcohol in large quantities so that was a normal occurrence. The after effects started a chain reaction in the youngest son's spiral downward. Drug abuse habits, such as snorting great amounts of cocaine up his nose, began. This, in turn, adversely resulted in a counterweight to Niillas' great physical and sports talents. It hurt Niillas in regard to better future career opportunities and prospects for him. The result was lack of an increased fortune making ability after the playing days were over. Mekkar's counsel regarding these matters was rejected outright and had no effect on his youngest sibling.

Other thoughts would flood Mekkar's head and there was always a sliver of hope that his mama and papa would let him know how they were doing. Maybe they could help and guide him from the other side? Mekkar continually asked himself these hard questions. The problem there was no definite answers or indicators of their awareness.

The young man subsequently attempted to cope the best he could by trying to focus on the earlier relaxing portion of the journey before they had rented the car. Mekkar still needed his full energy for other tasks at hand such as a forced adaptation upon his life. This included the long process of rehabilitation in the repairing of his own body. He was wondering if he would be able to play sports anymore at a relatively high level or even resume his just beginning future pro hockey career. There were whispers, and he heard about them too. The scuttlebutt was that Mekkar might never regain any of his previous athletic skills and abilities due to the accident. Some scenarios had Mekkar never returning at all as a player in any sport. Yet, Mekkar once again survived and would overcome. It just took awhile longer than he hoped.

As a result of broken bones in his legs suffered from the auto accident in Europe that also took both of Mekkar's parent's lives, his senior year sports season participation was curtailed. He didn't make it back until the latter part of the football season. A few of the naysayers were shocked that he was able to compete in fall athletics. They attributed it all due to his young quick recovery powers. His team duties were only two defensive and limited special teams plays. Even then Mekkar was still only about 75% of full capacity.

On one those defensive plays, in a road game, Mekkar barreled in on a blitz from his cornerback position on the line of scrimmage. He sacked the heralded opposition prep quarterback from the blindside. The walloping force of the hit from behind caused the signal caller to fumble the football and Mekkar pounced on it for the turnover for his side. This led to the winning score in a close victory for his squad. That was the highlight of the fall gridiron season for Mekkar. The result of hard work of putting in enormous amount of overtime during the rehabilitation recovery process paid off for Mekkar. This was after he would show up to class for awhile in a wheelchair with casts on both legs. His friends colored them with artwork and covered them with signage. At times, the young man pushed too hard and actually delayed part of his recovery timeline. His hard driving desire was to get back before the football season was over, that in which he succeeded. This meant almost no practice time for him, so he had to rely on natural athletic instincts he already possessed. Mekkar had to stay away from skating, hockey, or any physically related activities for a long time to get ready. It was killing him inside to not be able to play any games. The mental toll of inactivity was even more difficult for him to deal with.

These factors drove him from deep within and he has always possessed an extreme mentality to win anyway, in everything he does. Obstacles must be defeated and barriers must be knocked down which is part of his element overcoming, warrior personality. It was definitely his imbedded cultural Arctic background that gave him the view that most circumstances exist as part of a life and death struggle. The same scenario as his birth. The goal is to be able to regain everything at the same level as before and then improve upon that. Mekkar sees it as about the resolves stemming from one's will to defeat what is happening outwardly in an individual's circumstances. While at the same time, fight against being totally crushed inwardly. He knows it is easier to sometimes throw up one's hands and give up because it is the part of the path of least resistance. But, that is not Mekkar's way and his very nature is fight back with all that he has at his disposal in every realm. His brother, Alf, termed it as stubbornness and he is partially correct.

It was fortunate for him that his overall physical makeup and health constitution was such that it gave Mekkar an extra ordinary healing and injury restoration ability. Maybe there was a parallel between being partially named after a shaman and self-healing capability after all.

Another helpful tool in Mekkar's body arsenal was that his physical scars were less evident in his younger years. Large markings from various cuts, slices, wounds, and surgeries have seemed to shrink and be less noticeable on his body, even to him, as opposed to many others who had incurred similar injuries. He figured later on that it might be possibly being a guinea pig in the initial stages of development of the new liquid stitching breakthrough that was being tested. Having a good amount of hair on parts of his body also aided in covering some of the skin defects. Mekkar hated it at the time because it seemed to him that the process was longer. The long repeated trips for repairs were exhausting. Mekkar believes that the skin condition that affects him now, due to other health issues, has contributed even more to hiding the numerous flaws.

Unknown to him at the time, he did return to those aspects of his life earlier than anticipated by all. However, the long term effect was his athletic career was shortened. Before the end of his playing days, Mekkar seemed to be frequently hampered by an ever increasing list of ailments and injuries. Many years later his physical well-being is very affected by the compounded injuries suffered and diminishes his quality of life. His mind does question whether the sacrifices were worth the risk involved and very low financial rewards in comparison than the amount today's athletes receive. Mekkar doesn't blame anyone but himself. He feels that he could have been wiser and less reckless with his body. He says it was a product of youth and lack of experience in life. Mekkar attributes this to a belief that when you are young you feel indestructible. That view takes a position that neglects consideration of short or long term consequences. Mekkar knew the liability risks and chose to take that path anyway. It was something Mekkar was convinced he had some control over.

Even though Mekkar would be the only person in either vehicle to survive the accident, this incident still haunts him to this day. He still has issues about being in the back seat of motor vehicles due to this traumatic event. Due to the accident Mekkar will still refuse to get into a vehicle he deems as too small or unsafe. If he has to sit in the back seats there has to be a door next to him. He is always looking for a way of escape just in case. Otherwise, he begins to panic and other people who know him wonder why. Most of the time he doesn't bother to explain the reasons because he is trying forget. The whole idea is to shove those bad memories back deep into his sub-consciousness where they belong. Mekkar would prefer to walk instead or will look to accept another ride that meets his safety and exit access criteria.

The young man's life changed forever and toughened his personal resolve as a result of great challenges due to this occurrence. The event eventually fostered traits of more self-reliance and a greater distrust of others, especially of authority figures. However, due to his parents' early, unscheduled departure from this life they will be forever immortalized in Mekkar's mind.

Exploding Nuclear Plant and Effects

There are two subjects that Mekkar has great difficulty talking about in relation to all others in his life and this is one of them. Normally he tries to block out of his mind these negative experiences and painful events such as this. So, this was an arduous process getting Mekkar to recall and speak about it. It was a laborious task to extract a few of the details that affected him during this time. There were a wide range of emotions that went through his intellect while writing this chapter and it was excruciating to watch. Anger swells up, even to this day, regarding the rough treatment of him and those around him affected by this tragedy. By the way, the whole situation came about, by no fault of their own actions.

What is not common knowledge by most are the wind patterns and air currents that circulate in the upper cirrus clouds. These can blow around manufacturing pollution anywhere. Ash, from numerous volcanic eruptions around the world, has been found far away from the original source. The old tall smoke stacks rising from plants during the early part of the twenty-first century are examples of this. Tainted air also spewed out from heavy industry areas in the former Soviet bloc nations of Eastern Europe. Mekkar believes that the atmosphere traps pollution and forces it to spread to other parts of the world. Otherwise, that foul air would continue on into outer space and away from the planet. Liabilities in the air can strike anything that breathes because it can travel worldwide. Thus, it is surely able to affect Mekkar's home area also.

Of course, the young man from the arctic is not a weather expert but he has his own theories about the subject. On occasion, Mekkar's region might receive acid rain due to emanations from the old industrial cities of Europe and elsewhere. Growing up Mekkar saw the effects first hand of the residue as a result of using these old methods of production. Soot and dinginess are extensive in areas nearby this type of activity. A look at industrial centers such as Milwaukee, Pittsburgh, or West Virginia coal mining towns in the United States shows this plainly.

On previous occasions officials arrived from the national government with news to supposedly deliver help to his family, as well as, other inhabitants of the area. For example, they would tell them that they will put certain substances in the lakes, but excluded the larger faster moving rivers. The white coats, as Mekkar described them, would inform the locals that this method would keep the fish and more alive. They also claimed the action taken would preserve wildlife for a specific amount of time. Mekkar knew this was untrue because this was not the first time he heard these promises. The same exact hallow echoes were repeated over and over. He figured it wouldn't be the last time either.

The assertions of powerful lasting effects of neutralizing the negative aspects of the acid rain for long periods of time were false as usual. Mekkar read about other places that had used the same approach and the results were relatively short term or not effective at all. The young man also remembered the last time when the local aquatic life began to die much earlier than predicted. No real statistical evidence or acknowledgement by those in charge was published the last time this scenario was carried out. It was not in the official best interest and they did not care what the natives thought, is how Mekkar perceived it. Mekkar had a theory that this is just another example of another dominant culture attempting to destroy a much smaller native population. In this instance, forcing them to suffer from the cause and effect fallout due to grossly mismanaged errors of modern society. What was worse is these were not mistakes due to native ways and not by their own hand.

Mekkar read a story of the uniformed workers involved in the combat and cleanup process of the nuclear power plant accident. A food vendor on streets of a big city, which was nearby, made a reference to the falling nuclear fallout rain he saw around him at the time. It gave the impression to Mekkar that the kiosk operator felt that it was no big deal. This was part of an interview given to a journalist during the May Day military parade in the surrounding town. Unfortunately, there was a follow up story a few weeks later and it was revealed that the journalist along with the vendor both died excruciating deaths. Both had radiation burns all over their skin according to those close to them. So, much for trusting your government to protect their citizens, huh? Mekkar has a belief that governments will do everything, in their power, to hide their secret activities. Aspects such as incompetence, mistakes, and intentional actions against their own populations will be hidden as well.

When the explosion happened at the nuclear power plant, it transmitted the poison fallout in many directions quickly in all directions. Radioactive waste also travelled through the atmosphere. First, it traveled to nearby cities and nations and beyond. The harmful wind then directed itself due north into places no one could have guessed. Even some areas as far as 1,000 miles (1,609.34 kilometers) away were affected much more than anyone was told.

Mekkar heard that it was originally thought to have begun at a nuclear plant in a nation in the north. The guess was that since radiation was detected there and that nation has a few nuclear power reactors of their own. They later discovered that it came from somewhere else. There was a claim that a phrase out of reliance on this type of energy would be completed by a certain period of time. However Mekkar stated, "You know how governments are." Plus he added, "I will believe it when I see it'. He knew the lies were just beginning.

The native from the Arctic thought to himself that it is just another way the modern world behaves in a discriminatory fashion. He is convinced that those in charge desire to wipe out his native land and culture to gain domination over everything. Mekkar felt that it is ironic, that peoples that are frequently affected by pollution issues and this accident are the ones who cause little damage to the environment in comparison. Many native cultures see the earth as its relative with the idea of taking care of it. That is, if you want to enjoy its benefits. It is the total opposite of the "civilized" view of destroying the planet to gain resources with little effort toward replenishment for future resource usage.

Part of his maturing process was following the lead of his parents. Mekkar refused to accept limited reports from only one source. His distrust of potential censorship pushed him to probe further for more information from a different perspective. In one aspect, it was good that Alf was not in the area, but Mekkar could have used his younger brother's language skills right then. Even though this event occurred before the World Wide Web available to the general public there were other ways to find out information, if one were creative. Other reports on his monster sized shortwave radio poured in regarding the effects of this incident. Some the news was in languages Mekkar didn't understand. He turned the knob constantly looking for sources he could comprehend. Eventually bulletins and detailed discussions about the resulting fallout were found. Mekkar listened to reports about radioactivity moving and descending in Alaska,

Siberia, as well as other places far from the epicenter. He thought it was like the aftermath from the Mount Saint Helens volcanic eruption leaving remnants in many places.

A couple of Mekkar's acquaintances from the large city in the vicinity were directly involved in the operational crews. These were brothers around his own age whom he played hockey against and went to the same high school with during an international exchange program. He heard that part of the duties included having to directly remove radioactive material. Furthermore, without the proper clothing or equipment. Both soon died from the catastrophic after effects. Mekkar directly received the news, via telephone, that they both lost their lives about a week later. Their relatives described the physical agony of their condition in gruesome detail. Recounting the severe radiation skin lesions and the internal poisoning was difficult for Mekkar to listen to. Sadly, one of the end results was the two brothers basically coughed up their lungs.

It was not officially disclosed what exactly each of them were involved in or whether they were thrust into action immediately after the fact to fight further damage. This made Mekkar extremely sad for his friends. He became skeptical and wondered if the whole thing was poorly handled by the authorities on purpose. His suspiciousness was heightened by his growing belief of population control through direct elimination. His opinion is there will be more fear created episodes such as this in the future. Plus, Mekkar was already familiar with the story of the 1979 Three Mile Island meltdown in Pennsylvania.

Mekkar was soon listening from various sources and even saw some pictures regarding this tragedy. Alf, who was not there, translated underground news about the activity to his older brother. He related information over the telephone about the efforts to put out a fire in one of the reactors. There was talk about some of the firefighters were also sent into that risky environment without any hazmat suits. Proper gear was lacking and items to fight a regular fire were used, which was ineffective at best.

The native from the north was outdoors tending to his reindeer during portions of the radiation fallout blanketed his area. Janne mentioned to him that national government officials would be paying them a visit soon afterward. He described to Mekkar that they would help them with things related to the effects caused by the cloud. Mekkar thought that he knew what was coming, however, he was sorely mistaken. The first of the officials came about an hour or so after Janne brought the subject up to him. Mekkar assumed correctly that more white clothed people from the health department were on their way. One of the first doctor's and his nurse began to round up some the people. Mekkar was now imagining that he might be like one of his animals' in this scenario.

Before long, Mekkar with some others were being transported by truck to a hospice type building set up away from his village. The architecture appeared to Mekkar as if it were formerly some type of old folks home. It irritated Mekkar when the health workers kept spraying everyone in the group with a liquid based substance at regular intervals. He wanted to punch some of them to make them stop. No one told the herd of people what that particular compound was, even when Mekkar asked. His inquiries were readily dismissed. Mekkar growled a couple of times at the health officials. He nicknamed them the white rats. However, Mekkar concluded that his reality at the moment was that he was actually a rat in a cage instead.

When the group arrived at their destination, they escorted Mekkar along with ten other males to a shower area. Females were separated at this point. He was required to remove his clothing prior to the body washing. Commands were given to the assistants to make sure all of them were thoroughly scrubbed and cleaned. They were given this rough gritty soap that looked like lava rock and brushes with hard bristles. It was painful to the skin and created red blotches all over his body. Mekkar was unaware that the government representatives had taken and destroyed the clothes he was wearing beforehand. What Mekkar didn't know was that this would be the last time he would don his distinctive native clothing. Mekkar now especially disliked these authoritative robbers as he described them. He also wondered why they stole all of the personal belongings he had on his person.

The agent of the state claimed that they would compensate him for everything lost or destroyed during this process. But, Mekkar didn't believe them. He had heard adults in his village tell many stories about how his native people had been ripped off repeatedly. The northerner had also read articles regarding many times where the state took from his people. On the few occasions when the authorities did give back something it was never close to fair value in return. Mekkar felt that this was dehumanizing treatment on their behalf and there was no need for it. Yet, he and fellow villagers were in for further surprises to come.

So, Mekkar at this point had no quality clothes or at least some that weren't cheaply made along with no other items on his person. He told another person in the group, "Look at the cheap generic and common everyday clothing the white rats gave us". Following the cleaning procedure Mekkar got dressed in a lackadaisical manner. He hated the helpless feeling and the continual turn of events that were happening around him. The white ghosts (health officials) as Mekkar thought of them now directed his group to a larger room. Here each one of them had face to face sit down contact with a government representative. Mekkar was ready with questions and wanted some absolute answers and he intended to get them. Despite the fact he distrusted them.

This is where the agents of the government finally explained to Mekkar some of what was going on and the reasons for their actions. Mekkar wanted to cut through the lies and still had his doubts as to whether he was being told the whole story. He was still curious as to why they were being processed in this harsh manner like animals. Mekkar, at this point, was beyond perturbed and ready to kick some butt. Mekkar was at his breaking point with the overwhelming need to exercise his past sports demons on some government stooges. When he gets ticked off, Mekkar gets mighty ferocious and desires to get physical. Those hockey and fighter training skills were close to being exhibited in a harmful manner and he knew who his targets were – anyone in white.

Next, the white rats pulled out these old looking green canisters. They seemed to Mekkar as being from the World War II period. He could have sworn he saw foreign lettering on them, but couldn't identify them. Mekkar wished his brother Alf were here just then because he could read that info on the cans. Mekkar figured these were either Chinese or Japanese by the lettering. He remembered from his history lessons that Japan got nuked by the United States in 1945. Thus, Mekkar assumed the items were from there and they must be old. The officials handed out large spoons to each person and poured out this foul smelling liquid substance into each spoon. The stuff reeked like rotten fish. A government overseer told Mekkar to take what was in the spoon, pour into his mouth, and swallow it. The individual attempted to explain in a personal way. Just, as if your mama gave you cough syrup when you were sick. Mekkar put it into his mouth and spit it back out on the ground. It was gross and he let anyone within hearing distance know about it. So, when he had to do it a few more times, Mekkar thought that he was better prepared for the next round. He wasn't and becoming more irritated with each round.

One of individuals observing there told him that it was potassium iodine. They also added that it was supposed to help prevent thyroid malfunction and cancer. It didn't matter to Mekkar what they called this nasty stuff. It was supposed to help him? I don't believe it. He just knew when the liquid hit his tongue, it was absolutely awful tasting. Mekkar thought it was worse than when his godparents would have him drink a full glass of straight vinegar. Mekkar would then usually have to run to the bathroom and throw up. Mekkar thought that this iodine solution was much worse than the vinegar he remembered.

The white rats had Mekkar and others there in the group take five big spoonfuls of this iodine juice. Mekkar wanted some vodka to drink right then to wash down the dreadful flavor in his mouth. He was of the opinion that he would rather eat fresh steamy reindeer excrement in the future before ever having to ingest that horrific syrup again. Mekkar later learned the syrup gave limited protection and only helped to protect the thyroid. No other parts of the body would gain any benefit from the liquid. Thus, the compound was very limited in its scope of defense. Oh Great! Mekkar thought whether it worth the effort to endure the hideous taste that gave minimal protection to him. It probably wasn't worth the trouble at all.

Eventually, he did some research on the long term physical effects and consequences on the health of those exposed to the toxic particles. He checked out various sources, mostly at the library, to gather any information he needed. The data came from a host of various language newspaper articles, other media sources, scientific journals, and a few people he knew. It is important to note, the internet was less accessible back then and to enter it required some computer hacking skills. The internet itself is much older than the World Wide Web (www) which didn't even exist for public access until 1989. He could do this when he had access. Problem was that he didn't have his own computer and now Lasse's was unavailable. Mekkar dug deeper and sought information regarding scientist predictions on future outcomes. That is, for people in the distressed areas due to the nuclear accident and the after-effects.

During the initial cleansing process, the national health people stated to Mekkar that he had nothing to worry about. The he would not experience any major effects from this plague for at least twenty five years, if at all. Mekkar thought that this was all hogwash. He later came to the conclusion that this advice was not correct after receiving the news of what happened to the two brothers. They have suffered severely and died fairly rapidly as well as others who survived for short terms after the incident. The young man also reasoned that the government claims are all falsehoods and full of lies. Flat out, Mekkar didn't trust the government people. He was educated enough to know that anyone can make their case with statistical analysis alone.

He still had a nagging feeling that there are facts still missing and more that he is not being told. Mekkar wanted to ask a physician several questions. However, the doctor had to be outside of the current system and not employed by the government. It had to be a person who he felt he could trust a little more than these liars who arrived quickly on the scene. Mekkar's sentiment was how did they know when and where to show up so speedily after the crisis? He was conducting a thorough analysis to satisfy some of his own questions. The objective was tying together time frames between cause and effect. When and how the predictions or warnings came announced and whether the full consequences of errors could be avoided or not. Mekkar searched a wide array of sources. He knew, like economists, very few scientific experts in any field completely agree on all data gathered, its interpretation, and impending possibilities.

After the explosion of the reactor other future events arose to inflict more long term health concerns upon the residents. Whole areas and people were burdened way beyond the scope of previous predictions. Mekkar and others he knew in the surrounding area heard rumors and innuendo regarding other nuclear plants that might affect them. These were also constructed in a similar manner as the one that melted down. A number of these energy plants and various nuke reactor stations were not well known. Some were in locations not far away millions of people, but kept secret from them.

Not a small number of people were affected by this event. The fear is that it could get much worse over time. Likewise, if these other plants have minor leakage issues the results could be catastrophic. A large storm, a great wind, or extensive atmospheric activity could carry the pollution sources right to people's front doors in a hurry. It might seem as though the issue were caused next door, but not necessarily. If a population was previously affected, minor escapes of poisoned air is not such an insignificant factor upon a person's health. Added to the fact, would be a great number of these stations were poorly designed and construction was worse. Standards that wouldn't even meet minimal grades for similar power plant facilities in other parts of the world. Even first nations have problems with nuclear power technology and related energy generation.

Science has shown how acid rain can travel long distances to wipe out fish in lakes. This effect was due to antiquated manufacturing structures and policies of irresponsible nations who could care less about their neighbors. In the past, issues arose from a few of those alternative places were much closer to Mekkar's village. Unfortunately, this is a realm that is more powerful than coal and has the ability to do more destruction over wider areas. There was a secretive hidden agenda used before in not revealing who was adjacent to some of these facilities. What would stop this trend from continuing and having much more potential destructive capability? Would the public be better informed of what is going on around them or lied to some more?

There were also other suggestions of explosions occurring due to nuclear testing and various mysterious activities. Imagine this was happening near the largest military bases in the world. Unfortunately, no large international media outlets said a peep about these conceivable incidents. It seemed to Mekkar that no one seemed to care or bother to investigate these possible occurrences. Maybe the reins were held tight by those in charge? Alf continued to translate some more alternative sources to Mekkar, in a host of different languages. The material reported a few fairly hushed up activities and locations. Alf and Mekkar noticed a tendency concerning these accounts had a habit of being removed from circulation quickly after exposing their covert details. These incidents were quickly hushed up or hidden from public consumption. Just part of another country's rulers attempt to hide their misdeeds perhaps, thought Mekkar? Again being misapplied and all falling under the all-inclusive umbrella term of national security.

Mekkar's family ended losing everything they owned due to the fallout. Contrary to the answers given by the officials, no one he knew received any compensation from anyone for it. His home, vehicles, reindeer herd, business, and all personal belongings were destroyed. Friends, relatives, natives, and fellow citizens perished or were affected by this disaster. Mekkar's own personal health was affected also and still causes problems for him to this day.

A person that Mekkar met later on was an exchange student at the time in a university town not close to the event. That individual acquired type-two diabetes from the distant effects of the fallout that emerged. During the accident, a professional hockey player lived in a city nearby the plant in his youth. It was mentioned that he is awaiting any possible long term effects from the incident to eventually germinate. How can one fight against a force that is not well understood and we don't know when it might surface?

Later on, the United States supplied a few billion dollars toward encasing and sealing off of the damaged nuclear reactor. The hope was subsequent damage could be limited somewhat and wouldn't continue to be such a large problem down the line. Mekkar is convinced, however, that the governmental officials responsible for the plant at all levels stole most of that money. He thinks the cash loaned toward that securing and restricting the damage was basically siphoned off because many people had their hands out. The bureaucrats and officials kept a lot of project money for themselves through corruption, bribery, and outright theft. Now, Mekkar is of the opinion that is what government and their representatives always do.

Unbelievably, a few years afterward the incident some people in positions of power still wanted to reopen that plant. Thankfully it is permanently closed for power generation. Now, the local leaders there have the ambition to make the area available to attract tourists and rake in some cash to line their own pockets. What is forgotten is the fate of common people that were affected since they just get kicked to the curb. It is interesting to note that in 2003 fallout spiked in certain northern areas and reindeer had to be destroyed once again. The animal's food sources were still contaminated along with the local food supply chain. The earth and surrounding environments will be spoiled for a lot longer period of time. People are now passing the effects to their children and nearby cultures have been impacted forever. [Chernobyl – 20 Years, 20 Lives by photographer Mads Eskesen] Has the cost been worth it? Mekkar distinctly says No.

It is important to note that sometimes details become fuzzy to Mekkar regarding events that occurred long ago. One reason is that he doesn't want to remember when he had to basically start over. Another reason is that he has had multiple concussions with a number comparable to former pro athletes. Only their doctors probably know the extent of the full measure related to permanent memory and brain damage issues. All related to numerous and frequent head trauma. Mekkar at times describes it as the frustration of having short circuits in his head without the warning buzzer. He more often than not forgets what he is saying, while he is the middle of speaking. This is telling considering when he was younger he had a photographic memory and used it extensively. Mekkar is glad he was excellent at taking written notes.

Mekkar has said on occasion that people's minds are similar to computers. That is everything that happens to them in their life goes on the hard drive. That is the subconscious memory. Mekkar's trouble is with the accessible memory, the Random Access Memory (RAM), which is now faulty. That is the conscious memory that Mekkar is unable to control what he can remember at any given time. Mekkar figures that he is not the only one who has those same recall problems. He refuses to use the head impairment as a crutch because he knew the hazards and risks when he started. However, it is not so easy to replace or upgrade the brain Ram in human beings is it? There is the rub, maybe technology and scientific discovery can solve this issue in the coming future, perhaps?